The Prequel

SUBJECTED

Eye of God

G. F. Smith

Confluential Press

~ A Confluence of Influence

Acknowledgments

i.   Cover Image: *Eye of God Nebula* – Hubble Image with rights from Sky Image Lab
ii. Earth Image: NASA
iii. Cover Design: © 2012 by G. F. Smith, with Technical, Layout, and Creative assistance from Jonah C. Smith
iv. Graphic illustration of Fire-in-Eye (taken from Music Artist Jonah C. Smith's *The Graceful Fire*): © 2010 by Jonah C. Smith
v. Poem: *Why did he do it?* © 1979 by author, Michael Willever
vi. Man of Clay and additional Graphics: © 2011 by G. F. Smith

Convention: The Author has chosen to make a break with convention in regards to the usage of certain grammar and punctuation, especially in dialogue, and specifically regarding the usage of the Ellipsis: the three-dot (…) sentence break. Convention describes the purpose of the ellipsis as an "omission" of particularly unimportant or non-essential words. According to the Author's particular convention, this also indubitably includes unspoken *thoughts*.

In this writing, the effect is used to indicate (mimic) actual human speech, in where we frequently, and habitually, break our sentences to: think of what we want to say next; consider the ramifications of what we *are* going to say next; convey ambivalence, uncertainty, ambiguity; indicate a state of awe, or during the expression of emotion, as with fear, anger, happiness and love. We're human, and literary works which include human characters should…*read* like human, not just human English Scholars (with all due respect).

Warning! This book—by the author's own humble admission—is solar-plexus-deep in philosophical heaviness. This was wrought by intention, and when the Reader arrives at the end, he or she will also arrive at the understanding of just why that is—without giving it away, think P.O.V.

This particular work (the prequel in the Subjected Series) was written primarily for those who have traversed some heavy experiences in their lives, or who are deeply empathetic toward those whom they know presently are, or…will be.

Special thanks: to family, friends, and business associates who have given their support and encouragement throughout this endeavor. Enduring, not only the time it has taken for its creation, but the sometimes obsessive focus that was often required for its rendering. Thanks for understanding.

Life has its reasons...

Prologue

"Yes, that is the one thing everyone wants beyond all others...control! The desire results from a natural inclination," he said, shifting his gaze slightly before continuing.

"From an infant's first breath, to the dying's' last, the yearning underlies every hunger, wish, prayer, and aspiration. It is the quest of life itself, to garner control. To have our needs, wants, desires, yes even our dreams, fulfilled. However, I sense you've convinced yourself that, for you, these challenges are insurmountable?"

Although he spoke with an authoritative tone, his mercurial blue eyes exuded genuine empathy. He stood silent for a brief moment, studying the pain and frustration that haunted the young man's eyes.

"I assure you, you are not alone," he continued.

"There are reasons, exceedingly important reasons, for your position...for everyone's position!" He paused again. His eyebrows now sat lower. "Experience, knowledge, understanding...wisdom, through time, award us measures of control. Yet, it is the epitome of irony, I would agree, that it seemingly takes a lifetime of struggle to gain even a semblance of control, only to be lost in the end to the inexorable effects of entropy, decay...death?" He spoke the last part mockingly as a question. With clinched lips, he slowly shook his head from side to side, letting out a pithy laugh through his nose.

Then, perceiving the young man's disheartened thoughts, the distinguished figure suddenly smiled knowingly.

"Yes, well, what if we were to sufficiently illustrate for you the inherent purpose? Might you choose to participate then?"

Chapter 1

"What's going to happen is…is going to happen, Son, it's just the way things are! There's no changing it!" He remembered the velvety warmth of her hand as she held his, and how her lips quivered as she spoke. *"Life's hard, it's…just plain hard, I know. But it's got its reasons, Son. I need you to believe that!"*

Daniel Jeremy Sayer knew that he would forever remember the words she spoke to him on that day. He remembered them again as he lay there, as he had a thousand times. He wanted to sleep, needed to sleep, but he wasn't able to. His mind kept looping back through the previous seven years, over and over again, trying to reconcile the past with his thoughts of the future.

That one day still seemed like yesterday for him.

He wished he could have done something, and that he could have saved her somehow. He'd wished it, prayed it, and had even screamed it from the top of his lungs on numerous occasions. But for whatever reason, Old Man Fate—God—hadn't listened, much less answered. Life was just this way. And as a man now, he had to accept that. At least, that's what he kept telling himself of late.

Like most people, he couldn't recall ever asking, or ever wanting, to be subjected to this life, much less to its seemingly incessant pains and frustrations. And like everyone else, he had no memories of where he was before he came to be, and he had no idea what he was supposed to do while he was here.

And he surely didn't know what was coming up after his life here would be over.

All he seemed to know was the image in the mirror. The many pains and the few pleasures of his senses, and the experiences which he'd had since he'd shown up on the planet. And that life always seemed to want to go in the opposite direction from what Daniel Jeremy Sayer wanted. At least, it always seemed to anyway.

He often wondered if the assortment of frequent and sometimes bizarre experiences that he found himself having to endure throughout his seminal years might have been intentionally thrust upon him. By who, or what, he did not know. That they were somehow meant to ruin his chances at a normal, happy life, but *"what's normal...or happy?"* his mother repeatedly asked him.

She was good at that, getting him to think about such things.

He reached up and rubbed his sleepless eyes, and then once again, remembered her saying: *"You have to look at it from outside the box, Daniel! All experiences leave an indelible mark on us. How we choose to think about them, learn from them—make good out of them—is what makes all the difference."*

He lay there, quiet and still. Continuing to recount his life up to that point, again considering what she'd said to him back then. As he did, the images of his childhood solidified in his mind like video game figures endowed with a profusion of unnaturally resilient life spans: the insensitive teachers, the snobbish cliques, the heartless teasing school girls, and your usual predatory jock-typical bully-type figures. Which, like pimples, bad hair and uncomfortably-fitting underwear, seemed intent upon tormenting him throughout his early school experience.

Apparently, he just attracted that sort of thing—a little on the timid side, tall for his age, and somewhat goofy in stature, a prime target for the older, bigger kids who could only feel superior by making someone else feel inferior.

Through his formative years, he grew to despise bullies, on all scales.

Daniel Jeremy Sayer just seemed to be one of those unlucky kids, too. His stuff constantly ended up lost, stolen, dented or destroyed in some fashion. One odd summer when he was twelve, his bicycle seemed to develop a preternaturally strange magnetic attraction to stationary objects, causing him to wreck more times than he could remember.

That was the summer when he'd missed a corner and had ridden headlong into a concrete block wall, fracturing his collarbone. The really odd thing being, that he'd seen it happening in his mind mere moments before it happened. At least he thought he had.

A couple of his favorite pets died prematurely around that time, too—both under his own bike tire: a cute little tabby kitten on a Tuesday evening that tried to jump through the spokes just as he'd begun to take off down the sidewalk, and then his old dog Samson the following Saturday, as he raced home on his bike, trying to beat the heaviest part of a rainstorm that he had gotten caught in. Both animals died a painful, twitching death from broken necks, and he, nearly, from a guilt-ridden heart.

Another particularly difficult time in his life was when he had become extremely ill from a severe case of pneumonia. He was so sick that he had to use a wheel chair to get around due to the temporary loss of most of the strength in his legs and arms. He spent the better part of that entire summer at home by himself, just lying in bed, able to do nothing but watch TV and read.

The doctors couldn't figure out why his condition was so severe, since pneumonia routinely doesn't produce those kinds of symptoms. And apparently, they never did figure it out. Because by the time they thought they might have some possible avenues of research to pursue, he had recovered.

One day he could barely move, and the next it was like he was a new person.

But battles often raged in his young, maturing mind as to whether the things that kept happening to him were in reality his fault, or whether they had just descended upon him because of bad luck, or coincidence, or maybe something that someone else had done a long time ago—a curse, or something that had to do with DNA, or whatever. Either way, he tried to be determined enough to learn something from it all. At least, that's what his mother kept encouraging him to do. Up until the day she died.

He was eleven then.

Chapter 2

Jeremy awoke around six o'clock that morning. Long before his alarm was set to go off. In reality, he was awake most of the night just lying there, thinking about his life, thinking about life in general. Who could sleep knowing that, in just a few short hours, you were going to do something like jump out of an airplane?

He whispered to himself in a not-quite-awake elastic whine.

"I've never even been on an airplane, except when I was a toddler, I think. I don't even know if I like to fly…" He laughed and shook his head at the irony. "Now I'm going to jump out of one!" He closed his eyes tightly. A whining, laughing, rumbling sound escaped through his nose as he rolled over. He put his pillow tightly over the side of his face, as if to hide from the reality that was setting in.

But, he knew it was time, time for his life to change—big time.

Having just turned eighteen, and recently graduated from high school a few weeks earlier, Jeremy and his friends were about to celebrate his birthday and their graduation together in a boldly atypical way, a potentially indelible experience. That is, if they survived.

He and his friends were going to go skydiving, parachuting actually. It was something they had boasted about doing many times over the prior four years of their lives, with total lack of trepidation. It was also a pact the three of them had made when four years seemed like forever. Kids rarely think about forever though. But not with Jeremy, he was always thinking about it.

Jeremy sat on the edge of the bed and reached for the alarm, hitting the 'off' button with only a fraction of a second of its annoying shriek piercing his ears. It quickly faded back into the silence from whence it came. He took a deep breath. His mind swam, just imagining the coming day's events. He thought it would be best not to think about it right then. His gut seemed to be swimming, too.

He took another deep breath, got up, and walked sock-footed down the hallway to the bathroom. It felt good for him to walk, languorously stretching his all-but-atrophic muscles as he did so. He entered the small, green-tiled bathroom and shut the door slowly behind him. Before it closed all the way, he heard the familiar voice emanating from the kitchen.

"I think I hear someone stirring." Jeremy's Uncle Paul howled purposely toward the hallway. "Ready for a bi...g breakfast?" he hollered again, snickering under his breath, all the while knowing that Jeremy could hear him. He also knew fully well that as soon as Jeremy started to even think about food, his stomach would turn on him. He couldn't help but tease him a little.

"Bacon, eggs...pancakes! And thick, rich syrup! Come and get 'em while they're hot!" He smiled a pseudo-devious smile when he had said the thick-rich-syrup part.

In spite of his sometimes importune demeanor, Jeremy's uncle had a hugely kind and sincere heart, flanked on both sides by a pleasant and personable persona. Paul T. Usher was his full name. A medium-to-large-sized stout man, yet not at all portly. He had longish brown hair to his collar, and a short, well-trimmed beard. He wore thin-rimmed glasses. Paul was also well tanned from working outside, and ruggedly built like the quintessential mountain-trail-hiking outdoorsman, which many remarked he looked like because he was always wearing big-pocketed pants or shorts, flannel shirts, hiking boots, and brimmed, fedora-style hats when it was sunny or wintry.

He was the kind of guy who never left his house without his fold-up multi-tool hanging off his belt. And slung across his shoulder, his old leather backpack, which contained all sorts of survival-type items: bandages to beef jerky, flashlights to fishing kits, those sorts of things. The suburban Indiana Jones type—minus the whip—his neighbors often whispered and then giggled about in their private neighborhood gossip assemblies.

One of the man's favorite things to say was: "You've got to be prepared, you never know what might happen, what if?" Paul had always been like that. He and his sister—Jeremy's mom—had been a lot alike in that way.

Paul was also the kind of guy who was always thinking about possibilities and probabilities, and applying the techniques of extrapolation. That was one of his favorite words to use: *extrapolate*. "It's a good word to use," he'd say, "because the inference is that you're a thinker."

And because of his peculiar propensity toward being forward-thinking, he would answer virtually every question that Jeremy asked with: "Well, what do you think?" or, "What does your mind tell you?" or, "How do you see it?"

These responses were always given with the ulterior motive of encouraging his nephew to look deeper into things. To study things for himself, and to consider possibilities other than just the obvious, instead of just accepting, without any effort on his part, what everyone else believed.

Jeremy had a unique outlook on life because of this. But, this outlook was also in constant conflict with his tendency toward depression. What kid wouldn't be predisposed to a little depression after losing your mom—and then your dad, too?

That was another one of those indelible experiences.

Chapter 3

Jeremy stood there in the bathroom doing his morning business. And just as his uncle had suspected, as soon as he heard the word "food" and smelled the various aromas wafting through the air, Jeremy's stomach seemed to twist into a knot. In response, he quickly turned and sat down on the toilet. With great effort, he responded to his uncle's breakfast call with feigned excitement.

"Great, be out in a few minutes!" he yelled toward the closed door.

Thirty minutes later, showered and dressed, Jeremy entered the kitchen and plopped down a stack of books on the countertop next to the back door, which led out to the driveway. The food was on the table and his Uncle Paul was sitting in his usual chair next to the window, sipping on a cup of coffee, his breakfast already half-eaten.

"So, how's the new family daredevil this morning?" He smiled largely.

Jeremy didn't speak immediately, but finally got the words out. "Fine, just fine. I'm just taking a little longer to wake up than usual."

"Oh, I see," Paul said, still grinning from ear to ear. "Hungry?" he asked.

"Uhmm…" Jeremy paused, peered at his uncle.

He then realized that his uncle knew exactly how he felt—a little sick to his stomach. Not wanting to allow him any more ammo for his protracted teasing, Jeremy answered sturdily.

"Yeah, I could eat something, thanks." He paused again to gulp down some air. "So, what gives? This is not the usual toast or cereal breakfast we're used to. And what are you so happy about?" Jeremy asked, squinting at his uncle.

"Well, I thought I'd do something special since this is a special occasion. You know, the birthday, the graduation, the Jump! The let..." He paused abruptly, then resumed. "Uhmm, just everything. Excited? Nerrrrrvous?" he asked, drawing it out like a cow mooing.

Jeremy thought for a moment before answering.

"Yeah, well, yeah, thanks. I guess I'm a little nervous. Alright, a lot nervous! But, it's still going to be cool. A cup of your horseshoe coffee, and a few more deep breaths and I'll be good to go!"

"Yep, I figure you will." He grinned again. "I remember my first time. I felt the same way. Stomach a little twisted up there, huh? It's going to be a rush, there's no doubt about it. You'll survive." He then looked into Jeremy's weary eyes. "You're going to take more deep breaths today than you've taken in the past five years," he said, with extra emphasis on the last words.

They then grinned at each other, and simultaneously breathed in through their noses until they couldn't take any more. Then, with an explosion of air, they each burst out with a deep, guttural yell. They rocked and swayed in their chairs, flung their arms back to the side and behind their heads, as if they were in one of those skydiving, arched, freefall positions they'd practiced together, both acting as if they were falling through the air at nearly twice the nation's speed limit. They finished with a chuckle, and then at the same time reached for their mugs of hot breakfast beverage.

As Paul downed another swig of his coffee he looked over toward the countertop at the books Jeremy had loosely thrown down.

"You were up reading all night, weren't you? Get any sleep?" he asked.

"Yeah, a little, I think," Jeremy replied. "In and out."

"What were you reading?" Paul asked arbitrarily, squinting at the stack of books. He then spoke out a couple of titles: "*A Brief History of Time...Who Moved My Cheese? ...So*

You're Here, Now Where Do You Want to Go? Wow, long title, some light reading to help you sleep, huh?"

He let out another slight laugh.

"Yeah," Jeremy smiled back. "The top one is about physics. The other ones are about business."

"Yeah, I see that: *origin and fate of the universe, arrow of time, uncertainty principle,* yep, Stephen Hawking. I've read him. Too bad about his condition. The wheel chair and all, using a computer to speak, had to be rough—still around though, amazingly. *Who Moved My Cheese?* Spencer Johnson M.D, that's an old one, but a good one. Interesting, business stuff, huh?" Paul asked lightly.

"Yeah, some guy named Thomas Dorkin wrote that other one. It's…"

"Dorkin?" Paul interrupted. "Huh, now that's a name!" he added.

"Yeah, I thought the same thing. It was pretty cool though. Something about…well, the title kind of says it. It's about this business guy and his ideas of getting where you want to be in business, by figuring out where you want to be in life, first. You know? Goals and visions, dreams and stuff, I crammed it for one of my final papers."

Jeremy took a small sip of the still-too-hot coffee.

"I need to stop at the library on the way back and drop them off."

"Sounds like my mug of tea. I'd hate to have his name, nevertheless." Paul snickered again.

"Yeah." Jeremy replied.

"So, you ready for this?" Paul asked, referring to the jump.

"Yeah. *Yeah,* I think it's going to be awesome. Scott and Bass and I have been waiting for this for a long time. It'll be more than awesome!" Jeremy said as he tipped his coffee cup to his mouth and took a big gulp, wincing because of its hotness. "I want this; I…I *need* this." He choked the pain away, while flopping his tongue around in his widely opened mouth.

"You know it takes a lot of concentration—a lot of focus. It's kind of like…" His uncle paused, and then spoke the new thought that entered his mind. "What do you mean you 'need' this?"

He didn't say anything right at first, but within a few moments, Jeremy answered, "Well, you know." He considered his thoughts again, "I think I need this because, 'cause it's just something I, *we* really want to do, *accomplish*, you know? Like when we jumped off Miller's Bridge."

Paul tilted his head and looked over his glasses. "You jumped off Old Miller's Bridge? When did you, no, *why* did you jump off Miller's Bridge, for heaven's sake?"

Paul had a look of shock on his face; it then morphed into squinting displeasure.

Jeremy was genuinely glad that he finally told his uncle. He thought he could since he was an adult now—although it wasn't exactly being received like he thought it would. Jeremy winced at his uncle's expression, and at his still-burning mouth.

Old Miller's Bridge was a train trestle that towered over one hundred feet above the southern edge of a lake that went by the same name. It was out Finley's way, only a few miles from his house. Jeremy knew that he had never told his uncle about this little antic, yet he felt that now was the time. He spoke with trepidation, and understandable reticence.

"Uh, Scott and Bass and I did, end of last summer. Don't worry, the water was up from all the rain that week and we…"

Paul interrupted. "Listen, I'm all for fun and thrills, like today, for example, but." He paused, realizing he needed to control his obvious discontent towards his nephew. "Look, Jeremy, fear is something you know I consider, well, I consider it something to look square in the face. But, jumping off Old Miller's Bridge, well, it's foolish, Son. People are breaking their necks all the time pulling stunts like that. It's just plain…numbskullian."

He just then made up the word.

Jeremy smiled a smirky grin. "Where do you think we got the idea from?" He said, then smiled bigger, raising his eyebrows while imitating his uncle's usual mannerism of looking over his glasses when trying to make a point—even though Jeremy didn't wear glasses.

Paul knew he was caught. He suddenly remembered that he had told Jeremy a long time ago that he and several of his friends had done the exact same thing when he had been a young boy.

"Okay, you got me, it was just as stupid of an idea back then as it is today. Listen, there's such a thing as stupid risk, and then there is such a thing as…as calculated risk. The former leads to destruction and the latter leads to…" Paul looked up as if trying to find the correct words somewhere on an invisible marquee floating in space up by the kitchen ceiling. "Well, the latter could still lead to possible maiming, or death." He was trying to be dramatic for effect, looking over his glasses once again.

Paul realized he couldn't say much more. He knew exactly what Jeremy was thinking. In Paul's mind, he wanted to help Jeremy realize the difference between risks that can be beneficial, and other types of risks that are motivated by pretension and foolishness. But even though in his mind he was seeking to accentuate the differences for Jeremy, in his heart, he was really proud of him.

Not for the stupid thing that he and his friends had done, but that his nephew had found the courage and the determination to do it in the first place—Jeremy had always been sort of timid, not exactly the fearless type. But now he was thinking about Jeremy's past bouts with depression. He couldn't help but wonder if there was more to his nephew's newly-found fearlessness.

He shuttered the thought.

"I know what you're saying—" Jeremy spoke after a short, yet uncomfortable, silence. "We didn't just do it, you know, like on a whim. The water was up three feet. We dropped a line down and measured it! There was over fifteen feet of water down there, and we didn't go off anywhere near the top. You know, like some stupid people have. Anyway, it was cool, it was a rush!" He included one of his uncle's old, yet frequently used terms, trying to connect with him.

Paul thought back to *his* teenage years. He remembered

the day well. He was fifteen and thought himself quite the daredevil-type, too, back then. He even remembered the shirt he wore. He laughed in his mind. It was an old, tattered Superman shirt, blue with a big diamond-encased "S" on the front. And he remembered the confidence it'd given him— the courage—like Dumbo's magic feather. He wore it almost every day for two and a half years. Until it became so worn and ratty that, in a fit of frustration, his mom stole it out of the laundry and used it as fire starter in their burn barrel.

He remembered that he and his friends hadn't even thought about checking the water's depth when they had done it. They just dove in on mutual dares and from way up on the massive iron structure.

He also remembered the one boy who had died later that same summer, after jumping off the very top. He hadn't thought about that for many years. He quickly pushed it back out of his recollections. Jeremy and his friends must have given it considerable thought, he convinced himself. This helped reduce his anxiety—a little.

"So, okay, this *need* thing, you don't *need* to prove anything to anybody. What's your mind really telling you?" Paul, as usual, was trying to encourage Jeremy to look at things from all angles.

"I'm not going parachuting to 'prove' anything to anybody, exactly." He stared out the window for a moment, then resumed. "I'm doing it for the…for the *living of it*."

"'The living of it'," Paul repeated the statement and then tilted his head, making it a question.

"Yeah," he paused for a moment before continuing. "The guys and I watched this video awhile back. It had this skydiver on it and he said, something like: 'Some people say that skydivers have some sort of death wish, and that they're not afraid to die. The truth is, most skydivers *are* afraid of dying, but what skydivers are most afraid of, is *not* living!' I thought that was a pretty interesting thing to say."

"Yeah," Paul said, looking pensively into Jeremy's tired blue eyes. "I can relate to that. I've always thought the same way, I guess, *but—*"

Jeremy nodded his head, anticipating his uncle's reaction to the statement. "Yeah, *I* know," he said, smiling largely. "I've always seen that in you. It is something to consider, isn't it?"

"Yes, it is. Some things, you know, like that, can make life more valuable, more precious, if looked at the right way." He spoke slowly, reflectively, remembering all the times he had said these very things to his nephew.

"Yeah, I know what the guy meant. It's one thing to be alive, it's another to...to *truly live!*" He said it with a noted level of drama, intoning a lower voice, looking up in the air and holding his palm up to the sky. He quickly relaxed and then continued. "There are a lot of people in life who haven't figured that out yet, and I guess I'm one of them. People are afraid of stuff you know, so afraid that they spend a good portion of their time on this planet shying away from the very things that could give their lives some meaning."

Paul suddenly tilted his head down, struck with a thought. He was thinking of some of the things he was afraid of. Considering that maybe it was really some of these things that had kept him from finishing school, getting a degree, becoming a teacher, seeing the world, and lecturing like he had originally planned a long time ago. He found himself dispelling the uncomfortable thought.

Jeremy just sat there, his mind drifting on pulsations of sleepiness. He was unknowingly still nodding his head at his uncle's comments as he peered out the window. At first, he wasn't really looking at anything in particular, just observing the general panoramic view as he further pondered his uncle's words. Both became silent for the moment. Then, Jeremy began noticing the birds diving for insects in the grassy field next to the house, and he noticed that the trees off in the distance were gently swaying in the warm morning breeze. He watched in amazement as three brown squirrels jumped playfully from branch to branch, seemingly fearless while leaping the great distances between the tiny limbs.

Jeremy then heard his uncle's coffee cup make a pinging sound as it inadvertently tapped his plate in transit from the table to his lips.

Jeremy's mind quickly returned.

"Yeah," Jeremy replied after the short silence. He took a bite of his breakfast. "It's sad, but understandable; life's kind of scary."

"The interesting thing," Paul resumed, "is that people aren't just scared about living; they're scared to make choices about living. Because they know that once they make a choice, a huge amount of effort on their part must follow. Not to mention the unfamiliar terrain they're going to have to travel on, once they get off their butts.

"It's the fear and apprehension, the ambivalence that goes along with the act of choosing. Should I? Shouldn't I? Could I, even? Choosing is only half the battle. There's always that fear-of-failure thing going on, too. It really boils down to that: choices, and then follow-through, *grit*. That's what it all boils down to, true grit. Ever seen the movie? True Grit…John Wayne? Now that's a good flic—the old one—still timely, you should watch it sometime. Courage, faith, purpose, one man against all odds!"

Jeremy's thoughts started drifting again. Jeremy's thoughts started drifting again. His uncle's consummate philosophizing sometimes made his mind wander, especially when he was tired.

Paul used to be a devout and intensely serious student of religion and philosophy, and then of the arts and sciences. Although a long-time college student—he attended college for over seven years—he could never settle on a degree, or even a major. Yet, he was a smart man and intuitively deep in his own down-to-earth way.

He thought about entering the ministry when he was a young adult. Hugely influenced by his church-going parents—long deceased—but was dissuaded by all the strife between the different religions of the world, and what he said were "lives mostly wasted on endless arguments and debates over supposed truths that were mostly made up in the minds of men anyway, not God's."

Then he was going to be a scientist. Study the origins of the universe, advance the world's understanding of biology, of physics, and help define everyone's place in "life's big bowl of cosmic soup," as he would describe it. But for some reason, he just couldn't get the math part. Much less settle for a life full of what he called "academic manipulation." So, instead, he started a small nursery business and merged it with a petting zoo.

For him, it was a metaphorical microcosm of all that life was—a perfect example of the interconnection and interdependency of all life forms, on all levels. It's a combination that seemed to work well for him. He made a modest living. Had most of the winter off to read, and write his *Essays on being a Being*—a book he'd been working on for over twenty years, his personal dissertation—and he had the chance to meet all sorts of people and have conversations about, well, about everything.

That was the way he conducted his research. "For his life's work," he'd say. Paul sometimes felt bad that he hadn't finished school, and that he hadn't done something different with his life. This was a particularly recurring thought, especially after he took Jeremy in under his wing.

But, Paul still loved to ponder, and he loved to have others join in with him.

He would frequently ask some of his more interested patrons at his business, questions he had often asked of himself: "How many of us have cursed ourselves for not understanding something, or for not knowing something when we could have, or worse yet, *should* have?"

This one always seemed to make people look sideways in a contemplative sort of way, like they could relate to the thought. People really loved Paul Usher, and his unique way of encouraging others to think about such things.

<<< >>>

"It doesn't have to be jumping out of an airplane—or off a bridge." Paul looked over his glasses again. Jeremy returned his attention to his uncle. "It can just be the fear of trying something new. Like putting in for that new job, or choosing to further an education, learning to talk to people, or just leaving home and going somewhere, anywhere, really. Facing one's fears is only learning to face life's inevitable frustrations. Learning to face the anxiety that goes along with the frustration, I suppose. I guess it's just a natural part of who we are, of being human, just part of our nature. I can understand why people shy away from it."

Jeremy grabbed his cup of coffee. "Yeah, I guess so, me too," he said. "But I guess, in the beginning, if people hadn't faced their fears, then we'd still be starving to death hiding in caves, drawing pictures of life, instead of living it', huh?" It was a reference to something his uncle had said to him sometime back

"This is true," Paul replied, and then smiled proudly, acknowledging his nephew's reference to the memory. He then looked at his watch. "Hey, the clock's ticking," he said emphatically. "We'd better get ready to go if we're going to get there on time."

They quickly devoured their last few bites of breakfast and rose from the table. As they cleared the dishes and prepared to leave, Paul began humming some old song that just came to his mind from back in his youth:

"Uhmmm…uhm…ticking away…uhmmm uhm…uhmmm uhm an uhm day…"

Chapter 4

With the stops they needed to make, the trip to the Drop Zone would take them around an hour in all. The airport was on the outskirts of a small town just south of Indianapolis. It wasn't much of an airport. A flying field was about all it amounted to, located out amongst cow pastures and stands of corn. It had two large hangers, each with concrete floors. There were several rows of long buildings painted white with metal roofs which paralleled each other, all situated alongside a single paved runway.

The long buildings were each segmented into individual bays, with only a few even having doors. They were just under-roof graveled parking spaces for small aircraft, Cessna's mostly—and the occasional custom-made, single-seat, experimental flying-box with wings.

The largest plane there was an old twin-engine, six-seater Beech Craft. Owned and operated by the people who ran the airport. They mostly used it as a service for the farmers and locals to fly around the county so they could observe their respective properties from the air, and for the occasional chartered business or pleasure trip to a larger city like Chicago, Ill., or Louisville, Ky.

The Drop Zone was housed in the largest hanger. It had enough floor space to park two Cessna 182's inside, along with a huge carpeted area for the skydivers to pack parachutes on. It was out of the hot sun, easier on the knees when packing chutes and it was a great place for everyone to lie around at the end of a long, adrenaline-filled day of fun.

There was a small training room in the back where the students were taught the basics of skydiving: what makes up a parachute rig, how to enter and exit the plane, how to identify possible malfunctions, if, by chance, there was one, and how not to crap your pants and act quickly and accordingly if something unfortunate did happen.

The students also learned: how to follow radio commands, steer a parachute on descent, and how to perform a PLF—a Parachute Landing Fall—after their feet hit the ground, and for the more advanced students, the fine art of body flight—Free-falling, as most called it, but to some, the brief event was an artistic expression of athletic prowess and agility.

It was much akin to the famed Kata, performed for centuries by enthusiasts of Karate and Kung Fu. To them, free-fall was an aerial dance of form and articulate fluidity, delicately executed in the equivalent of a 120 mile-per-hour, hurricane-force wind. To others, the act was shear insanity. Only a small portion of beginning students ever reached that level of commitment, or courage.

Mounted in progressive stages on two of the walls of the training room were large laminated illustrations. These were used to help map things out for the students. On the largest illustration, saliently displayed on the wall to the left-front of the class, was the simple, yet primary tool of education that all the trainers used: a poster of the typical upwind, S-patterned, zigzagging flight path.

This method was the best way to bleed altitude and stay upwind until it was time to fly over the landing area, make the final 180-degree turn, and then land facing into the wind, always producing the safest, most controlled landings.

In the unlikely event of a radio failure, this was the most crucial piece of information the student needed to know. Since the sport started using advanced parachute design— typically a ram-air, elliptical flying wing—it could make the difference between landing like a butterfly and crashing into the ground at high speed.

There were seats in the training room for nearly twenty students, if necessary, but that was pushing the capacity somewhat. And there was a Video Center built into an angled wall in the front-right corner of the odd-shaped room, which featured three video-display monitors, one large main one, and two smaller ones, and below them, inset into the wall, the usual digital recording and sound equipment configuration.

The Video Center was where the trainers graphically displayed the dangers, as well as the thrills of the sport. This was also where the Jumpmasters made mini-DVD copies of the student's experience—for a nominal fee, of course. Just about everyone wanted a video, no matter the cost, mainly to have something to show their friends to prove that they'd actually done it.

<<< >>>

Jeremy and his uncle had stopped and picked up Scott and Bass before heading out of town. They were all nervously excited upon seeing each other. All three of the boys were obviously tired, too. Each had bloodshot eyes from not being able to sleep the night before. Paul giggled under his breath when he saw them. Just knowing what they were feeling made him feel the same excitement inside—just as he had felt his first time many years before.

He looked over at Jeremy, sitting next to him in the front seat, and then he quickly glanced back at Scott on the passenger side, and at Bass sitting behind him. He realized that each of them was sitting in nearly the same position: legs drawn together, knees touching, with both palms slapped together and their hands wedged in between their legs, as if they were cold, even though it was a fairly warm morning. All three were gently rocking forward and backward. Paul realized that he was the only one in the car who noticed this, and the thought of it made him giggle to himself again.

Jeremy looked over at his uncle, and sharply asked, "What?"

"What?" Paul answered back, like nothing in particular was on his mind. He laughed to himself again.

They drove on.

As the old model SUV 4x4 slowed to a halt at one of the last stop signs before leaving town, a middle-aged lady pulled up beside them in one of those sporty electric wheel chairs. It was purple and had big gray, knobby tires on it. She had a leash in her hand and at the end was a little mutt-of-a-dog, white with brown splotches all over it. It seemed to have the energy of ten animals its size, bouncing around like it was a kernel of popcorn in a hot skillet.

She looked both ways, up at the traffic light, and then with a forward push on the little joy stick mounted at the end of her right-hand armrest, she directed her motorized chair off the sloping curb, her dog anxiously tugging her across the street.

As she passed in front of the SUV, she glanced up over the hood. The familiar person in the vehicle brought a smile to her face. She grinned largely, and at the same time lifted her left hand awkwardly and gestured toward Paul, giving him a hearty thumbs-up. She looked at Jeremy, at Scott and Bass in the back seat, and then smiled even bigger, her teeth glistening in the morning sunshine. They all smiled back, nodding their heads.

"Hello, Mr. Usher. Out for a walk!" she said, still smiling as she made it to the other side of the road, wheels spiting road sand on the way up the curb, just as the light turned green. "Not sure who's walking who," she said loudly with perfect comedic delivery, her voice trailing off as she continued down the sidewalk.

Paul waved at her. "See you, Beth!" he yelled out the window, as he resumed driving.

"Who's that?" Scott asked, still watching her, head swiveled around and looking back through the rear window as they pulled away.

"That's Beth Rivers. She comes down to the shop on and off, volunteers, helps with the kids and the animals. Nice lady, got a lot of spunk, that one does!" he said, as he glanced at her one more time through the side mirror, obviously viewing some memories.

"Wow! She's just out, running around by herself?" Bass queried with amazement, his eyes still on her, watching her dog excitedly straining at its leash, seemingly trying to choke itself to death on purpose.

"Yep, why?" Paul replied, as if it wasn't strange at all.

"Man, I'd hate to be handicapped like that," Scott said, mostly to himself, now turning around facing forward.

"We're all handicapped, Scott." Paul heard the comment. "But the more politically correct term is: *challenged*. And we all are, in one way or another. What matters is what one..."

"Yeah, especially Scott!" Bass interjected abruptly, getting a scrunched-face smirk and a shoulder shove in return.

Paul waited for a moment until the giggles subsided.

"What matters is what one does with it," Paul said with extra emphasis. "She and I had a conversation once. She told me, 'You just gotta do the best you can do with what you've got, with what you've been given, or not given!' She's got a serious point there. Yep, spunky lady! Spunky dog, too," he then added. "That thing'd dig a hole just bouncing around if you were to leave it in one spot for too long!" He snickered at the image in his mind.

Jeremy just sat there, still watching the woman and her dog as they receded into the distance behind them. Something about her, or what his uncle just said, produced a sense of awe. He wasn't exactly sure why. His thoughts were then broken.

"So, guys, you ready for this?" Paul said exuberantly, changing the subject.

Scott was the first to answer in his characteristic, macho way.

"Nooooo doubt! Going to jump out of an airplane, toooooday, yep, going to fly like a bird. I've been waiting for this, seems like forever." He took a deep breath and exhaled hard.

Bass interjected.

"Yes sir, we're going to do it, just dooooo-it!" Bass said, imitating in an over-zealous announcer's voice, the new catch-phrase of the recent dog-park commercials. "Can't wait..." he trailed off to a whisper, "can't...wait..." The others didn't hear him murmur the rest of his comments, as he turned his head and again looked out the window. "Can't wait, but wouldn't mind waiting...I can't breathe...can't wait to breathe...just want to breathe." Bass continued murmuring it under his breath like a lyric to one of those songs that you can't get out of your head.

Jeremy just sat there, staring out of the window and looking up at the sky, apparently lost in thought, too.

Paul softly laughed to himself at the guys' inflated attempts at showing courage. He knew that all three were on the proverbial edges of their seats, and that they were experiencing some of the deepest and rawest feelings that they had ever felt in their young lives—just as he remembered experiencing. He was seeing the humor in it, yet, at the same time, he knew the intense psychological stress they were under. He was proud of them, proud of their determination to face something like this.

In a way, he felt like a tribal elder preparing the young boys for a ritual initiation. He hoped they were ready—especially Jeremy.

Chapter 5

Jeremy was an average school kid, at least on the outside. Tall, medium-length, light brown hair, average build with a little buff-ness from the hard work he did after school and on the weekends to earn spending money and to save for college.

He was a very articulate kid, loved to read all sorts of different things, good vocabulary, and a deep thinker, as his uncle and their old family friend, Finley, used to remark. On the inside, though, Jeremy was what his uncle called, "dazed and confused." Even though he was just an average kid, from an average town, he did seem to have an above average amount of tragedy in his young life. And this tended to push him into varying levels of anxiety, and depression.

Jeremy lived an extremely up-and-down sort of existence the years following his mother's death. Spending time with his uncle, their friend Finley, and Jeremy's two best friends were the up times.

Scott Ramses was an average kid, too, about 5' 10", and very athletic. Although he never went out for sports, he worked out on his own, "in spite of the jocks," he'd say. He didn't like their better-than-thou smugness any more than Jeremy did. Scott was always well tanned and had short blond hair, bleached from working outside in the sun on his parents' small farm just on the edge of town. Scott was a good kid, but he was always the one who was the most mouthy and mischievous of the lot.

He'd gotten them all in numerous dilemmas, numerous times, although not seriously—mostly pranks in bad taste, that sort of thing. Scott wasn't extremely smart, but he was genuine, and he had an uncanny way of expressing things of a deep nature in the most simplest of terms. This is what Jeremy liked about him the most.

Michael Fishman—"Bass" for short—was another good kid, though somewhat on the nerdy side. He was smart, had good grades, an inch or two taller than Jeremy. He had short, dark brown hair and wore glasses—although the last year of school he switched to contacts. "For the girls," he'd say.

Although he wasn't as built-up as Scott Ramses, he, too, was athletic. He played basketball all through junior high and high school, and even though he wasn't exceptionally good at the sport, he always seemed to make the team. No one tried harder, or spent as much time as he did practicing. He was just one of those guys who loved to play and just wouldn't give up. No matter what anyone said.

One time in a close game, he received the ball and everyone started to yell, "Go Fish, Go Fish." Then, with a profoundly ethereal feeling of control, unusual power, and clarity of mind, he executed the greatest moves he had ever done in his life: a behind-the-back blind dribble, spin around, bounce pass between an opponent's legs to himself on the run, and then topped it off with an amazingly timed, back-jumping, fade-away, three-pointer, buzzer-beating shot that won the game. It was the hallmark of his sports career, making him feel, for several days after, like Michael Jordan: the greatest all-around basketball player of all time.

To him, it was an unearthly epiphany, an in-the-zone, tapping-in-to-the-power-of-the-universe, kind of thing. It was the best he'd ever played, ever imagined he could play—but it was never to happen again. He always wished that he'd been given the Gift by what he called the "the great God of basketball," but he finally realized, after the many years of frustration, that the important thing, for him, was to just keep showing up and playing.

They called him Bass for the obvious reason—his name was Fishman, and the fact that, on a well-storied boating trip one summer with his family, a fish actually jumped straight up out of the lake and knocked Bass backwards into the water—the suddenness of it more than the impact, everyone quickly realized, causing the awkward spill—which, just as suddenly, sent everyone into uncontrollable hysterics.

Bass was never quite able to live that one down.

He'd been called Bass since he was in fifth grade, by everyone. After a number of years, even his own family members started calling him Bass all the time. He finally figured it was like what his father had always said, "You just have to accept what you've been given, Son, and make the best of it. Your legs just can't keep up with your mind! Or, keep you in a boat!" His dad would affectionately, albeit teasingly, rehash during every family get-together.

Even though he really didn't like the name, he became sort of proud of it after a while. It was this attitude that Jeremy liked in Bass. Every once in a while, Jeremy would call Bass by his given name, Michael, usually offering a wink along with it. Bass knew it wasn't just because it was his name, but also because of the old basketball player, Michael Jordan. They both, as Jeremy had once commented, had the same characteristic tenacity when it came to doing things. That always made Bass happy. It helped him accept his shortcomings, and his nickname, knowing that he had a friend who really understood him.

Jeremy played sports his first year in junior high school, too, but stopped after that, mainly because he also got tired of all the "better-than-thou" jock stuff that always went on between lots of the kids at his school. But, he still loved to shoot hoops with his friends, mostly because he liked the physics involved.

His uncle would always remind him that a sport was, in a way, like life: "you're trying to get to a goal. Something is always trying to keep you from it, blocking you. You make your mistakes as you go along, learn from them. You take your blows as those come, learn from them. And, if you concentrate hard enough, work hard enough, you eventually figure out a way to outsmart the opposition, at least once in a while. And, along the way, you find a few good friends— from both sides of the playing field."

Jeremy, Bass, and Scott were about as close as friends could be. They helped each other. They supported each other. Always pushed and prodded each other. And they loved to go on adventures. They would go fishing, camping, swimming, and exploring together. Sometimes they went hunting together, although they never really did ever kill anything.

Once, on one of their few hunting excursions, all three simultaneously shot their pellet guns at a young rabbit. But after they got close enough to the thing to look into its sad little eyes, they realized that they hadn't killed it at all. It had just been wounded in one of its hind legs. They never did figure out which one of them actually shot it, and neither of them could finish it off either.

In sharp contrast to what they had set out to do, that afternoon turned into a harried attempt at a great animal rescue. They quickly bandaged the wound, wrapped the poor thing up in Bass' favorite jacket, and, taking turns carrying it, ran over a mile to where they had hidden their bikes and then rode like the wind to the nearest veterinarian's office.

Amazingly, the animal survived.

One of their favorite adventurous things to do was to explore the caves west of town. Salamander and Buchner's were the largest, and their favorites. They had once gotten lost in the very back of Salamander when they weren't paying attention—the experience really scared the boys, especially Jeremy. After that, they stayed in familiar territory as they learned to be a little more careful, and calculated.

It was during one of those caving trips, the summer after junior high school, that they had made the decision to jump out of an airplane to commemorate their future graduations. The three sat around a small campfire just inside of Buchner's cave and made a pinprick blood-pact, agreeing that on that great and miraculous day, they would face this ultimate-of-tests, together.

This was the day they had waited for. It had finally arrived. This was going to be their day. The one they had all dreamed about for so long. This was their quest, their mission. It was going to be their epiphany. It was going to bring about their long-sought-after revelation of what manhood was supposed to be. They were going to "break the bonds of gravity and fly to new heights of understanding," they'd poetically articulate.

They were going to go down there. They were going to take that class. Then they were going to climb into that plane, fly three thousand feet up into the big blue sky, open that door, and then jump out. This was going to be their day of triumph! Their day of glory! Yet, they couldn't help but wonder—during all the tossing and turning the night before—which one of them was going to be going out of the door first?

Chapter 6

"So, you guys are all done with school now. Any new thoughts on careers, jobs, stuff like that?" He tried to make conversation to help relieve some of their obvious stress as they made their way down the road.

"I don't know, the big J's probably going to be a writer or journalist or something like that, since he's always got his nose in a book," Scott said with a laugh. "I'm going to college, if we can afford it. Don't know what for yet, but I'll figure something out. Maybe a brain surgeon, or maybe I'll be a CEO of one of those big corporations—sit around in my big, butt-comfy chair and make everyone else do stuff, while I rake in the money."

They all laughed.

"I'm thinking about sports medicine or sports training. I…" Bass began saying, but was interrupted.

"Yeah, sports, right, sporting goods maybe—he's going to sell basketball key chains in one of those little box stores in the mall," Scott joked. Everyone laughed again. "Naw, I'm just teasing you. You go for it Bass-man."

Bass continued, "Uhmm, I'm thinking about sports medicine, training, maybe, using computers and technology to help develop the right muscles, you know. Learning nutrition therapy, too, and maybe work with kids, early, to help them get better, so they'll be ready when they get older. I'm not sure. I think that would be cool.

"But then again, I'll probably just go to a business college like my dad wants me to. He's already got something 'cooking,' he says." Bass took a deep breath and sighed. Paul recognized the subtle, yet painfully obvious disappointment in Bass's airy expression.

Jeremy thought the sports idea really fit Bass, and that that would be a cool thing for him to do—help people achieve their dreams. But, knowing Bass's dad too, he figured Bass would end up a businessman or something. Just like Bass had said. Bass' dad was very persuasive when it came to his son.

"Nah, not me," Scott exclaimed. "I want to do something cool, like stuntman work or something. You know, wreck cars, jump off of buildings and bridges and stuff!" Scott laughed after the comment. "That'd be *really* awesome."

"That's nice, Bass," Paul said, addressing Bass first. "I could see you doing something in sports…" He paused. "And I'd bet you'd be good at wrecking cars, Scott." Everyone laughed. God help us, Paul thought, and then continued, "Soooo, you guys ever think just why you want to do this? The jump, I mean. I know that it's going to be 'cool' and all, and it'll be 'awesome' telling all your friends that you jumped out of an airplane, but have you ever asked yourselves, just why? *Why* you really want to do this in the first place?"

They were all silent for a moment, trying to contemplate some deeper reason than just the obvious. Then Scott hollered out, "Females!" They all laughed again, knowing what he meant. "The ladies just love this swarsh-buckling crap. They fall all over guys who do this stuff!"

Paul and the others laughed again, while shaking their heads, thinking that is just Scott. But they understood.

Jeremy spoke next. "I want to do it, well, I guess because it's just…*not* natural. I mean, like when we jumped off Miller's Bridge. After we did it, I felt so, well, kind of free. Kind of in control of myself, you know, like I could do just about anything."

Paul gave each of them that over-the-glasses look. He cleared his throat, and then quickly turned his attention back to his driving. The boys knew what Paul was thinking.

"Yeah, I felt the same way too!" Bass said. "You know, it was cool because after I did that, I think I got better at basketball. I mean, I wasn't so apprehensive about shooting three-pointers. You know what I mean? I was more confident, I think."

"Appre-what? There you go, Bass. You're using those big words again. Can't you just use regular language while you're down here on Earth?" Scott said.

Jeremy laughed. "It means, *Scott*, that you're not sure about something. That you're a little scared of doing something. So you hold back, you know. You're afraid of what might happen. And it only seems to be 'big words' if all you know are little words!" Jeremy looked back toward Scott and smiled as Bass punched Scott in the arm, laughing. Scott reared up, ready to throw a few punches of his own.

Paul laughed also, and then interjected, "Alright, guys!"

Jeremy responded, "Yeah, I know what you mean, Bass. I think I actually got better in speech class after that, too. Kind of more confident, like I didn't really care what anybody else thought. Because I just knew I'd do all right! I mean, I still got real nervous, but it didn't matter as much."

"Difficult things seem to do that, you know, condition us that way," Paul said.

Scott interrupted, "Oh, let's get all deep and cosmic, and brain-iacle. Not everything's got to do with everything. It's not all that, '*to be, or not to be, that is the question*,' Shakespeare crap. It's just to, or not to, do it, or don't, that's all."

Bass just shook his head. He rolled his eyes and then looked away again. Paul and Jeremy thought to themselves that Scott had, once again, made one of his profound observations. They marveled at its truth and simplicity, and then laughed at how he had said it.

Their minds returned to the thoughts of the event they were soon to experience. They all went silent, pondering their own reasons for doing it, until Paul offered them something else to think about.

"Hey," Paul said with a sober tone, leaning slightly toward the three, barely smiling. "If your parachutes don't open, make sure you land face down, okay." He paused. They all developed seriously concerned looks on their faces. "I'd hate to have to roll over your broken, smashed up bodies just to get to your wallets!" He snickered.

Jeremy scrunched his eyes at the macabre, off-the-wall comment, and then said, "You need to seriously think about finding you a good woman Uncle Paul, like soon. That was sick, really sick!"

Then they all started laughing and swatting at Paul in response to his joke. The laughs abruptly stopped with another single comment from Paul Usher: "Uh, we're here, boys!"

The three simultaneously halted the hysteria, quickly turned, and were now looking fixedly ahead toward a small plane, which was slowly taking off from the airport's distant runway.

Each gulped down a jagged chunk of the molasses-thick air.

Chapter 7

"Greetings fellow sky-gazers. How are all of you? I'm Godfrey Givins, and welcome to our skydiving center. I'm your host for today—and, by the way, I'm also the owner of this humble establishment, and, consequently, that's why I get the privilege of addressing you fine people with what everyone around here calls 'the Talk.'" The man made those familiar quotation mark signs with his fingers as his eyebrows went up and down. "Sounds a little ominous I know, but well intentioned," the tanned, athletic-looking man said jokingly, yet with recognizable seriousness.

"You can all call me 'Brake', that's what everyone around here calls me." He paused and smiled. "I won't be instructing this class today. I'll be leaving that up to one of our qualified instructor-types. But, what I do get to do is to hopefully teach you all a few lessons about awareness. Just a few things that will help you remember how important 'it' is—awareness, I mean."

He did the quotation thing again.

The man looked around the room and randomly pointed his finger at a spiked-hair young man dressed in contemporary neo-punk-style clothing.

"You, do you think skydiving is…" He paused, as if searching for a particular word, "awesome," then added, "dude?" He smiled.

The young man also smiled, slightly embarrassed. Realizing all the eyes in the room were on him. He sat up straighter in his chair. "Uh, well, uh, yeah, totally awesome. I mean, like, you know, it's like you get to jump out of a perfectly good airplane." He laughed and looked around the room, wondering if he had impressed everyone with his wit.

Mr. Givins laughed along with everyone else. He crossed his arms over his chest, shook his head side-to-side and looked down to the floor. As if he had heard that same supposedly witty statement about a 'perfectly good airplane' a million times—which of course, he had.

"What about the rest of you?" He scanned the room.

They all mumbled their own acknowledgements to the question. Jeremy just smiled. Scott spoke. "Yeah, awesome!" Then repeating what Mr. Givins had said, added, "dude." Bass and Jeremy laughed.

Everyone laughed at the somewhat nostalgic use of descriptors.

Mr. Givins continued, "Yes, skydiving is awesome. It's…cool. It's definitely an eye-popping, heart-pounding, mind-blowing experience. And because of that very *thing*…" he paused for effect, "it's very, very dangerous."

The class abruptly settled down, realizing that the man in front of them was getting more serious now. A stern smile adorned his face. His eyes became deeply reflective, the look speaking a thousand silent words. The class could suddenly see the years of experience emanating from this man's gaze. A strange mixture of frustration, pain, even loss, yet the look was softened by a sublimely radiant joy. They all got quiet. All sat up a little straighter, and each felt a strange reverence all of a sudden.

"Yes, skydiving is dangerous. Don't be fooled into thinking otherwise. Skydiving is like any other choice one makes in their lives. It has consequences, sometimes good ones, sometimes bad ones. That's what 'the Talk' is all about." He made those quotation gestures one more time. "And, I'll ask you to bear with me in this short discourse. Because it's about the only time I get to use some of the sociology and psychology stuff I learned in college."

Jeremy listened more intently now.

"The point that I really want to get across to you, is this: the quality of experience you leave here with today is totally up to you. Skydiving is not an amusement park ride where someone straps you into a seat and everything is perfectly choreographed for your entertainment pleasure.

"Oh, the equipment is packed for you—by professionals, mind you. The radios are charged, checked, and serviced regularly, as are the planes. And you're going to be instructed on the do's and don'ts of the sport by experts, who've pretty much seen it all. But, from there on, it's up to you. You're the one who will decide the consequences of the experience. How you act, how you choose to *react,* to what unfolds before you, is what will determine the quality of the experience you have."

The majority of the class was wide-eyed and silent. Most were thinking intently about what the man was saying. Many were already visibly suffering from a gut-wrenching fear. With a few exuding that stern-faced look of determination, attempting to cover up their intense anxiety with a forged appearance of courage.

Due to his years of experience, Mr. Givins could easily pick out the ones who were somewhat struggling for control, or who were in some way preoccupied. Scott Ramses was one of those who caught his eye. He noticed his distraction. Scott was looking past him at a poster on the wall.

Something about Scott's inattention sparked a thought in Mr. Givin's mind.

The man lowered his eyes to the floor in a sullen moment of contemplation. He was trying to decide whether or not he should say what was on his mind. Making the decision, he looked back up with what appeared to be memory-generated glassiness in his eyes and then delicately began telling a story.

"There was this guy I knew, once, in college. It was a long time ago. A bunch of us decided to go parachuting at a local Drop Zone. We had all gone three or four times that summer. All of us were still beginners. Well, this guy used to be a real show-off. Real cocky, you know the type. A real jerk, actually."

He looked to the floor again. Repositioned his arms and legs for comfort, and then continued.

"He was flying his canopy down, you see, and instead of steering toward the designated landing site, as he was instructed to do in class—as well as numerous times during his descent, via radio—he decided that he would swoop down and just fly over toward the buildings, over all the spectators' heads, and attempt to land in front of the awestruck people. You know, show off a little. Put on a big show, something to brag about back on campus."

He paused again, looked down once more, and then continued.

"Well, he didn't quite make it. The air turbulence around the hanger, as with all structures natural or man-made, created a low pressure area around him—simple physics. Anyway, he and his canopy dropped like a rock, right on top of several people that were standing there next to the concession area.

"He ended up crashing into a nineteen-year-old female college freshman with the force of a Hino delivery truck, slamming her against a picnic table. *She* ended up with a broken back. He sustained a broken leg, in two places, and several other people were bruised up pretty badly. One had a nasty cut on the elbow—took twenty stitches." Mr. Givins looked down to the floor again, and then bit his lip.

"That pretty young girl had to spend two months in traction, four months in a hospital bed, and over a year in rehab. They actually thought for a time that she would end up paralyzed. But fortunately, she wasn't. Many claimed it was a miracle—I *know* it was."

Jeremy heard sadness in his voice, along with joy, and then anger.

"That stupid A-hole—please pardon my choice of nouns here—was specifically told in class to avoid the buildings because of the danger of the air turbulence and lower air pressures inherent to them. He was told on the radio during the last few moments of his flight to toggle back toward the landing area. But he wouldn't listen. He *refused* to listen. He chose to not look at the big picture that he had been shown, and instead, chose to only think of himself, his own agenda, and his own pride.

"His self-induced blindness had dire consequences that day, for everyone involved."

Once again, he looked to the floor, swept his foot in front of the other, and then back.

"You see, the sport of skydiving is very serious business. I want you all to remember that. Please!" He looked around the room. A sincere, yet soft expression then molded his face.

Jeremy spoke. "Can I ask you a couple of questions, Mr. Givins?"

The man looked up and replied, seemingly glad for the interruption, "Sure, uh…" He motioned a gesture for a name.

"My name's Jeremy…Jeremy Sayer."

"Yes, go right ahead, Jeremy Sayer, ask away."

"Uh, you're the guy in the story, aren't you?" Jeremy asked and then smiled. The others looked over at him with curious looks on their faces.

Mr. Givins laughed softly out of his nose, shook his head from side to side, and then responded, looking deeply into Jeremy's eyes, "Well, yes, Jeremy, I *am* the guy. I was the big hole with the 'A' in front of it." Everyone looked up at him with astonishment. "Yes, everyone, I'm the one in the story. I'm the one who pulled that stupid stunt that day, and I regret it even now. But, things do have a way of working themselves out. Your next question is probably: why in the world am I still into this skydiving thing?"

"Yeah, that's one of them," Jeremy replied.

"Well, I see you picked up on that, too. Uhmm, let me try to explain."

He backed up and leaned against the desk, folded his arms over his chest, and began stroking the thin beard that covered his chin. For a brief moment, he stared at nothing in particular, just empty space, apparently viewing a mental portrait of the picture he was about to draw for the class.

"After the accident, skydiving was the farthest thing from my mind. For a long time, the thought of it sickened me. Kind of like when you accidentally eat something spoiled. You know, you don't ever want to eat that thing again. Even if it's something you once really liked, or even loved. In one way, it was the worst time in my life. Yet, in another, it was the best."

Everyone squinted and then slanted their heads to the side in confusion.

"I learned something valuable at that juncture in my life, extremely valuable: about myself, *and* about life. I learned how my actions, my choices, even my very beliefs, can affect others. And, that was an area of life I'd missed for the most part—at least up to that point. I missed the significance of how interconnected everything—everyone—is. I missed seeing the Big Picture, the whole action-reaction thing. Or, the chain-reaction thing, if that's how you want to look at it."

The class was mesmerized. Each person was thinking about their own experiences, relating them to what Mr. Givins was saying.

"I also realized that—like the old saying goes—'it's not the trigger's fault, it's the finger's fault.'" He looked around for acknowledgement, and then continued, "It wasn't skydiving that was the problem. It was me. In fact, months later, because of that stupid stunt, and because of the sport of skydiving, I met the love of my life—my wife. And, several years later, we started skydiving together. Now we both love it.

"She showed me so much courage during that time, that even though I was scared to death to do it again, I finally found the courage to face it, and the tenacity to keep with it. Doing so truly changed my life—as did she."

He smiled real big as the women in the class whispered subtle comments of how romantic it all sounded.

"You know, there are a lot of challenges in this uncertain world of ours. Whatever yours are, facing them is no different than what you're facing today. Life is full of obstacles, full of frustrations—walls—the majority of these being mental and/or spiritual in nature.

"I've found it very fulfilling to make a career out of helping others overcome these obstacles. Skydiving, for me, is like a school. It forces me to think, to focus, to learn, to prepare, to show respect, and once again, as I illustrated before, to consider consequences. It's taught me to consider my mortality, and live a better life because of it. And that's the salient issue here, salient meaning, 'the part that sticks out.'" He did the quotation gesture again.

"Skydiving is one of those sports that is, without a doubt, death-defying. You're going to be hanging there, way the hell up in the air, under little more than a strong, well-built kite, with nothing but the big sky to stand on. You're going to be totally alone—even though you'll have a radio—and yet you're going to feel utterly connected to everything else at the same time. Trust me. It will be a life-changing experience for you."

He stood up from his leaning position against the desk.

"Well, that's about all I have for you. I hope I wasn't too dramatic or daunting. Oh yes, and remember, don't forget to have fun! You have to have fun! That's one of the main reasons you're all here, isn't it? Right?" He pointed around the room with his index finger, smiled, and then looked at his watch. "Any more questions before I send in your instructor?"

Jeremy raised his hand, speaking at the same time. "Yeah, uh, whatever happened to that college student? You know, the girl from the accident. She was alright?"

Mr. Givins laughed as he grabbed his jacket off the chair behind the desk.

"Oh, yes, I forgot to mention that. You remember I told you about meeting the love of my life, a few months after the accident? Well, it was her, the girl. I married her!" He paused, smiling at everyone. "Strange how things work out, huh? I guess life has its reasons! Anyway, you're about to meet her. She's going to be your instructor for the day. And by the way, her name is Grace."

Everyone gasped, and their eyes widened abruptly.

"I had the privilege of sharing some *consequences* with you. Now she gets to go over the *choices* part. Be careful, everyone! And enjoy—"

He smiled a huge smile again, and then slipped out of the room. Satisfied, and always amused at how pliable eyebrows can be.

Chapter 8

Paul left for the five hours it took for the instructors to teach the class. He picked up something to eat, stopped at a little park to enjoy his lunch on a picnic table, and, after he finished eating, reread the letter that had come in the mail that morning. Enclosed within it was another sealed envelope, this one addressed to Jeremy. Paul thought it was the right thing to do, to wait to give his nephew the letter, a letter from Jeremy's dad. It had been a long time since Joseph had communicated with his son—nearly two years.

Paul wondered about its contents.

The letter addressed directly to him only briefly stated that Jeremy's dad had done a lot of thinking. That he wanted Paul to give Jeremy the enclosed envelope he had sent, and to make absolutely sure that Jeremy opened it while he was with him. Paul convinced himself again that it was the best thing to do—to wait until after the jump to give it to him. He didn't want Jeremy's head all twisted up with emotions on a day like this.

When he returned to the airport, he saw the guys and the rest of the class out in a large grassy area walking around with their arms high in the air. As if holding onto invisible parachute steering toggles—the two cords which, when pulled down separately, turn the canopy, and when pulled simultaneously, flare the back of the canopy down like a bird does with its wings, allowing a controlled, feather-light landing.

They were all practicing how they would react to the radio instructions from the ground: right toggle down halfway, let up. Left toggle down halfway, let up, and then, the very last few seconds, flare! Both toggles half-down...three-quarters down...all the way down!

Paul watched as various other skydivers flew around and came in for landings. He thought: today's rigs are much better than when his old friend Finley had jumped when he was in the military back before the Gulf War. Back then—at least with most military rigs—you came in pretty much straight down and generally had to fall to the ground and roll to the side to keep from breaking your ankles. With this Ram-air technology, you can swoop in like a bird and land as gently as a butterfly. Things sure change with time, and knowledge, Paul thought.

It was the last part of the class, and the students were going through their final rehearsals before rigging up. Paul wished that he were going up that day. He would have gone, but he knew they could only fit three students, a Jumpmaster, and a pilot, in the small Cessna aircraft. He wanted the three boys to all go up together—so they could see each other's faces. At least, that's what he told himself. He smiled from ear-to-ear just thinking about it.

He then noticed the students high-fiving each other and walking back toward the hanger. The class was over.

<<< >>>

A flurry of activities abounded around the Drop Zone: skydivers were inside packing their parachutes on the huge carpeted floor; people were sitting around on picnic tables, in lawn chairs, and on big coolers out on the edge of the tarmac; riggers were pre-checking the student rigs, helmets and radios; pilots and mechanics were inspecting the planes and the weather. People everywhere were talking and laughing, and many were just looking up at the sky with their hands over their brows to block out the sun, watching the experienced jumpers do their thing. There were even a few dogs running around scarfing up the scraps of food that people had either dropped, or had thrown down for them.

The old, yet still powerful music of Tom Petty was playing in the background—*Running Down a Dream*, and *Learning to Fly* were some of the favorites when the students were there. Four guys were suited up in identical jump suits and lying belly-down on mechanic's carts, practicing the simultaneous, sequential turns they would soon be doing while formation flying. Three of the students, knowing they would be on the first load to go, were already over at the prep station getting ready to suit up. Their faces were sheet-white.

Paul greeted the guys at the hanger's entrance.

"Hey, hey, how was the class?" Paul asked with excitement, eyebrows high, barely able to breathe himself.

Bass was the first to try to speak.

"Whew, I guess this is it." He took a deep breath, exhaled and then continued, "Class was good, a lot to remember," he said.

The others had the same difficulty getting their breath.

"Piece of cake!" Scott said courageously, watching the guys on the carts, trying to think of a joke to make about them.

"Good class," Jeremy said. "It's a little hot out, and humid. This is going to be great, though. *Whew*, well, I guess this is the place, huh! We're really here!" His eyebrows went up and down with rapidity.

Then, to fend off the weight of the anxiety, they all started shaking each other's hands, high-fiving again, fidgeting, stretching, loosening up, and verbally spouting off a plethora of nonsensical gibberish: "it's been nice knowing you," and "see you on the other side," and Scott cracked them all up when he said, in a very good, granny-like sounding voice, "I've fallen, and I can't get up!" They all laughed, even though the comment made little sense to any of them, other than they'd remembered Scott's dad had used it on occasion.

They felt awkward and uncomfortably out of place, so they continued smacking each other on the shoulders, punching each other in the arms, and saying stupid things to compensate. None of them was able to stand still in one place for any length of time. And they all felt like they had to pee yet again.

They automatically settled down as they watched the first load of students begin to board a plane, the Jumpmaster carefully double-checking each person's rig as they climbed in. They watched absorbedly as the engine fired and the craft started rolling along the pavement, its door still open. The guys could hear as the Jumpmaster loudly spoke above the drone of the plane's engine as he went over the final three commands that his students would hear from him after they were at altitude: PUT YOUR FEET OUT AND STOP…GO ON OUT AND HANG, and then the final command given, when the Jumpmaster determined that they were over the right spot…JUMP, which, for a student, meant, release your death-grip!

Upon the harrowing call, the student is supposed to: let go, spread their arms out over, and off to the sides of their head, spread their legs apart, keep their knees and elbows appropriately bent, and initiate a hard arching, belly-out type configuration. This body position allows the jumper to remain stable in the wind until the static line pulls out the student's parachute as the plane races ahead, ultimately leaving the jumper hanging there, safe under his open parachute.

The boys gulped at the thick air when they heard the Load Coordinator's yell.

"Load number three, you're up!"

They all looked at each other, eyebrows high, faces flushed, and cheeks puffed out due to a sudden and voluminous exhalation of breath that came from each of them. They gulped down more of the thick air. Together, awkward and stiff, they walked to the rigging area where the various assistants awaited them with enthusiasm. Jeremy was the first to meet his.

She was a fragile-looking, attractive young girl named Caitlin Dobbs. Everyone there at the Drop Zone called her CD, for short. She was about as tall as Jeremy, had a thin petite build, and long honey-brown hair. One side of it was layered back, with a small brown-leather ornament in the shape of a diminutive bird holding it in place. She had on low-waist jeans, and a tight, short-sleeved, light blue, frilly Vnecked cotton shirt, with a fine gold necklace around her neck. A bulky radio hung off of her blandly ornate belt— seemingly over-sized compared to her thin waist.

CD was a college student, preparing to start her second year, and working hard toward a degree in education. Her aspirations were of becoming a teacher, and maybe working with troubled youths. But she hadn't settled on anything exactly yet. She had been skydiving for about two years, and had jumped close to one hundred times. She wasn't a Jumpmaster, yet. She was still a little inexperienced, but she was licensed and packed parachutes to help out and earn free jumps, and always did her part to help calm the new students as she assisted them with their rigs, before and after.

Jeremy was glad that he got her as a helper. He liked her from the moment he laid eyes on her.

Bass got a somewhat different assistant. The man had long, greasy, blue-black hair. He was unshaven, and had tattoos covering most of the skin of both arms, including a small one of a falcon on his cheek under his right sideburn. He kept murmuring, "You're going to freak, man. You're going to freak," and then humming to the music that was playing in the background as his muscled body twitched to its rhythm.

He told Bass to call him by his Indian name: *Sky*. Said it was short for Sky Hunter, and that he'd been named that by his family after a short stint in the military—Air Force, of course—and because he'd clocked the fastest delta maneuver at that zone.

Bass wished that he had been as lucky as Jeremy.

Scott's helper was a short, balding, gray-haired older man who looked to be in his sixties. The man was wearing an old, worn, seriously baggie, flame-colored jumpsuit. Scott couldn't help but wonder if the man was actually a skydiver, thinking he must be too old. The man first said his name was Bond...*James* Bond.

He then laughed, followed by, "Not really, my name is actually *Thomas* Bond, but, you might as well have some fun, right?" Scott thought his comment was kind of weird, and that he had used too much musk-scented cologne that morning.

All three backed up into the parachute rigs that their helpers were holding out for them, slipping their arms through the padded shoulder straps. They felt nervous and awkward and out of place.

For some reason, right then, Jeremy noticed how different all the people appeared to be: there were young people there, old people, punks with spiked hair, and cowboys with big belt buckles, business-types, and several obviously military types. Some had long hair, some had short hair, some seemed rather dirty and disheveled, while others appeared as prim and proper as an English gentleman just off the golf course. And by the looks of the parking lot, there were the well-off as well as the not-so-well off.

It reminded him of a college campus, of being surrounded by a diversity of people from all over the world. Everyone seemed to be having such a good time, and friendliness seemed to know no class. He was lost in the image of it all until his attractive assistant, CD, spoke, breaking his train of thought.

"Hi…I, I'm CD." She pointed to her little nametag just under her left collarbone. Everyone on staff at the center wore a gold nametag that had a set of bird's wings engraved on one side next to the person's first name, and the name of the center in smaller letters at the bottom. "You okay?" she asked sweetly with a smile.

"Yeah, uh, yeah, I was just thinking about all the different people here—you know, young people, old people."

He was interrupted when the guy who was helping Bass circled by at that instant, still mumbling, "Going to freak, man, going…to…freak!"

CD finished Jeremy's sentence in a low voice. "Strange people." They smiled at each other, and laughed softly. "Actually, he's ok. He'd help anyone in the world, and he loves kids—has five of them himself. Works three, sometimes four different jobs, go figure. Huh?" She smiled with the comment. "He really gets off on watching first-timers—I guess I do, too. I love adventure," she said, smiling again.

He watched her lips as she talked.

"So, you cool with this?" she asked, checking his parachute rig's straps one more time. When she got to the ones that went around his legs, his eyebrows rose up high and he actually wondered if this beautiful girl—who was so close in front of him now—could hear his heart palpitating.

"Yeah...uh, yeah," he replied, looking back up to her eyes, thinking she might have noticed him staring too long at her mouth. "Yeah, I'm ready, I'm good." He smiled at her with a curious look on his face. He took a deep breath and blew it out forcefully.

She could tell Jeremy liked her. At least, that's what she thought. She was surprised at her realization that she kind of felt the same way, but then she started thinking that he was just another jumper, only there for the thrills. She put her thoughts back on the rigging job.

Their plane was at the fueling station gassing up, so they had the chance to talk for a couple of minutes while waiting. They did so with surprising ease, seeing how they were strangers, and even though it was a short conversation, mostly about adventure and on-the-edge kind of stuff, they both silently felt something click between them.

But with Jeremy, it was more like a big-bang than just a click.

<<< >>>

After the three were all rigged and ready to go Mr. Givins walked up to them, looking intently back and forth between their faces and their rigs.

"You go for it, guys. *Be aware*, remember what you learned, and have fun." He squeezed Jeremy's shoulder because he was standing closest to him, but everyone felt the sentiment. "This is your Jumpmaster," he said, and then put his other hand on the shoulder of the older man who had helped Scott to suit up. "This is Mr. Bond, Mr. *James* Bond," he said with a giggle. "Actually, just call him Tom. Follow his instructions and you'll have the adventure of a lifetime."

He nodded with a look of confidence, and then walked over to another group of skydivers. To the ones that were still practicing their formations on those little mechanic's carts.

"Well, gentlemen, nice to meet you all. The moment of truth, huh?" Tom said with a smile. "What do you say, get on board? Shall we?"

He motioned toward the blue and white Cessna now waiting out beyond the gathering of people. The guys looked at each other, raised their eyebrows again, blew out another deeply held breath, and started walking toward the plane. On the way, they stopped briefly. The man named Thomas then spoke loudly to compensate for the high-decibel sound of the plane's idling engine.

"Usually, the biggest guy goes first. Then the next biggest, and so on, but since all of you appear to be about the same size and weight, which one of you would like to be the first one out?"

There was momentary silence.

They all gulped as inconspicuously as possible, and then began looking back and forth at each other. Jeremy got the words out first, although he strained in the effort. Scott trailed him by only a few seconds.

"I'll go," Jeremy said. "I'll go first," he repeated. He was instantly shocked at the words he had just spoken.

Scott said he would go second.

Bass didn't say anything. He just smiled and nodded, took another deep breath and blew it out in a rush of air that sounded like a horse making raspberries in a water trough.

Once again, they began their slow walk to the plane.

Their legs felt weighted and numb, and everywhere they looked it seemed as if they were being watched. Just outside the hanger there was another group of spectators: a couple of moms, an old man, a kid with a toothless sock puppet silently putting on a show, someone's girlfriend, and a couple of regulars who were there every weekend just for the sun, the fun and the excitement.

As Jeremy passed the small group of people, the old man standing there caught his eye for some reason. As he looked at him, a twinge of familiarity piqued his mind. Then, oddly, the old man spoke boldly to him as he passed.

"Don't forget to arch there, *young* man. It's like faith. It's what keeps you in control. Remember that?" The old man smiled with an odd intensity and then stepped back as the group passed.

Suddenly, Jeremy's attention was now on the spinning prop that they had to navigate around to access the entry door on the other side of the plane. After passing the rotating, potential people-grinder, Jeremy turned and looked back at the crowd and at that old man, suddenly curious about the familiar feeling he was having.

'*Arch...Faith?*' he recounted him saying. He thought about it for another quick second and then his mind returned to the immediacy of the moment as he peered into the cramped space of the seat-less plane.

He swallowed hard.

Jeremy then glanced to his right. Off in the distance, he noticed that girl, CD. She was just standing there by some people out on the tarmac, looking right at him. She smiled and waved, and then turned away, apparently finished with whatever it was she was doing. Jeremy grabbed one more glance at her as she disappeared into the mirage-like haze of the spinning prop on her way back toward the hanger.

Jeremy smiled. His mind drifted.

Bass was instructed to climb in first. He crawled to the back and sat down on the floor facing forward. Then Scott got in and sat with his parachute against the back of the pilot's seat. Then, reluctantly, Jeremy climbed in, back first as instructed, and sat down next to the door opening facing the back of the plane. They all felt awkward, cramped up, uncomfortably pinched by their parachutes' straps. They felt like sardines in a can, as many skydivers tend to describe it. Their bodies all meshed together in the hot, stuffy, tightly enclosed space.

The man named Tom did another rig check on Jeremy. He then unfastened the static line that was strapped to his parachute's pack, and motioned for Jeremy to notice that he was indeed now hooking it to the metal eyelet securely bolted to the floor of the plane next to the door. Jeremy acknowledged it with a nod. Tom nodded back, climbed in, and told the pilot that they were good to go.

The idling engine roared to life with a push of the throttle. The plane slowly turned away from the hanger, taxied across the tarmac, turned yet again and started down the runway. When it reached the end of the paved path, the pilot whipped the plane around one hundred and eighty degrees, and faced it into the wind. Staying on the brakes, he pushed the throttle halfway forward. The plane shook violently as Tom slammed the door. Then the pilot said, "And away-eee we-eee go!" He let off the brakes and the craft lunged forward as if released by a catapult.

Tom yelled at Jeremy, just as the plane started lifting from the ground.

"You ready to change your life?" He laughed, grinning from ear to ear, and then looked out of the door's window.

Jeremy smiled, gulped down the dryness in his throat. He looked out of the window, too, and watched the haze outside oddly thicken with every passing second. His mind began to congeal, just as the atmosphere was doing there in front of his eyes. He felt his innermost self begin to quiver, and his stomach suddenly became sour. He closed his eyelids tightly, as if looking inside. As if trying to find some stillness—something, anything, to make the pressure that was squeezing down on him go away.

The climb to altitude would take about twenty minutes. A little longer than usual, the pilot had said, because of having to wait on several other planes coming in for landings at the small airport. For the majority of the trip up, Jeremy didn't want to look out of the window. He would close his eyes for a minute or two, and then open them for a quick glance, and then quickly close them again. Each time contemplating where he was, where he was going, what he was about to do—and wondering *why* in the world he was doing it.

No one talked much on the ride to altitude. However, Scott did manage to yell out a hearty: "THE MOMENT OF TRUTH!"

And Bass replied with: "TO INFINITY, AND *BEYOND*! YEAAAAH!"

But they had to yell loudly over the sound of the powerful engine to be heard. They all smiled at the comments, even Thomas. But for the most part, they remained silent and reflective.

When they were approaching jump-run, Tom gave the pilot a hand signal: a thumb to the right, and then all five fingers extended. This indicated a slight right course change of about five degrees.

As the plane turned, Tom gave him a thumbs-up, telling him to straighten out. Another few minutes went by. The guys all jerked with nervous reactions when Tom put his hand on Jeremy's left knee, slapped it, and yelled, "DOOR!"

Jeremy's heart about blew out of his chest.

With that, Tom opened the upward-swinging door, putting one foot out onto the small step. The guys wondered what he was doing, and then they simultaneously realized that he was looking down, spotting the landing zone to make sure Jeremy was let out over the right area—in direct alignment and upwind of the little airport, just as they had been taught in class.

They then remembered what Scott had said about their Jumpmaster back in the hanger. They hoped this old man knew what he was doing.

Scott and Bass could tell that Jeremy was afraid. 'Petrified' would be a better term. His face was grayish-white, having the pallor of an old, dingy-gray painter's sheet.

Tom checked Jeremy's static line one last time, showing him again that it was securely fixed to the metal loop bolted to the floor of the plane. He did another quick check of the back of Jeremy's rig.

Then, the dreaded command came.

He yelled it directly at Jeremy's face.

"PUT YOUR FEET OUT, AND STOP!"

Jeremy just sat there. He didn't want to move. He looked back at his friends who were grinning. He managed to grin back, but strained in the attempt. Then, slowly, carefully, he followed the instructions. He looked down for the first time, down through the thick air at the surreal scene below him.

He shook his head in disbelief.

He took another deep breath and swallowed hard.

The air tasted sour.

He felt the eighty-knot windblast on his feet as he gradually extended them out the door. Instinctively, he compensated for it with his strong leg muscles. He then placed his feet on the little step, precariously struggled to hang them over its edge, desperate to get a good foothold. He did so, and then stopped.

He waited for what seemed an eternity.

Jeremy's heart was racing.

His mind was spinning.

Jeremy couldn't believe his feet were actually out of the plane. He felt like he was imagining it all, like his sleep-less, tossing dreams the night before.

Then Tom started looking around jerkily. He was hanging out the door beside Jeremy, looking forward of the plane, and then behind it. *What was happening*, Jeremy thought. *What's wrong!* he wanted to cry out.

"GO ON OUT AND HANG!" Tom yelled suddenly.

Jeremy jerked in reaction to the loud call. He froze for a moment, but then somewhat gained his senses and slowly started reaching out, again fighting the violently turbulent prop blast.

He grabbed onto the wing's strut tightly.

He blew out the breath that he had been holding and quickly took in another—even deeper than before. It was sour, too. His heart was beating like crazy. He couldn't believe this was happening. That he was actually there. He looked back at his friends for one more glance. He saw their horrified looks. They were just sitting there with their mouths open.

Tom grabbed his attention again and motioned for him to proceed a little more quickly this time.

Jeremy then slid his hands out along the leading edge of the thick, painted-metal wing support, feeling the full force of the prop blast against his body as he stood there, hunched over, standing on the step. With a gasp, he gripped it as tightly as he could and let his feet slip off.

He and the others were shocked to see that he was now dangling in mid-air.

Jeremy glanced down, then forward, stopping his eyes on the plane's prop.

He just couldn't believe it. He couldn't believe it.

He exhaled and quickly took another breath, holding it in tightly as if he were getting ready to go underwater.

He looked over his left shoulder at Tom. Tom was looking down at the ground. It seemed that he was hanging there for too long. *What's wrong*, he thought again.

At that moment, Tom looked up, smiled another ear-to-ear, purse-lipped smile, and then, with a thumb high in the air, shouted the last command.

"JUMP!"

Jeremy tried to smile back.

He couldn't see the others.

He looked forward again, now really noticing the plane's prop; it appeared to be spinning backwards. He tried to remember where he was, what he was doing. If there was anything he might have forgotten from the training.

Brake...*Brake!* So, that's why they called Mr. Givins 'Brake', because of the accident. Because he couldn't stop...or, maybe because he "stopped" being the asshole he said he used to be. Jeremy realized how peculiar it was that he was thinking of all this now. Hanging there on the wing of a plane—strange, he thought.

Tom motioned again for him to let go.

Jeremy, remembering what he was taught, spread his legs apart, bent his knees, and then tightened the muscles in his back to arch.

With the greatest of effort, he let go.

He watched his fingers slip off the strut.

Felt his body, as well as his mind, start to drift.

He was falling.

He was falling through the sky.
And it seemed like it was all happening in slow motion.
He felt like he was going to pass out.
He felt like he was going to die.

Chapter 9

"Hello, Jeremy," a man with strange ethereal eyes and a serene smile, spoke. "You're quite startled, aren't you? You needn't be. Just take a moment to gather yourself. Take a few deep breaths. You're welcome to look around as much as you'd like. Please do. It will help orient your senses."

Jeremy looked up at the towering figure before him, and then slowly turned his head to look around, responding to the voice's encouragement. Everything seemed so large, and in contrast, Jeremy felt so small. Briefly, he had a strange feeling of insignificance, but then it went away as he turned back and began to notice the details of the person behind the voice.

The man had gray hair, cut short, and parted on one side. He wore an old-fashioned, yet crisp blue-gray suit with long, streamlined lapels. One had a small, odd-looking flower sticking out of a buttonhole. The man had a trimmed gray beard, grayer than his hair, and round-ish metal-framed glasses. He looked old, yet life and energy seemed to form his somewhat childish expression.

Jeremy didn't know where he was, and he didn't know this man.

His mind swirled as he attempted to bring it all together.

His eyes told him where he apparently was, but his mind kept telling him where he *should* be: in the sky, falling through the air. This made him confused, disoriented. He thought once again about how large everything around him was, and how distorted everything seemed to be. He felt small, suddenly sickened by the confusion.

He started feeling really scared.

"Yes, Jeremy, everything does seem rather enlarged and over-encompassing doesn't it. Just take a few more moments. You'll be fine!"

Jeremy continued to think of the airplane, and falling.

His memory seemed to oscillate.

It folded back and forth, from where he was, to where he was now.

This wasn't right, he thought.

"You're dealing with it, Jeremy. That's it. You just need to keep *choosing* to, and it will all come together for you. I assure you."

Jeremy looked around again for a brief moment, but then closed his eyes tightly.

Then, he quickly opened them again, wider.

This time, all that was around him, including the man, started to come into greater focus. He blinked rapidly, and took yet another deep breath, determined to understand. At that moment, everything started to—it seemed to—shrink down, and become more proportional, he thought.

"That's good, Jeremy. See, as I said, you're finding the way to deal with it. Let's just give it a few more moments, and then we'll start."

Jeremy thought: *Start…start what?*

"Start the session," the man spoke. "Yes, you're coming around nicely, earlier than most, actually. I assumed as much."

Jeremy noticed the man was moving closer toward him. He felt that it was difficult to turn his head to even look. He felt exhausted, drained. He tried to speak, mumbled in his mind a few words. *What…what's happening?*

The man spoke again, whispering softly. "You're one of my new students, Jeremy. A very…*necessary* one, I would include. One whose, contributions, before your experiences here are complete, will offer incalculable substance to, well, shall I say, everything?"

He smiled excitedly, letting out a pithy laugh.

"Not to imply that anyone else's contributions are of *less* importance, mind you. Everyone has that BIG role to play, before their work on Earth is complete." He calmed, then spoke again, slowly and deliberately. "You're in my study, Daniel Jeremy Sayer. This is where I begin many of the orientation sessions. You're feeling better now. Are you not?"

Jeremy squinted, lowered his head, blinked several times, and then noticed his hands and arms. He slowly turned his palms up. He looked at them. He was trembling. His thoughts kept asking, *is this real?*

"Yes, Jeremy. This is real, this place, this...*time*. You are real. I am real. What we are experiencing at this very moment, is all real. Trust me. As time always portends, you will see more clearly. Things will become more apparent for you very soon." Again, a sudden joyous chuckle followed.

As Jeremy continued taking deep breaths, everything around him, including the man, slowly began to reduce in size. But then, he wasn't sure if it weren't the other way around and that he was getting larger. Or maybe both were happening at the same time. It was as if the actual focusing of his mind had something to do with it. He tried harder. Until he, the man, and the surroundings, were almost proportional. Proportional not just in size, he concluded, but in intensity. Yes, intensity seemed the best way to describe it.

Jeremy thought how odd this was.

His amusement at the strangeness quickly passed when he once again remembered where he was, and where his mind told him that he should be. He still felt dizzy, shaken and weak. Everything around him was getting more intense again. It all seemed to start undulating, throbbing. Yes, throbbing, he thought. As if everything was coming at him, bombarding his senses in waves.

He suddenly felt his heart pounding.

"Jeremy...*Jeremy*, listen to my voice. Apply your mind," the man said.

Jeremy heard the man speak. He then put his lips together, folded them inside his mouth, and bit down. He sensed that he must be determined, determined to gain control. As he forced the thought of focusing, the throbbing pulsating intensities of everything around him began to settle down again. Everything seemed to smooth out: what he was seeing, what he was feeling, what he was hearing. The dizziness and disorientation started to leave. Yet, he realized that he had to concentrate to hold it all still.

What's happening? he thought.

Chapter 10

"Good, Jeremy, good," the man spoke. "Concentrate. That's it, concentrate. Well done. As I said, you've attuned more quickly than most. You're feeling better now, aren't you? It will still take a little while to stabilize, it always does, especially at your age." He smiled sensitively again. "Just listen to what I am about to tell you. Listen, not only to my words, but concentrate on their meaning."

He emphasized the words for Jeremy by placing his hands, fingertip-to-fingertip in the air. As if he were gently caressing and moving his fingers around the surface area of an invisible sphere.

"Your mind is beginning to fill up with questions, very good. This is a wonderful sign. You're coming around nicely, indeed. Now then, let me answer some of the more immediately relevant one's for you first. And then, later, during another period, we will talk about some of the, shall we say, deeper subjects that you'll find developing from our discussions."

Jeremy thought: *Discussions?*

"The first two questions in your mind," he paused and laughed slightly, "are whether you are dead, or maybe demented? And if not, where are you?" He smiled once more. "Jeremy, let me assure you," he laughed again, "you are neither dead, nor are you demented. You're quite alive, and in ways that you, as of yet, have no concept. As far as where you are, well, it's quite difficult to explain, in its entirety, at least for now. But, let it suffice to say that you are in my study, as it were.

"My name is Professor Timorous Vector. You may call me *Professor*, if you would like. This is where I often begin orientation with the new students."

He motioned toward the surrounding room.

Jeremy thought: *Students...Professor?*

"Yes, *yes*, Jeremy, but, labels are so superficial. Titles, names, they are so formal, yet not always indicative of who we really are, wouldn't you agree?" He giggled softly again, then continued. "The character, this is what is important. What someone is inside, who they are. That which drives what they do, that which weighs and chooses the decisions they make. This is the real stuff of a being!"

He looked at Jeremy, smiled again, and then continued talking.

"Jeremy, I'm here to help you. That should answer your next question. Think of me as a teacher, a guide, a messenger, if you would like. My mission is to help you learn. To help you understand. To help you develop and expand. By doing so, well, it will help you. It will help me. It will help everything, as I said."

Jeremy's head was still spinning.

He thought: *Mission? Help me...help everything?*

Did he see? He didn't see at all.

"Well, you will. You can trust me," the man said, with a soft gentleness resonant in his voice. He then smiled largely again. "We might as well just *jump* right in and get started, hadn't we?" The man sputtered a slight laugh again because of the word 'jump'. "Do you see that object, Jeremy?" He motioned to his left.

Jeremy slowly turned and noticed a wall, a huge wall that seemed to stretch up and down and to both sides as far has he could see. Immediately stunned that he had not noticed it before, Jeremy looked at it with concentration and deep curiosity. It appeared to be made of something he had never seen before, apparently—as much as he tried, he couldn't focus his eyes on its surface. It had a strange depth to it. Almost as if it was translucent, as if he could see through it to some degree, but yet couldn't. For some reason, he suddenly felt drawn to it, and as he stood there contemplating the strange feeling, the odd man started walking toward it.

Jeremy, now realizing that he had just been standing there the whole time, curiously found himself attempting to follow. He took a few steps, stopped, and looked down at his feet. Everything seemed normal, proportional, at least in size now, he thought.

He then looked up again, took a deep breath and once again started walking toward the man and the object. As he did so, he noticed a curious sense of heightened motion—accelerated motion. He moved his right hand up into his field of vision. He saw it move at an average, normal speed, but again, its motion seemed extraordinary, for some reason.

This made him feel strange, yet curious.

"You see, Jeremy, just a moment ago, your position was down *there*." He gestured downward with his hand, as if through the floor. "And then you were, *there*." He pointed over to where Jeremy had found himself standing a moment before. "And then you saw this object, *here*. It came into your vision. Once in your mind's sight, it overwhelmed your vision. You became curious, desirous, *hungry*...to know what it was, and why it is *here*.

"In order for you to satisfy your desire to know, to understand, you chose to initiate the motion necessary to bring yourself over here. This became your mission, you see. All experiences have their roots in these things: positions, visions, and missions. Do you understand?"

Jeremy shook his head, and concluded that he didn't. He still wondered what was going on.

"Ask yourself, Jeremy, what is the basic characteristic that everything in this material universe here, shares?"

Jeremy's eyebrows lowered, and then rose again in confusion.

"The answer is motion. Everything moves. Some things move quickly, some things move slowly. Yet everything, everywhere, is in motion. Look at this." He motioned towards the wall. "It seems like it's not moving, but it is. Its molecules, its atoms, its quanta, they're all moving, dancing their particular and necessary dances.

"Think about it. Its subatomic particles are vibrating at varying harmonic frequencies. They're all moving, as they should. Everything that makes everything what it is, from the large to the small, is moving to one gigantic orchestral movement."

The man touched—oddly caressed—the towering wall before them as if it were an ancient artifact, and he was enamored with being in its presence.

"Go ahead, Jeremy, touch it," the man said softly, gazing up at the object's immensity.

Jeremy wondered again what was happening.

With growing interest, yet understandable reticence, he reached out and slowly placed his hand on the object as this man was doing. He felt strange warmth, a velvety softness. It tingled, like a minute electric current was flowing through his hand. He felt as if he could push his hand deeper into it, but the more he did, the more resistance he felt, as if it were made of some sort of black foam.

He pulled back, looking at the spot where his hand had been. There was no visual evidence that his hand had been there at all. There was still no identifiable surface, no depression, no outline, yet he could have sworn that his hand pushed deep into it—*curious*, he thought.

Jeremy's mind then rebounded to when he was falling through the air, where his mind once again concluded he should be. *Why was he here?* He started to feel small and exhausted again.

"Now Jeremy, what if you found it necessary to go beyond this object? To do something—to *become* something—but you had to be on the other side of it for it to come to pass. What would you need to do?"

Jeremy thought about it, momentarily interrupting the feeling of smallness and exhaustion.

I'd need to find a way to go around it...through it, he thought.

"Find a way to go through it?" Jeremy was startled when he heard himself ask the question.

He suddenly became aware that he was talking now. His voice sounded normal, but strained, and coarse. He hadn't realized it before, but he had been communicating with this man only through his thoughts. He felt odd that he only now realized it—it seemed so comfortable, like it was just a natural thing. His eyebrows lowered with sudden awareness. He noticed that the man was now grinning at his realization.

"Very good, Jeremy!" The man smiled. "Very good! What if I were to tell you that the only way to get to the other side of this object was to do exactly as you say? But what would facilitate you doing so? What would you have to do to achieve this vision?"

Jeremy thought for a moment, made it a question in his mind: *Learn how?*

"That's right, Jeremy. You would have to learn how. This means that you would have to learn everything about the object, the wall—as you're thinking of it. You would have to understand it. You would have to learn of its essence: how strong it is, how dense it is, what it is made of, where it starts, where it ends.

"These answers could be discovered by finding out whence it began, what caused it, how it came into being, who made it, and *why*? We are speaking, Jeremy, of a mission. In order to achieve a vision, one must persistently and methodically progress through a series of missions. Learning is the mission, you see?

"Learning is what takes you from your current position, to your desired vision. It's all about the learning, Jeremy. Learning is growth. Growth is life. Life is in motion. Life, itself, is a mission, but, a mission to achieve *what*?" He paused momentarily, smiled mischievously, and then quickly resumed. "Let me ask you, Jeremy, why *are* there walls?" The man wasn't smiling now.

Jeremy thought about it, but couldn't offer an answer.

The man then answered his own question. "A wall, is nothing more than an intended barrier of resistance—an inhibitor—Jeremy, as with frustration. Sadly, ignorantly, people hate walls, and they despise frustration. However, I assure you, frustration—as with walls—exists for specific reasons, for specific purposes. They are part of the necessary structure of this universe. Walls, inhibitors, frustrations, they hold us back. Keep us in check. Even protect us, when needed.

"Yet they force us to *choose*! That's the key here, the solution, Jeremy! Oh, if you could only see the Big Picture right now. How all of this ties together, where it is all going. How it is all coming to fruition, even as we speak."

The man was smiling broadly again. A crazy, enraptured stare also molded his face as he looked to his left, and up. It seemed that his eyes were looking at something overwhelmingly wondrous, far beyond the wall, far beyond the both of them. His eyes glazed over with indescribable joy, inexpressible elation.

Jeremy looked up in the same direction and once more placed his hand on the wall. He immediately began feeling that electric tingle again. Then, the man gently touched Jeremy's shoulder at the base of his neck. Suddenly, Jeremy felt the same pulse of current from the man's hand.

He began seeing colors that he'd never seen before. They were deep and contrasting. He saw confluences of what he supposed were pure Matter and Energy—Spirit and Mind, he curiously intuited, not knowing how, or why.

For a brief instant, he felt intense joy, inexpressible delight—and love. He felt his mind spreading, growing, and expanding. He was beginning to comprehend what he suddenly realized must be other realities, truths, things that are wholly unknown to humans, ancient secrets of the Cosmos.

He was more than captivated.

He was awestruck by the experience.

Then, he felt the hand leaving his shoulder.

As quickly as it had started, it suddenly waned, and then stopped altogether. He realized he was just standing there looking at the wall. He was just staring at it, and yet for that brief moment, he had been seeing through it, beyond it—far beyond it. And while doing so, his deep breaths felt like pure nourishment.

Everything seemed to go utterly silent, and then he heard the voice again.

"Jeremy…*Jeremy*, the time will come. You've seen glimpses, yes, as if looking through the Eye of God, some have likened it? This is true. However, the things you saw, felt, *knew*, for that brief instant, well, trust me, they are only the start, only the beginning.

"There is much to see, much to learn, much to know. But, the wall holds you back for a reason," he said solemnly, pausing before continuing.

"You have many missions ahead of you. And you'll only understand this when you *choose* to understand this. This is what the illustrations are all about, and that is why I am here. I am here to help you with these experiences."

Jeremy's mind was swirling again.

He felt excited, then strangely sad.

Somehow, he felt as if he was supposed to be there, then not. It didn't seem to matter so much to him that he wasn't falling from that airplane now, but then it did. For some reason, he felt strong, then weak, and then strong again.

His thoughts again were broken by the man's voice.

"Jeremy, I brought you here for a reason. As I said before, this is where I often begin orientation with my new students. You see, Jeremy, life down there on Earth must be thought of as a school."

Jeremy immediately thought, *'Down there…Down where? School?'*

"We Professors like to call it the, 'School of the Blind'."

He gave a slight smile, and then realized that Jeremy did not understand.

"You will understand, Jeremy, in time. Anyway, everyone—every*thing*—down there, has a purpose. Everything is connected in ways that you have yet to comprehend. I'm not able to tell you the overall purpose of it, yet. You have insufficient knowledge and experience to grasp it, at present. But one day, you will. One day, you will."

He smiled again.

"Let it suffice to say, that you are an important part of that purpose, Jeremy, a *very* important part. My profession is to help you develop the realization of this fact, but most importantly, to encourage you to participate."

Jeremy didn't speak. He just considered the things that this man, who called himself the Professor, was saying. He started to feel small again, and tired. Yet, he was inexplicably absorbed in the moment.

Chapter 11

"You have an interest in history, do you not, Jeremy?" the man asked, pausing, smiling.

As Jeremy contemplated the question, his mind suddenly began churning with hundreds of images of textbook pictures. Scenes from documentaries, and other books he'd read at various times in his life. Good events, bad events, all sparking lucid associations of historic subject matter.

Jeremy was intrigued by the man's curiously pointed question. He noticed his own amazement at how it spawned such a cache of imagery in his mind—much like Jeremy felt at times when talking to his Uncle Paul, but, this was different. His memories seemed clearer, crisper than ever.

"*Yes*, I—I've always had a great interest in history," Jeremy found himself saying, curious as to what was coming next.

"Have you ever considered, Jeremy, that you *are* history? Not that you're just living at some point in history, but that you are a contributor *to* history? That you're an integral component of history? Curious thought, isn't it?

"However, let's regress a little. It's always a good idea to start with the fundamentals, and then move progressively upward. You've seen a few glimpses. You're becoming more curious. But foundations must be laid first, before building the framework for anything else, don't you agree?"

Jeremy realized that it was another rhetorical question, so he didn't answer. The man resumed.

"Please, sit down Jeremy, here if you'd like." The man pointed to a set of chairs just a few steps away. This was the first time that Jeremy had the sense about him to begin really noticing the other details of his present surroundings.

The chairs were nicely upholstered. Apparently made of smooth, comfortable, brushed brown leather, with high backs, and contoured wings at head level. The kind you would find in an old Ivy League college library. They were sitting side-by-side with a small, antique-looking table placed between them.

Off to the side was a huge wooden desk. It, too, was antique-looking. It had simple, carved edges and trim, and was the rich, dark brown color of walnut. Yet Jeremy only noticed a faint trace of grain in the material, if any at all. For some reason, everything around him looked old, but then it didn't. The strangeness of the thought made him squint.

Then he noticed that there were only sparse items on the large desk: a brass lamp with satin patina that shone soft light over what looked like a large appointment calendar, an old brass-and-wood pen holder set, a couple picture frames, both turned away from his view, and a long, seemingly gold-inlayed wooden name block that displayed the letters, PROF. T. VECTOR.

The chairs were turned a few degrees toward each other, yet both were facing another large wall. This one, sided and trimmed in the same wood-like material that the chairs, the table, and the desk were made of. In the middle of this other wall was what looked to Jeremy to be a large window. Yet, there were no panes of glass reflecting any light, nor any mullion partitions, or anything of the sort that Jeremy could relate it to. It was just a big, framed, dark rectangle that made him think of a window.

It was then that he noticed that there were bookshelves full of books, to the left and right. As he curiously glanced at them, he began noticing some of the titles, and he realized that many, if not most, were books that he had read at one time or another. He recognized the titles as his eyes fell across them, each stirring the recollection of their contents in his mind.

This, too, was odd, he thought.

Then, he noticed numerous other shelves farther along the walls, with all sorts of interesting things were on them, besides being crammed with books. Some things he recognized, like picture frames, and small statues of various things—items that reminded him of souvenirs of some sort.

Other things he didn't recognize, things that were oddly shaped and gave off subtle reflections, objects that folded in on themselves, shapes that seemed to have more depth than what they should have. Some of the things seemed to actually move, yet when he looked at them, he couldn't tell if they were moving, or if it were his eyes that were moving as he gazed at them.

These things seemed to draw his attention and he felt a strange elation while he was looking at them—the kind of feeling one would have when looking at the Grand Canyon in person for the first time. Again, odd, he thought, extremely odd. The association didn't make sense to him.

Amidst the sensations of awe, something else caught his attention. On one of the shelves, there was a picture of a young boy, probably around ten or eleven years old, sitting in a wheel chair on the roofless concrete porch of an old, white-painted, clapboard-sided house looking up toward the sky at sunrise, or perhaps sunset.

In the firmament, at about forty degrees above the horizon, a star or a planet was shining brightly, and a flock of birds could be seen above the distant trees, their black profiles stark against the deep blue, pinkish-streaked, twilit sky.

He noticed that the young boy in the picture was crying. Tears were streaming down his sullen face. Something seemed oddly familiar about the scene. And then, Jeremy was shocked when he noticed that the boy in the picture looked like him when he had been younger, at least that's what he thought.

He wanted to take a closer look, but his attention was redirected.

"Please, have a seat, Jeremy," the man said again.

Jeremy, startled by the resonance, turned in response, but then rotated back and caught another glance of the picture as he sat down.

He again remembered where he had been just a few moments before—letting go of the airplane wing. But for some reason, he wasn't as alarmed and shocked by it all, as he had been when he had first arrived.

Arrived? he thought. He then felt oddly numb.

He still didn't know exactly where he was, or why. He noticed that feeling of tiredness coming over him again. Then the strange man, who called himself 'the Professor', sat down in the chair next to him. He crossed his legs, leaned slightly towards Jeremy, and spoke again.

"Jeremy, I'd like to ask you another question. What do the words *innovation* and *invention* mean to you? Keep it simple now. Remember, we're talking foundations."

Jeremy thought for a moment. "I don't know, changes, changes for the better?" he answered, still taken aback by all that was happening.

"Very good, Jeremy, changes for the better, very good. Now, you've heard the saying, 'Necessity is the mother of invention', haven't you?"

Jeremy nodded his head slowly, thinking at the same time about its meaning, and remembering his uncle talking about it in the past, and from school. "Yeah, it means that if something is needed, or…necessary, then that kind of forces someone to search for a way to fill the need?" he said it like a question.

The man nodded after Jeremy spoke. "That is correct. However, there is a more fundamental point to observe here. What do people experience when a need, or a desire, remains *un*-fulfilled?"

Jeremy slowly shook his head from side-to-side, not understanding what he was trying to get at. The man spoke again.

"What do you feel, Jeremy, when you attempt to fill a need—especially something that is 'necessary'—but are, for whatever reason, restrained from being able to do so?"

Jeremy thought about the question, and then answered, "Anger…uhmm, resentment, frustration, I guess?" Jeremy said it lightly, still not sure what this strange man was after.

The man sat up quickly and spoke. "*Yes*, that's it, Jeremy, frustration. It is frustration—*not* necessity—that is the 'mother of invention.' You know what a crossword puzzle is,

Jeremy, right? All those words and their relative meanings, all connected, all tied together in some way, all following a theme of some sort.

"Well, all things in existence are connected in a similar way. Things overlap, contribute to, or are a part of, other things. Those things, in turn, contribute to, and are part of, something else. This is the way things are.

"Frustration, Jeremy, is one of those things. Yes, frustration can breed resentment, spawn anger, intensify fear. It even fosters hate. Yet, it can just as easily spawn the antithesis of these rudimentary, yet powerful forces. It is truly the progenitor of understanding, of courage, of forgiveness, yes, of love, even.

"When a being comes against a proverbial wall of frustration, there are two fundamental choices they can choose. The frustration can dissuade them from continuing on a path toward the fulfillment of a particular need or desire—or mission. Or, frustration can serve as a driving, steering, learning force that, in essence, becomes the matrix that births and perpetuates the ultimate fulfillment of that need."

Jeremy, although overwhelmed, somehow understood what the man was saying. At that moment, an image appeared in his mind, an image of fire. He thought about it, and wondered why he was thinking of fire.

His thoughts were interrupted again.

"Let me present some illustrations, Jeremy. Please, observe the…'window', as you choose to think of it."

The man pointed to the window-like object on the wall. Before he could wonder what might happen next, an image began appearing. Yet, it wasn't just a two-dimensional scene, like on a monitor, or a screen. It was an actual, life-sized, three-dimensional scene of a thick green forest, with mountains in the background, birds flying, trees waving with a gentle wind, a stream flowing down a mountainside into a lake.

It was amazing, beautiful, vibrant, and the sound coming from it suddenly pierced his ears with clarity and range. He could hear birds, the brushing of leaves in the wind, the crackling of twigs. Jeremy was dumbfounded, completely taken in by the depth of what he was seeing.

For some reason, the thought crossed his mind that maybe this room—the Professor's study, as he'd called it—might be a ship of some kind, and that it just materialized there in this beautiful place, and they were now looking out of a two meter tall, by three meter wide opening through its hull.

Jeremy blinked his eyes in amazement.

Chapter 12

"What…what is this?" Jeremy asked with a slightly trembling voice.

"You're seeing the Earth, Jeremy, for you, forty thousand years ago. Beautiful, is it not? Green and lush, *alive*."

"*What?* What…?"he asked in his mind, and then spoke, stuttering, myriad questions pummeling his thoughts.

"Keep watching, Jeremy. Remember, I said we would start with fundamentals. This one is quite important."

Within a few seconds, the scene started rotating to the left.

The images that came into Jeremy's view were in sharp contrast to the splendor he had at first observed. He began seeing a valley, initially shallow, yet dropping off and getting deeper as his eyes covered the distance to the right. But everything there was burned up, charred and black, still smoldering, still smoking, the apparent consequence of an intense forest fire.

The rotating panoramic scene then halted. He could still see the remaining fringes of lush greenery to his left, but it stood in sharp contrast to the grayish-blackness that was now before him.

In a clearing less than a dozen yards away was an outcropping of rocks set in a near-vertical hillside escarpment that wrapped around the base of a mountain. Embedded in the once verdant, vine-covered rock face was an entrance to a shallow cave; and Jeremy was astonished when he then saw a hairy, fur-clothed, barefoot man frantically jumping up and down, peering into the dark opening.

The hunched-over man was making strange sounds as he heaved himself towards and away from the cave's entrance, back and forth, back and forth, frantically swaying the tilt of his body from one foot to the other. Finally, hesitantly, the man ran into the cave and then quickly exited, dragging a small child by one arm. Its body was lifeless and limp. Its pale skin was charred in places and blistery, and its hair mostly burned away.

The man stopped, let the arm drop to the ground beside the motionless child. For a moment, he just stood there and stared, incredulity causing his eyes to blink spasmodically. He reached down and gently stroked the child's forehead. He then held his hand in front of his face, staring at the greasy, fleshy residue now sticking to his fingers. Quickly he stood up and rushed back into the cave. This time, when he returned, he was dragging a small, yet stoutly-built woman. She, too, was charred and her hair was mostly burned away.

The man laid the woman down next to the child. He looked at his hands again, and then slowly knelt beside them both. Suddenly, he began crying and moaning, his entire body exuding agony, frustration, and pain. Tears poured from his blackened eyes as mucous dripped from his nose and ran down onto his lips. His eyebrows were stretched high, and the muscles of his face were drawn tight, his breathing, shallow.

Then, he wilted down into a sitting, limply tilted position, and ran both hands through his grey-streaked, black hair. Stopping, and holding them on top of his head, he squeezed his palms against his temples, gritted his teeth, and clamped his lips as tight as he could. He just stayed in that position, seemingly frozen in time, rocking back and forth ever so slightly as he mourned his now-apparent and unalterable loss.

Jeremy was enraptured with the scene. He didn't know what to say.

What he thought he was seeing was perhaps the solitary survivor of a family and their dwelling place that had just been burned out by a raging forest fire. Jeremy suddenly felt sick. He sat there, nearly motionless, just staring at the horror, not being able to fully grasp what he was seeing.

He looked up at the Professor, and when he did, he saw tears in the man's eyes. Jeremy couldn't help but wonder what was going on.

"What *is* all this?" he asked quietly.

"Well, you see, Jeremy," the Professor began. "It started by lightning, and swiftly raced up the valley driven by the fierce wind. He was on the other side of that ridge there, just doing what he does, gathering food for his family, and because of this, he was spared his life.

"However, the other family members were caught by surprise because they were sleeping in the cave. They awoke and tried to run out, but there was nowhere to go but out into the heat, and flames. Frustrated, after their many attempts, they turned and ran back into the cave for protection, but the ensuing firestorm quickly sucked all the oxygen out of the shallow indentation in the mountainside. They suffocated as they burned to death. Had they endured the flames for just a few more seconds, and ran toward that larger clearing, they would have survived—if only they'd known. If only they'd had more time.

"Their lack of knowledge, and time, their…disempowerment, due to their fears and frustrations, sealed their fate." The man spoke with solemn graveness now. "You see, Jeremy, frustration is fueled by ignorance. Yet, the flames of frustration can be overcome, smothered out, by knowledge, *if* given enough time. This is why you're here. It's why we're *all* here."

The man paused and appeared to take a deep, sober breath. He then resumed.

"Time, Jeremy, is a peculiar thing. To some, time is slow. To others, time slips away before they want, or expect it to. To some, time and experience come earlier, to others, later. And, to a few, time is altogether meaningless." He smiled.

The Professor then gestured toward a small clock sitting on a table between them. Jeremy hadn't noticed it before. The second hand was moving, yet it was only clicking a half-second forward, then a half-second back, repeating the slight motion.

That's strange, Jeremy thought, as his eyes followed its peculiar twitching movement.

The Professor spoke again. "A lot can be squeezed into a fraction of a second, Jeremy, and a lot can be lost. This is one of the fundamentals I was talking about, one of the most important things to learn during your experience here. A moment can be just as critical as a lifetime, you see."

The Professor was almost whispering, yet his words resounded in Jeremy's mind. Jeremy sensed that there was something deep and true to these words, and he almost felt as he had when he had glimpsed the other side of that wall for that brief instant.

The Wall, he thought, and history, pain, loss, motion, frustration, fear, ignorance, knowledge, and time. These concepts swirled around in Jeremy's mind. They started to make him dizzy.

His head was spinning.

He started feeling sick again.

The Professor stood up, stepped around to the side of Jeremy's chair, and then spoke. "It's time now, Jeremy." He put his hand on his shoulder, gave it an encouraging squeeze, and then spoke almost imperceptibly in his ear. "ARCH! Jeremy. ARCH!"

Chapter 13

The thrashing, twisting violence was a sensory overload for Jeremy's brain.

He felt something hit him in the chin, and the tightness under his legs squeezed his groin area to the point of hurting in the worst, pinching sort of way. His body whipped one direction, and then another, and then back again. His chest was being compressed, as if held tightly in a harness of some kind.

His head flailed around uncontrollably, and he couldn't see anything except streaks of different colored lights flashing before his eyes—first to the right then to the left. He felt he was spinning, spinning violently. The sounds he heard were loud and thunderous. A swishing, roaring rush of cold air blasted his eardrums. It was excruciating. He heard his own voice begin to stutter.

"What…what's happening to…to me?"

He felt small, and afraid.

His heart raced; it was beating like a bass drum.

He started to tell himself that this must be the end.

He tightened his face muscles and felt his eyes roll back inside their sockets.

This is it, he thought.

A feeling of intense nausea overtook him.

Then, just as quickly as the torrential uproar began, it diminished into an airy calm.

He thought he heard a scratchy voice speaking to him. It sounded far away in the distance, small and almost imperceptible.

His eyes were closed and he listened intently.

He trained his ear toward the sound, listened closely.

"Jumper number one"…*squelch*, "reach up and pull down your toggles. Jumper number one, I said reach up and pull down your toggles."

Jeremy opened his eyes and blinked rapidly. His body jerked—a nervous reaction to what he saw. Before him were a big blue sky above, and a horizon of earthy pastel colors below, all blending together into the center of infinity.

What, where? he thought.

He looked up, around.

Above him was a large canopy of blue and white stripes. He quickly looked down at his chest at the thick black strapping that swathed over it. He felt the cold air cutting into his nostrils as he breathed sighs of relief—glad the violence was over.

He then realized where he was.

He was hanging in the air, under a big, puffy, rectangular-shaped, fully inflated parachute. He heard the faint hum of a plane in the distance, the plane that had just dropped him off on his jump run.

Jeremy was speechless.

…*squelch*. "Jumper number one, are you still with us up there? Reach up and pull down your toggles, you copy? Give me a sign!"

Jeremy looked down at his chest.

The radio, he thought.

The guy on the ground, on the radio, was Mr. Givins, Brake. He was talking to him. Jeremy looked up and, remembering the training, reached up with each hand and grabbed the yellow loops of braided strap and pulled down hard. He heard the sound of Velcro ripping apart, and in an instant, he had both steering toggles in his hands.

"Show me a sign, jumper number one. Give me a little right toggle. You copy? Right toggle, we need to keep you upwind for a bit."

Shaken, but recovering his spatial sense of location, Jeremy pulled down on the right toggle just as he had heard. He looked down and saw the outline of the airport below him—he could see the runway, and the long hangers. They seemed like small toys placed on an uneven checkered board of green and brown shapes, dotted with specks of shimmering color, engulfed in a thick surreal haze. As he pulled down he felt the parachute turn until the airport was behind him.

Mr. Givins spoke again.

"Good, you're alive up there, jumper number one. You had me worried for a minute. Now, let the toggle back up. Repeat, let the toggle back up."

Jeremy let it go back up.

The parachute stabilized and stopped turning. Jeremy just hung there. His mind filled with amazement. His face and hands were suddenly numb from the cold, brisk air. He was just hanging there, under a parachute, three-quarters of a kilometer above the ground.

He couldn't believe it.

He didn't believe it.

Yet, he was doing it.

He smiled.

He then felt tears well up in his eyes.

His mind quickly returned to the thoughts of the Professor, of the study, of the wall, and of that window. All of it raced through his mind at just that brief instant. He felt so strange. He felt like he must be crazy or something. He was wrapped in a moment of insanity. Again he felt cold all over, afraid and sick to his stomach. This can't be right, he thought, this just couldn't be!

"Okay, jumper number one—Jeremy, if I remember right. Let's have some fun. I'm going to steer you into a couple of left-hand full-turns to help you bleed a little altitude. We wouldn't want you to have to land in Mr. Clower's cow pasture. No one likes to clean poop off of parachutes—especially me!" The radio squelched yet again. "Now, pull down hard on the left toggle, and hold on. You're going for a ride." He said it dramatically. The last word resonated from his mouth as he slowly moved the radio away. He knew that to the jumpers, it sounded like a circus announcer's fading voice.

It's exactly what Jeremy heard.

Jeremy laughed slightly. It brought him back to some sort of reality. He thought whimsically: what is reality? It seemed that the coldness he felt was becoming more tolerable now. After a minute he laughed another laugh. It made him feel better. After all he seemed alright, he thought. He looked around, took several deep breaths, and noticed the Sun was now warming his face.

Then, surprising himself, he let out the biggest scream he had ever screamed in his entire life. Crazy or not, now he was beginning to feel as big as ten men, and at that moment, he felt like he could breathe in the whole sky.

Jeremy pulled down hard and the parachute immediately started into a steep left hand dive. At the end of the first loop around, Jeremy's body was swinging out past the parachute. It was the most thrilling sensation he had ever felt. Better than any rollercoaster in the world. His sense of inner control, and his courage, returned to him. He just knew he'd feel this way. It was imagining this feeling that kept him up all night last night, he thought. Yes, he thought again, it was just last night. For some reason, it seemed liked days ago.

"Okay, jumper number one, let's try it to the right, bleed a little more altitude, two full right turns this time. If it gets too much for you, let up on the toggle a little bit. I'll tell you when to stop. Copy that?"

Jeremy let out another scream and pulled down hard. He thought of his friends. He realized that he had forgotten them for a while. He smiled when he thought that they were just about ready to do the same thing he was doing. They would feel the same thing, the same exhilaration. He couldn't wait to share it with them, to talk with them about it. He completed both turns. The airport was behind him again. The radio crackled.

"Hey, jumper number one. Let the toggle up for a short while. We'll do it again in a minute." Jeremy complied. "Hey, I got someone down here who wants to talk with you, hold on."

"Jeremy," ...*squelch*, "it's me, Uncle Paul. Heeeeey, you're doing it!" He was looking up at the small dot in the sky that was his nephew. "Enjoy the ride, Son!" he yelled. He let off the button and started to hand the radio back to Mr. Givins, but hesitated. He pulled it back to his lips, pushed the button and quickly spoke again. "Hey Jeremy, don't forget about the wallet thing!" He laughed heartily and then gave the radio back.

Mr. Givins didn't get the point of the comment, giving Paul a funny look. He took the radio and then shaded his eyes with his hand as he looked back up into the sky. He let Jeremy play around up there awhile, doing turns and sweeps, diving to the right, then to the left, although not enough to really overdo it. After all, this was his first time.

Jeremy then steered his canopy right up to the edge of a thick white cloud—one about the size of three or four huge houses all clumped together. He couldn't see through the center of it, yet its edges were thin, wispy and translucent.

He was positioned just above and beside it. He marveled at the mass of it. He steered straight ahead to go inside of it, and as he did, he started to feel its moisture on his skin. Then Mr. Givins told him on the radio to stay out of it. It's always a flyer's best policy, he told him, because you never know what could be hiding in one.

Jeremy flew around its edge until he was on the other side and below it, looking up in awe at its wind-morphed majesty. Mr. Givins got back on the radio, and began giving Jeremy instructions for his final approach and landing.

"Okay, that's about it for the extreme stuff, jumper number one. Don't want to give you too much all at once, you're still a student, and we want you to come back." He always used this time for a little sales pitch for the center. Why not, he thought, you can't get more of a captive audience than this.

"Okay now, it's time to get serious, Jeremy, so get ready for your final turns when I tell you!"

Jeremy's mind raced back to the Professor's study. He remembered the remarks he had said about Jeremy being a new student. Weird, Jeremy thought again. He then wondered at that very moment if it really even did happen. His mind spun and spiraled with the thoughts.

The whole thing, it just drained him of energy. Again, he felt small, slightly nauseous, and tired. No, exhausted was how he felt, he suddenly realized. His eyes got big and blurry as he continued looking back into his unremitting thoughts.

Mr. Givins caught Jeremy's attention once more as he steered him over the landing area, turned him 180° into the wind and centered him up on his final approach. Jeremy glided in as smooth as could be, his parachute's cloth Slider flapping rhythmically in the breeze. Right at the last second, Mr. Givins yelled, "Flare!"

But Jeremy intuitively started before the call. Remembering the training, he pulled down on both toggles at the same time, with the exact needed progressive tension. By doing so, Jeremy landed as soft as a butterfly, still standing, without the slightest jolt.

Mr. Givins, along with the rest of the support staff, ran up to him, his uncle trailing the small group.

"Fine job, Jeremy! Yeah! You're a natural at this," Mr. Givins said. "I couldn't have done it better myself, good control...good control." He paused, and then added, "And I mean that. You got a knack for this kid, nice flare, nice landing...*nice* landing."

The others ran downwind and started grabbing up the parachute so the stiff breeze wouldn't catch it, as Mr. Givins started loosening up Jeremy's straps. CD was there and she began removing his helmet and radio. She smiled the cutest smile, just inches away from his face as she helped him get his helmet straps loosened. As she did, she whispered, "Cool, huh?"

Jeremy about melted right there in front of everyone, his mind totally on her at that moment.

"I can tell your plane exit shook you up a bit, but that sure was a nice landing. What an experience, huh, Jeremy? There's nothing like it in the world. Let's get you to the recovery truck, and you can relax a little while we persuade your friends to come on down," Mr. Givins said, smiling.

"Nice job, Jeremy," his uncle said, slapping him on the shoulder. "Nice job, Brake," he also said to Mr. Givins. "That was great, that was great!" He almost felt like he had just jumped himself. He breathed a sigh of relief, for both of them.

A few minutes later, Scott was on his final approach, yelling down at them as he flew over. They yelled back, waving with both arms and thumbs up in the air. Scott's landing was just about as perfect as Jeremy's.

Bass' landing was a little more comical. He wasn't responding quickly enough to Mr. Givins' commands. As a result, he flew way too far downwind and then didn't have enough altitude to make it back to the landing area. Mr. Givins had to talk him down into Mr. Clower's field. As soon as he touched down, they all jumped into the truck, drove over to the gate, opened it, and sped out into the field to get him.

On the way, Mr. Givins lifted the radio to his lips, smiled, and then spoke, uttering his best Schwarzenegger–style impression.

"Brake to DZ, Brake to DZ…he's dowwwn, he's dowwwn, bringing bock poop on da parachute," Mr. Givins informed the hanger with the news. "Get oud't da ho-ses…"

Everyone could hear the news reverberating through the Drop Zone's radio base unit. All the people who worked at the airport shared in the amusement. Scott, Jeremy and his uncle laughed so hard that they were about to bust at the seams.

Jeremy thought that it felt good to laugh. He looked over toward CD. She was helping Bass get up off the ground. She briefly looked up at Jeremy, stared for the longest second, and then smiled at him. Jeremy smiled back.

Jeremy looked up in the sky once more, and then closed his eyes. He felt the sun's warmth on his face again. He was so filled with the experience that he could just lie down and instantly go to sleep without even trying.

At that moment, time seemed to stand still.

<<< >>>

The trip back home was full of the rapid-fire sharing of their experiences. After a pizza-and-movie party at Jeremy's house, everyone decided to make it an early evening. With the exception of Paul, who went to the nursery to take care of some late-night work.

They were all spent from over-dosing on soda, adrenaline, and excitement. Everyone left around nine o'clock, after final hugs, slaps on the backs, and of course a sortie of jocular jabs at Bass' landing in the cow pasture.

When everyone was gone, Jeremy turned all the lights off except the one in the mud-room off the kitchen for his uncle to see to get in. He then went into his bedroom and slowly climbed into bed, moaning sighs of relief and satisfaction.

His body suddenly felt numb. He noticed through the open window that it was almost a full moon. By its reflective shine, he could see the tall grasses blowing listlessly in the field next to the house—different shades of moonlit gray and silver.

The scene, along with his thoughts and memories, entranced him.

Jeremy just lay there, silent for a while. He then closed his eyes. Instantly, his mind returned to the strange experience he'd had. *It just had to be your mind*, he thought. It couldn't have been real, he concluded. It was just imagination, that's all it was.

Any more, and he'd have to start believing that he had some real problems. That was the first time all evening that he'd had the time to think about it. Without some mental interruption like a friend talking, his uncle joking or laughing, or the image of that girl, CD, that now suddenly seemed to be burned into his mind.

He was glad for the image, though. Glad to have it to focus on, instead of the weird experience of that strange place and that strange person. Jeremy laughed a small, crazy laugh. He shook his head, and then softly murmured out loud, "Man, I'm the one who's strange." He laughed again, took a deep breath, intent on searching for that image of CD—it only took a split second.

He smiled at its softness, and then drifted off.

Chapter 14

The next day came after nearly eleven hours of the deepest sleep that Jeremy could ever remember having. He woke up at around nine thirty in the morning, but lay there in a dreamy state for another fifteen minutes, or so. He finally got up, meandered clumsily to the bathroom, and then stumbled into the kitchen. His uncle was nowhere to be seen. He looked around. On the table was a note:

....

THOUGHT I'D LET YOU SLEEP. DROP BY THE NURSERY LATER, I COULD USE SOME HELP BREAKING UP THE STARTERS. BUT, I CAN MANAGE.

JUST REMEMBER, LIFE IS A SERIES OF CHOICES. CHOOSE WISELY, GRASSHOPPER.

OH! YEAH! WE FORGOT TO DROP YOUR BOOKS OFF YESTERDAY. I PUT THEM ON THE SEAT OF YOUR TRUCK.

PROUD OF YOU, SON!

....

Jeremy made some strong coffee, sat down in his uncle's seat, and just sipped it while looking out the window. It wasn't as nice a day as it was the day before. It was storming off in the distance and Jeremy could tell it would make it to their area sometime soon.

The contrast of the sunshine, the white clouds and the blue sky next to the blue-gray darkness in the distance was picturesque, though. It was warm, about seventy-two degrees, with a light breeze. Jeremy started thinking about what his uncle had said in the note. They had talked about it numerous times.

Jeremy was a man now, and he needed to think about what he really wanted to do with his life.

He remembered his uncle saying that:

"Choices are like small steps. To go any significant distance, one has to take a huge number of them, even though sometimes it feels like trying to move a mountain with a spoon."

What should he do with his life now? he thought. What was he supposed to do?

He suddenly remembered the *experience,* and that Professor guy. He hadn't thought of it since the night before. He shook his head from side to side, laughed at himself through his nose as he contorted his face in repulsion at the crazy memory.

But, he couldn't help but consider the strange man's comments about purpose, about meaning, about destiny, and about...*frustration,* he suddenly remembered. Yes, he thought, frustration. Like what his uncle said about moving mountains with spoons, and people not wanting to do anything because there are too many steps to take, too many choices, and fear.

Jeremy felt weird, like it was somehow tied together.

Maybe it was just a dream, from last night. Maybe he just got everything all mixed up in his head. Yeah, that had to be it, he told himself.

He then realized that he was just sitting there in a daze.

He shook his head to force himself to snap out of it. He gulped down the rest of his coffee, trying to think about what he wanted to do with his life. He imagined some of the things he thought of as he was growing up: an astronaut...no, that would be cool, but he was too tall; a fireman...no, that would be cool too, helping people and all, but all he remembered really liking about it, when he was kid, was being able to ride on the back of the big trucks.

Then he remembered Finley saying once, "Try to do in life, the things that you really love to do, things that you have a passion for, because those are the things that you're usually supposed to do, are *meant* to do. Getting stuck having to do the things you hate every day—day in and day out—doesn't make life much worth living," Jeremy silently asked himself: *What do I love doing? I like a lot of things, but I don't know…I, I just don't know what I would love to do!*

He was going into a daze again, staring out the window, yet only seeing what was in his mind. Then his drifting thoughts were interrupted by a metrical noise that sounded something like tapping, or pecking on glass.

His eyes focused in on a small creature just outside of the window. It was a hummingbird, hovering next to the birdfeeder. It was right up against the glass, its beak just a fraction of an inch away. It was facing him, looking right at him, as if studying him, looking more with one eye, then turning its head slightly, and looking with the other. Its wings hummed a muffled rhythm.

Jeremy smiled. "Hello, you're a tiny one. What're you looking at?" he said, with a small hint of a Mafioso's monotonic drone. The small bird backed away a few inches as if it were reacting to what he'd said, yet it still hovered there, watching.

"Ah! Come back, come on back. I'm not going to hurt you, promise," Jeremy said gently this time, as if he were cooing a kitten. Again, seemingly in response to what he'd said, the bird flew back in closer to the window and looked at him more intently now. Jeremy, amazed, leaned closer. The bird backed up again a second time.

Smiling ear-to-ear, Jeremy leaned back in his chair. Once again, the little thing came back in closer to the window.

"Now, aren't you the curious one?" Jeremy smiled at the thought.

Then, the bird turned ninety degrees to the right. Tilted its head and looked at Jeremy with its left eye. A moment later, it gracefully spun around in mid-air to make a full circle. Then, it courageously returned to the window, even though Jeremy was now leaning up close to it.

Effortlessly, it floated up to the same elevation as Jeremy's eyes, hovered slightly forward, and then tapped the window again with its tiny beak. Then, it slowly flew backwards, turning as it went, and finally flew away and out of sight. Jeremy smiled, and then spoke out loud to no one in particular.

"*Wow*! I'm going to love telling Uncle Paul this little story."

Jeremy's uncle loved animals. He had a special attraction to them, as did they to him. He had told Jeremy several stories about the strange behaviors of some that he had witnessed over the years. Like the one about the mouse in the dog food bag.

Jeremy remembered it as he sat there.

Paul had heard something stirring around inside an almost-empty twenty-five pound sack of dog food. It wasn't well lit in the part of the garage where the dog food bag was kept, so he grabbed a flashlight off the workbench. He walked over to it and shone it down into the bag. When he looked inside, he saw a little field mouse at the bottom, obviously trapped, not able to climb up due to the slick waxy paper lining. It had a big red ball of food in its mouth— about half the size of its diminutive head.

It was jumping straight up and then falling back down, apparently trying to grab hold of the bag's zip-string that just happened to be hanging down—the string that's used to open the bag. It froze when it saw the bright light now shining on it from above.

Paul spoke to the mouse. "Go ahead, you little thief, if you think you can do it!"

The mouse resumed its desperate jumping, and on the fourth jump, it landed a single claw in the string. Paul's eyes swelled in amazement as it swung there—the ball of food still in its mouth. It actually climbed up that thin little string, with the greatest of effort and resolve, almost losing its hold several times. But it just kept climbing, toward what must have appeared to it as a blinding light from heaven.

Then, it stopped on the top edge of the sack and looked straight at Paul. It was breathing so hard that Paul could see its little ribs with each deep breath. It seemed as if it were saying to him: "Are you going to knock me back down? Are you going to kill me?"

Paul spoke to the mouse as he backed up slightly to give it room. "Go ahead, little guy, you sure earned it."

After a slight pause, the mouse leapt off the sack—ball of food still in its mouth—and landed on the pile of junk next to it. It quickly scurried down and disappeared under some old boards that were stacked on the garage floor. Paul shook his head, marveling at the feat.

Just as he was getting ready to go back to what he was doing, the mouse reappeared from behind a box—the food *still* in its mouth. Paul said that it looked right at him, turned its head slightly and seemed to nod a little. At least it seemed that way. Paul got the distinct impression that it was saying thanks. Then, it just disappeared.

Jeremy thought about this intently.

His uncle sure loves to tell that story to the patrons at the nursery—it always brings a smile. He laughed subtly to himself, thinking of the mouse story, and of the little hummingbird's behavior. The thought crossed his mind that there's a lot more going on than what we realize, a kind of connection, or something. It made him start remembering what that strange Professor guy had said, what he imagined him saying. Had dreamed about him saying, he decided again. He shook his head once more, thinking he was crazy.

Jeremy realized that he was just sitting there in a daze.

He shook his head once more, stretched and popped his neck. He got up, poured another cup of coffee, and then went into the bedroom. As he dressed, he thought again about the bird, the mouse in his uncle's story, and their strange behaviors. He suddenly wondered what kind of hummingbird it was—*never seen one like it before, have to pick up a book on them at the nursery,* he thought.

That reminded him of the library books he'd forgotten to return the evening before.

He rapidly decided that he'd drop those off on his way over to help his uncle get the season's batch of starter plants ready, as he was asked to do in his uncle's note. His uncle really did need the help, and he owed it to him.

He sat down on the bed to put his shoes on, and then started thinking about his uncle again. Jeremy thought of all his uncle had done for him over the past many years. He had sacrificed a lot to raise him, he thought appreciatively.

He then thought of the Continuum, his uncle's vocation, and his pride and joy.

It always amazed Jeremy how many folks would take the time to travel out there beyond the edge of town, and most with their children, to frequent the place. Going out of their way, when they could go to a more commercialized place in town and be quick about it.

But, as his uncle put it, "It wasn't just a place to go to buy things. It was place to come and experience things." He called it Life's Continuum: a place for plants, animals, and people, "or whatever else might show up." His uncle would always say it with those vibrating eyebrows.

The establishment sold plants and fertilizers, and just about everything that had anything to do with gardening. It also marketed unique pieces of pottery, and landscape art, all handmade at the Pioneer Artist's Colony a few miles down the road, and miscellaneous items like wind chimes and yard ornaments, natural pest-control concoctions, and an assortment of other things that pertained to animals: books, cages, feeders, live traps, etc.

And of course, it had the petting zoo. It was a pretty good-sized one, too: a large, rustic pole barn housed the animals, and at each end of it, there were two spacious, fenced-in areas landscaped with huge rolling mounds, boulders, rocks, logs, and trees, with numerous benches lining the intertwining pathways for the patrons to sit on while visiting the animals. All built and lovingly cared for by his uncle.

Kids of all ages adored the place, and it was quite a frequent occurrence in the summer and fall to have busloads of them come out there on field trips just to learn about, and interact with, the animals. It even featured a small, fenced-in cemetery for the zoo animals, strategically placed next to a compost generation area.

Only a few visitors caught the significance of that one.

The parents could shop while the kids stayed occupied, playing with and feeding the zoo animals, or spending time marveling at the variety of insects displayed at the Bug Emporium—a carryover from a science project that Paul had done during high school. The joy on the kids' faces at the diversity of life never ceased to amaze Paul Usher. He loved teaching them about the animals, the plants, and about life, too.

Paul would always find the occasional opportunity to discuss some of his philosophies-of-life with the various patrons who would listen. It was his way of sharing, or "giving something back, to life," he'd say. "There's just something special about two strangers conversing about some of life's deepest subjects."

Paul had little conversation starters—small printed signs—stuck everywhere in amongst the plants: quotes, axioms, adages, proverbs, etc. They were displayed in various sizes and types and colors. If one of the patrons commented about one of them, then they could find themselves in a half-hour-long discussion about it, and for the most part, they all loved it, especially the more frequent customers.

He could tell the people who did, or didn't enjoy conversations of that nature. Paul Usher had a unique sense about people, and how to communicate with them. He wouldn't push his ideas on anyone. It was as if he and the other person were just standing side by side, observing the world together, and then they would discuss what they were seeing.

"Conclusions," he'd say, "are up to the concluder, besides, I've yet to run across a final one anyway!"

People would often find humor in Paul's witty, though frequently offbeat comments. And he had a uniquely humble, yet jolly candor about him, along with a joyously contagious laugh. Just about everyone who knew Paul Usher, loved Paul Usher, in spite of his abstract goofiness.

Jeremy suddenly realized that he had just been sitting there in a daze again.

He took a deep breath and then a sip of his coffee. It was cold. He looked at his watch. Nearly half an hour had passed while he had been sitting there. He looked down; one shoe still remained to be tied. He scrunched his eyes at the sight.

"*Wow*, space-case there, Daniel Jeremy Sayer," he said out loud to himself.

Chapter 15

Jeremy drove to the library to return the books he'd forgotten the day before. It was understandable that they had forgotten to swing into town to return them. They were all filled with such excitement from the day at the Drop Zone. He pulled into the parking lot just as it started to sprinkle a little rain. He grabbed the books, slammed the truck door, and ran to the overhang which covered the main entrance. He darted inside, put the books in the return area, and scanned the multi-level, cavernous expanse—there weren't very many people there.

Jeremy couldn't ever just drop off books at the library, and he rarely ever used the night deposit slot. He almost always had to go inside and check out more. And even though he was out of school now, it didn't change anything. He loved to read, and this day was no exception.

A book on hummingbirds would be a good start, his mind reminded him.

He crossed the atrium, punched a few keys on one of the library's computers to get a reference number, then went up the stairs to the nature section and started looking around. He already knew where he was going; he'd been there a lot over the years. He'd done all sorts of research on plants and animals throughout school, so he immediately knew the general area of where to start looking.

He quickly found several books on a shelf to choose from: an old, quite large volume on ornithology that was full of hand-painted illustrations, published back in the forties, or fifties. Then there were numerous contemporary books with photographs, and several smaller handbooks and field guides on the subject, all neatly arranged right at about eye level. He picked up the old book with the illustrations and started skimming through the section on hummingbirds. Then he heard a voice behind him—a slightly familiar voice.

"Hello, jumper number one!"

He thought he recognized the voice, but wasn't sure. It sounded gentle—sweet, actually. He slowly turned to see whom it belonged to. He about croaked when his eyes fell on CD—Caitlin Dobbs. His mouth fell open. He suddenly became as still as a stone statue.

"Hi," she said again.

Jeremy just stood there, staring. He noticed her eyebrows going up in a look of confusion.

"Hi, uh…hi," he managed to mumble. He was shocked. His heart was racing and he felt like he couldn't breathe all of a sudden. His head began to spin. He immediately felt sick to his stomach.

"Imagine meeting you here," she said. "Are you recovering alright from your jump yesterday? You did good! But, you seemed pretty shocked by it all, at least right after you landed. So, did you like it, or did it…'*freak*' you out too much?" she asked with a smile, lifting her eyebrows again, twisting her upper body back and forth rhythmically to throw her long brown hair back over her shoulder, slightly nervous herself, for some reason.

Jeremy remembered the strange tattooed guy at the Drop Zone—Sky, he remembered his name—saying: "you're gonna freak, you're gonna freak!" He knew she was referring to him in her question.

"No, uh…no, I mean, yes. It was great, really great. No, it didn't freak me out, too much." He laughed, then for a split second, remembered the Professor and his study.

"Good," she said. "Uh, so…uh, I'm glad you had a good time. It's a neat place up there, a lot of great people." She paused, waiting for a return comment.

Jeremy just stared at her.

He couldn't believe she was standing there. She's so beautiful, he thought. He felt himself start to go numb all over. He just couldn't believe that she was real.

"Uh, you okay?" she asked, her eyes squinting.

"Yeah," he stammered. "Yeah, it's just...it's just really nice to see you—" He couldn't believe he'd said it. It just came out.

We don't even know each other, he thought. He felt embarrassed, felt the blood rush to his face, thought that she just had to notice his head spinning around in big circles.

"I mean, what a coincidence meeting you...here, I mean. This is a long way from up Indy way!"

Every word seemed to come out wrong.

"Cool, uhmm, it's nice to see you, too. Yeah, it is a coincidence, isn't it? Pretty amazing," she replied crisply, surprised at her own comment, and feelings.

Jeremy nearly fell over when he heard her say that. He realized that he had better get a grip. He didn't want her to think that he was a dork or anything. He leaned against the bookshelf to get his balance, trying to act calm and collected.

"So, I...I guess you must live around here, huh?" he asked quickly.

"Yeah, I do, just north of town, Griffy Lake. I go to I.U. What about you?"

"Yeah, *really*! Uh, yeah, I do too, not in town. I live east, actually, out toward Nashville, in Brown County. Cool...I.U. huh? Wow! I think I'm going to go to I.U. next year, too. I'm...I'm thinking about going to I.U, anyway, next year, I mean."

He cleared his throat, and felt like shooting himself in the head.

"That's awesome. I'm just finishing my freshman year. I like it, *big school*, but it's a great school!" she said, twisting side to side again, nervously. "I'm lucky to live nearby. People from all over the world come to IU."

"Yeah, it's big," he replied, "and it is a great school. I know lots of people who go there...went there. My uncle went there. So...what are you taking?" Jeremy asked, starting to feel only slightly more comfortable.

"I'm working on a degree in education. I'd like to be a teacher someday, maybe even a professor, of something." She rolled her eyes. "At least, I think. Teachers don't make much, but I'd really like to do something that helps people.

You know? Do something that does some good for people."

She smiled, a little embarrassed at revealing some of her deepest desires to a total stranger. But she started to realize that, for some reason, she liked Jeremy. She thought he was nice looking, and had a nice personality—at least what she saw of it back at the Drop Zone the day before. But, he's acting a little goofy now, she thought.

"A teacher, that's awesome. My mom was a teacher. My uncle says we're all teachers, you know, in a way." He still stumbled with his words. "We all have experiences, good ones, bad ones, and when we share them, then, they just might help someone else, and they might, in turn, help us, you know, 'cause we helped someone else, you know?" Jeremy thought he must be sounding like a dork again.

He felt so inadequate.

"Yeah, you know, I totally agree. That's a cool way of thinking about it." She smiled. "Your uncle sounds like a wise man."

Jeremy remembered the note that his uncle had left him. He'd called him—as he had several times—'grasshopper'. It was taken from that old show his uncle used to watch, back in the seventies or eighties, about a wise old Chinese man and his young protégé student.

Jeremy thought about the Professor again; his mind drifted.

"What are you reading?" CD asked.

"Uhmm, a book!" Jeremy answered.

"Okay, sooooo, what's it about…the book?" she replied, smiling.

He struggled to think straight.

"Book, yeah, uh, it's about hummingbirds," he said.

He was suddenly mortified; he couldn't believe he'd said it. But what was he supposed to do? He had it in his hands. Girls think guys are supposed to read stuff about sports, or adventure, or cars and stuff. Not about hummingbirds. He wanted to shoot himself in the head again.

Just as his ego began to sink down to the point of staining the carpet, she spoke.

"Really," she voiced with enthusiasm. "That's really cool, I *love* hummingbirds. I've got two feeders outside of my bedroom window."

She stepped toward him, turned, and stood beside him. The inside of her elbow touched Jeremy's arm as she nudged closer to look at the book he was holding. He opened it wider and held it between them so they could both see it. Jeremy smelled the faint scent of shampoo, or body wash. It was a clean smell.

Jeremy couldn't feel his toes; they'd just melted off inside his shoes, he thought.

"Yeah, uh, we've...*I* had one show up at our feeder this morning, and it kept tapping on the window with its beak. I'd never seen one do that before, so I thought I'd ...I'd look it up," he said.

He was staring at her face just in front of his.

"Neat." She looked up into his eyes. They both became still for a moment.

Then, she stepped a little farther away, thinking she might be invading his personal space. Jeremy thought the exact same thing, at the same time, and proceeded to step sideways a little as well. They both smiled. Then, to Jeremy's total amazement, she said something that just about floored him.

"Hey, you want to go get a cup of coffee or something?"

Jeremy's heart sputtered.

He could have sworn that it had stopped altogether. He imagined a likeness of himself hunched over his own chest, pumping out compressions, one a second, on his lifeless corpse, shouting, "Not yet, not yet, don't you die on me now!"

"Yeah, uh, yeah!" He swallowed hard. "I'd like that verily much, *very* much, I mean...very much."

They both smiled.

<<< >>>

Jeremy never made it to Life's Continuum that day.

He and CD shared several cups of coffee together, along with toasted bagels with honey on them. They lost all track of time while sitting in the little booth at the small coffee shop around the corner from the library. They talked for hours, easily, about all kinds of things: hummingbirds, flying, books, parachutes, freefalling, music, college, movies, the world, and about what each hoped to someday do in life. They kept amazing one another with subjects that each knew, or in some way had experience or interest in.

After three hours in the coffee shop, they walked in the drizzle together. Not really going anywhere, just walking, and talking. And then they drove in Jeremy's old truck to the north side of town to check out the park that had just recently been renovated. It featured a small lake, a lot of exotic plants engineered as a biological filter to clean the runoff, and a cantilevered deck that extended out over a waterfall.

It was a beautiful setting, and they just couldn't quit smiling about it all—or at each other. When it began to rain hard, they ran to Jeremy's truck, finding that he had accidentally locked his keys in it. Peering over the truck's hood at each other, they started laughing hysterically as the rain came down harder and harder. Jeremy looked over toward the little Mandarin Buffet just across the street, then back toward her.

"Hey, can I buy you dinner?" The rain poured harder. Jeremy, more confident now, smiled.

"Sure," she replied, looking over at the restaurant, and then added, "I just hope their egg drop soup isn't all watery." They both looked intensely serious for a moment, and then burst out in hysterical laughter again as they made for the restaurant.

Chapter 16

The following summer, Jeremy and CD were inseparable. And, according to Jeremy's own proclamation, he was the happiest he had ever been. Being with her renewed him. Made him whole, he'd say to his uncle. The summer seemed to fly by, for both of them. They each worked full-time to fund their college expenses—CD's second year and Jeremy's up-and-coming first.

Jeremy worked at Life's Continuum potting plants, weeding plants, watering plants, dusting plants, anything and everything that had anything to do with the plants. He also took care of the grounds, worked with the animals, and helped to build the new addition on the south side of the main building.

CD worked as a teacher's aide at a year-round alternative school, and she had an evening job three days a week at the Drop Zone, doing everything from hanging signs and pictures for advertising, to cutting grass, sweeping up the hanger and the grounds, packing parachutes, or cleaning puke out of the airplanes. She was a real hard worker and Mr. Givins treated her like a daughter. The daughter he and his wife could never have—another consequence of the accident all those years back.

Scott and Bass were busy, too. Scott worked on his father's farm, and Bass worked with his dad in his retail business. And like Jeremy, Bass was gearing up to go to I.U., too. The school had one of the highest-ranked business programs in the country, and it was right in their own backyard. Both could go there and not have to live on campus and pay the high rents.

Scott's family said they couldn't afford I.U., so Scott was preparing to go to a good, but less expensive technical college. His parents thought that something to do with computer technology would be best, since everything was about computers these days. Scott somewhat agreed with them, but he still felt kind of left out of the gang, what with everyone going to Indiana University.

Throughout the summer, the group got together as much as they could, and CD fit right in. Scott and Bass liked her a lot, especially after one particular Sunday afternoon when they snuck onto the grounds of an old limestone mill and went quarry diving. They were temporarily speechless when she dropped her pants and top right there in front of them— sporting a tight-fitting, yet modest bikini—and was the first one to dive in off the twenty-foot high cliff.

They were obviously jealous of Jeremy's good fortune. Because as soon as CD leapt off the overhang, Scott and Bass started poking and punching Jeremy, and saying things like: "you're a dog, you're a lucky *dog*, a freakazoidial, mucous-covered, mutant-faced, space-slug-dog. How'd you end up with such a fox; it's not *fair*…it's just not *right*…no way Jose! This must be a grand cosmic error! Error! Tilt! Error! Must destroy anomaly! Must destroy error! Must destroy!"

Then, acting like completely out-of-order zombiefied automatons, they both reached down, each grabbing one of Jeremy's legs, still mouthing insults in robotic-sounding harmonious monotones, attempting to throw him off the cliff into the water. But Jeremy cinched down on both of them with a death-grip, a head under each elbow, and all three, quite out of control and lacking any sort of form, fell, upside down, all twisted together, slamming into the water, with Bass and Scott still gurgling out their bubble-muffled robotic insults.

CD yelled at them after they rose to the surface.

"Nice dive, boys. Let's see that one again!"

They all whooped and hollered and high-fived each other as they climbed back up the cliff.

It was a great summer.

But like all summers, they give way to fall.

Chapter 17

"So, what about your family?" she asked, after a fairly lengthy discussion about her own. She had suspected that it might be a sensitive subject for him. They had been together for almost six months, and he had rarely spoken of it.

She knew that Jeremy's mother had passed away when he was only eleven—from some sort of cancer. And that his father was a long-distance truck driver who hauled stuff for the government, or for companies that contracted with the government, or something like that.

She knew his dad mainly worked out West, between Arizona and California, and only rarely made trips back to Indiana. She knew that much because she saw postmarks on some letters and cards that he had sent Jeremy a few years back. This was all she knew about his family. Except that Jeremy had some relatives—from his dad's side—who lived in the northern part of the state which he had only met twice, when he was a small child, and hadn't seen since. And that his mom and uncle's relatives were all gone now. That was about it. She wondered the most about his dad.

Reticent, and with a slight nervous stutter, she asked the question, "What happened with you…with you and your dad, Jeremy?" She placed a loving hand on his forearm and, with a sheepish expression, continued, "I'm just curious. If you don't want to talk about it, that's okay—" She squeezed his arm softly.

He was looking down, gazing stoically, as though seeing through the floor and into the Earth at the buried memories he'd hidden there a long time before.

She was just about ready to speak again when Jeremy started. "No...no, it's okay. I knew it'd come up sooner or later."

He looked up, smiled a sad smile out of the corner of his mouth, and then turned his head back down. He began to tell her the story. She didn't say a word. She just sat there and listened.

"Well..." He took a deep breath, blew it out with puffed cheeks, and then began again. "It's kind of a long story, starts with my mom, actually. I guess I had just turned about ten years old when they found out that she had leukemia. They suspected that it was related to this toxic dump place, out near where she worked. At least that's what some people speculated.

"Anyway, Mom used to work at this nursery, over on the west side of town. It was around a bunch of factories, and the one where the dump was. It made big electrical devices, transformers, and stuff. It was real close to where we lived at that time, too. She worked at that nursery part-time for almost twenty years, mainly during the summers when she wasn't teaching.

"She loved working with plants, growing things, like Uncle Paul does. The PCB's, which they think must've given her the cancer, leached out of this company's dump into the creek that ran through the nursery. It ran behind our house, too, actually.

"I guess the company buried all of that junk back in the mid-forties, and then just forgot to tell anybody about it, or didn't want to tell anybody about it. The nursery used the water from the creek to water all the plants and trees they sold—pumped it straight out of it. They just didn't know, I guess didn't have a clue, at least back then. There were some lawsuits years later, but nothing ever came of them, I guess, for my mom anyway.

"So, she got real sick and the doctors told her that she only had about six months to live, or whatever, but she fought it for over a year before she died. I guess she suffered a lot, from being sick and all. You know the effects of chemo, and all that stuff. I only remember seeing her sick a few times, but I was only eleven when she died, and I didn't know she was even going to die until the last couple months, when she was in the hospital. No one told me. I wish they had, now. I could have spent more time with her. Better time, you know? But, I guess they did what they thought was best."

Jeremy's eyes started to well with tears. He just sat there, silent for a moment.

CD remained completely still, and tears began welling in her eyes, too. But she didn't say anything. She just sat there, and waited.

He continued, "To top that off, the big kicker was what happened the last month, before she died." He took another deep breath, blew it out slowly. "My uncle finally told me—when I was about fourteen, I guess it was—what happened. He said that he wasn't sure if he should've told me or not, but he did anyway. You see, up until then, I never knew why my father was always gone.

"I was told that he was just busy, you know, with his driving and all. That he had some important jobs to do for the government, or some crap. They made it sound like he was some sort of secret agent or something. I was pretty naïve back then, I suppose.

"I was even proud for a while, that he was gone. You know, doing secret stuff for the government. I imagined him hauling missiles around, hiding them from the enemy, or...or hauling around one of those secret mobile labs or something, ready to set it up at the least sign of trouble, help direct our Air Force in the event of a war, or whatever. I was pretty stupid.

"I lived with Uncle Paul for all those years, and I guess he just didn't have the heart to tell me. I guess he just wanted to wait until I got older. I can understand that, now. If I had known, then I would have probably been pretty confused and angry—who knows how I would have reacted at such a young age. Maybe it would have been better to have told me back then, maybe not at all, I don't know."

Jeremy wiped a tear with his thumb. "Anyway, one day Uncle Paul and I were out at Finley's lake, fishing off of the dock, and as difficult as it was for them, I guess, they just came right out and told me.

"My dad wasn't, *isn't*, my real dad. You know, by blood."

CD's head turned abruptly. She looked straight at Jeremy's face. Both had been looking toward the fireplace, but now only Jeremy was watching and listening as its embers glowed and crackled. She wondered if she'd made a mistake in trying to get Jeremy to talk about it. She could read the look on his face. She was hoping, praying, that she hadn't gone too far. But after another deep breath, Jeremy continued.

"I guess…I guess back before my mom and my dad got together, my mom had been with someone else. She told Uncle Paul about it shortly after she told Dad—about a month before she died. I guess she was with this other guy, but he didn't really want anything, you know, long-term. So, I guess in order to get back at him, or whatever, she went out with my dad, and the other guy just went on his own way. I guess she really did like Joseph, my dad, and eventually did fall in love with him.

"Then, along came the news of me. They were happy, I was told. I had a sort of normal childhood, and…and I loved my dad, I guess. We used to do things together, some things, at least at first, but he was gone a lot of the time, I remember. I don't remember doing much together, actually. He's been away for a lot of years now. I've only seen him, maybe, three or four times since back then, you know?"

Jeremy was visibly on the edge of sobbing now. CD realized it, too. She wanted to end it, to stop talking, but she knew that it was too late. She had started something that Jeremy was going to have to finish himself. All she could do was sit and hold his hand and squeeze it to let him know that she was with him. She felt so stupid, and sorry for bringing it up.

Jeremy went on.

"I guess she found out from some blood tests that were done. Since she was getting checked out and all, back at the beginning of her illness, she suggested that Dad might as well get a physical done, too. They did blood work on him, and I guess she asked the doctor to do a paternity test.

"No one knows how or even if she might have suspected anything. I guess it must've been a mother's instinct, or something. Anyway, it was her family doctor that she'd known for a long time, and he agreed to it, and to discuss the results only with her, I guess.

"She must have lived with the news for the better part of a year, you know. It was only the last two months of her life that she finally chose to tell Dad the truth—no one knows why. When she did, he couldn't take it. He was losing the woman he loved, and now his son, it turned out, wasn't even his own flesh and blood."

CD's eyebrows rose, then contorted. She was crying now, as was Jeremy. In Jeremy's heart, he could feel the pain that his dad must have felt, all the hurt, the anger, the resentment. His dad probably wished that he could turn back time, but that was impossible. CD felt his anguish as if it were her own. It only made her cry harder.

Jeremy struggled to continue.

"I guess after Mom died…" Jeremy wiped a tear away. "Dad began drinking, a lot. Uncle Paul said he was always drinking, that he was drunk most of the time after Mom was gone. He said he'd found him on his knees more than once, just crying, praying.

"It got to him so bad that he lost his job with the company he worked for here in town—he was in an accident, or something. I don't remember much about it, actually. Only being alone a lot, and my uncle being sad, and starting to spend a lot of time with me.

"I guess Dad finally went and tried to get some help, a program, counselors, you know. But, I guess it didn't really help much. So, I guess he just had to get away, away from the house, town…*me*. I guess I don't blame him. That's got to suck! Life just sucks sometimes—for a lot of people," he said, now wiping the flood of tears from both eyes.

CD slowly shook her head from side to side, and then bit her lower lip. Tears rolled down both her cheeks. Wiping them didn't seem to help. Jeremy was now hunched over in her lap, and she was holding him and rocking him gently. They were both crying, one of those deep, lonely types of cries.

They were so absorbed in the moment that they didn't hear Paul Usher drive up and come in the back door. He caught the last minute or two of their conversation from around the corner. He knew instantly what it was about. Paul silently slipped back outside before they became aware of his presence. He didn't want to embarrass them, or interfere with this important time together.

Alone in the backyard, Paul walked slowly to the fence line of the large field behind the house. The crunching of the frozen snow crystals under his boots was deafening in contrast to his somber, reflective thoughts. He stood there with both hands gripping the fence's metal gate tightly, twisting his gloved hands one way, and then another. It was cold, really cold, he realized.

He took a slow deep breath, blew it out, and watched the vaporous plume form a large wispy cloud that drifted slowly across the fence. He shook his head in disgust, rattled the gate with a hard push of frustration, and then withdrew his hands. He then stepped back, took another deep breath and then blew it out ever harder, making a growling, grunting sound. Then, teary-eyed himself, he looked up at the cloudy winter sky and prayed, "God, sometimes…*sometimes*…" He didn't finish; he just let the tears and the blasts of his hot breath coming out of his nostrils do all the talking.

Chapter 18

Monday was another day full of classes for Jeremy. He finished up the day attending a lecture by a visiting professor, and then dropped by the library to pick up a few things. Then he went out to Life's Continuum to see what he could do to help his uncle get ready for the holidays.

"Hey, Uncle Paul," Jeremy said, as he walked up to him. Paul was in the back corner of the warehouse, assembling some new feed dispensers for the animals.

"Jeremy, *hi*, I didn't expect to see you out here today. You're not scheduled until this weekend."

He looked at Jeremy. He could immediately tell that something was on his mind.

"*So*, what's up, school okay?" he asked.

"Yeah," Jeremy said, "school's fine. I just thought I'd come out and see if you needed any help, you know, get ready for the holidays." He reached out and straightened a pot that was sitting crooked on a shelf, not looking in his uncle's eyes, but looking everywhere else.

"Help, huh? Yeah, I guess I could use some help. But, you didn't really come out here to work, did you? Come on, what's up?" He could tell that Jeremy wanted to talk. And he suspected it had something to do with CD. "Hey, what do you say we go in and get warmed up by the stove? I could use a cup of coffee. Want one?"

"Yeah, I...I do." Jeremy smiled. "Thanks."

Paul had a small garage-sized extension built onto one of the smaller pole barns in the back used for working on vehicles. It was away from the public areas, and quiet. The addition only had one window in it, a large picture window. It looked out toward the back of the property where there was a nice-sized stand of oak trees, some shrub bushes, and a small perennial flower garden.

Surrounding it all was an old split wood fence, grayed from the weather and sun. Beyond that, the property dropped down into a flat-bottomed valley where there was a large cornfield, and beyond that, an old gravel road that followed the winding path of a gently meandering creek.

The room served as his private office. It was more functional than fancy. Insulation could still be seen in one of the walls, and it had an unfinished concrete floor. There was a big woodstove in one corner, and a door to the outside where the wood was brought in.

There was a desk, a few filing cabinets, and an antique wall hutch—which used to be Paul's great-grandmother's. There was an old table in one corner that had a small TV on it, a few fold-up chairs leaning up against the wall, and an old, dark-blue, tattered, but clean couch with a rough-hewn, slab-wood coffee table placed in front of it.

Paul went to the wood stove, stoked it with a few pieces of split wood, and then fixed up a coffee strainer with a filter and some dark roast. He grabbed the pot of hot water off the stove and started pouring, letting it drain into a glass carafe that he had sitting on a ceramic plate on the stove.

He poured two mugs and offered one to his nephew.

Jeremy was sitting on the couch, looking out of the big window at the panoramic scene—there was still a significant portion of the year's first snow around, and it made the valley's features more picturesque.

He received the cup, said 'thank you', and then set it down on the rough-hewn table in front of him. He watched his uncle as he sat down in his office chair behind his desk. This was a familiar scene for Jeremy. They had done this many times. It was where they talked—but, more importantly, it was where they listened to each other.

"Uncle Paul," Jeremy paused, picked up his cup, and stared at the steam rising from it. He was silent for a long moment, obviously gathering his thoughts. Then he started. "Why do you think Mom had to, felt she needed to, you know, tell Dad about me, about that other guy?"

He took a drink, swallowing hard between his words.

"I mean, why did she feel she had to? I just thought about that last night, when CD was over."

He paused, looked up at his uncle, and then added, "I told her, about Mom, and about Dad—"

He focused on the steam again.

Paul listened, sipping his own coffee, but he abruptly stopped. Somehow he knew that Jeremy was going to bring up this particular subject. He'd sensed it as soon as he had shown up. He said a short silent prayer for wisdom, and sensitivity—as he always did at times like these.

He answered slowly. "Jeremy, no one can know what your mom was thinking at that time. But I'd suspect it was because she knew she was going to die, and she wanted to leave this world being honest. I reckon she must've felt that Joseph had a right to know. And, maybe, she couldn't leave this world knowing that someday, some *way*, he, and eventually you, might find out. I don't know. I'm not saying it was the right thing, or the wrong thing for her to do. I'm just saying why she might have done it."

Jeremy didn't say a word. He just sat there, thinking.

His uncle continued, "You know, Jeremy, there's not a human being alive, or dead, who hasn't done something that they regretted doing. So much can happen in a moment's time—a moment of anger, of passion—and sometimes, most of the time, there's no turning back. She really loved this guy—your real dad—but he turned out to be one of those types that probably only really cared about himself, I guess. I don't really know.

"She really didn't talk about him much, and I only met him a few times. He seemed like a nice guy." He paused again before continuing. "But he left her for some reason. I don't know why. And we'll probably never know.

"When he left, apparently, and I don't know if you remember me telling you this or not, but, she went to see some friends, for comfort and consolation or whatever. You know, and there was Joseph, your dad. He was just a friend of a friend of your mom's who'd happened to be there.

"They talked; he immediately liked her, I guess, and she ended up liking him. I suppose he was lonely, too. She was hurt, and lonely, and the circumstances were right, for both of them, and so, they got together. In a way, it was what each of them needed, at the time, I believe.

"Anyway, neither knew the news, you know, about you. All they knew was they needed each other and that they felt good together. They eventually came to believe that they were meant to be together. Your mom told me that one time. He loved her more than anything."

Paul paused after he'd said it, but he couldn't retract it. He went on.

"Your dad is a really a good man, Jeremy. He's just...*is* just, still really confused, and hurt. I don't think he was angry with her, or with you. I just think he's...he's just angry at the world, at God, probably, most likely, for allowing all of this to happen.

"And when someone's mad at God, there's really nowhere else one can turn to for help. You know? So, I guess your dad just turned in on himself. It happens to a lot of people.

"Your mom didn't do anything bad, Jeremy—with that guy, or with telling your dad the truth. Your mom was a great person. She'd help anyone, any time, and I don't think for a minute that she meant any harm in what she did.

"She was just reaching out for...*love*, to be loved, and trying to set things right, while she had the chance. She was just human, like the rest of us. She didn't mean to hurt you either, Jeremy; you've got to know that."

Jeremy gritted his teeth and cinched his lips at the comment.

A big part of Jeremy was still hurting and still angry that his dad had left. That he hadn't seemed to care about anything, much less him, for the last six years of his life. But, on the other hand, when he thought about how he would react if something like that had happened to him, he just didn't know.

Maybe, Jeremy thought, he would have done the same thing, if it were him going through it. Jeremy hurt for his dad. He truly did. He didn't think it was fair—that he lost his wife, or that his son turned out to be someone else's. He tried hard to put himself in his dad's shoes, but it wasn't easy.

After all, he didn't ask for this to happen, either. It was all just really difficult to understand. He wanted to hate his real dad. He wanted to blame him for all this, but then he thought, maybe he never even found out that his mom was expecting a baby. Maybe he doesn't even know that he has a son out there in the world—*Me*, Jeremy thought.

"Did my real dad ever know about me, mom being pregnant with me, I mean?" he asked, looking up at his uncle.

"I don't know, Jeremy. I honestly don't know." Paul read something in his nephew's eyes. After a pause, he continued, "But, I don't think so. I really don't think so. There's no way he could have. Your mom didn't even know—though she might have suspected back then. But, he wouldn't have known, because he'd already left.

"Maybe he had a good reason for leaving? I don't know. Whatever he was thinking, whatever the reason, he left. Who knows, maybe if he had known that you were on the way, that he was going to be a father, maybe he would have done the responsible thing and stayed around?

"Who knows what might have happened if he would have just made one different choice? Maybe to stay another month or two, try to make it work, or whatever. What if Joseph hadn't chosen to go be with your mom's friends that day, who knows what the outcome would have been then. Who knows? All we really know is that it worked out, the way it worked out!"

"Yeah." Jeremy only said. Then, shakily, he asked, "Do you know his name, my real dad? What he was like, anything about him?" Jeremy looked at his uncle squarely.

Paul looked at him, nodded, although reluctantly.

"Yes, Jeremy, I do." He paused, and then started again after clearing his throat. "It was Johnston, Phillip Johnston. He was in the military…Marines, as I remember. From a family of military people—going way back, I heard. That's all

I know. The last anyone saw of him was around 9/11, I think."

Jeremy didn't ask any more. He just nodded in return.

Both sat there, silently looking out of the window, sipping their coffee, and wondering about how things work out, and about life. Neither knew it, but they both thought it: if it had not worked out this way, then *they* might not have been together.

Neither could imagine that—not being together, that is. They were truly, in every sense of the word, father and son. But, more than that, they were friends.

"You know, Jeremy, some things just happen. Who knows why? It's frustrating when you really think about. I can think back and remember all sorts of things that I did, things that happened, for one reason or another, and no matter how much I wished that they would have worked out differently; things just wouldn't be the same as they are now.

"What if I would have gone into the ministry, like I'd considered years ago?" He peered out the window again, a distant look in his eyes. "Sometimes, I wonder, what if I would have hit the books harder and put up with all that academic bull crap. Who knows, maybe I'd be doing more good in the world.

"Maybe I would've been a teacher, or one of those professor/lecturer types by now, instead of a small businessman who bores people with my philosophical rantings, while trying to sell them a dead tree at Christmastime to hang little baubles of their own past memories on."

He shook his head slowly from side to side, and then sipped his coffee.

Jeremy looked up into his uncle's eyes, then out the window again. Something his uncle said made him remember that Professor character. That strange experience he had imagined when he and the guys had gone skydiving earlier in the summer. He hadn't thought of it for some time.

He hadn't wanted to think of it.

"It's all a big conundrum, Jeremy, why things work out the way they do. Why sometimes things seem meant to be, and then sometimes they don't. Like in that old Christmas movie: *It's a Wonderful Life*. How would things be, if things hadn't happened the way they did? If people weren't who they were, or are? It kind of bends the old mind, if you know what I mean.

"There's a term for it, you know. It's called the Anthropic Principle: if things weren't the way they are, and they were some other way, then we wouldn't know what it was like now, *if* it was some other way. All we know, or *can* know, is the way it *is*...like it is...*now*! Never both at the same time" Their eyebrows stretched up nearly to their hair lines.

They smiled at each other.

"Yeah," Jeremy said. "It's strange. Like meeting CD, she just popped into my life, and everything's changed. I think differently about things now. I think more about the future and stuff. She encourages me, helps me, and ...and loves me, I think!"

"Yeah," Paul replied. "I could tell. That's good." He smiled. "I really like her, too. I can tell you're both getting pretty close."

He wanted to tell Jeremy that he had heard part of their conversation the night before, and that he'd seen them crying together, but he knew that he should just leave it alone. It's something that he didn't need to say, he thought.

They just sat there for a little while, pondering things, about the past, and about the future. Then Jeremy got up, reached out his hand in a handshake gesture. Paul reached up and took his nephew's hand. Jeremy shook it hard, and then pulled his uncle up out of his chair.

"Come on," Jeremy said. "We've got Christmas trees to unload. People need a place to hang up their memories, you know!"

They both smiled at the bittersweet thought.

Chapter 19

Christmas was less than a week away. It was Jeremy's and CD's first one together and they wanted it to be special. They had decided to drive up to the big city of Indianapolis to do some shopping, and then go out to eat. They discussed maybe going to one of those nice places downtown where they had a couple of people wait on you at the same time. Dine in candlelight and use cloth napkins.

But they decided against the idea.

Jeremy had wanted to make the evening special for her, but he was honestly glad to find that they were both genuinely of the same mind about it. With school expenses and everything, they just couldn't justify spending all that money for one meal. They settled on dinner at Steak-n-Shake, finding that they both loved the chili there, and, being that it was so cold that day, a hot bowl of chili sounded great to them.

Following a nice dinner together, they went to the Circle Center Mall downtown, and after most of their shopping was done, they decided on a walk around the Soldier's and Sailor's monument on the circle in the center of town. The monument was, as it is every year, strung vertically with lights all the way to its top. It was huge, and back in the day, used to be heralded as the biggest Christmas tree in the world. Jeremy laughed when CD said, "This one'll do. I'll get the axe and start chopin', you back up the truck!"

They then thought about taking a horse-drawn carriage ride to end their evening, but decided it was too cold to just sit there behind a huge animal that had been on duty all day and seriously needed an appointment with a high-pressure, industrial strength bidet.

As they started home, CD commented that she wanted to make one more stop—at a bookstore—if that was alright with Jeremy. He frowned and rolled his eyes as he spoke his answer: "Books! Seriously? I *hate* books. Okay...*okay*, I suppose, if I must!"

She laughed at his goofiness.

CD wanted to get her mom a book on Natural Foods and Holistic Health for a Christmas present. She told Jeremy that her mom was getting worried that "something was going on inside of her that didn't feel right," and she had thought it would be about time, due to her age, to straighten up her diet a little. Jeremy acknowledged the point, thinking about his uncle in the same light.

They decided to stop at the Barnes and Noble's bookstore before leaving town. Upon arriving, they saw that they had well over an hour before the store would close. Plenty of time, they agreed. They went in and Jeremy followed CD back to the Natural Foods section, reading book title after book title as quickly as they passed his line of sight.

Then, Jeremy noticed something going on over by the café. People were standing around a long table, and there was someone behind it sitting in a chair. The person was shaking people's hands.

It was a book signing, Jeremy suddenly realized. He quickly wondered who it might be. He had only seen something like this on TV, and he thought it was really interesting. CD looked over too, and having already picked out the perfect book for her mother, suggested that they check it out before leaving.

They went up to the counter, paid, and then meandered over to the small gathering of people. On the other side of the table, they saw a well-tanned, middle-aged man dressed in casual clothes: brown jeans, a comfortable-looking tan corduroy shirt, worn under a coarse-stitched, light-brown, tweed jacket.

He wore small, wire-rimmed glasses that sat way down on his nose, and he had longish, graying brown hair that was tucked behind his ears. His face was somewhat scarred from what might have been teenage acne, and he had a pleasingly humble, yet oddly somber look on his face.

They stepped up a little closer as the people thinned out, until they were only a few meters from the table. Then, a rather large woman shook the man's hand, turned, and walked away. After the lady left, the two noticed a small poster-board sign sitting on the end of the table that read:

Author: Thomas Dorkin

Book Signing: 7-9 pm

Jeremy smiled. "That's weird," he whispered to CD. "That's the guy who wrote that book I read awhile back: *So You're Here! Now Where Do You Want to Go?* I read it, at least most of it, again, the night before the guys and I went skydiving that first time. It was pretty good. It was about choices, life choices, about deciding what you wanted to do—are destined to do—in life, and then figuring out what you needed to do, you know, to get there."

"Cool," she whispered in reply. "He looks like a nice guy." She paused. "Let's go meet him."

Jeremy looked down at her, then back at the man. He hadn't thought of that, but why not, he said to himself. He looked at the table again and read the rest of the sign. It had the title of his new book on it: *Some Things Meant, Some Things Not.*

"That's strange," he murmured.

"What's strange?" she asked, also in a whisper, barely hearing what he had mumbled.

"Uh…" He looked down at her again. "Something my uncle and I were talking about. About how some things are meant to be, how things work out, and stuff."

Jeremy's mind was swirling. He was remembering what he had read in this guy's book, along with things that his uncle had said in the past. And, suddenly, to his astonishment, even some of the things that that Professor guy—the one he'd dreamt about—had spoken of.

"Well, let's go meet him," CD said, interrupting his thoughts.

"'Meet him?' Uhmm, okay! Yeah. I...I suppose we could—" He jostled his head back and forth slightly as if the idea was a small ball, and it was rolling around in his head.

They walked over toward the area and stood behind a man who was just finishing a conversation with the author. The man turned, nodded at CD, and then walked away. They stepped up to the table. Jeremy was nervous for some reason. He felt like he was in a daze, or something. He didn't know why.

The man looked at them and then reached out his hand toward Jeremy. Jeremy looked down, all of a sudden realizing he was going to shake his hand. He reciprocated by slowly offering his hand.

"Hello, Thomas Dorkin," the man said, gripping firmly.

Jeremy noticed that his hand felt strong and calloused, not at all like he thought a writer's hand would feel like.

"Hello, uh, I'm Jeremy...Jeremy Sayer. This is..." He looked down at CD, paused and then smiled. "My girlfriend, CD, uh, Caitlin Dobbs," he said proudly. He was shocked for a moment. He had never introduced her before as his girlfriend. He noticed that she smiled though, when he'd said it.

"Well, nice to meet you two. Jeremy, Caitlin. Thanks for stopping by. Have you had a chance to read my newest book?" he asked.

Jeremy replied, "Yes, it was good. I mean, I read your other book, your last book. I haven't read your new one yet. But, I liked the last one. It was good." Jeremy was searching for something to say. For some reason, he felt like an idiot. "I read it, again actually, the night before I went skydiving, back in the spring. It was cool, the book I mean, well and the skydiving. I really liked the part about..."

The man stopped Jeremy's comments short. "Oh really, skydiving? I'm into skydiving, too. I haven't done it for, well, let's see, a couple years I guess it's been, but I thoroughly enjoy it. Actually, I've recently thought about doing it again. Just last week, I was thinking about it. Huh! That's interesting," he said, pausing. "So, where do you go? Local, I'm assuming?"

"*Go*? Oh, go, skydiving you mean, uhmm, local, yes, local, uhmm, Givins Skydiving Center, just south of town here. It's just a little flying field, actually, mostly grass, one runway, but really nice. The center's not real big either, three planes, and there's only…" Jeremy was cut short, again.

"Yep, I know the place. I've more than heard of it! Godfrey Givins owns it, right? At least he did several years ago. I jumped there, back when he first started up the business. I actually know Godfrey. Did know Godfrey, pretty well, it's been years though. We were in college together, down at I.U…" He saw the look of astonishment on their faces. He paused for a moment, thought about it, and then continued, "Small universe, isn't it?" Then added, "To some of us, it's smaller than you think! How's he doing? Brake, Godfrey, I mean. Does he still own it?"

CD and Jeremy were amazed that he knew Godfrey, and about the center. And he even knew his nickname.

"Yeah, he does. He's doing great," CD replied. "The center's really growing. I work there in the summer, when I'm not in school. How'd you ever end up down there, I mean, knowing Brake and all? Oh, you said that you went to school with him? What a coincidence?" she said. Jeremy thought so, too.

"Well, I'm originally from out West, but I went to I.U. for my undergrad work. I met Godfrey there, I guess it was during my second year. It was funny, how we met, actually. He had an odd name, God-free…Givins, you know. And I had an unusual name too—Dorkin. As you can imagine, I got ribbed for mine, a lot. Godfrey did too, for his. And because of that one thing in common, we became friends.

"We hung out together for most of our college years. I remember him being rather a showoff, and," he paused, leaned forward and whispered, "and quite the asshole at times." He laughed, and then looked around to see if anyone else had heard him.

No one had.

"I think he tried to over-compensate for the name." He laughed again, as if teasing him even though he wasn't even there. "I'm about finished here." He looked at his watch; it was right at nine o'clock. "Say, would the two of you care to join me for a cup of coffee, or hot chocolate perhaps? I'd like to hear about how Brake's doing. I've got a little time. What do you say?" He smiled a big smile at them, opening his arms wide as if he wouldn't take no for an answer.

"Sure," they both said at the same time, looking at each other. "Cool," they also said, simultaneously.

Thomas Dorkin picked up on their synchronicity.

"Cool," he replied back. "Shall we?"

Chapter 20

Jeremy, CD, and the author, Thomas Dorkin, sat at a corner table in the back of the bookstore's little café. Each had a steaming cup of hot cocoa in front them, only sipping intermittently as they waited for them to cool. Jeremy had picked up one of Professor Dorkin's new books, which he'd signed for him.

The two of them thought he was real nice, actually conversing more about them, than himself—he turned out to be a very humble guy. Not like what a lot of people might expect for a guy who was a famous published author. He talked to them as if he was just any other ordinary guy.

They talked about skydiving, about Godfrey, about his wife's accident, and how they ended up getting married as a result, and that it'd been several years since the author had actually seen his old friend.

And, oddly, he told them how the story about Godfrey, and how he had met his wife, was one of the inspirations that led him to write his most recent book.

"It is a story that's stranger than fiction. Falling out of the sky, crashing into a stranger with a parachute, causing her to be laid up in the hospital for months, threatened with life-long paralysis, and then ending up marrying her. It seems like it's just all too unlikely, doesn't it? Something out of the imagination of Hollywood," he said.

It did seem unlikely, Jeremy thought, but then he realized that he and CD were sitting there, a couple of teenagers, talking with an acclaimed author, and, Jeremy having just recently read his book, and they having just happened upon this bookstore, at exactly the right time, and then ending up knowing someone that he knows. And, *that* someone just happened to be part of the inspiration for his newest book, which, by the way, was about fate and destiny.

"Stuff like that happens every day..." Jeremy said with a conspicuously deep sarcastic intonation. It's no wonder they were a little frazzled by it all. The strange thing was that Thomas Dorkin didn't act as if it were all that unusual.

"So, I'm glad to hear Brake's doing alright. What a coincidence running into you two, *if* you believe in coincidence, I mean."

They curiously looked at each other, then at him. "What do you mean?" CD asked. Jeremy nodded in agreement with her question.

"Well, I explain my thoughts on the subject a little deeper in that book there." He pointed down to the copy on the table. "But, the idea is that we might just live in a world—a universe—where things happen because they are supposed to happen, a deterministic universe, where all events, from the motion and direction of a galaxy, down to the motion and direction of each of our individual lives, happens for a reason. It's been created that way. Just because we don't see it all the time, or understand it when we do see it, doesn't mean that it's not happening."

Jeremy was beginning to understand; he was remembering his high school classes on the subject. And what Thomas Dorkin was saying was almost exactly what he and his uncle were talking about just a few weeks earlier. And it was what that Professor guy had said, the one he'd dreamed. For some reason, it made sense, but how could it, he concluded.

"I know it sounds strange. It delves into the realm of philosophy, metaphysics, and religion even." He searched for the best words. "There is definitely more going on in life than what meets the eye, and most people only rarely catch a glimpse of it, if at all.

"People—people including all the great philosophers of history—have tried to speculate on the subject. Objectively speaking, the topic leads us to wonder whether there really is such a thing as fate or destiny, or predestination, as some would call it, and how that could exist at the same time as free will, and individual choice. It's a subject that has driven many insane. Just look at history!"

Jeremy and CD listened intently.

He continued, "On the one hand, if everything is meant to be, if everything in nature is somehow locked in place, then the Agamemnon's, the Attila's, the Hitler's and the Hussein's—all those psycho-killer-madman types—are meant to be as well. They couldn't be any other way, even if they wanted to, and so it goes with all the other nasty things humans have to endure at times as well, like: earthquakes, volcanoes, floods, starvation, pestilence, sickness, disease, all the things in creation that bring about loss, heartache, pain, suffering…death.

"If these things are meant to be, if people like Hitler were meant to be, then people—us, *we*—could just go on our merry way and say to ourselves, 'Oh, I'm just bad, I'm just evil, and since I'm made that way, then I don't have to take any responsibility for my actions—who I hurt, or what I do.'

"But, I'm sure you can agree. We must all be responsible for our actions, for the impact we have on others, and on the world. We must choose to be different, choose to be better, to *not* do the things we know we *can* do, once we realize that a lot of the things we *can* do, are essentially wrong. To learn from the mistakes we make, and from the mistakes others make.

"It's a difficult thing to grasp, to think about, actually, once you start to think about it. I hope you find some insight on the subject during your stints in life. If you do, let me know; maybe I can rewrite that book with more answers, instead of mostly just questions."

He laughed heartily, looking at his watch.

Jeremy and CD were mesmerized by his words. They had only briefly thought of such things. But what he said made sense. They both believed, as they'd been taught, that there was a reason for everything. They felt, rather uncannily, that they were supposed to be there, right at that moment, right at that time. They felt strangely large, yet small, at the same time.

Jeremy remembered that feeling.

It was like feeling happiness and sadness, being smart and stupid, all at the same time. Like you were just beginning to see something great, but were still blind to it. He immediately remembered the wall, the one in the Professor's study. He remembered touching it, glimpsing something on the other side of it, but he couldn't remember what he saw.

"Well, folks, I'd best be going." He looked at his watch again. "I've got to catch a plane early in the morning. I'm flying back to Oregon for the holidays. This was my last signing. In fact, I wouldn't have even been here if my agent hadn't messed up my itinerary and my plane schedule. I was supposed to leave yesterday, but since I was here anyway, he worked out another signing on the spur of the moment, not a bad turnout actually, for little or no advertising." He stood up and pushed his chair under the table.

"Listen, it was nice meeting you two. We might see each other again. I'm planning on coming back this way in the spring. And now that you guys have got me thinking about Godfrey again, I think I'll *drop* by his Drop Zone and see him on my next trip through. Be sure to tell him we met, and that I'm going to do that, okay, alright? Maybe you'll both be there. I'd love to see you again, too. Thanks for keeping me company, and for reading my books. Take care now. You be careful driving home."

He shook their hands and, after putting his coat on and talking with the bookstore's manager for a brief moment, exited the large glass doors of the main entrance, giving them both a quick smile and a wave before disappearing into the night.

Wow, they said to each other with their eyes. It took them a few moments, but then they realized that they'd been talking with this fascinating man for close to an hour, and that they, too, had better get going.

On the drive home, they didn't talk much. They just thought about things. They both felt really tired, for some reason.

Chapter 21

The next day, CD went over to Jeremy's to get a head start on wrapping presents. Later, they were going to go to a movie. They started on the presents, but they never made it to the movie.

"I was talking to my uncle about, you know, my mom and Joseph, and my real dad, and after talking to Professor Dorkin, I kind of look at things differently now.

"If my real dad and my mother hadn't gotten together, I wouldn't even be here, I guess. And if he had stayed around, you know, he might have found out that I was going to come into the world. It would have been totally different. He may have been a good father, and I might have grown up to be a doctor, or something really cool.

"Then again, the guy might have been a bad father. He might have been abusive, beat me—*and* mom—and we might have been miserable.

"As a result, I might have grown up to be a mean, uncaring, drunken deadbeat, living in jails and in alleyways, and stuff. Maybe I would have been a…uh…a serial killer! Yeah, a killer!"

He looked at her with pretend evil eyes, started walking over to her all creepy-like, looking up and down at her delicate, fragile body, breathing hard and slow and making eerie, wheezy, gurgling sounds.

She immediately jumped into a karate pose and did the bring-it-on finger gesture that the character Neo did in that old movie, *The Matrix*, which they'd recently watched together.

"Aaayaah!" she yelled, with a Bruce Lee, cat-like cry coming afterwards. He lunged for her. They grabbed each other, faking a struggle. Then, she pretended to turn into a helpless Southern Belle, crying softly.

"Help me, help me," she said, with the back of her hand on her forehead as if she were about to faint.

He sniffed at her as if he were a monster ready to devour her very flesh.

Then they smiled, all goofy–like, and then kissed passionately. He let her up and they resumed wrapping presents.

They laughed at their silliness.

"You know, there are a lot of things that could have turned out differently, if something simple had just been changed, or, you know, went a different way," she said. "Like that day you and the guys came out to the Drop Zone to jump. I wasn't even scheduled to be there that day."

"Really?" Jeremy asked.

"Nope, I was supposed to go with my mom to take care of some family stuff. But she called me that morning and canceled because she didn't feel well."

Jeremy asked. "Was she alright?"

"Oh yeah, she's been having these female problems, on an off for a few years, you know, *women* stuff." She rattled her eyebrows, and tilted her head to get the point across.

Jeremy slowly shook his head way up, and then way down in a gesture of final acknowledgement, rolling his eyes when the full realization hit.

"Anyway, I decided to go on out to the DZ just because it was such a beautiful day that day. Remember the big fluffy clouds, the steady breeze—? That's the best time to go skydiving, when there's something up there to fly around, or over, or under, something to see instead of just air. It really gives it all a three-dimensional aspect to it, more depth, you know, instead of just emptiness."

She noticed Jeremy staring into space.

What she said made him remember the Professor again. He was thinking about telling her. He thought she would understand. That she wouldn't think he was crazy or anything. Then, for some reason, he remembered how long the experience had lasted. It wasn't just a few seconds, or even minutes, it seemed like it had lasted for hours. He could remember a lot of it, he thought, but then he couldn't—or maybe it was that he didn't want to.

No, he said to himself. He better not tell her.

What if he *was* a little off, or maybe had some medical brain-thing going on? He decided against the idea. He just sat there, motionless, leaning back in his chair, kind of looking up toward the ceiling. For a moment, he felt frozen, like he couldn't move even if he wanted to, even if his mind told him to. He started feeling small again, that strange feeling, again.

"Earth to Jeremy," she spoke, snapping her fingers.

Jeremy was still staring. He realized that he hadn't said anything for a long time. Then he remembered what they were talking about. He sat up quickly, and began speaking.

"So, if you hadn't shown up that day, if you had gone with your mom, then we might not have ever met?"

"Yeah, that's what I was thinking, strange, huh?" she said.

Then Jeremy remembered something that he had thought of the night before, but hadn't mentioned.

"Here's something strange, too. Remember the day after we jumped, when we met at the library?"

"Yeah, why?" she replied.

"Well, the reason I went to the library was to return that book by Thomas Dorkin! I'd had it for several weeks, and actually reviewed it again the night before the jump, and that was the day I returned it. I had just dropped it off at the counter minutes before we met."

"You're kidding. You never mentioned that!"

"I remembered it last night when we were talking with him, but then I got sidetracked with all he was saying. And the really weird thing is, that we took the book, along with a few others I had, to the Drop Zone that day and we were supposed to return them on the way back, but we forgot. It was all the excitement, I guess. We just forgot. Weird, if any one of those things had happened differently, we might have never met there, at the library."

CD's eyebrows went up in the air. They both got a spooky feeling.

"What if, like Thomas Dorkin said, 'there's more going on than meets the eye'? Well then, what could it be? A big experiment maybe, a big game?" Jeremy asked rhetorically with a mystic tone, thinking about the Professor again.

"Maybe it's a big play, or an elaborate story being acted out, and we're the characters? Maybe God's a playwright, or a movie director, or something?" CD added.

"Yeah, maybe, but what about the freewill we have? What if I decided I didn't want to play the part of, say, a gardener or a…truck driver, or whatever. Say I wanted to play the part of an author, like Thomas Dorkin, or a world leader or advisor, or something? What's to stop me? With freewill, I can change my destiny, if I want to, right?"

"Yeah," she said, "unless not changing your destiny, *is* your destiny." She smiled deviously.

"Yeah, but then I could still change it, if I really wanted to," he said, shaking his finger at her.

"Yeah, unless not being able to *was* your destiny, too!" She smiled again, contorting her eyebrows, like she had just placed him in check while playing a game of chess, trying to look all wise and sly.

He was stopped in his tracks this time, also making weird configurations with his eyeballs and eyebrows. He thought: this must be what they call circular thinking.

"I can see why he said that if we figured out anything to give him a call, and he'd rewrite his book with answers, instead of just questions." They both smiled again at each other.

Suddenly, their metaphysical amusement was broken by the earsplitting shrill of screeching tires.

The two of them looked at each other, quickly got up, rushed over to the window and looked outside. Scott Ramses had just pulled up into the driveway and was getting out of his car, its rear end still smoking from the burning rubber. He slammed the door, and wiped away what looked like tears from his eyes.

He started walking toward the house, hesitated, and then turned back, put his hands on his temples for a moment, then turned again facing the house. He wiped more tears away, and then hurriedly ran up the walkway to the front door. Jeremy was already heading there to receive him. He opened the door just as he knocked on it. Scott rushed in. He was really upset about something.

"Scott, hey, what's up, you okay?" Jeremy asked, shutting the door behind him.

"Hey, Scott," CD followed. "What's up?"

Then Scott began talking. He was almost screaming. He paced the floor frantically, into the dining room, then back into the living room, then back again.

"I hate him, the son-of-a…I hate him!" He blurted it out, stopping his comment short, noting that CD was there.

Jeremy asked, "Who? What? Who do you hate?" He looked over at CD.

"My freaking dad, that's who, the prick kicked me out of the house. Said I was no good, said I wouldn't amount to nothing if I didn't straighten up, or some bull crap!" Scott was spitting as he talked. He had been crying for some time, and his nose was running.

"You two had a fight, huh? It'll be okay!" Jeremy said, trying to calm him down however he could.

"Yeah, and if the son-of-a…if…if he would have touched me, I would have taken him out!" He screamed as he shook his fist in the air. "The…the prick…" He put both his hands on top of his head and combed his hair back with his knuckles, still pacing.

"Calm down a little, and tell us what happened," Jeremy said. CD just stood back behind Jeremy. She had never seen anyone so mad and upset—except in a movie maybe.

"The asshole said I was just wasting his money, that I wasn't getting good enough grades for him. He said he wasn't even going to be able to pay for the next semester, anyway. So I might as well just go and get a job somewhere, 'cause he couldn't afford to even run the farm anymore either, much less waste money that he didn't have on someone who's just playing games.'" He sniffed and wiped the mucus from his nose with his hand, and then smeared it on his pants. "I ain't playing no games, the prick. Let's see him learn all that techno-crap, see if he could do it better. I hate the son-of-a...B."

Jeremy stood next to Scott now. He put his hand on his shoulder to comfort him. He looked back at CD again. Jeremy suspected that what happened was that Scott's dad had gotten mad at him because he wasn't putting out the effort that he probably should be in school.

Jeremy knew how Scott felt about tech school. Scott hadn't liked it from the first month he was there. From past conversations, Jeremy also figured he was just barely hanging on anyway, much like his family's farm.

He knew that Scott's dad had been struggling to make it profitable, but that it wasn't even close to being that way. He had borrowed all he could to try to turn it back into a good business, like it was back when the boys were growing up. But, with the way things are, a small farm can't survive—no matter how good the manager is who's running it. It's been happening everywhere for decades. Now it was happening to them. He figured the stress of it all must have been hitting them hard.

"Take it easy. Things will cool down between you two."

"Cool down!" Scott screamed at Jeremy before he could finish speaking. "Cool freakin' down, the F' kicked me out. After all the work I did for him on that stupid farm, for all those F'n years. He called me ungrateful. He told me I didn't appreciate anything, and that I didn't care about anyone but myself. He's the one who doesn't freaking care, the freakin' dictator.

"He said that I always left messes around the house. I always borrowed his stuff but never put it back where *he* wants it! *I* never help do chores without having to be told, and that I always did a half-assed job! Well, screw him! I'll never do anything for him again, the prick."

He wiped more tears away.

"Listen, I'll do whatever I can. You want me to call him? I'll..."

Scott interrupted Jeremy again. "No, just…just forget it. I'll handle it. I'm tired of this crap, this…this freakin' crap!"

He walked back over to the front door, opened it and ran out, slamming it as he left. He moved so fast that by the time Jeremy got the door open and was able to run outside after him, Scott was already in his car, motor racing, tires smoking as he backed out of the driveway. He took off and didn't even look back at Jeremy and CD running out to the road, yelling for him to stop.

They just stood there in the yard, speechless.

After a minute, they walked back in the house and shut the door. Jeremy thought for a moment, and then explained to her what he had suspected. She could see how it would all unfold that way. The pressures from the farm, Scott's non-caring, sometimes cocky attitude, on top of the low grades he was getting.

Jeremy knew Scott's father—Harland Ramses—pretty well, so did Uncle Paul. Harland and his uncle had been friends for years. Scott's dad was a good man, a hard-working man. But he'd had a hard time growing up, and had gotten into a lot of trouble at a young age. Fights, and brushes with the law, and had even spent some time in jail.

He used to be a member of a motorcycle gang over about a ten-year stretch, from his twenties through his thirties. And he had a hot temper. He was one of those typical rebellious types from the early nineties. But time had softened him to a large degree.

Harland was a big man: 6'2", two hundred and thirty pounds, barrel-chested, and strong. He had numerous tattoos on his arms and still occasionally wore a bandanna around his head to hold his long, graying, dark brown hair out of his eyes, especially when he was working. He wore glasses, and he still carried one of those big leather wallets chained to his belt—as he had done when he was younger.

They called him Harley back then, partly because of the famous motorcycle, and partly because of his name. He finally wised up, he had said, when he hit thirty years old. Said he'd had enough of that hateful, cause-trouble-for-everyone-just-because-you-hated-life kind of attitude.

He finally quit carousing and moved away from California—where he lived for those ten years—and started working on a farm in Indiana. Said he wanted to get away from cities, bright lights, noise, and all the pissed-off people out there. He ended up meeting Scott's mom a year later and they were married. They had lived in the country ever since. Harland was fifty-three now.

Jeremy knew that all Scott's dad really wanted was for his son to be successful. To be able to make it out in the world, and not get caught up in all the crap that he went through in his day. He wanted him to be smarter, and not make the mistakes he had made, or was making now, by trying to earn a living as a small-time farmer. Jeremy remembered Harland telling him and his uncle about it one time while they were sitting in a diner, eating breakfast on a Saturday before a long day of fishing.

He remembered Scott's dad saying that he knew the farm was slowly going down, but that he didn't know what to do. It was all he had known for the last twenty years. He just hoped and prayed that it would turn around. But, it hadn't, Jeremy then realized.

He and CD wondered what to do next. They figured that it would be best to call Uncle Paul. Maybe he would have an idea. Jeremy had never seen it this bad between the two of them before—he was really worried.

He called his uncle, and Paul said he'd go over to the Ramses' farm as soon as he was done at the Continuum. Jeremy could imagine how their conversation would go. His uncle was really good at talking with people—and listening.

Chapter 22

Paul pulled up to the Ramses' house, got out of his truck, and walked around to the back. Everyone who knew the Ramses went to the back door. Harland's wife answered the knock.

"Hey, Paul," Karen Ramses said with a smile, knowing why he was there. "Harland's out in the shop. I told him you was stopping by." She motioned with her head toward the barn. "Paul," she paused, "thanks for coming over." She forced another smile. Only this one had a bittersweet appearance.

Paul nodded courteously, smiling back.

He walked over to the barn and around to the side where Harland had his workshop. His shop was the size of a two-and-a-half car garage. It had two over-head doors along the length of the building, and two walk-in doors, one on each end of the old structure.

One of the bays held two motorcycles, parked side by side. One without tires was sitting up on a couple of concrete blocks, the other leaning on its kickstand: an old Indian, and a Harley soft-tail. Harland had been restoring them, although he hadn't touched them in years—no money for parts. Both of the bikes were old classics. They just sat there with dust on them.

There were motorcycle parts scattered everywhere, enough to build three or four bikes if all the parts would fit together. They were hanging off the walls, the roof trusses, and packed in boxes stacked on one another, and on the workbenches—all from years of yard sales, farm auctions, and dream projects that Harland swore he'd get to, one of these days.

That's where the Indian came from, from an auction. The Harley soft-tail was from his old days in California. There were years of memories stacked there. He still loved motorcycles, always had, but just never had the time or the money to mess with them anymore.

In the other bay of the shop, there were more workbenches, areas where he'd work on the parts off his farm machinery that had broken down. And in the smaller, half-bay, there was an area set up with wood-working equipment: a band saw, a table saw, a drill press and more work benches against the wall—there was always something to work on when you owned a farm.

In one corner, there was a large wood stove made out of a 55-gallon barrel; it heated the entire shop. When Paul entered, Harland was just shutting the door to the stove, having just stoked it.

"Harley," Paul said, shutting the door behind him.

He called him 'Harley' for a reason. Usually, he would call him 'Harland', but on occasion, he'd use 'Harley'. He intentionally used it this time as a way to start their conversation off by helping Harland remember that he was young once, and had done a lot of things out of anger.

Harland knew exactly why Paul called him that. He said "Paul," as his greeting. They both smiled. Harland took a deep breath and blew it hard out of his nose, looking down at the stove.

"The damn kid," Harland started with a snort, shaking his head. "Don't know what he's doing."

"Yeah, I heard you guys had a little falling out again. Just thought I'd stop by, you know, talk if you want," Paul said.

Harland had known Paul for long enough that it didn't seem to bother him to let a tear or two roll down his cheek. In truth, he was glad he had a friend that close.

"He don't know what he's doing, Paul." He paused. "He's just playing around, not thinking about the future, not giving a crap about how he's going to make it out in the world. For some reason, he's just got it in his thick head that life owes him, and if it don't give him what he thinks should be coming to him, he'll just get all pissed off and blame everyone else, blame me! Says that I'm a dictator, and that I make him do all this crap, chores and work, all this crap, because I just have to be the Big Boss all the time.

"Says that I've always been this way, nothing is ever perfect enough for me, that I expect everyone to do everything exactly like I want." Harland wiped another tear from his right eye, tried to regain his composure. He was still looking down, just standing there with his hands in his pockets.

Paul had walked to the other side of the stove while Harland talked, and was now standing opposite him. He took his gloves off and stretched his hands out over it to warm them. He remained silent, knowing that Harland would continue.

"Part of the problem is…is that his mother has always thought I was too hard on him. She'd always interrupt when he and I were in the middle of something, when I was trying to make a point. And she'd always take his side, telling me that I was just going off on a tangent again, that I was expecting too much, expecting—" He paused to think for a moment.

"Expecting *too* much," he said. "Who should be the judge of what's *too* much, or *too* little. I mean, who's to say that my level of expectation, *expectations*, are too high, and that hers is just the right amount? I mean, if I…if I think my son should do, should do, X amount of chores a day, and she thinks it should be only half, then who's to say she's right and I'm wrong? The world expects a lot, Paul, a lot.

"If I believe Scott should work harder in school and get A's and B's, instead of C's and D's…F's, why should I be condemned as being over-bearing or dictatorial?"

He paused, shook his head from side to side, realizing that he was getting louder than he should. He calmed himself, and then continued.

"Scott's a good kid, I know that. He tries. He works hard at stuff; the stuff he wants to work at. I just want him to realize that you have to work hard, even at stuff that you don't want to work hard at. *Life's* hard. It's full of stuff we don't want to do. Stuff we have to do, whether we like it or not. He just can't see that yet. Don't want to see it, I reckon.

"I mean, he's always leaving his crap around the house. He won't keep his stuff in his room, much less in any type of order—never has. He won't help out by doing his own dishes. He just thinks that, for some reason, dishes are a parent's job, I guess, and his mother just does them for him. She just goes ahead and does them so she won't have to deal with it! What's that teach him? And he just lets her do it. It's just laziness, that's all it is. He's got little or no concern about how his life affects others—*ours!*

"He'll borrow my tools, Paul, and leave them wherever he wants. Not consider'n the fact *I'm* the one who worked for them, earned them, *bought* them, and that I should have the right to choose where they should be kept. And it's not that I don't want him to use them; all I want is for him to let me know first—in case *I* might need 'em—and put them back when he's done.

"But he doesn't, and then he forgets where he left them because he's so disorganized. And he won't even consider where that leaves *me*, if I did need something. And if I say anything about it, then I'm the one who's being unreasonable, nit-picky…*selfish.*" He pointed at himself with his thumb.

His anger was building again.

Paul slowly shook his head in agreement. He understood—he has asked himself the same questions. Who should be the judge of what is right or wrong when it comes to choosing a way of living, or a level of achievement?

He promptly remembered one particular professor from back in college. The students referred to him as the "Drill Sergeant." His often cold and seemingly insensitive expectations had made Paul and the rest of the class angry and rebellious.

"You want to know why I am the way I am?" the man had asked the entire class one day. Paul seized on the memory. "Life is about advancing, not just surviving." The man angrily defended himself after hearing some students murmur something about how "anal" he was. "It's about applying your own life, instead of just using others! You've got to give back to life, not just take from it! You've got to learn, in order to give, and give, in order to learn! At least," he said, "I care enough about everyone in this room to try and help you see that."

Paul thought of how angry and rebellious he used to be about things, and how, at that time, he hadn't even considered or cared about how his life affected others. He remembered that it took a number of years before he saw the big picture. Paul knew that was what Scott and his dad were going through.

"I know it's not all Scott's fault," Harland humbly admitted. "I know I've got a bad temper. I guess I inherited it from my dad—he could be a real asshole." They laughed. "—and from the life I used to live." Harland shook his head. He had a lost look on his face. "I've tried to work around his mother's expectations. She's a good woman, and I love her, and I know she wants the best for Scott, too. I guess I just expect more. I want more for Scott. She just doesn't know, or just can't remember how hard it is out there in the real world. What it takes to survive, to do more than just survive.

"It's tough having people tell you how to do something, or what you can do, or can't do, what level *to* do it. And having to just smile and take it. Just so you can keep your damn job, make a few bucks. She hasn't had to work out in the real world for twenty-some years. Now that's probably going to have to change soon!" He got quiet for a moment, thinking about what he had just said.

Paul remained silent.

"I know I've got my farm, and I'm my own boss, but I haven't forgotten what it's like to have to kiss butt just to survive. Just to keep a paycheck coming in. And I still have to, you know, even owning my own farm and being my own boss. Nobody's his or her own boss, really.

"We all have to meet expectations, give respect, whether we like it or not, to our customers, to our bankers, to the people we depend on, and especially to those who depend on us. Scott's not thinking about that part of it. He's just thinking that life's all about him, that it owes him.

"Just wait until he gets out there for real, in the real world. College will help, if he'll let it, but he won't even do that. He's not even trying, Paul. He just thinks it's a big game, and he just doesn't want to play right now! That's what he told me. That's exactly what he told me!

"He doesn't realize what will happen if he doesn't take it seriously, if he doesn't think about the consequences of his actions, or his lack of actions. The kid just doesn't seem to care." He paused and looked down. "Now, I can't even afford to send him, even if he did want to take it seriously."

Paul immediately noticed the different look on Harland's face. It changed from anger and disappointment, to one of fear and foreboding. He knew that something else was going on, and he figured he knew what it was. But, he didn't say anything. He just stood there, and waited.

"I'm going to lose the place, Paul. I can't pay my bills. They're going to foreclose. I found out the day before yesterday. First of the year, we'll know exactly when. They'll probably give us sixty, maybe ninety days, I don't know. I'm not sure what the law allows. But I'm going to have to do something. I'm just not sure what that might be." He was talking at a near whisper now, a tear streaked down his cheek.

Paul wasn't exactly shocked. He had seen it coming. All he could do was shake his head. "I'm sorry, Harland. I wish there was something I could do—" Paul didn't know what to say. He realized the stress Harland's family was going through. He understood how he and Scott could have reached this point. Why it all of a sudden seemed to blow up. He just stood there.

"It's my fault," Harland said. "I should have gotten out years ago." He turned to the side, his head still down. "Maybe Scott was right. He said that I was stupid for staying in something that wasn't going to work. I was determined to prove him wrong. Maybe it's just that I was too scared to try something else, something different." He paused for a long time, and then continued.

"Maybe computers aren't what he should be doing— maybe it's not meant for him. But I just wanted to get him to realize that he has to do something, to choose something, even if it's just for now, until something else comes along. I just want the best for him, for him to care about himself and to appreciate what *we're* trying to do for him. I don't know. I guess I'm just going about it wrong. I really do want the best for him, Paul, that's all."

Paul could tell that Harland was at a point of mental exhaustion, trying to figure out what was happening in his life. He felt it was time to say something.

"Maybe he's scared too," Paul said. "You know, to do something different. All he's known is being a kid and going to school. Growing up is scary, all the responsibilities. Maybe, even though he knows he's got to grow up, maybe he's having a hard time facing it.

"So…he blames others, instead of facing the truth. Heck, I couldn't finish school, much less decide on what I wanted to do, and I sure wasn't able to do it when I was his age. But, one thing did happen. Life rolled along and I finally did do something. I'm sure Scott will too. It'll just take some time, some patience."

"Yeah," Harland replied in a near whisper. "I know what you mean. I guess in a way. I'm kind of where Scott is now. I've got to make a choice to face reality, *life*, even though it seems to be kicking me in the face right now." Harland just about burst out into tears, but he held it back. He struggled to continue. "I…guess it's about time for me to change, myself—" he said.

"Harland, it's not your fault, the farm, I mean. It's the times. Things have changed so much over the past hundred years—what with machines, technology, corporations and such. People have had to just learn to adapt and use their heads if they're going to make it.

"Like what you just said about Scott. You've always been a hard worker; you can fix anything, make stuff from nothing." He looked around the shop as he spoke. "Why, I just know there's something out there you'll probably find that you enjoy, even more than farming."

Paul didn't realize how true his words were.

Harland smiled a little. "Hell, Paul, I haven't enjoyed farming for years. I just did it because I...was doing it. Because it was just what I was...what I was doin'—" He went silent.

Harland had never really admitted that to himself, until that moment. And whether he liked it or not, he was going to have to change it. He was going to have to do something, whatever that might be. He felt real tired all of a sudden. He realized that his son must feel the same way—wherever he was.

He turned away from Paul. His tears were too many now.

Chapter 23

No one had seen or heard from Scott for three days. He had just disappeared. Jeremy called everyone he could think of who might have possibly seen him, or might have an idea of where he could be. Jeremy was really worried about his friend—everyone was. He hadn't slept well the past few nights because of it.

Scott's mother was the one everyone was really worried about. She was beside herself with fear. She knew how Scott was. She knew that he had a bad temper, and that sometimes he would do things, and say things that nobody really knew about, except her. She, of course, knew him in a deeper way than anyone else. Most mothers do with their sons.

Jeremy remembered, about a year ago, when Scott and his dad had gotten into one of their big arguments. The next day, in the school parking lot, Scott had told him about it. He had said that he was "going to quit school and go to Florida or North Carolina and get a job at one of those fancy car shops or something."

What worried Jeremy, as he sat there in the kitchen remembering, was not that Scott had threatened to leave. What worried him the most was what Scott had said after he had made that statement, "...or drive off a cliff or something."

Jeremy then thought about what his uncle had told him at breakfast just before he left for work.

Paul had gone over to the Ramses' farm on the second day that Scott was missing, just to check in on them, but he never made it inside the house to see them. When he went to the door, he heard them fighting. They were arguing about who was to blame.

Paul had listened as Harland yelled, telling her that she was too lenient when it came to setting standards, that the boy needed to be more responsible when it came to the house and chores, and school, and that she wasn't helping by tolerating his bad behavior, simply because she was too afraid of confrontation.

He insisted that if they would have been more together on what they expected Scott to behave like when he was younger, and enforced it together, then he wouldn't have turned out to be so disrespectful, unappreciative, and always playing them against each other.

She'd yell back, telling him that if he had been *there* more, instead of always out working in his shop tinkering with those stupid motorcycles, or hanging out over at his friends' in *their* stupid workshops, or if she would've had more help in raising their kid, then maybe they would have *been* more together, and that if he weren't such the loner-type, then maybe Scott wouldn't have been the same way. Maybe they would have been closer, too. She hadn't married somebody to be a single mother, she had yelled passionately.

At that, Paul left; he knew it wasn't any of his business, and that he shouldn't be listening. They hadn't known he was there at all.

Jeremy remembered Scott telling him that Harland didn't mind being alone; in fact, most of the time, Harland preferred it. He remembered him and Scott speculating one day about it. That after all that Scott's dad had gone through in his younger days—all the craziness, the hate, the anger— he just preferred to be by himself most of the time. He would rather be on a tractor, or out in his workshop tinkering, than going to school functions or hanging out with his wife's church friends at pitch-ins or cookouts.

He remembered his uncle telling him that Harland Ramses and he had a lot in common. They both believed deeply in God, had gone to church for a while when they were a lot younger, but both had become turned off by organized religion and all the hypocrisy.

Harland had confessed to Paul, once, that it was God who saved him from all that crap he was caught up in out there in California. And that if it were not for God in his life, he would probably have been dead by now.

Harland had a great respect for others. It wasn't that he didn't like all those people his wife knew and associated with. Or that he thought they were just a bunch of fanatics. He knew they were good people. They did a lot for each other, and the community.

He just couldn't feel comfortable around them. There was always the thought in the back of his mind that they were in some way judging him, because of his past maybe, or thinking less of him because he didn't want to go to church twice a week like they did.

Harland believed that a relationship with God was a personal thing. He believed that God was in the heart, that we are forgiven because of His Son, and that a lot of those people in church don't give God, or other people enough credit.

Jeremy remembered Harland saying once, "It's His spirit that calls on a man's heart—not necessarily a preacher's. And it's got little to do with paying weekly dues to help pad pews, or make payments on fancy new carpet or churchy backdrops. Yet, I can still understand why people needed fellowship, and, if that's what makes them feel closer to God , then they should go."

Jeremy just sat there looking out the window, thinking. Suddenly, he could see Scott's face in his mind—it had a look of anxiety and fear on it. Then, the ringing sound of the phone interrupted his thoughts. He got up, walked to the counter and picked it up.

"Hello," he said. "*Hey*, Mr. Ramses, any word from …what…*what?*" He just stood there and listened intently for the next few minutes as Harland told him what had happened to his friend.

"He's okay, that's what's important," Jeremy said with relief. "Really? Man… Yeah… Just call…are you sure we don't need to come down there? It's not a prob… Well, okay… Alright… yeah, just hang in there… I'll be praying, too… Okay…alright, bye, Mr. Ramses!"

Jeremy hung up the phone. He just stood there, staring. Once again, he saw Scott's face in his mind, the same image as before, and he thought how strange it was that it had happened right before the phone rang. Almost like something had made it happen. He shrugged the thought.

Chapter 24

Harland said that he'd just talked with the Tennessee State Police before he called Jeremy and his uncle. He told Jeremy that his son had turned up in a hospital, in another town, in another state, but he was far from okay—he'd been in a serious car wreck. Scott had apparently decided to run away to somewhere down south, just as Jeremy had remembered him saying.

Reportedly, Scott had been drinking and the officers on the scene said that they had found alcohol in Scott's car—he probably just walked into a store and purchased it himself. He could pass for drinking age, they speculated. According to Harland, Scott had drained his savings—all two hundred and forty-seven dollars' worth—which Harland had discovered the day before.

Harland went on to say that Scott had been spotted by some people who had witnessed him driving erratically—knocking over orange traffic cones along the interstate in a construction zone, speeding, swerving from one lane to another for no apparent reason, and pulling up to other cars in the passing lane like he was trying to get them to drag race.

The people who witnessed the wreck reported that he had jerkily veered off the side of the highway and was aiming straight for the starting edge of a guardrail that led up to a bridge that spanned a deep gorge. It was as if he wanted to go off the road on the other side of the railing. But, they said, Scott's car seemed to swerve back onto the road at the last second.

They said they saw him try the same thing again a few miles down the highway at another location. He came so close that time that when he tried to swerve back up onto the road, he hit the guardrail, and sparks flew off the side of his car as it scraped up against the corrugated barrier.

The impact was severe enough that it blew out the passenger-side rear tire. That's when the vehicle started fishtailing, shot across to the other side of the highway, and he lost control.

The car went down a semi-steep hill of loosely packed soil covered with patchy clumps of grass and weeds. It slid sideways, hit a clump of exposed rocks sticking out of the ground, and then rolled over several times.

People in two different vehicles witnessed the event, and stopped.

Apparently, no one's cell phone would work in that area, so one of the cars containing a mother and her two completely astonished kids, sped off to the next gas station up the road to call it in while an elderly gentleman carefully made his way down the hill to see if he could help. His fretful wife remained up by the road to wait for the authorities.

There was no fire, and no threat of explosion. The gas tank, it turned out, was almost empty and neither it, nor the gas line had ruptured. The car was still running when the elderly man finally got down to it, and it had apparently landed back on its wheels, after rolling over two full revolutions. The gentleman remarked to the state troopers that it had happened just like it might have been choreographed in some action movie.

Scott hadn't had his seatbelt on, and the thrashing around from the roll-over beat him up pretty badly. He was extremely lucky that he hadn't been ejected from the car. His left arm was broken in two places. His right leg was broken, probably from hitting the steering wheel. And his left ankle was broken, most likely from hitting the emergency brake pedal. He had a serious concussion, and numerous cuts and bruises over his face and arms and his left hip.

The gentleman also reported that when he got to the driver's side door, Scott was just sitting there, looking into the rearview mirror, trying to wipe the blood out of his left eye with his tee-shirt. He was mumbling something like, "I'm so stupid...I'm a wuss...a freaking, stupid wuss! But man, that...*that was awesome!*"

The gentleman reported smelling alcohol on Scott, as did the troopers when they arrived at the scene. The officers said that, ironically, it was probably the alcohol that saved his life. Anybody who would have taken a beating like Scott had would have been a lot worse off—even dead—if they had been all stiff and tensed up. Scott, it seemed, just rode it out, rolling with the car.

The incident happened about five-thirty in the afternoon, just before sunset. By the time the emergency crews got there and took him to the nearest hospital, it was around seven in the evening. Scott's parents had driven all night to get there.

He was stable and coherent by the next morning. Other than having a real bad headache, being extremely sore from the bruising he took, and in a lot of pain from the broken bones, he would be allowed to go home after staying one more night. His parents stayed there at the hospital with him, sleeping on the couches in the waiting room.

<<< >>>

Late that night, long after Scott's mother had fallen asleep, Harland went into his son's room and started looking through his belongings. He didn't find any maps or brochures, or anything to indicate what he had been up to.

In his wallet, he found seventeen dollars, a receipt for a hotel room for a two-night stay somewhere in Kentucky—along with the room's key card—and a folded-up piece of notebook paper.

He looked at the folded paper curiously as he took it out of the wallet. Suddenly feeling flushed with anxiety, he shook his head slowly, and pursed his lips, attempting to vanquish the thoughts rushing through his mind.

Harland carefully unfolded the paper to read its contents. His breathing stopped abruptly. He stared at the paper. He felt a strange quivering sensation in his legs. He backed up slowly, clumsily, and sat down in a chair. He looked over toward Scott, and then back down at the paper. Then, he began reading the handwritten suicide note:

> *Goodbye. I'm sorry I couldn't be what everyone hoped I'd be! I guess I just don't have what it takes! It's my fault, not anyone else's! Sorry Dad, Mom. I love you both, and always will.*
>
> *Scott*

Harland started crying.

Again, he looked over at his sleeping son, knocked out from the painkillers. He didn't know what to do. He just sat there, staring, tears dripping down his face. He was so glad that he had found the note this way, and not when Scott's mother was present. This would just kill her. He sat silent, his thoughts weaving in and out of time.

He then thought of those days in his own life when *he* had considered killing himself. Back when he was at his lowest, back when it seemed that he hated everyone and everything—especially life. He remembered the times when he'd prayed and cried out to God for help, for a reason to live, for some purpose, any purpose, just a reason to get up out of bed.

Instantly, like a spark, he remembered something that had happened back in those dark days. It'd been years since he'd even thought of it. Why had he forgotten it for so long, he wondered. Why had he thought of it now?

In the lucidness of his memories, he relived that time when he was riding his motorcycle down a country road, late, on a clear and starry summer night. He'd been drunk, and stoned. He was just out, riding. He wasn't riding to anywhere, or from anywhere—he was just riding.

He remembered thinking that everything was a waste. That no one cared about him, or anyone else, for that matter. The world was just one big vortex of chaos, in motion for no apparent reason, full of nothing but pain and frustration, suffering, and then death.

He remembered looking up at the stars as he rode, gazing at them with awe, and thinking of the incomprehensible vastness of what was up there. Thinking of the miracle of it all, and yet at the same time, wishing he were dead, or that he'd never even been born.

He then felt the motorcycle bounce up and down a little, the sensation momentarily turning his attention. He instinctively slowed the machine, and as he did, he looked down and noticed that there was no pavement in front of him, only rocks and dirt, and clumps of grass were passing into his field of vision.

Sluggishly, he brought the machine to a halt, his indifferent, drunken haziness making everything seem surreal and dreamlike. Slowly, but surely, he concluded that he'd nearly fallen asleep, and that he had ridden the motorcycle off the road.

He had been riding down a walking path, parallel to a cliff's edge, and about ten to fifteen meters down, he could make out a tree line, and just on the other side of that, he saw the moon's cloud-covered light reflecting up at him off a distant river.

He was suddenly breathless when he realized that the cliff beside him, not more than a few meters away, followed the bend in the river, and there, straight in front of him, not more than another thirty or forty meters away, was the cliff's edge. There was nothing but blackness directly beyond and below it. He then starkly realized that if he had not stopped when he had, in just a matter of a few seconds, he would have driven off the precipice and into the darkness.

Harland just sat there in the chair, staring.

He suddenly remembered that experience, in all its detail, as if it had been yesterday. And because of it, he couldn't help but think—as he had done back then—that there must be more going on in life, more than what we know. That, perhaps, there is a reason for it all, for what was happening to him, and for what was happening to Scott.

He looked over at his son, and then whispered, "Thank you for saving my son, God…thank you."

Harland folded the letter carefully and quietly. He placed it in his pants pocket, and then put the other contents back in the wallet just as he had found them. He returned everything to its prior location, sat down again in the chair, and then quietly resumed his reflections.

He thought once again, back to that time in his life when he had wished he were never born, when he had wished that he had never even existed. But then, he thought, if he were not alive, then Scott wouldn't be alive either.

Chapter 25

Jeremy sat alone in the kitchen, his mind awash with the thoughts and images of what Scott might have gone through, spontaneous suppositions of what he was probably thinking about and feeling before the crash. From Harland's report, it sounded like Scott was lucky—very lucky—if luck had anything to do with it?

Something inside told him that Scott had tried to commit suicide. Partly from Harland's recitation of the police and witness reports and partly from the things Scott had said to him many months back. The thought of it entranced him for some reason.

He began thinking about the conversation that he and CD had had about free-will and destiny. Jeremy felt tired and disoriented. Adrenaline crash, probably—he thought.

He was staring at a spiral-shaped knot in one of the wooden cabinet doors in front of him. Suddenly, his eyes became very heavy. He closed them for a moment to rest. He felt like he was spinning, as if he were in a car rolling over. He recognized the feeling. Wait a minute, he said in his mind.

<<< >>>

Jeremy tried to open his eyes, but they felt like thick, heavy clay pottery lids.

By shear force, he pried them halfway open, and when he did, he saw something wholly different than what he'd seen only a moment before:

He saw the blurry figure of a man.

He torqued his eye muscles to get them to focus better. His eyebrows sank down. He wasn't in the kitchen; he wasn't where he had been. It was then that he realized what he was seeing—it was that Professor character again. It was the man he'd seen—had imagined, dreamed—back when he had gone skydiving.

Once more, he began having that strange feeling of being small. Everything around him seemed to pulsate, became larger and smaller, smaller and then larger. Things started to spin, oscillating sporadically—he began to feel nauseous. He couldn't think straight. Suddenly, he became petrified with fear.

No…no, he thought. *This…this can't be*!

His eyes began to roll back into their sockets and his head began to get heavy, tilting back as if it, too, were made of heavy clay like his eyelids.

Then he heard a voice.

"Hello again, Jeremy, it's good to see you. Don't worry, that awkward feeling will pass, as it did before. Look at me, Jeremy, that's it, look up. Look at me. That's good, see, it's beginning to pass, just as I said."

Jeremy struggled to focus. He looked at the man, trying to keep his head straight, trying to center on the man's eyes. He had kind, yet mysterious eyes, Jeremy thought. And in thinking that, in what seemed like only a few seconds, the nausea began to leave him, and everything that had first seemed so large, now seemed more proportional. He remembered this from before—*before*, he thought. This had happened before. He had felt this way before.

He gritted his teeth, forced his eyes to look at the man, at this Professor Vector. He remembered his name, he realized. His mind, again, was rocketing between extremes, pulsating, swaying back and forth between anxiety and calmness, weakness and strength, fear and courage. His whole body trembled with each diametrical reverberation. Then, it settled, and the raw sensations again began to fade.

He realized that he was back in the Professor's study. Before him was the desk with the nameplate on it: PROF. T. VECTOR. There were the shelves, the books, the chairs, and that big window, and opposite that, the Wall, that strange Wall. Jeremy looked around in astonishment.

"Yes, it's a dynamic ride, isn't it? Going from one extreme to another? That's where the dizziness comes from, from the acute motion of change. It's somewhat akin to a flatlander being forced to go for a jaunt in the mountains. The lights and shadows, the peaks, the valleys, the warmth, the cold, the senses are inundated with change; they're overloaded with experience." He paused, smiling, seemingly saying something with his expression.

"People are so used to their areas of control. Leaving them can feel so traumatic and disorienting. It's why people like to stay where they are, you know? Change is frustrating, difficult. But, it is purposeful, I assure you. You're finding your center again, good, very good."

Jeremy thought again that this just couldn't be happening, not again. It couldn't be real—he must be going insane. He felt the nausea returning.

"No, Jeremy, you're not insane. This is real, as I said before, during our last encounter. Please, have a seat, won't you?" The man motioned toward the chairs.

All of a sudden, Jeremy was sitting in one of those big brown chairs. He didn't even remember walking over to it, or sitting. The Professor was now sitting opposite him in the other chair.

It all just happened.

"Jeremy," he said, speaking again. "You're welcome here. Trust me. You have no reason to fear." He cleared his throat. "I've brought you here again to share some things with you, if that's all right? You're feeling better now, aren't you? The transition is virtually complete, this is good.

"Now Jeremy, I would like to ask you something. Would you be interested in attending a discourse—a lecture, if you will? It should prove very interesting for you. I didn't want you to be too alarmed. This is why I brought you here to my study, first, to help you get your bearings, as it were.

"The discourse—which by the way, *I* will be facilitating shortly—discusses the relevancies of causality. I will be presenting many enduring, as well as current perspectives about the history of reality, including the efficacy of choices, of consequences, of purpose and reason, change, and of course, *frustration*, and how these help steer us along on our journeys of learning.

"It is officially, and quite fittingly entitled: Subjected: a discourse of...*Course*." He paused and laughed at his play on words. Jeremy didn't respond, so the distinguished man cleared his throat again, appearing slightly embarrassed, and then continued, "Yes, well. It's a serious discussion, somewhat witty, yet peppered with a touch of humor. It's intended to be this way, as you'll see. Levity, as well as gravity, is good for the spirit—keeps it soaring, while at the same time tethered, you understand. However, I don't want you to miss the overall thesis being presented. It's quite important. I'm sure you'll find it interesting. What do you say?"

Jeremy just sat there and stared.

He felt a strange feeling of whimsy for some reason. The nausea was completely gone now, although he still felt that pulsating feeling. Strangely, he felt a kind of elation at the Professor's words. Yet, he thought again that this was so weird. He couldn't yet grasp that this was happening to him—again.

There just had to be something wrong with his brain: a tumor, a blood clot, something that was making him dream, or daydream, or something. He looked back into his mind, searching for reality. He felt oddly comical in his attempt. It was such a strange feeling. He thought it very funny, and inside, he began to laugh at his apparent lunacy.

"Yes, Jeremy, I'm sad to inform you that, well, that you are...you are as loony as they come!" The Professor had a most serious look on his face. "Yes, the epitome of looniness, as they say!" He smiled an awkward grin.

Then, with an eruption, he burst out laughing hysterically, flailing around in his chair as if *he* were the lunatic. He opened his eyes as wide as he could, framed them with both palms, and rolled his eyes all around. And then he started mumbling an assortment of nonsensical gibberish, laughing as he did so. He bounced up and down in the chair, and slapped his hands on his knees as if they were drums.

Jeremy started to laugh as well, softly at first. He thought that he may be crazy, and that all this might be images of his lunatic mind, but for some reason, he didn't fear it as he once had. The Professor calmed down from his intense show of craziness, and then he spoke again.

"Jeremy, Jeremy, we're *all* crazy, in many ways, different ways." His smile molted, leaving a look of sincerity. "Yes, there is sadness and tragedy, suffering and pain. Yet, one must remember that there is another end of the spectrum. And it is the entire spectrum, or Continuum, if you'd like, that must be observed, in its totality, in a balanced sort of way, you see?

"When the balance swings too far and remains unnaturally, and/or too long, at one extreme or the other, then there is much cause for concern. Yes, much cause. And that's when change must take place, as we're preparing for now. And trust me when I say, the coming change for all life on planet Earth goes far beyond what you can even imagine at this present time. As you progress—as our time together progresses—you'll begin to see this."

He paused and smiled again, as if waiting for a response.

Jeremy was taken aback at how simple and childlike the Professor could be, and yet how apparently deep in understanding. He was fascinated by the contrast. Strangely, he felt as if he was supposed to be there, and that he was supposed to go to this thing that the Professor mentioned. He suddenly realized that he was more than just interested; he was extremely curious about it.

He thoroughly enjoyed going to the lecture halls of the university, listening to the interesting speakers. He always seemed to get a lot out of that type of experience. Just sitting there observing, listening, learning. *Where would it be?* he wondered. *How long would it last?*

"How would I get th…?"

Chapter 26

"Hello, and welcome, everyone. I deeply appreciate all of you having chosen to accept my invitation to attend this discourse."

The Professor's voice resonated.

Jeremy flinched, not just at the more distant yet dynamic voice of the Professor, but at the images he was seeing before him. In the time of a single eye blink, his surroundings had dramatically changed again—to somewhere that was hugely different.

And 'huge' wasn't a big enough word.

He was in what looked like a gigantic auditorium. Its ceiling was dome-shaped, like an egg, perfectly round. As he scanned the environment, it became clear that he was in an enormous sphere of some sort. It was immense, several times the size of a large, modern sports arena. The entire ceiling, the top two-thirds of the sphere, was framed in the same kind of ornate wooden-like trim that was in the Professor's study.

It was laid out in squares, rectangles actually—like the stones of a pyramid. Large ones along the sides, twenty-five meters wide by fifteen or so meters tall at least, all stacked one on top of another, and parabolic in shape, yet all proportionally getting smaller, and more numerous, as they rose to the apex of the dome.

They reminded Jeremy of latitudinal and longitudinal grid lines on a globe—in fact, it suddenly looked as if he was actually inside a mammoth globe.

Strange, he thought.

At the peak, there was what appeared to be the bottom quarter of a smaller sphere hanging down from the top. It was translucent and gave off a gentle light. All the square areas along the walls and ceiling seemed to give off the same subtle glow as well. Jeremy realized these lit the entire auditorium. The light was odd, though—soft, yet penetrating. Each square reminded him of the window in the Professor's study. It, too, had emitted the same type of light.

Jeremy realized that he was sitting in a seat, on an aisle, and there were rows upon rows of seats, each row higher up and staggered from the ones below them. They extended about a third of the way up the sides from the bottom of the sphere, and they wrapped all the way around to the other side, opposite of where he was sitting. Jeremy was seated about twenty or so rows up from the center.

Then he noticed that, in the middle of the sphere, at the very bottom elevation, there was another half-sphere dome-like object, measuring at least fifty meters across and twenty-five or so meters high. It was huge, and black and fuzzy. It had the appearance of the wall that he had seen in the Professor's study, he remembered, except spherical. It had no observable surface and he realized that he couldn't focus on it. He could only see it when he looked slightly to the side, and away from it.

This thing was where the Professor's voice was coming from. Then, just as he thought the thought, the dark sphere started changing. It was becoming translucent in different spots. Emitting colors Jeremy couldn't remember ever seeing, yet still mixed with that indefinable fuzzy blackness.

It seemed to pulsate with a convoluted motion. Then the sides of it, beginning at its zenith—as if a growing hole were forming at the top of a dome—started slowly floating down, like an immense circular curtain being lowered. After it finally receded all the way downward into the floor, Jeremy saw a large, elevated, circular platform, or stage, on which the Professor stood.

All around the large platform, the fuzzy blackness—still emanating patches of luminescence—remained, the only remnant left from the sphere's recession. It was akin to a moat made of velvety, vibrating blackness which circumnavigated the entire platform, seemingly alive with motion and energy.

Suddenly, Jeremy realized there were other people everywhere. He hadn't noticed them before. Strange, he thought. He realized that only about half the seats were filled. And many of the people looked odd. He noticed weird and wonderful expressions on their faces. Some were curiously looking around as he was, while others just sat calmly, looking down at the Professor.

There were young people, old people, people from all different races, and bizarre people. Many were dressed in clothes that he recognized, while others were dressed so oddly, and their faces looked so peculiar, that he thought they had to be from other planets.

There were thousands, perhaps tens-of-thousands of people there.

Then, Jeremy noticed a particularly unusual man off to his right, almost in the same row, yet thirty or so meters away, around the slight curve of the globe. The man's profile was all that he saw. Jeremy thought to himself that he looked like something that he had seen in a science fiction movie once—or a dream. Not monster-like, but quite the opposite. He had the countenance of a man, yet his appearance seemed advanced and otherworldly, as if he were from some other universe altogether.

His features were striking, fine-looking actually, and he was giving off subtle light, radiating something, it seemed. Jeremy couldn't identify the particular glow that was emanating from him either. It was so faint, delicate. He couldn't decide if he was actually seeing anything, or not. He realized that he couldn't even begin to describe what he was seeing, even though he thought about it with focused concentration.

The being seemed pleasant though, not in any way frightening, and Jeremy felt drawn to look at him. He felt strangely blissful when he did—looking at him gave him a sense of joy, and serenity, yes, serenity, he realized. Then, almost instantly, seemingly in response to his lucid thoughts, the man abruptly turned, looked right at Jeremy, and smiled softly.

His eyes were penetrating. They were like windows, windows that exposed huge volumes of knowledge and wisdom. They shone with intense joy and sublime happiness, yet they somehow revealed that they understood sorrow, and sadness, misery and suffering—and all at the same time.

Jeremy got the distinct impression that the man was giggling or laughing in response to Jeremy's astonishment at the man's unusual appearance. Not exactly laughing at him, but kind of like an adult does while watching a newborn baby. Jeremy thought this was very odd. The man, still smiling, nodded in acknowledgement of Jeremy's curious gaze, and then turned his head back toward the Professor.

"Most of you are newcomers to the school, to this place, and to our series of discourses." The Professor looked around briefly, and then continued, "Some have been here many, many times. Some of you were here when the school started. We welcome all of you, and trust that you will find something valuable to take with you as you continue on your Quests for the Experiential. This, as you old-timers already know, is what the school is all about!"

He went silent for a moment as a requited applause arose.

The Professor then glanced up at the unusual man who, a moment before, had looked over at Jeremy. The Professor smiled at him. They were both smiling. Both were seemingly saying something to the other with just the look in their eyes. Then, the unusual man turned and spoke something to someone seated next to him, a very tall man.

Jeremy couldn't see this other man's entire face because of his angle of sight, but something seemed familiar about him, strangely familiar—he, too, emanated some sort of subtle light, or radiation. Then, the Professor began speaking again.

Jeremy turned to listen.

"Our discourses are intended to inspire you to be curious, to encourage you to contemplate, to hearten you on…on to higher levels of aspiration, and to persuade you to search…to search for your own answers…answers to life's most enduring questions. However, as I'm sure many of you are beginning to comprehend, the journey is *not* without its frustrations."

Again, he paused and smiled—a devious-looking smile, it appeared to Jeremy. Another slight applause erupted. After a moment, he continued.

"In your journeys of learning, you're also beginning to appreciate—I'm just as sure—that the act—or *action*—of seeking answers, is almost as important as securing the answers themselves. There is a tendency to only focus on the end of the adventure—the destination sought, the answer revealed.

"However, one must learn that the search for answers offers so much to the seeker. The seemingly incidental aspects of a search, *give* so much to the seeker. Much is gained as one plans a search, embarks upon search, and navigates a search. So much is learned along the way. A search, in and of itself, is an adventure in learning.

"Ponder, if you will: where would patience and temperance come from if answers were always forthwith? How would gratefulness, gratitude, and appreciation be developed, if all answers were immediate?

"At first thought, having answers when we need them, or seeing every angle when we want to, or knowing every turn, or predicting every probability, seems like the state to achieve. Yet, I implore you to consider these questions: What about the journey? What of the quality of the journey? What about the subtle nuances experienced as one travels on a journey? What about the sustained value that comes from noticing things during the seemingly insignificant—oftentimes frustrating—detours and stops along the way?"

He smiled again.

"Would the substance or essence of a being be the same if understanding were given without effort, without some level of exertion or expenditure of energy? Doesn't life itself promulgate the premise that life is not life if it is given without earning it? Doesn't this fact make life itself more valuable, more precious, more worth the experience?

"Isn't the loss of life more saddening, if the lost life was arduously earned, and deserved? Doesn't life itself require, nay demand that something be given back as recompense or reimbursement? Are the gifts of deliverance, salvation, of revelation, given without some cost being paid somewhere, by someone?"

The Professor, turning as he spoke, again stopped his gaze on the unusual man who looked over at Jeremy. He nodded, and then paused for a moment. He then reached down and picked up a small, odd-looking, clear glass receptacle that had appeared out of nowhere, on a thin, baseless stand positioned next to him. He then took a sip of its clear liquid.

He smiled, looking around intently at all that were gathered there, appearing overwhelmingly satisfied from the drink. He closed his eyes, seemingly blissful at the joy of it.

He then continued, "Many say there are those who are just born lucky. The universe has apparently deemed them fortunate, auspicious, blessed. And then there are those who are apparently born unlucky. They are labeled as the unfortunate, the ill-fated, even the damned.

"And no matter how hard either of these people try, or don't try, their fates appear to be sealed. They appear predestined toward their respective ends, no matter what. At least, that is how it seems!

"Then there are some who say that there is no sealed fate. We are the masters of our own fate! *We* make the decisions, and if there were some sort of predestination, some sort of determinism in effect, then we would not be creatures of free will. We would be only puppets, manipulated by some ethereal omnipotent being that moves us and animates us only according to his, or her, or its desire. So, *are* we autonomous in our decision-making? Are we truly the creators of our own destinies?"

His eyebrows were now set high! He was smiling broadly.

"It is known that when the time comes for an epiphany, it arrives on the wings of a revelation. A new knowledge is discovered, a previously unknown, yet eternally present, substantive property of existence comes into focus and is revealed, as when light suddenly illuminates a dark region of your mind, and that which you might, or might not have suspected as being there, all of a sudden blossoms into an understandable and now-apparent ubiquitous reality for you.

"However, no understanding, no revelation, no epiphany, comes to us without frustration."

He paused. A solemn, bittersweet look shaped his face.

"In reality, frustration feeds the fires of creative thinking—of Creation itself—and using fire as an analogy, it can comfort, as well as burn. Yes, this is true. Its warmth can lift you, and yet, its depths can destroy you." He paused for a brief moment, looking straight at Jeremy, and then he quickly resumed.

"Frustration, experienced at all active levels of reality, can metaphorically be thought of as a two-edged sword: it is a dubious catalyst for destruction, it can devastate the faithless and drive the timid insane. Yet, at the same time, it is an irreplaceable tool for segmenting many of the various problem areas of life. It is, in its most useful form, a discovery device, *the* article for identifying hidden knowledge, undeveloped intuition and imperfect understanding.

"Without frustration, without its propensity to force the mind and the body to strive, then all species on Earth would have sadly died out long ago. In truth, we would not have even come into existence without it. The very hunger that all species endure is but a form of this frustration. It mysteriously engages the body, mind, and spirit, and encourages, in varying degrees, the animation that defines life itself.

"Without motion or motivation, direction or destination, or any such animator, there would not be any reality, or any forces to even perpetuate conscious existence in the first place. In understanding the reciprocal of this fact, one can see that life itself exudes meaning, purpose, and reason— simply *because* of its animation, simply *because* of that which animates it. Label it as you wish. Name it as you will.

"There is, as you shall find, a cosmic and spiritual purpose for the existence of ubiquitous frustration. It can best be understood by viewing it in some of its more simple forms: for instance, the struggle of a butterfly exiting its cocoon, painful as it actually is for the delicate creature, is by its very essence the tool which forces the blood to the outermost edges of its wings—if this were not endured by the diminutive creature, it would never be able to fly, and hence fulfill its purpose.

"Its instinct, its nature, its compulsion to overcome its frustration *is that which gives it flight*…that which gives it…its freedom!"

The upward-facing palm of the man's right hand reached up and out in front of him as his voice resonated with the words, shaking to the vibration of his voice. Then, his arm slowly descended back to his side. He resumed, speaking quicker than before.

"If people were not frustrated by the weather, then they would not have built shelters. If people were not frustrated by persistent coldness, then they would not have sought methods to seek or create warmth. If people had not been frustrated by persistent offensive tastes, then they would not have searched for more palatable meals. If people had not been frustrated by a persistent inability to understand, then they would not be seen in the habit of craning their necks toward comprehension."

He quickened his pace of articulation even more.

"If people had not been frustrated by the persistent presence of objectionable odors, then they would not be seen in the habit of turning away to seek fresher air. And, if people had not been frustrated with persistent darkness, then they would never have begun their journeys in search of light.

"It is because of all the various forms and intensities of frustration that our senses are exercised, and we experience true aliveness." He paused briefly, but then quickly continued.

"Frustration is often thought of as a consequence of disappointment. It is believed to be only a feeling that is caused by something else, not a purposeful tool that, once recognized, can be used effectively and intentionally to perpetuate a spiritual human being through the various stages of growth.

"Frustration can also be thought of as being like the 'burn' that athletes of all ages and eras experience while working-out: a runner senses it just before their second-wind kicks in. A weight lifter, just as the force of their muscles and the force of gravity reach equilibrium. That burning sensation, that wall of impediment, that fiery frustration, often leads people to want to quit; however, it is precisely that feeling that, once a position beyond it is reached, provides the most benefit and value.

"Frustration is a beckoning voice that calls us to step beyond the edge, to learn what we need to learn, to believe that we can be more than we presently are, to have faith that there is a greater purpose for the pain that we presently endure!

"Things that are easily attained have little value. Things that are attained, only through sustained and decisive effort, have much value. Isn't joy less joyous, if it is wrought by meager effort? Isn't love more full and complete, when it is genuine, pure, and deeply felt through the absence of that which is loved? And, has it not been said that 'the food that satisfies a terrible hunger, satisfies indeed.'

"Although seemingly ambiguous in nature, frustration is the birthing place of hope. It is the causality of courage. It is the progenitor of love. It is synonymous with being baffled, circumvented and disappointed, and yet, antonymous with knowledge, fulfillment, and satisfaction.

"It, in reality, is responsible for every great leap that humanity has ever made. It was, and still is, purposely intended by the Creator of creators. It drives life, steers life. It is supposed to be! It is only our lack of understanding of it that moves us to dread it, to deny it, to hate it so.

"I'm sure that all of you are experiencing certain levels of frustration, even now. Especially those of you who are asking in your minds…when this discourse might, in fact, be over?"

The crowd suddenly roared with laughter. The Professor walked around in a large circle, acknowledging everyone as he passed. A large smile spread across his face. The crowd then started settling down.

He began again.

"This course is intended to help you force your way into what you will find is the real world, the real life, the real purpose for being. Frustration is a catalyst for this, you see. It is fundamental. It is foundational.

"Frustration, *Life*, has its reasons!"

He stopped once more and enjoyed another swallow of the liquid, and as before, he beamed with delight.

"You genuinely want to know. You honestly want to understand. You've been given many answers; however, they're not exactly the ones you expected. And so, you still have many more questions. Perhaps it is your perception, of the answers that have already *been* given, that are incomplete? Consider this, too."

He again paused and looked around, as if trying to look at every individual. Jeremy thought that the Professor presented himself like an old-time orator, as what he imagined the venerable Mark Twain must've been like back in his day.

Jeremy was captivated. He listened intently as the Professor started again.

"In a moment, you will be afforded the opportunities—through the Illustrations—to go on some journeys to seek out more *inclusive* answers. But let me remind you now. Many valuable incidentals are discovered on the journey to revelation. I encourage you again, not to think of these as superficial.

"Let me ask you," he queried, "which holds greater value, a thousand answers derived from one question…or *one* answer, derived from a thousand questions?" He paused again to let them think.

"I encourage you to consider the latter as the greater answer—I can ask it another 999 times, if you wish." The Professor gave a large radiating smile as he again looked all around.

Many chuckled at his comment. Several could be heard speaking softly and applauding. Jeremy also laughed. He thought of what that young preacher had said to him all those years back: "Just don't stop asking!"

His thoughts were halted as the man resumed.

"When one chooses to embrace frustration, one finds that their wise choice ultimately leads them down a meandering road of seemingly never-ending experiences. And these…these produce steering effects as a result: groups of experiences that serve to shape and mold us, often times, by squeezing us, and sometimes, necessarily, by inflaming us."

Jeremy's head tilted with the curious statement.

"Let me mention seven of the most familiar:

"Conscience…Creativity…Coincidence…" He counted them off on his fingers as he spoke.

"Calamity…" He paused again to emphasize the particular word as he scanned the audience with his eyes, smiling, again stopping his gaze on that unusual man. Then he continued once more.

"Consequence…Concentration…" He paused yet again, held his fist up high as if ready to upper-cut a small giant's jaw, then again spoke with added force.

"COOOOURAGE!" He let the sound resonate.

"All of these things can, and do, provide an impetus for change in altering one's course during a quest for an answer. Sailing these Seven C's can take you around a world, and through a universe, but one must remember. They do not, in any way, promise an easy voyage, or an effortless journey.

"On the contrary, these things have the tendency to thrust us in directions, and at velocities, that shake us at our very foundations. They often inundate us with fear and trepidation, while amazing us with wonderment and surprise.

"And, often times, the course changes they spur become a grievous and frustrating provocation, which can taint the most temperate with an inordinate amount of fury. You may have your own, shall I say, *colorful* words…to describe this phenomenon?"

Again, chuckles could be heard from the listeners.

"However, even this is intended to incite us to look at situations and circumstances differently. They force us to choose alternate courses. And as difficult as change is, the inevitable fortitude that results becomes extraordinarily valuable. I highly encourage you to look upon this as virtue—a thing of substance to be treasured."

He paused again, took another sip of liquid from the glass, closed his eyes with elation, inhaled deeply, and then started up once again.

"You have asked these questions: Why do just beings unjustly suffer failure, loss, and humility, while others, who are unjust in their character, experience so-called good luck, providence, and blessing? Why are the undeserving, at times, afforded greater opportunities, while the deserving often find few, or none at all?

"Surely, a good person deserves his or her portion of goodness, and inversely, a not-so-good person deserves his or her reduced portion. Common sense says that portions on any level should be proportionate, but, it isn't always that way, is it? Why are we subjected to this—?

"This dichotomy of loss and gain, this lack of expected or desired fairness, this seemingly grotesque distortion of right and wrong, and the resultant frustration that spawns from it, is, nonetheless, an integral and intended part of the School of the Blind. Nay, we say, it is imperative!"

He paused once again, scanning everyone with an intense authoritative look on his face. Then he waved his hand and motioned everyone's eyes toward the area of fuzzy blackness that surrounded the platform, and then up to the walls of the auditorium.

"The very law of entropy forces us to presuppose that, sooner or later, things will break down. Systems will fail, and eventually, everything erodes and decays and dies. Now, it may seem—for young minds—that this is the end of it all. It may seem that there is no escaping the inevitable, the unavoidable, but…" a large smile grew across his face, "I assure you, it is NOT! There is more going on than what you presently know. MORE than you can possibly…yet…imagine." His smile was broad, defined and certain.

"Please, observe now your choice of the Illustrations."

The Professor lifted his right arm again, and, slowly turning in a full circle, motioned everyone's attention toward the walls of the great sphere. The light inside immediately began to soften, and the large, framed, window-like areas began displaying all sorts of images, each a different one. Scenes of people, places, and events came vividly to life for all to see; the diversity of images in vibrant color and full motion were too many to count.

As Jeremy chose a scene to focus on, he was amazingly thrust into it, or drawn into it. He couldn't tell which. It felt as if it were both. Like he wanted to be a part of it, yet, at the same time, *it* was drawing him.

Within moments, he was able to observe it as if he were, in actuality, there—just like through the window in the Professor's study. The scenes weren't just mere pictures or images. They were the real thing. There were real people, real motion, and real sensations being felt. He could hear, and smell, and even taste the air, he realized.

This startled him. He pulled back, pulled his mind back. Somewhat shocked by the experience, he looked around at the other people in the large auditorium. At least half had disappeared. Many seemed to be popping in and out of existence—there, then gone, then back again. Many were smiling though, dreamily. It seemed pleasant for them. And yet, many seemed distraught and fearful.

Though apprehensive, Jeremy blinked, shook his head, and anxiously chose a different scene to begin viewing. He felt drawn to one in particular, for some reason. He didn't know why. He immediately became engrossed in its substance—being drawn deep into its essence.

He heard the Professor speak as the immersion began.

"Yes, that's it, look, feel, listen, learn. Everyone, experience that which is necessary for you at this particular time in your life's history. Yes, this is the way it is, and has been, since the school began. What you are going through is what you need to go through. You may not know it. You may not choose to acknowledge it, yet. But nevertheless, this is where you are, and it is your journey.

"What you are experiencing is what you need to experience. I encourage you, look past the usual, see beyond the surface. Enrapture yourselves in the seemingly incidental portions of your experience. For therein lies the greatest lesson, the greatest value to be gained.

"All things are meant to be, even if what is meant…is meant to change. Don't look to me for the answers. Look to your experiences as you travel on your journeys, for therein are the answers you seek. At every turn…ask the question. At every high…ask the question. At every low…ask the question. And keep on asking…everywhere in between.

"You are part of life, and life is a part of you. You were given breath, and mind, and spirit, by the Creator of creators. Through these, you are empowered to search out and progressively fulfill your intended purpose. Your questions will lead you on the path to *finding* your own purpose. So again…ask, and never quit asking.

"Great adventures await you all!"

Chapter 27

The scene that Jeremy was now a part of was curiously interesting to him. He was observing a young boy, around ten or eleven years old. He seemed extremely familiar to Jeremy, but he couldn't quite put his mind on it. The kid was in some sort of old-fashioned store, eyeing some chocolate candy bars in a box on a shelf.

Then, Jeremy just seemed to realize the circumstances. He somehow sensed what was going on. He was in a European country, somewhere, sometime during the First World War. The boy's parents had just recently died, leaving him impoverished, starving, and desperate.

Jeremy knew the boy was thinking about stealing those candy bars. No one was looking. No one even noticed that he was there. The kid struggled in his mind between hunger and fear. He swayed between thoughts of sweetness in his mouth, the filling of his starving belly, and the pain of being beaten if he were caught. Somehow, Jeremy knew this. He could read it in the boy's eyes. Yet, he also felt it deep inside, oddly, as if he *were* the boy.

It was more than just empathy, more than just compassion. Jeremy suddenly felt the deeper, life-altering conflict that the boy was going through. Not just imagining it, but knowing it profoundly in his mind and spirit. He felt the boy's anger, as if it were his own. He felt hatred at being forced by the circumstances into the situation, hatred at being born into that position—that life.

There was more to it than just the hunger, more than just a desperate little boy wanting food. There were seeds of trust, and faith, and rightness growing in his soul, battling for a stronghold, fighting for a place in his future. Jeremy felt them severely in his own heart, and in his now-twisted stomach.

Then the boy began experiencing heartache, overwhelming anguish, and a deep longing for understanding. Jeremy recognized the feelings. And again, it wasn't just for food, or the satisfying of the senses. It was for control, not only of his circumstances, but for control of his very life. Jeremy sensed that the boy—that *he*, too—was at a defining point. At an edge that would determine both their lives from that moment forward.

Jeremy watched, and felt, and listened, from both perspectives.

The boy started to reach for the candy bars. But then, abruptly, his hand stopped in mid-air. And then, without reason, the lad suddenly looked up. It was as if he were looking right into Jeremy's eyes. As if he somehow sensed a presence. That someone, or some*thing*, was looking at him.

Quickly, the boy withdrew his hand from the shelf, rubbed it as if it were sore, and began to cry as he did so.

He promptly turned, and ran away.

<<< >>>

Jeremy pulled back out of the scene.

It seemed so real, he thought. He shook his head, took a deep breath. He thought for a brief moment about what he had seen and felt. But then, before he could contemplate it to any great extent, he was immediately drawn into another image.

This scene was of a wilderness area, and in it, Jeremy suddenly realized, was the caveman who had played with the fire. This time, the scraggily-haired man was sitting on a rock next to a raging river, his broad frame gently rocking back and forth. He was watching a small spider traversing a single thread of its web, droopily strung between the two trees. Again, as in the prior scene, Jeremy began to feel the feelings of this man. He began to think what the man was thinking. Even see through his eyes.

The man was lost in thought, pondering the relationship between the spider and the thread. He began to consider the notion, crudely asked the question in his mind: if the spider were his size, then wouldn't the thread be longer than the river's gorge is wide?

The hairy man looked across the racing water to the far bank, up toward the cliff walls that surrounded him, back at the spider, and then across the river again. He then began drawing with a stick in the sand, tilting his head sideways in a pensive response to the concepts that were being constructed in his developing imagination.

Soon, he had drawn a picture: a rough, end-on view of a canyon. And then, with a spark of brilliance, and a sweeping motion of his hand, he drew a single drooping line between the two cliffs, spanning the great chasm.

Jeremy realized what the man was considering. He recognized the ideas that were emergent in his mind. He felt the man thinking, asking, and pondering: how could he make his own web? How could he get across the chasm that separated him from where his deepest yearnings drew him?

Suddenly, Jeremy felt overwhelming frustration, and then anger.

With swift abruptness, and eyes that could kill, the man suddenly turned and looked around, as if sensing a presence. He quickly stood, took several steps, and looked crazily in Jeremy's direction as if sensing that someone or something was watching him. The man reached up with both hands and pressed them to his temples. He stood there, rubbing the sides of his head and grunting.

Suddenly, Jeremy was struck with morbid trepidation, and an overwhelming feeling of oppression. He reactively and swiftly pulled himself out of the scene. Moments after, Jeremy found that he was breathing hard and was extremely anxious, for some reason. Then a strange sound caught his attention. It was a sound that he thought he knew. It wasn't just a noise, for it was somewhat melodious in nature—like a ringing.

The familiar resonance made Jeremy look around. He shook his head and took a deep breath again. He sat there quietly, and then the thought crossed his mind once more:

was he choosing the images he was observing, or were they somehow choosing him?

He became absorbed in the realization that he was somehow personifying the thoughts and feelings of the people he had just seen. Oddly, he felt as if they were a part of him, and he, a part of them. He wondered what was happening, why he felt such a link to their experiences. Then, he became curious as to what he might see—or *feel*—next. With this thought, he looked up, and though reticent, allowed himself to be drawn into another image.

<<< >>>

This scene appeared peaceful and serene. That's why he chose it. Nothing in particular seemed to be going on as he focused on it. He went into it slowly, yet freely. There was no sense of any fear, or anguish, or remorse in this one.

Jeremy's mind soon became immersed.

The scene was of a small village, in some faraway eastern country. Perhaps Japan, he thought. It was a beautiful day. The sun was shining, its rays were warm, the breeze was cool, and the air smelled clean and fresh. He noticed the fragrance of flowers, and the scent of food cooking somewhere—and the ocean, he thought. He smelled the ocean.

Jeremy found himself walking down a winding mountain path. He was actually there this time, it seemed. He could see snowcapped mountain peaks off in the distance to his left, and behind each and above, a rich blue sky dotted with wispy white clouds. He felt the warmth of the sun on his face and arms. He closed and opened his hands, feeling the cool mountain air squish between his fingers.

To his right and down through a valley, the translucent blue-green color of an ocean harbor came into his view. He heard soft music playing—a flute, he thought—and someone humming pleasantly to the melodious tune. He looked down the mountainside, toward where the path led, and saw a village of simply-constructed buildings. Single-story structures of wood and stone, most with rust-spotted metal roofs.

Jeremy stopped, smiled, and then slowly turned around three hundred and sixty degrees to fully take in the scene. He seemed to inhale the beauty and serenity that was before him as a breath of fresh air. The people in the village below appeared to be going about their daily business: walking, talking, hanging freshly washed laundry on clothes lines, or sweeping off their little wooden porches with frayed whisk brooms.

Vendors were trading fruits and vegetables and other various items at stands placed intermittently along the hard-packed dirt streets—baskets of produce were laid out on tables and on blankets on the ground, as if there were a recent harvest. Others were carrying sacs filled with just-purchased goods. Many were sitting on benches, eating fruit, playing board games, and laughing.

All were enjoying the warm sunny day.

Children were playing in small grassy areas between the buildings. An old man sitting in a chair was shaking his finger at a couple of children standing defiantly before him, while another young one was furtively making bunny-ears with her little fingers, along with goofy faces, behind the old one's head. The old man suddenly reared back, grabbed the young one up, pulled her over his shoulder and into his lap and proceeded to tickle the surprised child, the act culminating in a crescendo of high-pitched screams and joy-filled laughs and giggles from all of them.

Jeremy laughed, too.

He took a deep breath, and then exhaled.

He didn't know where he was, or what was going on, but he was certain that he liked it. There was warmth and freshness in the air, and everything around him radiated peace, and joy, and harmony.

But then, quite unexpectedly, in stark contrast to the harmony of mind that he was experiencing at that moment, Jeremy heard deep rumbling sounds coming from somewhere off in the distance. The sounds didn't fit the moment and he suddenly felt an inner anxiety from their discordant reverberations, their percussive effects now penetrating not only his ears, but his very bones, causing him to flinch and blink at the onslaught.

Reactively, he turned and peered down the valley in the general direction from where the deep echoing thuds were coming from. His eyes narrowed, focusing intently on the distant harbor. He then saw numerous airplanes flying in from the ocean. Suddenly, all around the waterfront area, he began seeing flashes of light and explosions.

Large columns of fire began reaching up into the sky, and peeling off them, rolls of blackness, twisting and convoluting horizontally into great billowing clouds of oily black smoke, which began casting dark shadows on the ground.

Everyone in the village suddenly became distressed.

Looks of fear molded their faces, as they, too, peered down the valley. Then, Jeremy heard sirens—loud and whining. He heard ringing in his ears. It was that sound again. He looked toward the buildings on the edge of the village where the sirens were, and saw soldiers pouring out of them by the dozens.

They were frantically uncovering small guns and artillery pieces which were placed all around the village, and covered by green canvas. They were frantically trying to load them, rushing to prepare them to fire. The people in the village began frantically running in all directions. Some ran into the buildings. Many ran up the sides of the mountain and into the woods.

Some just stood and stared at the sky.

Jeremy looked again and saw three planes rushing up the valley in single file, hugging the landscape, a mere fifty meters above the ground. Before he realized what was happening, the first plane dropped a flurry of incendiary bombs on the part of the village farthest down the hill; it immediately banked left and whizzed over Jeremy's head, the sound of its combustion engine-driven propeller dropping in pitch as it roared past.

No sooner than the first one had unleashed its fiery terror, the second and third plane banked and did the same thing with accurate precision, each on a different part of the village.

Within an instant, the entire area was engulfed in a storm of flaming debris and rolling black smoke. The squall of destruction quickly rushed up the hill toward Jeremy. He immediately felt its intense heat. He jumped back, instinctively covering his eyes and face with his arms. He felt something hit him square in the middle of his shoulder blades, something seemingly holding him from retreat.

Jeremy heard the ringing sound again.

He felt dizzy, nauseous; he started to shake. He opened his eyes. He could not believe the images he saw: people being blasted to the ground by the bombs' percussive effects, smashed up against buildings by the torrential walls of flames rolling speedily away from the epicenters of the explosions.

People all over were all of a sudden burning to death with no hope of escape. He saw their flesh instantly blistering from the flames that engulfed them. Shocked, yet quickly gaining the awareness of what was happening, they all started screaming, trying to get up, and trying to run away. But there was nowhere to go.

They were all on fire.

Not just their clothes, but their very flesh. Jeremy saw several children, white with astonishment, trying to wipe the flames off their arms and faces, and he noticed their horrified look when their skin came off in the attempt. A young girl looked toward Jeremy as if to cry for help, and then she turned and ran inside a building just as the glass from its windows blew out and the structure exploded, collapsing down upon her.

Jeremy stared, wide-eyed and horror-struck.

People were rolling around, beating themselves on the ground, not believing what was happening to them. They were breathing in the fire, and desperately blowing it out, trying to get it away from them—they looked like dragons, like lost demons from hell, suffering a wrath of judgment. But these weren't demons. These were just people, just people.

Jeremy defiantly grumbled, *why?*

Why this calamity?

Why this tragedy?

He felt sick.

He felt hate, and disgust, as he saw more planes, dropping more bombs on the already devastated village. Jeremy now smelled the sickening fumes of the cruel fires of inhumanity, and he hated it. And he suddenly found that he hated himself for even being a member of the species.

Why...*why?* he asked again.

He instinctively knew that he was seeing war. He was seeing the inhumanities of war.

He felt hate and disgust.

He screamed with rage toward the sky... "*Nooooo!*"

He heard another ringing sound; the sirens were still blaring sharply in his ears. His head was swirling. He felt as if he was going to vomit, and then another ringing sound, louder this time. He opened his eyes. His head jerked. His back again struck something, holding him from retreat, as his body wrenched from the horrendous assault on his senses.

He began shaking as he realized what was happening.

He gasped for air.

He was...he was...

He was sitting in a chair in the kitchen—he was home.

He was just sitting there.

He stared, eyes quivering, blinking rapidly, unbelieving, his head spinning in a vortex of uncertainty.

The phone rang again.

Jeremy looked over at it, eyes as wide as saucers. He just sat there, trembling.

The answering machine played its recorded message as Jeremy listened.

After the message came a soft and familiar voice:

"Hey DJ, thought you were home? Call me when you get back! I just wanted to know how your day was going! Talk to you later. Love you! Bye."

Chapter 28

Everything changed.

Scott gradually recuperated from his injuries over the following months, though it wasn't comfortable, nor was it easy. However, he and his dad did grow measurably closer because the ordeal; having done a lot of talking through what Paul and Harland had aptly referred to as: the solemn times.

The Ramses did finally have to give up their farm. They had no choice, nor any control over the situation. The bank, which wasn't even located in their state anymore, foreclosed on them with little more than a "sorry, it's just business" type of approach.

There were many months of sadness and pain, not only from Scott's ordeal, but from losing their home—the house they'd lived in for all those years. They suffered the embarrassment and humility of losing virtually everything that had defined their lives for the previous twenty years. After selling at auction, all the farm equipment and a goodly portion of their most valuable belongings, they moved into a rental house in town.

It was the hardest thing they had ever done.

But, they managed to survive.

Oddly, their whole family grew closer as a consequence.

Harland worked odd jobs for many months, though he wasn't very happy. Yet, with Scott's mom back in the working world—running a growing day care business in a partnership with a close friend—they paid their bills and slowly adapted.

As providence and coincidence would have it, though, things changed once more.

One day Harland walked into a Harley Davidson motorcycle shop to look around. During casual conversation with someone who worked there, he'd shared a few stories about his days in California—just basic biker talk. Quite by chance, it turned out that the person had an uncle who had been from the same area in California that Harland had been from.

Amazingly, Harland actually knew the guy because they had ridden together way back then. Harland had even helped the guy out in a bar fight once, when he had inadvertently hit on some other guy's girlfriend. That was how they had met, it turned out. Harland was just there and saw that the other guy was going way overboard, due to his jealousy, and the guy and his big friend, started wailing on this guy's uncle.

Harland just stepped in to help even the score a little.

It was a small world, they both commented, astounded at the probability of their having met. Harland was amazed when he heard that the guy's uncle was now a guitar-playing, born-again, youth pastor in a big biker church out in Southern California.

Although younger, the guy at the shop and Harland quickly became friends. And, again, as providence and coincidence would have it, one day, he introduced Harland to the manager of the place.

When the guy learned that Harland knew motorcycles inside and out, he immediately offered him a mechanics job, due to an abrupt opening he'd had because someone had just recently quit. Harland was a much better candidate than anyone had first thought, and a mechanics job was only the beginning.

Harland was a perfect match for the business.

People, it seemed, started frequenting the new shop just because they liked Harland, and loved his stories, along with his big, yet humble personality. For some reason, they trusted him, as much as they liked him. Harland—or Harley, as everyone started calling him again—in short order, became a part of the persona for the business, even employing him in some of their commercial advertising spots on local TV.

He had mentioned to Jeremy and Paul one day that it was strange how things worked out. If he hadn't literally lost the farm, he would never have been in the position to get the job at the motorcycle shop in the first place.

Ironically, in the latter part of that summer, Scott went to work at the same motorcycle shop, working part-time with his dad, having decided to hold off on college for a year or two, until he figured out just what it was that he really wanted to do with his life. He loved motorcycles as much as his dad did—along with cars—they both soon realized.

After all that happened, Harland didn't press Scott like he had, about going to college and getting a formal education. He figured that Scott, at some point in time, would find the type of career that he really enjoyed the most, just as *he* had, it seemed. Both Harland and Scott came to understand that choosing a life isn't easy. Having to live in one you hate, that's even harder.

<<< >>>

Jeremy was ready for his second year of college, CD for her third. They both worked hard during the summer, seeing each other as much as they could. But, with school starting and both still working full-time to keep up with expenses, there just never seemed to be enough time in the day.

School suddenly became all-consuming again.

One Saturday morning at the kitchen table, after reviewing course content on the environmental movement, for a sociology class, and astrophysics and astronomy, for a science class, Jeremy suddenly realized that he wasn't able to get his mind off of the people he'd seen in that big sphere, or auditorium—or whatever it was. And though he'd sought over the months to drive those thoughts away—still thinking something was really wrong with his mind—it made him wonder all over again about where they might've all been from, and where the Professor was from, for that matter, or, if they were really from anywhere, other than his own mind.

He had kept telling himself that the whole thing was just a part of his own vivid, messed-up imagination. That it was something caused from his lonely childhood after his mother had died, or from some DNA, genetic, brain thing. Or, one of the dozens of other possibilities he'd read in a psychology book recently. For some reason of late, his mind kept reeling back and forth with the issue: Was it real? Was it not? Was all that terrible stuff he had experienced a product of a sick mind? *His* sick mind?

Regardless, he just couldn't get all those people out of his head right then.

After studying his current course material about space and time, and the universe, and especially a section about the mathematical probabilities for life on other planets, he realized that he couldn't get one other particular question out of his mind: *How could we be the only ones in the entire universe?*

For some unknown reason, Jeremy kept thinking about that—a lot.

There's just got to be other life out there in the cosmos somewhere. There has to be. It just makes sense. Maybe that was where the Professor and all those people came from! From out there! Could it be?

Or…or maybe they were from God, heaven, another dimension maybe! It could be, couldn't it?

He'd always wanted to know these things, had always asked about them, even prayed about them more times than he could remember, though no answers ever came.

That thought suddenly stunned him.

He sat there in a daze, continuing to argue with himself inside his mind.

What if the Professor *was* real? *No, it couldn't be.*

What if all those people he saw were real, too? *No way!*

Maybe he was somehow transported to those places. *Yeah, right,* he thought.

Maybe he was unique in some sort of cosmic way, and he was chosen to be let in on some of the secrets of the universe. *Oh yeah, that's got to be it! I'm special!* he thought sarcastically, laughing and rolling his eyes.

Then he thought about it from another angle.

Maybe this happens to a lot of people, but no one ever talks about it because everyone will think they're crazy. He shook his head and laughed again. That reminded him of when the Professor joked about being loony—again, he wondered if he was.

He sought a reality check in another gulp of hot coffee just as his uncle entered the kitchen.

"Hey, " Jeremy said, startling himself out of his mental narration.

"Hey," his uncle returned the greeting.

"How are you doing this morning?" Jeremy continued, sitting up a little straighter. He was glad for the shift in thought, and reality.

"Okay, I would speculate…got in late. It was a long day yesterday, long week, actually. I haven't seen you since Wednesday, I guess? How're things?" He didn't wait for a response. "Man, am I sure glad it's the weekend. It's been a busy one." He grabbed a cup of coffee and threw a couple of pieces of whole-wheat bread into the toaster.

"Oh, everything's cool, I guess," Jeremy answered. "I got a lot of studying to do. They swamped us right off the bat. It's only been two weeks in, and I got another project due Monday!"

Paul laughed slightly.

"Yeah, well, they'll swell your head every chance they get. It's their job! Hang in there. Just look on the bright side, it'll only get worse!" He snickered as he smacked the toaster to stop it from over-doing his breakfast. He slapped some butter on the toast, and then threw them on a plate.

"You want one of these?" Paul asked.

"Sure," Jeremy replied.

Paul grabbed one and slung it through the air at him like a Frisbee.

Jeremy reached up in a quick reaction. "Whoa, incoming," he said, as he pinched it out of the air.

"Hey, you won't believe what I saw last night!" Paul said as he grabbed his coffee and toast, straddled the back of his chair with his left leg, and quickly sat down.

"What?" Jeremy said, curious, eyebrows dropping.

"I saw a UFO," he said, pausing for a moment to observe his nephew's reaction. "*Really*, am not kidding," he continued, as he took a bite of toast.

"I was out back of the pole barn, trying to catch Roberta, and I looked up over toward the tree line, on the other side of the valley, and there was this thing, this…light-looking, thing, underneath the clouds, kind of milky and translucent.

"I froze. It just stayed there in one place and didn't move and neither did I. I couldn't move a muscle. Totally astounded! I just stared at the thing for about ten seconds or so, you know? Then, I moved my head, just a little, to focus on it better, and wouldn't you know it, just as soon as I moved, it moved, too," he said slowly, dramatically.

"Then, it changed shape right there before my very eyes, like it was extending a part of itself, a pod of some kind, a translucent light-shaft kind of thing with a bulbous, glowing blob attached at the end of it, beaming it down to the ground, it seemed, real slow and morphing-like.

"I tell ya, I was frozen. It really freaked me out. It was soooo weird. I thought, what the heck. Then, I realized." He shook his head up and down slowly. "I saw it for what it really was. I was dumbfounded! I just couldn't believe my eyes!"

He paused for a moment, and then added, "It was a tiny drop of Roberta's snot that had flung up on my glasses, when I jerked her little rabbit-butt out from under the shed!" He displayed a large grin. "An Unidentified *Fluidic* Object!" he then said, and just looked at Jeremy, believing that what he had said was humorous. He then did his familiar vibrating-eyebrow thing.

Jeremy didn't say a word.

He didn't even smile.

He just sat there in a daze, looking back at his uncle.

Paul just stared back.

"What?" his uncle asked, taking another bite of his toast, crunching loudly, and then slurping down another swig of coffee, looking intently at his nephew, that devious grin still shaping his face as he chewed.

Jeremy realized that he was staring with wide eyes and eyebrows high. He forced himself to squint, and then spoke. "Nothing, nothing! Snot, huh?" he said, laughing softly out of his nose. "You had snot on your glasses?" He paused.

"You're a goof, Uncle Paul. You know that, a *goof…ball*," he said, again pausing for a moment, and then added, "You know what you need…you need to find you a good woman." Jeremy shook his head and laughed a little hardier. He took a bite of his toast, thinking silently, how weird.

"Yep, big ball of goof." Paul agreed, and then thought, *Woman? What's that supposed to mean?* Paul considered it, but decided not to comment about it. He rolled his eyes. "So, school's tough already, huh? You'll get through it," Paul remarked, downing another gulp of coffee.

"Yeah…yeah, I'll get through it." Jeremy paused, thinking about the coincidence of his uncle mentioning UFO's. With reticence, he asked a question. "Do you really believe in UFO's, Uncle Paul? I mean, you know, real ones, people on other planets, extraterrestrials?" He took another bite, trying not to seem too anxious about the question.

"UFO's, sure! Aliens, stuff like that? Yeah, I think there's a lot going on out there in the universe that we don't know about. I don't know if I believe that they're all monsters, or little green and gray, naked, boy-like creatures with long arms and wormy fingers, like the ones you see in the movies, or on TV. But, *yeah*, there's something going on out there." He took another bite of toast. "Why?" he asked.

"Oh, I was just wondering what you thought about it. We haven't talked about it, you know, for a long time," Jeremy said.

"No…no, I guess we haven't." He looked at his nephew curiously, and then continued, "You, *we*, used to talk about it a lot, I remember, back when you were a kid." He paused to think about the subject. "I don't know. I guess when you think about it, after all the recent knowledge that has been gathered, you know, from science, about space and stuff, the last hundred years or so, it makes sense.

"I mean, there's just so much out there, vast distances, trillions of stars, billions of galaxies, common sense tells you that we're not alone in the universe. I mean, why would we be? Chances are, us *not* being alone, are greater than us *being* alone, I believe, anyway. Who knows, maybe those probes that are on the way back from Mars will tell us something."

He took another bite of toast before continuing.

"Some people, and I guess I'm one of them, believe that the whole idea, or existence, of God, has to do with all that, in some way or another. Is God an alien? Jesus...the angels? Demons?" he said with an ominous tone.

"I don't know! Ancient Astronaut theory, a lot of people call it. We read some of that, back several odd years ago, Daniken...Chariots of the Gods, all that. Remember?"

Jeremy nodded, and then Paul quickly resumed.

"When you read the Old Testament, like when Ezekiel saw the visions of those wheels-within-wheels things or, when...when Moses saw the back of God as he passed over the mountain, maybe they *were* real things. Maybe that was the only way ancient people could describe those things, after they saw them. Maybe they were just visions, who knows? Maybe they were visions *from* God!"

He stared out the window, realizing that he hadn't thought of those things for years, since back when he was doing his religious studies.

"*Yeah*, stuff like that's in the Bible, I remember," Jeremy said with great attention.

"Yep, it's full of it, highly confluential stuff, too!" Paul replied.

"Yeah, I—I...*what*?" Jeremy started on another train of thought but then paused, thinking for a moment. "'Confluential?'" He repeated the word. "*Confluential*, is that even a word?" Jeremy asked his uncle, puzzled.

Paul smiled.

"Yep, it's a word, *my* word. I made it up, I think! It ought to be a word, anyway! I made it up back in college. God, religion...*science*, space-stuff, all that, you know, it comes from the word *confluence*: a merging or, or convergence, a...a coming together. And, *influential*: having an effect, a significant or pronounced effect." He thought for a second, and then, having searched his memory, explained further.

"It means: the coming together of streams of matter, or energy...or spirit, which initially creates turbulence and chaos, yet ultimately results in a greater, more synergistically, uh, dynamic system of life and reality, or whatever! That's the definition I gave it, at least, again, a long time ago. Needs some work!

"Things of this nature," he continued, "have an enormous influence on us, on people, on society, whether we see it or not. It always has. Memes, they call it. And more so now, I think." He had a smirk on his face, and then the corners of his mouth rose to a plump smile, quickly receding back as abruptly as it had been produced.

After a brief pause and no return comment from Jeremy, he went on.

"You know, Jeremy, I believe in God. I believe in His Son, that He sacrificed His life for us, and I believe in the Spirit of God, that it can dwell in us, manifest through us…all that.

"All that is our example to follow in life, and it's there for a reason. *I* believe. I mean, I believe I believe. I think I believe. I want to believe, anyway. I mean, if everyone gave as much as God's *Son* gave, then we'd all have everything we need. Laying down your life to save others, I mean, wow…that's the ultimate. You know?

"I do think that we're all tied to a spiritual nature, in some way, and that one day, we'll all reap what we sow." He looked Jeremy square in the eyes. "And, I believe we truly know very little about it all, contrary to what a lot of people claim to know. They're welcome to their opinions, their interpretations. Maybe they're right."

He started rehashing in his mind his old feelings about God, the Church, faith—*and* science. He paused, said a quick silent prayer for humility and understanding, as he always did when he would find himself in conversations about such things, and then he continued.

"You know, it's said that we are 'Children of God', and that we'll one day go to Heaven, and have eternal life. I've always wondered where heaven *was*. Back in the old days, before science revealed what the universe was like, it was understandable for people to think that heaven was some cloud-like place that's full of wispy-winged beings, and that it didn't have anything to do with this rotten life on Earth. But, nowadays, it doesn't seem so farfetched to think that God,

Heaven, His Son, the angels, and all that other stuff, is somehow part of the big universe that we now know exists.

"Personally, I think our human-kind has been on an educational journey since we began. Like back in the ancient days, maybe, we were like babies, or infants—metaphorically speaking, you know. Back then, we didn't know diddly-squat about anything. Then, as the ages and eons passed, we grew up, a little, and became like…like small kids, toddlers, playing with toys and always fighting with our brothers."

Paul saw that he was losing Jeremy, but continued anyway.

"Then, it seems like, maybe during the Renaissance period—like with Galileo, Isaac Newton, those guys, and all the way up to Einstein—we, as a race of beings, became like teenagers or young adults. And, maybe, as time goes on, we'll grow up even further and inherit—what a preacher I once knew called—'the real world.'" He smiled at Jeremy, thinking he might think that he was a bit weird for saying what he had just said.

Jeremy was intrigued, though.

"I think I see what you mean," he acknowledged. "What exactly do you mean by, what'd the *preacher* mean by, by the real world?" he asked curiously.

"Well," Paul paused to sort his thoughts. "I haven't exactly voiced this opinion for a long time, but, it's kind of like this. When you're young, you play with toys: toy cars, toy boats, toy airplanes, toy *guns*. These are only representations of real things. When you reach a certain age, you're allowed by society—the culture you grow up in—to use and implement the *real* things. You earn the privilege of using these *real* things, when before you were only allowed to play with them in toy-form.

"Now you are considered an adult and the responsibility falls in your hands to use these things wisely. If you don't, you could easily injure or kill someone with them, know what I mean?"

Jeremy nodded.

"I think, one day, one eon maybe, we, God's children, will reach a maturity that will give us the ability to understand—probably through tons more schooling and training-type stuff—how to really use the powers of the universe, for real, I mean.

"Think about it. Like, take this as an example: people have reached the understanding of the immense power bound-up in atoms, right? When we learned how to release it, we made nuclear power. With one result being: the atomic bomb. The power of that first bomb, although it seemed so large, is only a spark, compared to the enormous power and energy that the sun burns off every second, times that by quad-trillion, gazillion other suns." He fluttered his eyebrows.

"Somehow, for some reason, I think God is allowing us to play with a little bit of fire."

He held his hand up and pinched his fingers together, and squinted his eyes at the same time.

"Kind of like when a father lets his son stir the coals of a campfire, play with a burning stick. You know, swirl the stick around in the air, hold it close to his eyes, blow sparks off it—burn bugs." Paul giggled. "The son feels such power. He's amazed and curious, intrigued by the forces that he holds in his hand. But, a good and wise father will keep his son within certain boundary limits—so as not to allow him to go too far, if you know what I mean.

"I think, in the same way, God is allowing His children—down here on Earth—the same leeway, limited, mind you, for similar reasons. We're all riding around on this little eight-thousand-mile-wide ball of wet, fungus-laced dirt, playing with minute portions of matter and energy, learning the basics of God's universe, in preparation." Paul abruptly paused.

He realized that he had never expressed these things like he was doing now. He amazed himself at how simple it seemed, how easily it flowed out of his mouth. He remembered trying for years to express his feelings about it all—and rarely being able to find the right order of words. Now it just seemed to flow out. He was beside himself for a moment. He felt that feeling that he hadn't felt for a long time—that alien feeling.

"'*Preparation*'...preparation for what?" Jeremy asked.

Paul looked up at him, startled by the question. He realized he didn't know the answer. "I...well, I don't know. You tell me. Maybe, probably, something bigger, something better, I'd hope." He remembered something that he had studied in the Bible years ago. He took a sip of coffee, and then continued.

"You know, Jesus was recorded as saying something interesting about that. He said, 'The things that I do, ye shall do, and even greater things.' Maybe He meant it for real. I mean, He reportedly walked on water. He calmed storms. He healed people, lots of people, and He predicted things in the future. He could change His appearance so He wouldn't be recognized, and He even appeared in rooms where all the doors were locked. Once, He turned into a Being of Light, and then in the end, He was raised from the dead. There were countless other things He did, too, throughout His life, and, apparently *after* He died."

He paused for a moment, searching his thoughts, and then continued.

"The last time He was seen on Earth, after He rose—it was recorded anyway—that He...that He, floated up into the air, and disappeared into the clouds." His eyebrows vibrated again. "'Real...fantasy, you be the judge!'" Paul said for effect, imitating an announcer from one of those old pseudo-documentary TV shows.

"I don't know. Maybe He's the example of the mature adult that we all have the potential of being, one day. You know, like He's an older brother, and we're His little pip-squeak siblings. He tells us the truth about how stupid we are, how we're going to end up if we keep acting like jerks, and how the world—the universe—is going to eat us alive if we don't smarten up.

"I mean, if we're children of God now, then...then what will we be like when we *do* grow up? Personally, I don't think we'll reach that point in our lifetime. Maybe a hundred years, a thousand, I don't know. I think people are still too child-like to be able to handle that kind of responsibility, that kind of power.

"I mean, a good father wouldn't let his kids play with dynamite, you think? But then again, who knows, maybe when we die, we grow up a lot. I know I'd sure like to buzz around the universe like Superman, I'd."

He abruptly paused again, felt a twinge of familiar strangeness. A sensation he hadn't felt for many years. He took a deep breath and exhaled slowly before speaking again.

"You know, Jeremy, I used to have these feelings like...like I was seeing things with...alien eyes. You know?" He paused, squinted his eyes, trying to find the words.

Jeremy's brow lowered in response.

Paul stared blankly at the five-pronged fork next to his plate, and the piece of toast with his own teeth marks visible on its edge. Then, he looked at the open palm of his hand. He slowly, mechanically, flexed his fingers. He stared at it for a moment, and then spoke again.

"I—I haven't felt this way for a long time. But, this feeling, it's...kind of hard to describe. It's as if, at times, I'm looking at things through the eyes of an alien—seeing things, abstractly, as if I were not really a part of what I was seeing, like I'm just an observer, a visitor. Like the things I'm seeing are foreign, distant, kind of like they're old, archaic. And even though I know in my mind that what I'm seeing are everyday things: forks, toast, hands, simple things, even eating, they seem strange and curiously alien, you know?

"But, not alien in the sense that I don't understand them; alien in the sense that I'm really from somewhere else and I'm...I'm having glimpses of where I'm...where I'm really from. Like, while I'm here, it all seems common, but that's just because I'm here, and used to it, when a deeper part of me is actually from somewhere else, and I've just forgotten it, or something.

"I don't know, strange, huh? I don't really know how to explain it. Yet, it feels so real, you know, when it happens. But then, I'd find myself back in the sense of the present, and reality sets back in, and then it's all familiar again." He paused, just staring at the table. He looked up, smiled at Jeremy, and wriggled his eyebrows once more, but only minutely this time.

Then, in order to interject his usual measure of levity, Paul put one clenched fist to the side of his left chest. He stretched the other fist out as far as he could reach over his head, and then launched himself out of the chair like Superman, while trying to imitate a slow-motion, weightless effect.

"Want some more toast, Earthman?" he said, flying over to the toaster, making swishing, and rushing-air type sounds out of his contorted mouth.

Jeremy snickered at his uncle. He always had a way of making Jeremy laugh—and think.

Chapter 29

CONFIRMED: EVIDENCE OF ANCIENT LIFE ON RED PLANET—WE'RE NOT ALONE!

~*The WORLD TOMORROW* - Publication

That's what all the headlines read and the news programs touted. It was everywhere: every newspaper, every magazine, and every talk show—even every church service.

Once the news was announced, it made its way around the world as fast as the speed of light. Fossilized and chemical evidence of ancient microbial life had been found on the planet Mars. A planet some two hundred million kilometers away once had life forms on it, the same type of basic life forms that are found on Earth.

Two little robot probes dug them up, pointed their little microscopes at them, and sent the pictures beaming back through space. The images allegedly revealed what appeared to be fossilized structures. Years later, another dual exploration mission was sent there. These more-advanced robots scooped up a few kilos of soil and rocks and brought them back for scientists to study here on Earth.

And there it was, life—irrefutable, conclusive evidence of ancient life on Mars. People were captivated with the news. They were gripped with the excitement of the awesome revelation.

"This was truly a turning point of history," the news-people proclaimed. "If ever there was a so-called paradigm shift in thinking, this was probably the greatest one of all history."

Other creatures once existed—lived—on another planet. The implications were staggering. The discovery established, once and for all, that humans were not the only living creatures in the universe; where in the past it was only thought of as probable, now it was evident.

For many, this news came like any other—it barely raised an eyebrow.

"So what? Big deal," they'd say.

For others, it became an epiphany. It was a vision of a connected universe, filled with life, of which we are a part. To some, it was a revelation from God. And yet, to others, it was all lies and deception by the world's governments—simply another way to get people to pay more taxes.

The year following the worldwide announcement of the discovery was, to say the least, Earth-shaking. Everything changed, everywhere. Many people were excited, filled with elation, thrilled at the thought that we are probably not the only intelligent beings in the universe.

Some, at first, were lofted into a state of mind that could best be described as being awakened from a long sleep—they were just now beginning to feel connected, connected to everything here on this planet, and especially, to life out there.

However, many were thrown into a state of fear.

People reported feeling naked and exposed—vulnerable. They felt that the whole universe was watching them now. That it was somehow staring at them, even spying on them.

Everyone had their opinion, and the repercussions were broad and far-reaching.

Jeremy and CD, in discussing their own opinions, found that they both believed that it was possible, even probable, and that it just made sense. It was just logical to assume that there was life out there, somewhere. And now, apparently, their assumptions were true.

Their lives changed because of this, like everyone else's. The two were in the middle of the first semester that year when the announcement came, and the following winter filled their attention with amazing events happening all over the world.

They watched the news daily as if it were some sci-fi drama unfolding before their eyes, every day being a new twist in the story, followed by another suspenseful cliffhanger.

Some of the things were wondrous, as when the peace rallies started. People were getting together to celebrate their place in the cosmos and ring-in the New World, as they called it. Many facets of world government, at least at first, were finding the impetus to reconcile their differences and work together to prepare for the bright new future believed to be ahead.

Budgets requiring exorbitant amounts of money were being approved for world conferences, peace initiatives and grandiose, collaborative space programs. Even some of the world's religions rejoiced because of the news, believing that God was awakening the world to unknown realities of creation.

But, there were many negative sides that resulted from the announcement, too.

Millions of people were thrown into disagreement around the globe, and because of this, the media had a heyday, betting on both sides of the coin.

There were televised public debates, talk show arguments, street rallies, and riots popping up everywhere. The result was chaos in many of the large cities of the world. There were rising cases of gang war confrontation, mounting numbers of random beatings and deaths, all due to people fighting with each other because of their fierce disagreements over the nature and origins of reality.

The topics that fueled the rising tensions were many.

They were arguing, fighting over things like government spending, environmental degradation, over-population, faith and religion—and in ever-growing numbers, over the very future of the planet itself.

Conspiracy theories abounded.

Public figures rose and then fell from power seemingly on a daily basis. New leaders were coming out of nowhere to have their shot at taking control. Not just from political parties, but from the public and private sectors of society, as well.

These spawned what the media called: "The new-extreme, Extremist Groups."

Many of these were highly organized and well-funded. Chapters were springing up in most of the developed countries, and they quickly drafted charters which defined their position on global affairs. Several of the larger ones surreptitiously planned global campaigns for profit and dominance, strengthened by the fears of the masses—as had happened in countless centuries of the past.

These groups prophesied that: "We"—meaning all the people of Earth—were going to be taken over soon, invaded by extraterrestrials, that the governments have known this for a long time, and that they've hidden the truth from the people.

One particularly dominant group proudly called themselves: "Earthlings First."

It was not only their advertised name. It became their politicized slogan, and their battle cry. They posited that the Earth must prepare for the eventual coming of aliens—intrinsically hostile aliens, they believed.

Again, it was like a science fiction movie, its plot unfolding before the eyes of the planet. Groups of all types started appearing around the globe, with all kinds of contrasting and disparate beliefs. Some of these groups' beliefs even seemed to parallel the Arian movement during the Second World War: preaching separation, touting ethnic-cleansing, hyping the absolute necessity for racism and the purity of an unadulterated human race in order to survive as a species.

Propaganda campaigns espoused unequivocally that: "we are not only being watched from the sky. These beings are already here, and they're pretending to be us. They have been here for decades. They look like us. Many hold high positions in the world's governments, with most furtively planted in amongst the rich upper class."

These groups preached that: "they have been taking us over from the inside, allowing us to destroy ourselves through the consumption of things, and annihilating us from within by allowing us to slowly destroy the environment through our greed, stupidity and materialistic consumerism." And, from some of the groups' own media mouths: "to be rich—or even just well off—meant that you were probably one of them."

Most of those groups seemed to emerge from isolated sects of the foremost religions of the world—Islam and Christianity. Some more exuberant chapters believed, even preached publicly, that these weren't aliens that were coming, they were demons—fallen angels bent on trying to destroy God's work here on Earth.

They said that most, if not all, of the old ancient stories were, in some form or fashion, true. They said it was understandable that we conjured up feathery wings, halos, horns, tails and pitchforks, and stairways into heaven, to explain the stories we heard throughout the ages. But now that we've broken the barrier of knowledge through science, and experience, the truth has come out.

Chapter 30

People were demonstrating by the millions. Advocating for their groups and supporting their positions on one of two major themes, both of which were in near diametrical opposition to each other. The first, which was growing with ever-increasing intensity, was the Environmental Movement —of which the "Earthlings First" groups were the most radical.

These groups were convinced that the world's economies, fueled by big corporations and their lust for profits, must be curtailed and that rampant economic growth must be immediately reversed.

The argument included the fundamental beliefs that over-population, the insatiable hunger for consumer goods, and the arrogant disregard for the natural world's limits, were all contributing to the exponential consumption of Earth's finite resources.

The obvious by-product of this, as their positions held, was irreversible damage to Earth's fragile biospheres: the atmosphere, the oceans, the plants and forests, which are the systems that all biological life depends upon and need to survive. The progressive destruction of these, they believed, would be the precursor to global environmental collapse.

And this, they proclaimed adamantly, was what must have happened to Mars in the far distant past.

These fears—ironically portrayed in science fiction books and films over the prior decades, of a planet being decimated by its irreverent and mindless inhabitants—were fueling the anger and violence displayed in many of the demonstrations.

In growing numbers, people believed that doom was awaiting the planet, and that it was just a matter of time.

It seemed that the Mars announcement turned people into activists—radical ones—bent on saving the planet for future generations, at all costs.

On the other side of the controversy were those who felt that the reduction of consumerism, and the resultant worldwide economic depression that would follow, would itself send the world into a downward-spiral of chaos. Their belief was that this would cause worldwide starvation, disease, pestilence, and wars—unthinkable wars. This, they argued, would hasten the destruction of the world itself, and plunge the planet's populations into another period like that of the Dark Ages.

Chapter 31

Jeremy and CD would talk for hours about all that was going on in the world. They joked about it, at first. That is, until it arrived in their own hometown with some acts of horrific violence occurring near campus, resulting in several tragic deaths.

One particularly appalling ritual-torture death occurred, performed on a Korean business owner after his small imported food business had been ransacked and destroyed. The word ALIEN was spray painted on the front window of his establishment—and across the poor man's bludgeoned body.

It was around that time that CD started to call Jeremy by his first name—Daniel.

She said that it was more of a man's name. It wasn't that she didn't like the name Jeremy. It was just that the name, Daniel, always made her think of a courageous man—a man who faces challenges, a man who faces his own fears and doubts. Along with the fact that she had learned that Jeremy's mother had also called him Daniel most the time and she had liked that.

Jeremy's mother preferred to call her son Daniel, after his great, great, great...great, grandfather, Daniel Tecumseh Armington III. The man was one of those genuine unsung hero-types, a true-blue solider on the Northern side during the Civil War.

He once saved the lives of twenty-some slaves who had escaped but were then caught, and were facing brutal beatings and hangings. After emptying a rifle and a pistol, he fought all five of the remaining Southern soldiers with nothing but a knife in one hand, one of his cavalry boots in the other and, reportedly, such a courageous display of tenacious grit that it, as the story went, sufficiently frightened one of the Southern soldiers so bad with the fear of God, that it caused him to have a heart attack right there on the spot. Jeremy's multi-great grandfather was shot twice and stabbed in three places during the skirmish, but miraculously survived.

CD's decision to start calling him Daniel began as an infrequent gesture of love followed by a cute giggle, but then, to her, it became his everyday name. Jeremy liked it when she called him Daniel, and of course it reminded him of his mother—it was the last word she had spoken to him before she died, after she had said the word 'goodbye'.

Jeremy started using his first name after that, signing his name Daniel Jeremy Sayer, instead of just Jeremy Sayer. And from then on, CD frequently remarked that he was her DJ, and she was his favorite CD, and that they made beautiful music together. Because of this, he became more than just fond of the name Daniel. He became extremely proud of it. He loved the way she treated him—he loved everything about her, everything.

<<< >>>

Jeremy was in his third year of college, CD in her fourth. She had decided on going forward to earn her Master's in Education the next year, and was already working with groups that were oriented toward international educational projects and ministries. Groups that took seriously the belief that knowledge meant not only survival, but growth and success and freedom.

CD wanted to travel around the world. She wanted to teach, to help set up schools, and to help change the world, she'd say. She'd get so excited when she talked about it.

Jeremy had similar dreams and imagined the two of them traveling and working together on all sorts of things. They both knew that life wouldn't be as easy as they had oftentimes imagined, especially with all the craziness that was going on around the world. But they agreed that they would encourage each other through it all, and together, they felt that they could make a difference, that they *would* make a difference.

They often talked about getting married, and having children. But they decided that they should wait until they were done with school—for some reason, although it was a difficult decision, they just knew it would be best. CD's parents were glad of this, and so was Uncle Paul.

They didn't know, at the time, just how glad they all would be.

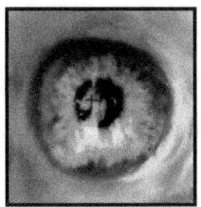

Chapter 32

Jeremy and CD were just about done with school, at least for that year. CD was finishing her undergraduate work and had a busy summer planned before jumping headlong back into the academic thick-of-things the next fall. She had been accepted by the university to work on her Master's degree in education.

Her parents were so happy for her, and they were busily getting ready for their daughter's commencement and graduation party—they'd planned and saved for the better part of a year for the occasion. CD wasn't into all the hoopla, but her parents really wanted her to go and receive her honors and enjoy the fruits of all her hard work.

They were so proud.

They sent out the invitations months prior, and were planning on sending reminder notices a week before the event, just to make sure that everyone remembered. A local band had been booked for the occasion, and they had the people at the Drop Zone scheduled to do a Demo-Jump right into the Dobb's own backyard—smoke, sparklers, and the works.

Godfrey Givins was all for it and he was going to participate in the jump to surprise her. CD had been a favorite there for years, and everyone was really proud of her, too. It was going to be a big day. All CD knew about the event was that her parents were going to have a little get together. At least that was what they told her. She was in for the surprise of her life.

It was a busy spring, for everyone.

Bass' parents were preparing for a big spring sale at all their stores. They were calling it the "Year-of-Jubilee Sale." The Fishmans were Jewish, so they decided to incorporate a modified version of an ancient tradition. They wanted to do something that would give back to the community, and at the same time, attract more customers. The Jubilee sale, they thought, would be the ticket.

In Hebrew tradition, the year of Jubilee happened every fifty years. At that time, according to the tradition, all debts in the land were supposed to be forgiven. This allowed everyone to start fresh with a clean slate, and was supposed to inspire an economic boon for the land.

The Fishmans were going to have a one-day event where an existing credit customer could come into their main store between 11:00 and 12:00 on the day of the sale, and all they would have to do was to ask—actually sign a paper—and 20% of their credit bill would be forgiven. Of course, it was only good for those customers who had a credit line, and it only applied to the balances prior to the announcement of the sale.

Also, on the day of the sale, every purchase that totaled over $200 would receive a 20% discount. The Fishmans sold furniture, lawn and garden accessories, and just about anything that had to do with sprucing up a house—inside or out. They had grown steadily over the prior ten years and were very successful, even in competition against the big super-stores, but it took a lot of hard work and good management on their part.

The announcement for the event went out in the papers and on local television weeks before the sale. It was well advertised, maybe too much so. On the day of the sale, the place was packed, actually slightly exceeding the required capacity allowed by law for the commercial building's occupancy level.

The Fishmans were a little taken aback by the overwhelming response, but they just knew that it would boost their business to the next level; maybe it would even become a franchise someday, like Wal-Mart. That had always been the Fishmans' dream.

It was going to be a big day for everyone.

<<< >>>

The music bellowed throughout the building. The food booths in the store dispensed free hot dogs and sodas. The kids played on swing sets and with yard toys on the Astro-turf laid out in the central atrium area, while their parents shopped.

The younger children were being vigilantly watched over by local caregivers who volunteered for the event as part of their own advertising. Each sported a specially printed tee-shirt with their daycare business' name on it. Karen Ramses' business was proudly represented by two of their best hired helpers. And all the children got free arm bands, not only to link the kids to their respective parents, but to commemorate the occasion as well.

The winners of the drawing would be announced at exactly twelve o'clock noon. Someone's lucky receipt numbers were going to win them a five-hundred-dollar grand prize shopping spree. Three would win one-hundred-dollar shopping sprees, and twelve others would win fifty-dollar gift cards.

There were close to three hundred people there—elbow to elbow in some areas. Most had made their purchases earlier and were back in the store, awaiting the drawing. Many played with their kids in the Lawn & Leisure department's cordoned-off play area, while others hung out at the food courts. There was a lot of excitement in the air.

CD and Jeremy were in the House and Home area, shopping together. She wanted a large, solid-wood bookshelf for her room. Something nice to display all the things that had made her life so special since she and Jeremy had gotten together: her books, her pictures, the music box he had gotten her, the little stuffed alien head Jeremy had won out of one of those claw machines that no one ever wins anything from, and the angel collection that she had inherited from her grandmother, who had died a year after she and Jeremy had gotten together—one of the angels being gifted to her by Jeremy a few days before she had died.

She soon found the perfect one, quickly deciding what would be on each shelf. It was a large piece of furniture, already assembled, heavy, and stood nearly two meters high.

They'd gotten Bass to help them, and together, they'd perched it on its side on one of those low-slung rolling carts with a bent-pipe handle attached to one end. They all worked at maneuvering the big thing through the narrow aisles, slowly making their way through the crowded store to the checkout.

On the way, Bass almost steered the cart right into the backside of a big-bottomed lady in a blue and white dress that was blindly backing out into the aisle, apparently oblivious as to where she was going. The end of the bookshelf narrowly missed her by what seemed like a half an inch. Bass quietly murmured some reference to the Titanic and an iceberg, and they all cracked up, laughing as they continued on their way.

After making it through the checkout, the three rolled the cart out to Jeremy's truck and they carefully loaded it up and wrapped it in old blankets. CD was going to stay with the guys and help get the unit tied down and secure, but Jeremy told her to go ahead and go back into the store. Maybe she'd win something, he'd said—it was almost time.

She walked back to the entrance, opened the big glass door, and then turned around and faced the direction of the truck. She waited a second until Jeremy noticed that she was looking back at him.

He smiled an exaggerated smile so she could see his expression from far away. She waved, and then blew him a kiss, her way of saying, 'Thank you for the shelf.' He felt proud and waved back at her—a wave that said, 'You're welcome. I love you too, and go ahead and go on back in the store to see if you won,' all at the same time. She smiled big, too, and then disappeared through the glass doors.

Bass looked at Jeremy and shook his head with an airy laugh escaping his nose, then looked back at the knot that he was tying in the rope and grinned as he shook his head.

"What?" Jeremy asked, grinning also.

Bass shook his head again, smiled broadly. "You're a lucky man, my friend…a lucky man!" They both smiled at each other and then went back to tying knots.

Then, with the suddenness of a clap of thunder, a horrendous sound and a great eardrum-shattering change in air pressure overcame the two. Their reaction was natural, instinctive. They both fell to the pavement beside of the truck, quickly covering their heads with their arms. A rush of wind and debris immediately smashed into them and they felt the stings of dozens of little objects hitting them in the face, neck and arms. They heard sounds like Velcro ripping apart, thunder, and hissing. They were stunned, shocked, summarily steeped in ignorance as to what was going on.

"What the *hell!?*" Bass yelled over the roaring reverberations.

"Something...something's exploded!" Jeremy shouted.

In their minds, they imagined a gas truck driving by and blowing up, or a gas main somewhere that might have ruptured on some construction site or something. Jeremy then imagined a plane crash, but thought he hadn't heard any plane. At least, he didn't remember any. *What the hell was going on?* they thought, as they huddled down away from the roaring noise.

Jeremy felt a small pain coming from the right side of his neck. He lifted his hand and touched it, and he immediately realized that there was something small and sharp sticking in his skin. It hurt. He looked at his hand and there was blood on it. He reached up again and pulled the object from his neck—it was a small sliver of glass. Glass, Jeremy thought. *Glass...!?*

Then, with an explosion in his own mind's eye, he saw the image of CD walking through the glass doors into Fishmans' store. He immediately felt sick. He put his arm over his eyes, stood up, and peered through the still-swirling debris, toward the store.

Where the glass doors had been, there was a huge blast-furnace-sized fireball rolling out of the opening. Thick black-and-gray plumes of smoke curled up into the blue sky. Above the roof, Jeremy noticed other huge pillars of billowing smoke and fire rolling up into the sky, coming from the other side of the building.

The whole structure was on fire. Then there were two other explosions, almost simultaneously. The earsplitting, percussive sounds sent the two back down behind the truck. Debris, again, started flying all around them. Seconds passed; they seemed like hours. Everything seemed to shift into slow motion.

Jeremy's mind rushed to the thought of CD—she was in there. He stood up to take another look, not covering his face this time, not even considering it. All that was in his mind was CD. He screamed, *"CD! CD!"* and then started to run around the truck's tail gate. Just as he rounded its corner, another blast sent him to the ground. This one seemed to come from the other side of the building.

"No...Nooooo!" Jeremy screamed with all his breath. All he could think of was that CD was in there. She was in there. Bass made it around the truck to Jeremy, dove down beside him, and grabbed him with both arms.

"Stay down, Jeremy, it may not be over yet!" Bass yelled to be heard above the roaring noise, a noise that sounded like the rumble of several powerful locomotives straining to gain speed. Within moments, seconds, the entire building was engulfed in flames.

The two looked up and saw people running out of the building. Many were on fire, clothes already burned away, and what was left of their hair, smoking. They were rubbing their eyes. Some were so dazed that they just stood there, not even seeking shelter, like they had, all of a sudden, became lost and couldn't find their way.

One man was so overcome that he just walked slowly, seemingly looking for his car keys in his pocket, on the way to the parking lot, not even realizing what had happened, or that he was on fire.

Some lady grabbed the man and threw him to the ground and started rolling him around in an attempt to put out the flames that were consuming his back and his right arm.

Jeremy stared in awe. Yet all he wanted was to run to CD, into the building. Bass knew this and told him that he couldn't do it. He kept yelling it at him, "You can't do it! You can't do it!" Bass held him with all the strength that he could muster. Jeremy was stronger, but Bass knew if he let go of him, Jeremy would try to do something stupid. He had to hold on, had to fight him, had to keep yelling at him over the roar.

Jeremy finally slowed his struggle. His fears were now realized. He kept shaking his head, saying "no...no, Caitlin...nooooo..." He cried it out with all his might and breath.

He finally gained some sense of what was going on. He looked squarely at Bass, as if hoping that he would convince him that she was alright, that she was somewhere safe.

Bass knew what Jeremy wanted. His eyes welled up with tears as he returned Jeremy's poignant gaze. Bass just slowly shook his head, fighting to hold back his own emotions, wishing that he could say something to Jeremy, wishing it was not happening.

Then, the thought hit Bass with a jolt.

It hadn't entered his mind until right then.

He was so engrossed with the horror of what was happening, and with Jeremy's reaction, that he hadn't even realized his own apparent loss—his mom and dad were in there, too. His mom and dad were in there amidst the flames, along with CD, and all the other people. It just hit him. Hit both of them, as they sat there holding each other, shaking with every thunderous heartbeat on the hot, debris-littered pavement.

The building was soon a raging inferno. Part of its walls and roof were beginning to collapse, falling in on its contents, falling in on the people. There are hundreds of people in there, Bass thought: mothers, fathers, children, friends, and girlfriends. *Hundreds* of people, and now they're all gone. They're gone, in just a matter of a few minutes. How could this happen? How? Why?

Sirens began to blare amidst their agonizing and confused thoughts. The sounds of screams and people yelling could be heard everywhere. They both noticed that the roar was getting louder; at least, it seemed that way. Maybe their eardrums were recuperating from the initial sound of the explosions.

It seemed that everything was in slow motion.

The resonances they heard seemed otherworldly, deafening, yet distant.

At first, none of it seemed real, or made any sense. But now it was becoming coldly apparent. The building had blown up, and there were hundreds of people in there, in the midst of it.

Jeremy and Bass felt tired, real tired all of a sudden.

They just sat there and stared.

They couldn't breathe.

Then, the tears began to flow.

Chapter 33

Within mere hours, the confusion surrounding what had happened was replaced with stark certainty. The explosions were a deliberate act of terrorism. The authorities had immediately ascertained what had happened, but the knowledge was not derived from the talents, proficiencies, and/or exhaustive investigative work of professionals.

It came directly from those who had purposely made it happen.

Simultaneously, as the cowardly terrorist act was being unleashed on the unwitting participants in the Fishmans' Jubilee extravaganza, numerous explicit electronic letters were being dispatched around the country, with some to other countries as well—Europe, China, India, Israel, South Korea, Taiwan, and Mexico. The e-mails arrived at exactly the same time that the Fishmans' building was exploding. The same time many other buildings were exploding, too.

The explanation was unequivocal.

It was quickly determined that twelve buildings in all, each located in a different part of the United States, were rigged to blow at the same time. Only one hadn't. This one was located in a small, nondescript college town in Texas. Apparently, the authorities there got a tip from someone— an anonymous caller—and the perpetrators were stopped the night before while rigging the explosives. The authorities had no idea that what they had stopped was only part-and-parcel of a well-planned, nationwide terrorist attack.

All the explosions were strategically located in small college towns—colleges that were primarily business-oriented—and all were rigged at small-to medium-sized companies that sold consumer products, mostly businesses that predominately sold imported goods from the developing countries of the world—primarily Asian in origin.

The letters, it was later realized, were sent to most of the major news networks, several to political groups, and many to government offices. Within a short time, it had been determined just who had sent them, and from where. The multi-addressed correspondences were sent from a site just a few miles out of town from where the Fishmans' store was located.

When authorities raided the place, they easily found the man who owned the computer, and the internet address of origin. Along with him were two other men, and a woman, all in the same static condition of being bound and gagged. Two had serious injuries to their heads, from having been beaten.

The people turned out to be cleaning service employees who worked for the company which contractually cleaned the Fishmans' store in the late hours of the night after closing. When questioned, they reported that they were abducted from the store the night before and brought there. They related how one of them had left the store to go to a twenty-four-hour fast food place to get some coffee—as they did virtually every night when they took their breaks.

When the man returned with the coffee at the back of the Fishmans' store, he was overtaken by three people in dark hoods wearing green masks. The three men had medium caliber, semi-automatic pistols and they forced him to get into a van that was sitting behind the building in the shadows.

Soon, the whole cleaning crew was in the van and tied up. Two of the workers tried to resist and they were shocked with one of those electric stun guns and hit in the head with small clubs—night sticks, reportedly, like the police use. Two of the hooded men spent about half-an-hour or so in the store, and then the entire group was driven to a secluded piece of property, the home of one of the cleaning crew. They were silently marched inside, allowed drinks of water through straws, and then tied up to the furniture. This was where they stayed until the police arrived.

The cleaning crew had no idea about what had happened at the store, or to its occupants. When told of the explosions, the fire, the number of people lost, they were all but entirely overcome with emotion—the woman becoming physically ill and vomiting right there on the floor. Apparently, the woman had family who attended the store's event. She herself had planned to attend with them, and would have, had not the person who was supposed to work that night called in sick. To her original chagrin, yet to the salvation of her life, she had been the scheduled replacement.

This similar MO was carried out all over the country. Each store's cleaning crew was abducted, and the terrorists just walked in and set up their explosives, uninhibited due to the disabled security. All the bombings were timed to go off when the Fishmans' place went up. It was believed that the Fishmans' job was the hub of the nationwide operation— their Jubilee Sale, and the fact that they were Jewish may also have had something to do with it, the FBI surmised.

The e-mail that was dispatched was brief and to the point:

....

To: The World
From: Earthlings First -Tactical

Scientists around the globe have confirmed beyond a shadow of a doubt that the exploitation of natural resources through overpopulation and rampant consumerism are not just fueling, but are hastening the inevitable demise of our planet.

Our plea is to raise the awareness of the common man to a level of understanding that will foster immediate change, with the goal of saving the world now, before it is too late.

The examples of this day—the Twelve Points of Light—as well as others to follow in the near future, are intended to illustrate on a small scale, what the entire planet is destined for if action is not taken immediately. A consuming fire is spreading out of control across our

planet. Consider these actions as a series of backfires that are being set in order to extinguish the larger inferno which is threatening the existence of everyone on the Earth.

We regret the collateral damage. However, all wars have this as a by-product. This battle is no different. We call on all to recognize the insidious path the world is blindly traversing, and plead with you to join this frontal attack on the political, corporate, and economic conglomerates that are responsible, so that we may save our Mother Earth—our only spaceship amongst the stars.

A wise man once said, "One day, even consumption will be consumed."

....

At the Fishmans', the authorities found no fingerprints, no complete footprints, or any identifiable items left behind by any of the perpetrators. The surveillance cameras at the store were no help because all the recording equipment was destroyed by the intense fire that had engulfed the building.

No one questioned during the investigation remembered seeing anything except the cleaning van, which was always there late at night. The only clue found was a faint tire tread on the edge of the road next to the house where the crew was found. The cleaning service employee's house, where the e-mails were sent from, was out in the country with no other neighbors in sight, which, the authorities suspected, was why they had used this location for this part of the crime.

They supposed that they had followed all the employees to see where they lived, and what their life habits were in order to make their plans. Ironically, no cleaning employees were killed anywhere in the country—a twisted showing of humaneness on the part of the terrorists, the media suggested.

When authorities deemed it safe to allow access to conduct investigations, it was conclusively determined that the arsonists used a form of napalm to create their bombs.

And from the eye witnesses who saw the building explode, it was also determined that there were several bombs that were employed, all detonating nearly simultaneously.

Also from the accounts of the witnesses, and a few survivors, it was determined that the bombs were most likely placed in the trash cans that were staged at the entrances and exits of the building. Because of this, few had the chance to escape. The authorities surmised that this, too, was intentional.

It was also determined that a smaller bomb was used to destroy the main line supplying water to the sprinkler systems. This was why the building went up so fast. The number of people who died was indeterminable for weeks. It finally settled at around two hundred and seventy at the Fishmans' business alone.

Around the country, the total number of dead exceeded twelve hundred. This was the first mass destruction with the loss of life intentionally perpetrated by so-called Eco-Terrorists. Also significant was the fact that they didn't strike in large populated cities, but in small towns, across the rural heartland of America.

Chapter 34

"Hi, Jeremy," Finley said solemnly. Finley instinctively knew how Jeremy was feeling.

"Hey, Finley," Jeremy replied with the tone of an airy whisper.

"Come on in. I knew you'd be coming out to see me at some point." Finley lovingly placed his hand on Jeremy's shoulder as he entered the foyer. His eyes immediately began to tear up as he looked at him. He took a slow, deep breath and then spoke again. "Life can be cruel, son, I know," he commented softly as Jeremy walked past him into the quiet, log and timber cabin. "Let's go out on the back deck. We can talk," Finley said.

Finley was an old man now. He used to make his living as a gardener, after retiring from the military, and he was a part-time preacher when called upon by his church. He had been a friend of Paul's from way back during Paul's college days. Paul had worked with Finley during that time and had become—according to Paul's own words—a dear friend and mentor.

Long since those days, Finley had retired to his farmhouse by himself, out in the country east of town, his wife of twenty-one years having passed on, and his kids having grown, out living their own lives: a son named Jonathon, who also sought a career in the military, and a daughter named Shannon, who worked in politics in the nation's capital.

When Jeremy had been younger, he and his friends had routinely hung out at Finley's lake, having done so just about every weekend of every summer while he was growing up. There they had fished, and swam, and camped, and relaxed the summers away together—as well as learned from Paul and he, about nature, and friendship, and life.

Finley cycled through some of those old thoughts and memories as he and Jeremy silently walked through the ascetically decorated, rustic living room. He remembered how much he enjoyed all their conversations, especially when it came to watching Jeremy appease his own curiosity by asking questions, questions about all sorts of interesting things.

Questions like: "What makes the spaces between the ripples on the lake's surface when you throw a rock in it?" Or, "How is it that there are so many different life-forms in just one drop of lake water?" Or, when looking up at the night sky, after filling their bellies with fire-grilled brats and home-made chocolate brownies, and reclining back in Finley's over-sized deck chairs, "How far is it to this star, or to that star? And where did, or does, light, energy, and space really come from?" and the really big one, "Where did we come from?"

He was always wondering about one thing or another, Finley remembered: the Big-Universe stuff. Finley recollected how Jeremy had once asked his uncle and he how the universe began, and whether it had a boundary, a place where it ended. "It was something I read," he'd said. "And, if it did end, like a big wall somewhere in space, what was on the other side of that?" And, "if there isn't a boundary, or end, how could it just go on forever?"

Why was he thinking about that now? Finley silently asked himself as they walked.

For some reason, he remembered the time that Jeremy had remarked that he would close his eyes and imagine himself flying, superman-like through space, past a nebula, then a black hole, and then he would imagine that all the universe, and everything in it, might just be a single cell in God's vast brain, and that he was in there, in his own little corner, just looking around, too small and insignificant to understand it all, but still wanting to.

He remembered that Paul had once remarked to him that he didn't know if it was such a good thing—Jeremy thinking all that much—or whether it might push him farther down into his often-recurring depression. Eventually, he just figured that it was Jeremy's way of dealing with things.

It was around that time that Jeremy found a small country church to frequent, and he got baptized there, just like his mom suggested he do shortly before she died. He got saved, decided that there were a lot more questions to ask, then set out asking them.

Finley softly laughed inside when he remembered what Jeremy had commented about once, about what he'd asked the preacher that one morning: "If God's so big and huge, and smart, and glorious and all, then…then He won't mind a few questions, will He?"

Reportedly, the preacher laughed, said he agreed, and then told Jeremy, "Just don't stop asking!" Much of his questioning started, understandably enough, soon after his mother died.

The thought sobered Finley immediately.

He knew that when the time was right, Jeremy would stop by to see him. And here he was—so the time must be right. He also knew that when the questions started, they were going to be some of the toughest that any human being would ever ask, or ever try to answer.

<<< >>>

Jeremy walked through the rear hallway that led to the kitchen and the back door. Finley trailed him, still recollecting, head bowed with his fingers stroking his lips, as if he were somehow trying to prepare what he would say. What should he say, what *could* he say, to this young man who had been like his own son, and having already gone through so much in his life. He sensed the heaviness of an overwhelming despair growing in Jeremy, and he silently prayed for wisdom. He pleaded for the right things to say, the right way to say them.

"You want some tea? A good hot mug of tea would sure do me fine right about now."

"No, but thanks, Finley," Jeremy replied, looking down to the floor.

"Ah, come on, have a cup of tea with me. It's my own mix, grew the herbs myself. What do you say, a mug of Finley's special blend?" Finley said, trying to sound encouraging.

Jeremy stopped at the entrance to the kitchen. "Sure, I guess I'll have a cup, thanks."

"No problem, the water's already hot, just takes a few minutes to steep."

Finley turned into the kitchen and walked over to the stove. He loaded the tea ball, put it in the handmade pottery tea pot sitting on the counter top and poured the hot water. They both watched as the steam rose silently, associating it with the brevity of life. Life itself was like a vapor, born of fire and water, and only here for a short time.

The old man placed the pot and a couple of matching mugs onto a tray and they both went outside onto the deck. Each took a seat in one of the old, grayed, Adirondack chairs that faced the lake. The scenic panorama before them drew their vision as it always had—for some reason, it seemed more ethereal than usual.

It was a warm evening and the sun was just about to set in amongst the distant cumulus clouds creating a pinkish, yellow-red haze that reminded Finley of the countless times that he and Paul and Jeremy had enjoyed other sunsets together on that deck. They both, just as they had done with the vaporous steam in the kitchen, silently associated the sun going down with the intrinsic brevity of life—its cycles, its changes, its mysteries.

Jeremy accepted a mug from Finley, and then broke the silence.

"So, you knew I'd be coming out to see you, huh?" Jeremy said softly, painfully.

Finley smiled, took a sip of his tea, and then, with elbows firmly on the chair's armrests, held the mug with both hands just a few inches from his lips.

"Yep, I figured you would, sooner or later. I've always enjoyed our little talks." He took another sip, and then rested the mug on the chair's arm. He sat silently, waiting for

Jeremy to talk again—he noticed the tears welling in the young man's eyes.

Jeremy wiped the moisture from his cheek with his thumb.

"I…" He paused. "I just can't figure it out, why it happened. Why she had to die? Why God would take her? She was supposed to be here. She was supposed to be here, with me!" He wiped other tears, this time from both eyes, and then he wiped his nose on his hand, and then his hand on the side of his pants. "Why? It doesn't make any sense! She was so good. She was going to do so much with her life. She wanted to help the world. She wanted…she wanted to help make the world a better place. She *did* make the world a better place. Why'd God have to take her? It doesn't make any sense, you know?" Jeremy finished, and then started to weep.

It was strange, all the years he sat in this same spot musing at Jeremy's unending questions. He wanted to cry himself at the sad, ironic contrast of the moment. Finley dipped his head, grabbed his mug again, sat up a little straighter, leaned forward and put his elbows on his knees. He looked out across the lake for a moment. He struggled to keep his own tears back. He struggled to find the right words. Then, looking down at the weather-beaten deck boards below his feet, he spoke.

"Son, I can't pretend to know the answers. I wish I did, but I don't. Caitlin was such a good girl. She did a lot while she was here. Maybe, probably, she's doing a lot of good right now, right now as we speak. This is something that every man, every human, must go through sometime in their life, losing something precious and dear to us. All the way back to the beginning. History's full of sorrow, full of pain and loss. No one person is immune to it. It's a part of life, whether we can accept it or not." He stopped, sipping his tea again, searching for more words as Jeremy sat listening, crying. "Jeremy, all I can do—the best I can do—is to offer you my bent on things, what I see is going on. True or not, for right or wrong, I can only tell you what I think, what I believe."

Jeremy just nodded in response, wiped more tears.

"Son, the way I see it, is that God allowed this. He allows us to go through these things, for a reason—has since the beginning. A lot of people will argue with me, have argued with me. But I believe God's plan is for us to go through things like this. He's letting it happen, letting us humans go through it! Why? Well, we can only give it our best guess, but I believe it's probably got more to do with our lives after we die."

Jeremy murmured. "Yea, if there really is an after!"

"Well, I believe there is, but that's me," Finley said confidently. "Everyone has to decide on that for themselves. The way I see it, there are only two things that it can be: either there isn't any life after this one, and if that's the case, then all we have is what's here. And if that's the case, then we ought to make the best of it while we *are* here—for ourselves, and for everyone else.

"On the other hand, if there is a life after this life, then this life here, well, it must be a preparation of some sort, don't you think, for the next one? In fact, I believe everything we go through—*everything*—is intended to condition us, to prepare us, for that future, for that tomorrow, in the next life."

Jeremy remained silent, taking a sip of his tea, considering the words, and then, with a raspy voice, he spoke. "How could CD's dying be a preparation for anything?" he said indignantly.

Jeremy's mind jostled from one way of looking at it to another, from anger, to sorrow. He knew life was hard—he had already lost his mom, and then his dad. For some reason, he started remembering all of the bad fortune he'd had over the years. His life, he was now realizing, had been full of loss, full of frustration. Frustration, he thought—he remembered the Professor again. His thoughts were interrupted when Finley resumed talking.

"Well, maybe it wasn't all for *her* preparation. Maybe, probably, it's for yours as well. Maybe it's…for all of us. She inspired a lot of people, Jeremy. She had courage, conviction, and she had a conscience, and a love and respect for people that few have in this sorry world. She was fortunate to learn those things early in her life, and she touched a lot of lives with those things. You know?"

Jeremy shook his head in agreement regarding CD, but then reversed his head's motion in angry defiance of any purposeful reason for her dying.

"No! It's still not fair! It doesn't explain it. God's just mean! He sits up there in His…His place, wherever He is, where everything is perfect, and then forces us to have to go through this crap, just because He can! Why doesn't He come down here and go through it? Why doesn't He lose someone that He loves with all His heart, and see how He likes it!"

"Well," Finley responded quickly. "First off, I don't think He allows all this 'just because He *can*,' like you say. I think there's a bigger picture, one that only He can see now, but unfortunately we can't. And I know, it's like there's a big wall between us and…and this other reality, like a dark window, and we just can't see through it. But I believe that one day we will. And I'm just like you. I wish I could see through it, now…and know, truly know. But like I said before, I can't pretend to know the answers. 'Cause I don't. I just believe what I believe.

"And by the way, He did lose someone He loved—His own Son. But that was only for a time, think about that. What I mean is that someday, I'll see my Emma again, and you'll see CD. I believe that."

He stopped to think for a moment. He sipped his tea, and then began again.

"Let me ask you, Jeremy, and this may take some thinking. If you had died and were up there," Finley pointed to the now-darkened, yet star-lit sky, "and she was down here, what would you want her to do?" He paused, knowing Jeremy would think deeply and honestly about it.

Jeremy looked up in the direction that Finley pointed, and at that very moment, a light—most likely a distant star— flickered, got brighter and then stayed bright. Jeremy stared at it, thinking of the coincidence of it. He knew the answer to Finley's question—he would want her to go on with her life, and he knew that he would wait for her, if he were up there. He began to weep again. He couldn't describe it, but he felt her presence, her touch, and could even smell her, he thought. He wanted to be with her so badly. Tears started rolling down his cheeks.

They both went silent.

Jeremy lowered his head into his hands and began crying like he had never cried before. All the years of loss: his mom, his dad, all he had been through, all of this welled up inside of him and burst out. His cries were moans of agony. It seemed too much for him to bear, and he couldn't stop. He felt so alone. Finley reached over and held him. He sobbed like a baby in his arms. Finley rocked him back and forth, encouraging him to let it out, assuring him through his calm, wise voice that it would all be all right, that everything would be alright.

Finley looked up in the sky, and with tears washing down his cheeks, too, prayed these words: "Lord, help us see through this dirty window."

The two of them sat there, silent, just crying together. Jeremy needed this more than anything right now. Just to cry. Just to let his love pour out for this person he adored so much. For all the heartache and loss he'd endured all those years. It was painful, but it was a good thing, Finley told him.

Almost a half hour had passed. At least it seemed like that, maybe more, maybe less. Then Finley started talking again, had just felt like it was time.

"You know, Jeremy, life is hard. The only way to endure it—at least for most—is to find some good in the experience, and then concentrate on that. It's been said that 'life is like a box...like a prison, and we're all condemned to life.'

"Some seem to get special privileges, while others are forced to live with just the basics. Others still, deserved or not, are branded in some way and are forced to live in solitary, everything precious to them taken away—it's the saddest and loneliest of existences.

"The only way to endure our particular 'sentence' is to, as I said, find some good somewhere in it. If we don't, we live in despair, depression, a state of hopelessness. But, suffering is only suffering if we let it remain suffering. To some, hard physical labor is suffering. To others, it's a joy to have the opportunity to get pumped up. To some, work is a burden, to others, it's play! It's how you look at it!

"If people can't find some good to dwell on in the midst of their 'prison' experience, then they have to choose to create the good, themselves. This is said to be some of the greatest wisdom: if 'good' can't be found, then we must 'create' the good. People who can create good from what is bad, are the most cherished and honored in the universe. In fact, I believe it is the reason that God put us here in the first place, and it is why He allows the pain of frustration in the first place: to force the creation of good, in us, and through us.

"We're His children and He wants us to follow His example. He wants us to be little creators—creators of good. This is why we must choose to make life better, to make it good, both here and in the hereafter. This way of thinking is the difference between living in Heaven, and living in Hell."

Jeremy's sobbing finally stopped. He just sat there, looking up at the stars, listening to Finley. What he was saying made some sense. He thought how uncanny it was that the words Finley was saying sounded so much like what he had heard during those strange visits from that Professor character.

He again began to wonder about all of that stuff. It had been over two years since it had happened. He still wasn't sure whether they were even real, or whether they were his imagination, or some brain disorder or something. He wished that he had mentioned them to CD.

Jeremy felt better, sort of. Thinking of CD still stirred up so much emotion, yet strangely, he now felt that he was somehow just going to have to accept it—whether he liked it or not. But then, he felt his anger swelling in rebellion against the thought. He didn't want to accept it! He wanted to push it all out of his mind. He wanted to scream at God. He suddenly felt like two people, locked together in battle.

Finley sat silent for a few more minutes, and then asked, "Jeremy, I know you've thought a lot about the universe and stuff, have you ever asked yourself how it is that us puny little humans down here on this puny little planet have anything to do with the rest of the universe up there? I mean, think about it." Finley pointed up to the star-filled night sky, and then continued.

"We live on a wet, fungus-covered little dirt-ball, in the middle of a relatively small solar system. It's only the tiniest part of the galaxy—a speck of dust in a whirlwind, really.

"The Milky Way galaxy is huge—it takes over a hundred thousand years for light to travel across it from one side to the other. On farther out, there are billions of other galaxies. Many are thousands of times the size of our own. These galaxies are all floating out in a big bunch of space that scientists say is expanding. And they just recently discovered that this space itself is not only expanding, but also accelerating faster and faster in its expansion.

"It's all going somewhere, or into something. Where, no one knows yet. My point is this: we are a part of it, whatever it is. We, with our little three-and-a-half pound brains, have the ability to see it, to measure it, to learn about it, and even change it—at least on our own little microscopic scale."

Finley was intentionally trying to help Jeremy think about other things, about a bigger picture. It was working, for now.

"What do we have to do with it all?" Finley continued. "Are we just a fluke, a tiny pocket of cosmic disturbance that has no meaning or purpose? No, Son, I don't think so. I think we're here for a reason. I don't believe we're just a random occurrence that popped up out of nowhere, destined to fizzle out at some point in time.

"Look at the complexity around us, on the microscopic scale and the large scale. Everything is tied together—linked in ways that we can't comprehend. No, we may not know what's going on in the grand scheme of things, but at least we have discovered that there *is* a Grand Scheme of Things—it's all around us, and in us. And we are a part of it.

"Son, I truly believe that you're a part of it, that I'm a part of it, and that everyone who has ever lived on the Earth, is a part of it, and CD, well, she's still a part of it, too. Just because we don't know *how* all of the pieces fit together, doesn't mean that all the pieces *don't* fit together. You know what I'm saying?

"We have to decide in our own hearts whether this whole picture is good, or whether it's bad. Personally, I'll go to my grave believing that it is good—and the reason is because I choose to make it good, to create the good. But that's my choice, and whether you know it or not, you, along with everyone else on the planet, is faced with the same daily decision.

"I guess the reason I'm saying this is so you'll see that what happened to CD will inevitably force you to choose— to choose to make good out of it, or bad out of it. And whether you like it or not, your life will become a culmination of those choices. There's no sugarcoat'n here, Son; it's just the way things are. You're going to grieve for a long time, but you're also going to go on. I know CD would want you to." Finley smiled and placed his hand on his shoulder. They both looked up to the sky again. It was time for a few more tears.

Chapter 35

Jeremy felt somewhat comforted from his talk with Finley out on that old deck, those many weeks before. But he just couldn't seem to calm his anger. It just kept building the more he missed CD. He ached and festered because of it. It started to make him mad when he thought about what Finley had said: the part about being in a prison and having to create some good out of it.

All he could think of was that he had lost his mom. His dad didn't give a crap about him, and now he had lost the only person in the world who really knew him deep down inside. The world around him just kept beating him down, and yet he was supposed to keep his chin up and bear it with a smile on his face just because it's "just the way things are!"

Jeremy tried to keep his head on straight, but it was becoming increasingly difficult. He had never felt such anger in his life. He felt overwhelmingly oppressed by it. As the weeks passed, he became extremely depressed and moody. He would snap at everyone who tried to encourage him with positive thoughts and comments—even at CD's parents when they would call to see how he was doing.

He was also starting to get on the bad side of his uncle. Once, he yelled obscenities at him and used God in the reference because he had tried turning his mind by citing some humble adages from the Bible, something about Job, the patriarch, and all the loss and suffering that he had gone through.

Jeremy quit school that year, even though everyone encouraged him not to when he had first mentioned his intention of doing so. They all tried to get him to hang in there: Bass, Scott, Harley, Finley and Paul, even Brake from the Drop Zone, who would call him every once and a while to see how he was doing. All had noticed him turning from a once calm and happy young man, to someone who was becoming increasingly apathetic and despondent.

But no matter how hard they tried, he wouldn't listen. Jeremy was a different person, changing day by day—he just seemed to quit caring. All the years of silently accepting everything that had happened to him just turned into a building rage.

He didn't work anymore, not even at the Continuum. He would just lie around the house all the time, and stay up late every night watching movies—any movies, it didn't matter, just something to occupy his mind. He slept all hours of the day, and sometimes all day. He didn't clean up after himself anymore either, leaving dishes in the sink, clothes on the bathroom floor, even trash in the refrigerator and on the counters.

This went on for nearly three months after CD passed. And even though Jeremy's uncle tried to understand—did understand, for the most part—he just couldn't find it in himself to continue to accept Jeremy's behavior anymore without saying something about it.

One day, he challenged Jeremy and told him that he wanted him to clean up the house, because he was tired of having to clean it up himself. His uncle tried to express his genuine understanding of how Jeremy felt, but he also tried to get Jeremy to understand that his behavior was forcing someone else—*him*, in this case—to have to live in a way that he didn't want to live, especially in his own home, and that wasn't fair to him.

Paul tried to use reason, but it was to no avail. Jeremy just simply blew up on virtually every occasion in response to his uncle's emergent disapproval. More than once, Jeremy had rashly told him outright that he didn't really give a damn, and to leave him alone, which Paul had done, for the most part, not knowing what to do or how to react anymore.

Finally, after most of the summer was gone, Paul Usher had enough. In the heat of an argument, he told Jeremy that he wanted him to realize that he was a full-grown man now, and that he was sorry, but he wanted Jeremy to move out, and that it was time for him to make his own way in life.

Paul tried to ease the conditions that he had abruptly stipulated by telling Jeremy that he could take a couple of months to prepare. That he would help him find a job if he could, and maybe an apartment or something. Somewhere else where he could live that Jeremy might like better, and could live the way he wanted. But all his sincere efforts were for naught.

Laced with cutting disrespect and innumerable obscenities, Jeremy vocalized his feelings one more time by saying that his uncle was just like everything else in his life: always being taken away, leaving him, turning on him, just because "that's the way things are," and that it really didn't surprise him to find out that his uncle was no different.

The shocking sentiments really hurt Paul, badly. Jeremy had no idea how badly, and he didn't stay around to find out.

<<< >>>

Jeremy left the very next day.

He took his TV, his stereo, his music collection, the rifle that his uncle had given him on his twenty-first birthday, and just about every other possession he had that was of any value, and sold them wherever he could. All he got for the stuff at the local pawn shops in town, and from a few college students that he knew on campus, was a little over five hundred dollars.

Then, Jeremy emptied all the money out of his savings account, money he had saved for school—close to four thousand dollars. Everything Jeremy owned, everything his life had amounted to up to that point, was now under the camper shell of his old Toyota pick-up truck.

Sitting inside the cab, Jeremy opened the atlas that he had just purchased. He sat there, slowly shaking his head from side to side as the tears glistened on his cheeks. After the longest time, he picked a direction. West was as good as any. He looked one more time at the small photograph that he was holding tightly in his hand—a picture of CD.

He drove out of town, mumbling words spawned by loss, anger and fear. He was still crying sixty miles later as he merged onto the interstate. He didn't know where he was going—who really does, who really cares, he thought.

He pushed the pedal down harder.

Chapter 36

Daniel was startled at the question.

"What? What did you say?"

"I asked what that letter J stands for? John, Joe...Jock?" Laughter followed.

"Jesus...I know, Jesus? No...no! How 'bout Je...ho...vah—you one of those Jehovah's Witness dudes?" the other guy asked with a belch, and then more laughter.

Daniel looked at the two of them in his own foggy, stoned, and drunken state of mind. "No, no it doesn't...and I'm far from one of those guys." He paused reflectively, and then spoke again. "Je...re...my, Jeremy, it stands for Jeremy," he said, looking at the small, inch-wide tattoo on his upper-arm. He hadn't used the name for almost ten years. In fact, he hadn't even heard the name used except when he called his uncle back in Indiana. It had been at least a couple years since he had even talked to him, he remembered—it gave him a bad feeling. He took another drink. He didn't like feeling bad. The evening was over as far as he was concerned.

"What's the C...D part?" the guy spoke as Daniel stood up.

"Never mind, Dog Breath, finish your beer and go home. We got a new job to start tomorrow and we'd better be there early or the boss' going to be pissed," Daniel said, emphasizing the word as he rose from his chair. "Later, Clooney, thanks for the birthday bash, really!" Daniel said to the other man, and then threw some cash on the table.

The man called Clooney immediately picked up the bills and stuffed them back in Daniel's jeans pocket as he walked by. "Nope, nooooo, on me, I said. Happy...happy birthday!

And all that shit——." He mumbled the rest, unintelligible, as he gurgled down another swig of beer from his glass.

Daniel motioned his thanks with a simple facial expression and a half-hearted waving gesture. He turned and then left the small tavern. He got into his pick-up to drive the five and a half miles through the back roads to the little rented trailer that he lived in. It wasn't much by any standards. But it was comfortable, secluded, provided nice country to look at, and for the last several years had been his solitary refuge from the rest of the world.

Daniel had been gone from his home, his uncle, and his life back in Indiana for just short of ten years. When he thought about it, it surprised him that all that time had slipped away. Then, on the other hand, it didn't—you lose a sense of time when you short-circuit enough brain cells.

He had started drinking heavily a few weeks after he left his uncle's.

It seemed to help.

It didn't keep him from thinking about CD, but it did serve as a painkiller for the heartache—at least to some degree, he convinced himself.

He drove slowly, carefully. His mind spun with the thoughts of his uncle after thinking about him back at the tavern. He pulled into the short driveway, got out of the truck and leaned against it, giving his inebriated legs time to remember what they were connected to his body for.

The air was still and clear and the stars seemed to energize everything with a subtle glow. This was the one thing he liked about the desert areas of Nevada: the quiet, the mostly clear nights, the open country, and the big sky. For some reason, it made him think, even though he came out there to stop thinking. That evening was no exception. And because of the fact that it was his birthday, it made it even worse.

Daniel just couldn't keep himself from reminiscing about the previous ten years: losing CD, the falling-out with his uncle and his old friends, all for no good reason—on fate's part, or his part. For the life of him, he still couldn't figure out why he'd done what he had done. He was just numb to it now, he supposed. And there was no changing it. He had buried the guilt and embarrassment a long time ago. Best not to think about it. But the thoughts paraded before his mind's eye like scenes in a movie that he couldn't turn off.

Birthdays will do that, he thought.

He hated birthdays.

He hated life.

Yet, life was simpler now—numb, at least.

But that was not always the case.

Daniel stayed on the move for the first year after he left Indiana. He had made his way up to Montana for a time, stayed in the mountains, then Wyoming, and then he traveled down through Colorado. He stayed in Colorado Springs for a while, then Denver.

It didn't take long before all the money that he initially brought with him had run out. At first, he stayed in hotel rooms every night. Ate whatever he wanted, whenever he wanted, and drank a lot. But within about three months, it was all gone—then reality set in. He then found himself doing odd jobs, menial jobs, whatever he could find that would make him a few bucks to buy some food.

When winter came full force that first year, Daniel had an extremely difficult time finding enough work to support him—as a lot of people did. Things had quickly gone from bad to worse throughout the country. Unemployment was up, jobs were scarce, and everybody had their opinions as to why.

The negative numbers just kept rising, and it seemed that on every street corner, in mostly every city that Daniel traveled through, doomsayers were preaching from their soapboxes that the world was, in one way or another, coming to an end. He usually didn't pay much attention to them though.

For him, it already had.

After about starving to death during a long stretch in-between jobs and a period of time when he was at his lowest of lows, he headed farther south and finally ended up in Nevada. It was warmer down there, and he found a job doing construction work in and around the Yucca Flats Nuclear Waste Storage Facility.

The controversy was great concerning the facility. One year, they were going ahead with the construction of the site, and the next year the project was shelved. It stayed this way for a stretch of about twenty years, where one year it was unequivocally determined inadequate for the purpose, and then after a new government administration had come to power, all of a sudden, new tests apparently determined that it was more than adequate, and construction had begun again in earnest.

No one really wanted the facility there at Yucca Mountain, but the government had to put the stuff somewhere. They said it was the only place that the highly radioactive waste could be stored in a stable environment that wouldn't change over the course of ten thousand years. Everyone everywhere questioned the logic: "How do they know that something won't *change* in ten thousand years? It's ten thousand years they're talking about," they would sarcastically say.

Daniel wasn't sure either. But, he didn't really care what people thought. He asked himself numerous times what in the world he was doing there, why he was working around that stuff. The only answer he could arrive at was that he was just there to make a living, trying to survive like everyone else.

It wasn't like *he* was making the stuff, and trying to bury it in somebody's backyard, he thought. He was just working and trying to get along like everyone else. The country was racked with ever-increasing unemployment, and he realized he was extremely fortunate to even have a job.

He had felt bad when he saw the mass of protesters there that one hot afternoon during his first month working out there. Especially when that guy set himself on fire at the gate and died the next day—a fully clad, suit and tie, live human effigy of the government. But people were doing stuff like that all over the world—strange self-destructive things just to make a point about something they believed in, or didn't believe in.

After working as a laborer, carrying lumber and materials, and what-have-you, Daniel eventually took on the trade of a rough carpenter—the people who build the actual framework of a building. Their job is to bolt the first piece of material to the foundation and finish with the last piece on the very top—and everything in between. It was hard work, especially out in the sun in the 110-degree summer heat, but Daniel became unusually proficient at it.

He had built numerous projects with his uncle in the years past, and since he'd had prior experience—and almost three years of college—the small construction company he had applied to gave him a try. He was surprised when he got it because for every job that was created at the site, there were hundreds of people who had applied for it.

Daniel was thankful for the providence.

There were people with Bachelor's degrees working behind fast-food counters making less than he was, and he knew it. In fact, everyone knew it. That's why the small construction company was successful out there, too— because everyone at the company worked as hard, as fast, and as efficient as they could, just to be competitive and get what little work there was.

"No excuses," the boss would say. "If just one person slacks off, then no one will have a job—or any money." The company had fired dozens of people, some for no better reason than just being a few minutes late to work. It took Daniel awhile to learn this important lesson, years he remembered as he stood there, thinking about the past and his birthday. He was somewhat glad, thankful even, but he hadn't thought that way when he first took off from Indiana—his thoughts back then were entirely on something else.

He shifted his position a little, stared at a different set of stars. His mind, seemingly of its own accord, rehashed it again: the wasting of all that money the first few months, getting drunk, staying drunk, and walking out on countless jobs just because he didn't want to be there on that particular day.

Daniel remembered one time when he was down to his last few dollars. He needed money, and he couldn't find a job anywhere. It was about that time that he actually started thinking about robbing a gas station, or someplace. He had even found himself considering the rudiments of a plan once, but just couldn't bring himself to do it.

He then took the last few dollars he had, bought a little pot, rolled it all up, and sold it by the joint on the streets in some of the big cities that he stopped in. It didn't make him much money, and he knew that he didn't want to keep going down that road. He was desperate, but he wasn't totally stupid. At least for his sake, he convinced himself that he shouldn't stay that stupid.

That sparked another memory as he stood there—the memory of the two weeks he had spent in jail for being in the wrong place at the wrong time.

Chapter 37

The seventeen-year-old girl had artificially-silvered black hair, was slender, and very pretty. She had picked him up while he was down to hitchhiking that one day. He was thumbing a ride to the small town south of Denver where he had gotten some temporary work driving cars through an auction block. She had offered him a ride without hesitation. And their conversation had gotten deep within the first few moments of meeting, he remembered.

"Hey, what's up?" she said as Daniel got in.

"Uh, not much, my truck is broke down and I'm trying to get to work, down in Littleton. Thanks for the ride. I really appreciate it! I'm Daniel," he said, as he climbed in and shut the door.

"Sure, no prob! Hey there, I'm Christi. That's Christ, with an 'I' on the end, not a Y. Like Corpus Christi, in Texas. Corpus meaning 'body, or a body of works, like writings, words—even lyrics—of or about Christ,' that'd be Christ Jesus," she said, with pointed emphasis.

Jeremy narrowed his eyes at her long, drawn out comment.

"Cool, nice to meet you," he said, with a feigned and a slightly exaggerated pleasant tone.

"Littleton? Well, hmmm," she continued. "Let's see, I can drop you off at one of two spots. I'm going past Littleton, actually, a few miles further south—dropping something off at my aunt's, only take a minute—and then I'm turning around and driving right back into Littleton. I can drop you at the off ramp, on the way. It'd be a couple mile walk into town, or, if you want to, you can ride along and I can take you pretty much where you want to go! Up to you!"

"Uh, on into town's cool! I got enough time. Thanks," Daniel said.

"Like I said, no prob! So, where do you work?" she asked, while accelerating back on to the highway.

"I'm working at an auto auction place, Buyer's Auto Auction, actually, down on South Piedmont. You know where it is?"

"No, can't say I do, but I think I know where the street is. I'll get you there. Lord willing!"

Daniel looked at her and the question occurred to him: Why would this young, attractive girl pick him up? Wasn't she at all scared? Is she stupid or something?

"So, what do you do?" Daniel asked, trying to be polite and make conversation.

"Me? I rap! I'm working on my own DDR's (Downloadable Digital Recordings). I got a producer-slash-publisher and I'm going to get my own stuff out there for the world to hear—" She said it with pride, nearly singing it.

Daniel's eyebrows lowered.

He turned and looked out the window.

She continued, "I ain't into none of that gangsta rap or nothin'. I'm rappin' for Jesus!" she said with an equal sense of pride and confidence.

Daniel somehow knew immediately where the conversation was probably going to go. It wasn't that he was so offended by other people's beliefs. He just wanted to not have to think about things. He tried to avoid thinking about anything like that in his life, especially anything that brought back memories, memories that led him to tears, or anger. He quickly thought of something else to ask in order to change the subject that he suspected was coming up.

"So, where are you from, around here?"

"Nope, Indiana," she said.

"*Really?*" Daniel exclaimed. "Me to, whereabouts?" he asked, honestly curious.

"Central, actually. But I haven't been there since I was a baby. You?"

"South central, Brown County, actually. Huh, what a coincidence," he said.

"Ain't no coincidences," she replied, with a smile blossoming on her face.

Daniel sought to change the subject again.

"So, aren't you afraid of picking up strangers? I mean, you know, being a woman." He thought about what he had said. "No gender bias here, sorry, just that, well, you know, you're not exactly *un*-attractive. And you're not exactly big and scary, either. Doesn't it worry you? You got a gun under the seat, or something?" he asked, somewhat jokingly.

Daniel thought he probably succeeded in steering the conversation elsewhere, but soon realized that he had done exactly the opposite.

"Yeah, of course, I'm not stupid, and thanks, by the way." She smiled as she glanced over at him. "God told me to pick you up! Said, you was an alright guy! Well, was He right? *Are* you an alright guy?" She looked at him again, back at the road, and then at him once more, smiling larger with her big white teeth.

Daniel was caught off guard. He didn't want to think about God, much less talk about Him, or explain about why he felt the way he did.

It was still all too fresh in his memory.

"Yeah...*yeah*, I'm an alright guy. I just don't want to talk about...about, God stuff, okay! That's all, no offense."

The anger came back on him like a torrential rain pouring down into his soul, the pressure building quickly as if filling up behind his man-made dam. He should have just listened and smiled at her and not said a word, but for some reason he hadn't, or couldn't. He hated thinking about God, about how He took CD from him.

He fought to retain his composure.

"Listen," she struggled for the right words to say. "God can take care of everything, take care of anything. I can promise you that! Why are you so mad at God, anyway? It's people who're the problem, not God!"

The young girl, as Daniel remembered, kept talking and talking, saying that she felt led to say this, to say that—it almost started sounding like a rap song to him. Daniel's anger once again began to boil.

"Please, listen, I got no problem with you, or, or…you just don't understand. Just let me off right up there. Okay!" Daniel said hastily.

"*What?* I said it's no problem running you into town! I'm sorry if I said something I shouldn't have—in *my own car!*" she added, moving her head from side to side with each word, now a little perturbed at the changing demeanor of her once-pleasant passenger.

"Listen, I really appreciate the ride, but you haven't been through what I've been through, okay. You just don't understand! No one understands. Just let me off…*here!*" he'd said to her, pointing up the road a ways. She pulled over immediately and stopped the car. He abruptly got out.

Before she drove off, she pulled herself up and out of the open window and sat on the door, looking at Daniel across the car's roof. A genuine look of empathy blossomed on her face. She smiled, added an intentionally somber expression, and then spoke one last time:

"Hey, listen, no matter what happened, you're gonna have to forgive God for it, someday!" With that, she smiled again, winked, and then sped off, leaving Daniel on the side of the road.

That was only the beginning of the troubles that Daniel faced that day.

Chapter 38

He rubbed a single tear from his eye.

He just stood there, leaning against the truck, his memories as lucid and flowing as his blood was from all the alcohol.

The next ride he received stood in sharp contrast to the previous one, he remembered. Two guys picked him up, and they were obviously an unruly pair. They were on their way to an early Saturday get-together at some friend's, they had said. And they were ready to party, they'd also said, snickering and looking at each other strangely, silently, furtively saying something between them.

And even though the guy behind the wheel drove too fast, ran a stop sign, and even screeched the tires a time or two, Daniel felt somewhat more comfortable with them. At least that's what he thought at first. But, by the end of the day, he'd wished that he'd chosen to continue riding with that young Christian rapper girl.

Daniel laughed at the coincidence of it. It was one of those bittersweet experiences. More bitter than sweet, he remembered.

He had only been riding in the car for maybe a couple of miles when they stopped to pick up another hitchhiker: a guy who was a little older than Daniel, dark disheveled hair, kind of hippy clothes, and a big nose. He had a distant look in his eyes, but seemed nice. They all said hi to each other as he climbed into the other side of the car, sitting the small backpack he was carrying on the floorboard as he settled in. They then sped off again, spinning the tires in the roadside gravel.

Daniel had first thought that the two men in the front of the car were just a couple of nice guys, helping out two people who needed rides. Later on that day, he had figured out what the real reason was: those two guys had just robbed a pharmacy in another town, shot someone in the process, and were fleeing the authorities. The police were looking for just two men. The guys in the car must have figured that four people in the vehicle would go unnoticed—they didn't know that the police already had a make on the car, and a partial license plate number.

The guys seemed all right, at first. They lit up a joint and started to pass it around, seemed to want to celebrate something. Daniel, along with the new guy in the car—he had told everyone to call him Whiz—joined in and was having a good time. That was, until three police cars took off after them, lights flashing and sirens blaring. The old car they were driving was no match for the new police interceptors, or the radios.

They tried to run, weaving in and out of traffic as they raced down the curvy road. Daniel and Whiz endured a harrowing ten-minute car chase, all the time thinking they were going to die, imagining the car careening off a cliff, or rolling over twenty times down a boulder-laden hill. Images of severed body parts from the car's torn metal filled their heads.

As it turned out, the driver had panicked and slid off the road trying to make a corner, ending up getting the car stuck in a big pile of limbs and branches that a tree-trimming crew had left on the side of the road.

The police immediately surrounded them.

The two in the front seat began arguing about which of them was the most stupid for getting them into the mess. Then, the driver started shooting at the police while frantically trying to free the stuck car. The other man yelled at him to stop, telling him that he was an idiot because there was no way they were going to get out of this alive if they didn't give up.

Reluctantly, as the bullets flew, the guy admitted defeat as everyone ducked for cover. Reactively, he threw his gun out the open window and gave up, all the while cursing under his breath. After a cautioned approach, the police angrily dragged everybody from the car, roughed them and cuffed them—including him and Whiz—and then took them all away.

Not only because they were in the acquaintance of robbers, but because the car reeked of marijuana, Daniel and Whiz were thrown into jail with the other two. It took almost two weeks before they could convince the police that they were just a couple of innocent hitchhikers, in the wrong place at the wrong time, and that they didn't have anything to do with the two guys in the car, or the robbery.

They were questioned vehemently numerous times, accused of other crimes that they knew nothing about, and were constantly harassed by the majority of the guards while in jail. But, due to the testimony of the eye witnesses to the robbery and the getaway, they couldn't hold them anymore, so they let them go.

While they were in jail, and with little else to do, he and Whiz had had some long conversations about their lives, Daniel remembered. After a few days of silence, then intermittent talk, the two had begun to converse freely. Daniel found out that Whiz was a poet. He was actually quite good, Daniel remembered. After that, the discussions came fairly easily, especially after he found out that Whiz had been from Indiana, too.

Daniel was suddenly stoked with astonishment as he stood there thinking. Those two people—the Christian rapper girl, and Whiz, his partner in no-crime—had both been from the same state that he was from. He had never put the two together, until right at that moment as he stood there next to his truck. The reflection seized him. That was years ago, he thought.

"What the hell," he said out loud, shaking his head side-to-side in disbelief, scrunching his eyes in inebriated amazement.

As he stood there, looking at the night sky, again thinking about the strangeness of the coincidence, and seeing only his memories, he remembered the words of the poem that Whiz had given him shortly before they finally parted company.

Daniel still had it in a drawer somewhere:

. . . .

Why did He Do It?

To allude to a purpose is like grasping at straws.
For we've yet to discover a plausible cause.
The life we observe is a wondrous thing,
From a worm in the earth to a bird on the wing.

The power to animate permeates everything.
In the lowliest of forms it is seen.
Humanity is different; we can think for ourselves.
Yet we don't very often unless it concerns gaining wealth.

Destruction comes easy; solutions are few.
We'll rape all the good until we are through.
We are left to our outcome like rats in a trap,
To wallow and sputter and drown in our crap.

The reason is missing; we don't have a clue.
I know that you're out there. Is this what you do?
Why won't you answer and show us your face?
Would your countenance remove us without even a trace?

Are your reasons beyond us? Is your work undefiled?
To the point you avoid your questioning child?
I guess I must trust that you know what to do.
So far you've protected and drawn me to you.
In the end, will I know why this all had to be?
As soon as I'm ready, would you please answer me?

. . . .

Daniel remembered the poem, almost word-for-word. He had read it many times. He remembered how uncanny he thought it was, the part about 'why this all had to be?' It made Daniel think of those Professor imaginings. And as he stood there, holding himself up against the truck, it also reminded him of that one guard at the jail—the one who secretly, against the jail's policies, gave Whiz paper to write on.

He was a big, jovial black man who said that he was an R&B musician in his "*other* profession," as he put it. He was a very articulate man and said that his favorite subject, other than music, was philosophy. "A lot of philosophical talk takes place in jails and prisons—almost as much as funerals," he'd said, with a laugh.

Daniel also remembered him saying something about serving his purpose in life by being there to help protect the *good guys*—the generally good people who were in jail just because they made a few stupid mistakes in their lives during a time of weakness—from those who prey upon others out of the evil in their hearts.

"I guess you could consider me a…a guardian, of a sort," he remembered him saying with a sober, gurgled laugh. "There has to be people like me, to help turn the tide for those who can't yet turn it for themselves." Then Daniel remembered the last thing the guard had said to him, asked him, actually, "Are you the kind of guy who lets your *position* in life dictate your disposition? Don't you think it ought to be the other way around? Most of these folks in here, are in here because they got it backwards."

Daniel narrowed his eyes and then looked down at the darkened ground, kicking some gravel with his foot in an effort to redirect his thoughts. The effort failed. Again his uncle entered his mind.

Daniel had been thinking about him for the past several months, knowing that his birthday was coming up. And, just like every year, he knew he'd receive a card or letter with a picture of his uncle kneeling next to, or holding some small animal—a new addition to the petting zoo, or one that had grown up.

He knew his uncle well. The significance of the animals in the pictures that he sent each year was his uncle's way of expressing some metaphorical meaning. Saying that life goes on, or that it can change, or that we all live in some sort of prison, or zoo, and, like the animals, even though we live in our cages, we're still being taken care of—even if we don't realize it, or like it.

Daniel thought of that guard again. He then thought of his own present position in life, and his disposition—it was still bad. He mumbled the rhetorical question that Whiz's poem's title paraphrased, "Why did you do it?"

He didn't expect an answer.

He just stood there, staring up at the sky again.

He hadn't opened the birthday letter that his uncle had sent to him yet. He wanted to wait until after work. It was still sitting on the coffee table. Daniel took one more look at the night sky and then walked somewhat unsteadily up to the door, unlocked it and then went inside.

He sat down on the tattered couch and grabbed the letter.

He took a deep breath, and then opened it. Sure enough, it contained a picture. He pulled it out of the envelope, realizing it was face down. He took another deep breath and then turned it up so he could see it.

The picture wasn't of an animal this time. It was of a little white cross sticking out of the ground next to a humped-up pile of fresh soil in the animal graveyard. Daniel held it closer to his eyes. On the cross was the name, Bessie.

Bessie was the petting zoo's most favorite attraction, for the kids especially. She was a burro, a beast-of-burden, a kind and gentle animal. His uncle had gotten her when she had been just a baby, and over the last fourteen or so years, she had hauled literally thousands of kids around the Continuum's grounds, bringing them great joy in doing so.

The animal loved the kids, too. She always seemed to get excited when they would show up. It was as if she actually anticipated the fun they would have together, like she accepted her own place and purpose and found joy in them.

Daniel picked up the letter and started reading.

Bessie had died of a heart attack a month earlier. All the kids in the area, along with their parents, came out to her funeral. It was advertised in the paper. There must have been close to a hundred people there, his uncle wrote.

Some in attendance had ridden her and had their pictures taken on her when they were just children themselves—now they were grown-ups with their own kids that had befriended the gentle animal. It was a sad day, Paul related in his handwritten words, a sad day for everyone.

The rest of the letter only related the usual things:

Happy Birthday, hope you're all right, love to hear from you. But instead of the usual "Miss you!" his uncle wrote:

"*Missed* you!"

Daniel caught the significance immediately.

Ten years…*ten years*, he suddenly thought again.

He lay there and just stared blankly at the stained ceiling above him.

A tear ran down his cheek as he drifted off to sleep.

Chapter 39

The day broke with a beautiful sunrise.

It was already hot, too hot for early May. Daniel drove the twenty-five or so miles to the new jobsite while clearing his head from the night before with strong coffee and a couple of aspirins.

They had finished up two jobs that past week, and were getting ready to start this new one out on some big estate east of town. It was going to be a ten-thousand-square-foot house, built for one of the executives of a company that was contracted to manage the logistics center of the nuclear waste facility.

Daniel hadn't seen the prints yet, but his boss had told him about it: big place, complex job, a lot of work, and some new building techniques were going to be used, at least new to them. Daniel thought about it as he chewed on a piece of toast and drank the last of his coffee.

He had left a little earlier that morning to make sure he would be on time. As he approached the location, he was amazed at the size and beauty of the property. There were already two large houses up there on that ridge and this was going to be the third, and the largest.

It was at the end of a long lane that snaked around hill after hill of cactus stands, boulders, and brown-rock landscaping. The development of the land itself revealed the class of house they were going to construct. The house was being built just up the side of a hill from a seven-acre, s-shaped lake. An oasis in the desert, really, nestled down in a tight valley with sharply inclined, cliff-laden walls, with a large beach and landing area situated near each parcel of property.

It was a scenic, beautiful place. The nicest Daniel had ever worked at.

Daniel arrived and parked beside his boss's truck. Because he had made it a priority to be early, he was doing fine on the time, so he didn't rush. He just sat there for a minute, looking around, feeling sort of out-of-place in his old beat-down pick-up. All the other vehicles there were new, it seemed—shiny, with no rust, unlike his. But he didn't care, he told himself.

His boss saw him and waved. He then motioned for him to come over to the area where the construction trailers were parked. There was a large, off-white, circus-style open-air tent positioned there next to them, with six picnic tables placed symmetrically underneath its expanse, each separated by about 5-6' feet of space.

Several misting fans were hanging around the perimeter of the tent, blowing water mist over the tables for cooling. A rare and unusual set-up for a construction site, Daniel thought, even in the desert.

There were several people standing around. Most were at the far end of the tent, peering over a couple of the tables that had blue prints strewn across them. At the end of one of the tables stood a very attractive woman—she, too, seemed out of place on a construction site.

Daniel got out of his truck and headed over to the shade of the awning, to the table that his boss was standing by. He walked more upright than usual, his chest filled with air, head back and chin out, trying to present himself to all these unknown people in a confident and professional light.

He approached his boss. They both said their good mornings and nodded. After being introduced to two other contractors that he hadn't met before, his boss began showing Daniel the prints that they were going to work off of. Daniel studied them intently, looking up infrequently and only in reaction to the relevant parts of conversations that were going on between the other contractors.

Then, someone familiar caught Daniel's eye.

Standing directly across from him on the other side of the tent was a man who looked like Thomas Dorkin, the author. At first, Daniel thought it had to be someone who just looked like him. Surely, it wasn't, he thought. Daniel moved sideways a little to get a full view of the man—it *was* him. It was the author he and CD had met at the bookstore in Indianapolis, over twelve years earlier. He looked a lot thinner than he remembered. But it was him. There was no doubt.

He had sunglasses on, a leather-banded wide-brimmed coarse-weaved sun hat, rugged-looking baggy hunting-style pants, and a thin, sweat-soaked, double-pocketed, tan cotton shirt. He looked as if he had just gotten back from safari in Africa or something. Daniel just stared for a minute. He couldn't believe that it was him, after all those years. What was he doing out there? This was a strange coincidence, he thought.

Daniel noticed his boss's curiosity at his sudden lack of attention concerning the blue prints, and at his obsession with the people on the other side of the tent. Leaning down, Daniel whispered toward his boss's ear, "I know that guy, the guy with the hat and the shades."

"Really?" his boss said with disbelief. "You know Thomas Dorkin, the author?"

"Yeah," Daniel said excitedly. "Yeah, I met him years ago, back home, at one of his book signings. We talked about skydiving and a mutual friend we had that crashed into his wife…uh, the girl that became his wife…after breaking her back." Daniel muttered nonsensically, still staring across the tent, momentarily stunned. He was so astonished at seeing the man that he didn't even realize that he was making little or no sense to his boss. "Wow, this is weird!" Daniel confessed in a whisper.

"'*Skydiving*…broken back? Crashed into his *wife*,'…what?" his boss repeated, intending for him to clarify a little.

As the word 'skydiving' reached the other side of the tent, Thomas Dorkin turned his head out of curiosity to see where the familiar word had originated. In doing so, his eyes fell right on Daniel. He looked, leaned his head to the right and took his sunglasses off, placing them on top of his hat. He stared at Daniel for a moment, then smiled and spoke.

"Jeremy? *Jeremy*, is that you?"

Daniel's boss looked across the tent at Dorkin, and then back at Daniel. His boss was more puzzled than before.

Thomas Dorkin rounded several picnic tables as he moved quickly across the tent. He had his hand out in front of him fifteen feet before he even got to Daniel. When he was in range, he thrust his hand out farther to grab Daniel's in a handshake fashion, shaking it with excitement and vigor. Daniel's boss was not the only one surprised at the gesture— Daniel was shocked that he even remembered him.

For some reason, he now treated him like a long-lost friend.

"Jeremy, it is you. It's good to see you! What on Earth are you doing out here? What a surprise! I knew I'd see you again, someday. I figured it'd be in a different place, but here you are. What are you *doing* out here?" he repeated, still shaking his hand.

"Uh, hi, Mr. Dorkin, Thomas, it's…it's good to see you again, too. It's been a long time, hasn't it? Uh, I work for the construction company here. We're going to build the house, frame the house, actually, is what we do." Daniel just stared at him in amazement. "And, uhmm, oh yeah, this is my boss, Ben Southern. Uh, Ben, this is Thomas Dorkin," Daniel said out of courtesy, motioning each to the other.

Thomas reached out his hand to Daniel's boss, shook it, also out of courtesy, saying it was nice to meet him, and then immediately focused his attention back to Daniel.

"Framing…framing, you say. You're a framer? A builder, that's interesting." He smacked Daniel on the shoulder with his other hand, letting his hand linger there for a moment, and then smacking it again before removing it. "I can't believe you're actually standing here in front of me right now!" Thomas said excitedly.

Daniel thought this was strange as well.

The man continued, "Listen, I heard about CD! I'm so sorry, really, really sorry! When I found out, I was torn up for days. I only knew you guys from that one time we met, but I looked up ol' Godfrey about a year after the fire and he told me all about it. I read about it, too, the bombing and all.

I was as stunned as the rest of the world. I had no idea she was in it—until I heard. I'm so sorry! So sorry!" He shook his head as if seeing it happening in his mind. "I guess it's happening all the time now. The world's gotten pretty bad, hasn't it? Terrorists, abductions, the bombings, crazy people!" He suddenly realized he was rambling. He looked at Ben Southern and apologized. "I'm sorry. I'm holding you guys up, aren't I? How inconsiderate of me, I apologize. You've both got work to do."

He paused, thinking for a moment.

"No...well, well yes. Daniel and I have to get some...some logistical issues worked out here, before the crews show up." He chose a big word, since he knew that he was talking to an author, and he wanted to appear more educated. "But, that's alright," Ben said, trying to be polite.

"No problem, back to work it is. Just one thing, uh, listen, Jeremy." He paused again. "Oh, oh that's right, you're going by your first name now, aren't you, Daniel. I remember. Listen, Daniel, here's my cell number." He pulled out a card from his wallet as he spoke, handing it to Daniel. "Call me tonight when you have some free time. I'm in the area. I'd like to get together and talk. Would that be alright? What do you say?" He looked Daniel straight in the eyes. It was a look of joy, compassion, and of excitement, all at the same time.

"Uhmm, sure, maybe...maybe we could meet in town, or something, I guess," Daniel said, wondering how he knew that he was using his first name now.

"Good, I'll see you then. Give me a call, later, okay? *Please* do!" He reached out his hand, once again shaking Daniel's with excitement. He shook Ben's again as well. "Good, until then. I'll let you guys get back to work, and have a great day!" He nodded, turned, and then walked away.

Immediately, it occurred to Daniel that he had no idea why Thomas Dorkin was even there at the building site. Daniel asked quickly before the man took two steps away.

"Uh, Thomas," Daniel was surprised he called him by his first name. "What are you doing here? I mean, here, right now?"

Thomas Dorkin turned to respond. "Oh! Yes, I know the owners here. And I'm here to write my lassss…my latest, book. Great place to think, to write, the desert!" He paused, seemingly holding back a thought that he was about to speak. He looked to the ground, and then back up. "I'll explain more when we get together. You guys need to get back to work. It's going to be a hot one, I'm afraid. So, until then, okay!"

With that, he smiled and nodded, then turned and walked out from under the tent and over to a large white SUV where several people were apparently waiting for him, including the attractive lady that Daniel had first noticed upon arriving. Then all of them got in the vehicle and drove away.

"Wow, that was weird!" Daniel said, looking at his boss.

"Yeah, I'd say that. You're full of surprises, aren't you?"

He shook his head and noticed that several of the other contractors were waiting on the two of them to get the day started. Ben looked up at Daniel and motioned that it was time to go back to work.

It was hard for Daniel to concentrate that day.

His mind was somewhere else—in the past, and the future.

Chapter 40

In the late afternoon, Daniel drove home. All he could think about that day was running into Thomas Dorkin. What a coincidence, he kept thinking. Twelve years later, a totally different part of the country, and he not only remembered him, he treated him like he was an old friend.

The peculiar thing, he remembered, was that throughout all of Thomas Dorkin's books, he was always talking about things like unusual coincidences, and strange patterns in life. The really strange part about it all, was that it almost seemed like it was supposed to be happening.

Once home, Daniel got cleaned up and then he immediately called Thomas. Daniel noticed that he sounded extremely glad that he had in fact called him as he had requested. After a brief conversation about the coincidence of meeting again, Thomas invited Daniel to come out to the house that he was renting and join him for dinner. He said the place had a nice little backyard that looked down through a valley—a great place for conversation, he said.

Daniel accepted, and was given the address.

For the first time in years, Daniel was surprised at the fact that he looked forward to doing something that he hadn't done for what seemed like forever: talk about something other than the heat, the quality of lumber, and what the next job might be.

As Daniel drove through the valley that took him to Thomas Dorkin's house, he couldn't help but reminisce about the past again. He remembered when he and CD had met the author just before Christmas, and afterwards they talked about life and especially how there seemed to be some bigger plan going on. That everything could quite possibly be happening for some big cosmic reason, yet most people were just not aware of it.

Daniel, again, felt that familiar tinge of anger because of the subject of the past. He had worked so hard over the years to drive it from his mind. He still couldn't bring himself to believe that losing his mom, his dad, and then CD was in any way part of some Big Plan.

He didn't want to think about it anymore. But, for some reason, he just knew it would come up that evening. Something told him that he was going to have to deal with it all over again. He felt the urge to turn around.

Something steered him on anyway.

Chapter 41

Daniel found the place without any trouble. It was right at the end of the road that Thomas had directed him to. In fact, the road actually ended in a narrow gravel driveway that took him straight to the house. When he pulled up, he was surprised at what he saw. Daniel expected some big fancy residence, all landscaped and new.

Instead, what he saw was a little cottage made out of stones and rough-hewn timbers. There was no landscaping to speak of, just a little flower garden where a few yucca plants grew, running parallel to a hand-laid stone walkway that led to a side door of the house, and along the walkway, a tall, wooden privacy fence.

Daniel parked his truck between some big pine trees, next to an old-model Jeep 4x4. He noticed that the Jeep was rusted along the bottom and it looked like it hadn't been washed for months. Pine needles stuck to the paint, amidst splotches of sticky sap. His old truck was in the same shape, except for the pine needles, Daniel thought, as he closed the door of his truck.

As he turned away from the parking area to start down the path, Thomas Dorkin was already out the door and walking toward him, a big smile on his face. He swiftly approached Daniel with his hand already extended to offer a handshake; he grabbed Daniel's hand with both of his and shook it hard and firm—just like he had done at the jobsite earlier.

Again, Daniel considered how coincidental it was that their paths had crossed after all those years. But most of all, he wondered why he was treating him like a long-lost friend.

Daniel returned the shake. For some reason, he used both hands, too.

"So glad you came out," Thomas said. "I was hoping you wouldn't change your mind." He shook hard again, then let go and put his hand on Daniel's shoulder. "Let's go out back on the terrace. I've got some food on the grill for us. I hope you like steak and chicken?"

He waved his hand in the direction of the path and they both started walking. As soon as Daniel rounded the corner of the house, he was greeted by what he thought was one of the most beautiful views he had seen in the area. It was all but blocked by the house, the hill, the fence, and a dense patch of scrub trees.

The property was located at a point where two desert ridges came together, or split apart, depending on your point of view. The taller ridge was on the right, and the shorter one on the left. As the ridges spanned out, they drew farther apart and Daniel could see for what must have been ten to twelve miles.

Down in the valley, there were some flat areas covered with patches of green vegetation and a few stands of trees. Daniel could make out the figures of some large animals grazing—cows and horses. Close by the animals were two small lakes that reflected the hills off farther in the distance.

The only signs of human activity anywhere were a couple of fences way down in the bottom of the valley, some irrigation sprinklers blasting water over the small field next to where the animals were, and a small dusty dirt road. The rest was typical desert scenery—rock escarpments showing layered strata in different shades of light brown and gray, sparse vegetation, and lots of sand and parched dirt.

"Wow!" Daniel exclaimed. "This is nice!"

"Yeah, it is, isn't it? I come down here to get away and write. Climate's dry, it's quiet and no one bothers me. The neighbors never come around. I haven't seen them for months. I've been coming here for years, on and off. My wife's brother—*deceased* wife—owns the place. I've been renting it from him for some time now. Still won't sell it to me. It doesn't matter now, anyway."

He paused, looking at the view with distant eyes.

Daniel turned his head sharply when he heard the comment about his wife.

Thomas continued, "He owns a lot of the land you see out there—better than a thousand acres. People have been trying to buy it up from him for forever, but he won't sell it. He wants to keep it just like it is—I don't blame him."

"Wow!" Daniel said again. "He must have a lot of money."

"Yeah, I guess he does. The house you're building belongs to him. Actually, it's his wife who wants it. She's into big spreads like that. She was the pretty lady you probably noticed out there this morning. Nice gal, a little pretentious for my taste, though! Don't tell her I said that, okay!"

They both smiled.

"I heard that the guy who's building the house, your wife's—your deceased wife's—brother, sorry!" Daniel almost lost his thought using the word, "is some sort of executive? Has something to do with the nuclear waste site?"

"Yes, that's right. He's one of the head honchos up there on the logistics board. They make all the decisions on how the stuff is to be hauled in, transported around the site, safety, planning, procedures, stuff like that. There's a lot to it, actually. It's pretty nasty stuff. Hey, I need to get these steaks on. They'll only take a few minutes. Hungry?"

Daniel nodded.

The two discussed general topics while Thomas grilled a couple of sirloins. The chicken had already been cooking for some time before Daniel had shown up. Thomas asked how long Daniel had been out West, where he lived, and what he'd been doing these past years.

Daniel asked more questions about the view, the property, the house, and about Thomas' old Jeep—he'd always liked Jeeps. They had just begun eating when Daniel asked Thomas a more pointed question concerning the vehicle.

"So, you've been pretty successful at writing, I've read, anyway. What gives with the old Jeep? I figured you'd have a new SUV or truck or something, kind of like what I saw you get into back at the jobsite."

Daniel watched Thomas' expression turn.

It instantly became more solemn at his comment.

Daniel then thought to himself: What a stupid, insensitive question! He had asked it so hastily, just trying to make conversation.

"I'm sorry, that was a pretty tacky thing to ask; I was just wondering. I really like the old Jeeps, actually. I...I guess I've been hanging out with a lot of tacky people the last few years, I—"

Thomas interrupted, "No...no, that's alright, nothing wrong with the question." He paused to gather his thoughts and finish chewing, seemingly savoring the bite. He let out a sigh of satisfaction after swallowing, and then spoke. "The Jeep was my wife's. I just like driving it." He smiled a sad smile, and then continued, "As you get older, at least for some, perspectives change, you know. I used to have newer, flashier cars, and places to live. I've been fortunate to be able to have about anything I've wanted, go anywhere I wanted, still can. It's just...it just doesn't mean as much to me anymore, like it used to. Let's say, I just learned some things along the way that changed my values a little. "

"Like...what, what do you mean?" Daniel asked, immediately knowing the question would change the tone of the conversation.

For some reason, he just knew it would happen. He even thought about it earlier that afternoon while he was at work—it's why he couldn't keep his mind on the job for most of the day. It's why he'd felt like turning around and not even showing up.

Thomas knew as well.

In fact, he knew the first moment he saw Daniel that morning on the other side of the tent. It was why he was so exuberant in his greetings. He had been waiting for this for years—he'd even prepared for it.

Daniel had no idea what he was about to hear.

"Let's get rid of these first," he said, picking up the dishes and placing them on a tray sitting on a stone wall next to the table. "I'll get some coffee made—I make a great cup of coffee. Sound alright?"

Daniel didn't speak. He just nodded.

"How about building us a fire in that fire pit there, while I get some brewin'; it'll get cool when the sun starts setting." Thomas motioned over to a stack of wood and a pile of kindling. He smiled and then picked up the tray and headed into the house.

Daniel didn't like fires much anymore; he hadn't for a long, long time—he started it anyway.

Chapter 42

Thomas turned the outside lights on when he came back out with the coffee. They ringed the stone terrace with a soft, golden glow. The sunset was beautiful. There were still a few clouds in the sky to the west, and the huge orange disc of the sun was visible to the last second, its face streaked with the multi-colored slivers of the effervescing cloud vapors.

Thomas started where he had left off—answering Daniel's question.

"Life's funny, you know, Daniel. It used to be that I wanted all that stuff: new cars, houses, nice clothes. I used to be driven by the desire for all that stuff. In fact, I started writing as an edge to get all that stuff.

"My first book was business-based, you know? I guess it was a new way to address old methods of business psychology—nothing's new under the sun, just a different way of looking at it, really. But, it worked, and it was somewhat successful. However, none of that matters to me now."

He shook his head sideways and made a clicking sound through his teeth.

"I know you've been wondering about my reaction when I saw you today. Both of us were, to a great extent, I believe, surprised, but honestly, I wasn't surprised at all, at least in some ways." He looked at Daniel with one of those, it's-going-to-be-tough-to-describe kind of grins, and then he proceeded.

"Let me explain—and I hope you're ready for this. Remember when we met in the bookstore in Indianapolis, I was leaving to go back to Oregon for the holidays? Well, the plane I was on crash-landed in Montana. It came down in the middle of a highway of all places, a few miles short of the airport, emergency landing.

"It wasn't a real bad crash, really, as it turned out—no loss of life. The plane was having trouble staying level, multiple hydraulic failures, they had said. It just kept nosing down on descent, and shaking badly, but somehow the pilots managed to pull it up the last second.

"Nonetheless, the plane hit hard, and the front landing gear collapsed. We skidded a good ways, sparks flying everywhere, took out several of those aluminum light poles, but we finally came to a safe stop. There were so many sparks flying up past my window. I was just sure we were going to explode.

"The interesting thing was…was that the only thing in my mind during the crash was you and your girlfriend, CD. I kept thinking how I wasted a large portion of *my* young life doing things that, now, I can't even imagine doing. I guess my life sort of passed before my eyes, as they say. I really did think I was going to die, you know?

"Anyway, after the crash, the images of the two of you were stuck in my head. To me, I guess you were the quintessential examples of youth—you know, facing life with curiosity, excitement, joy, full of promise, and the future. At least, that's how I remembered you guys.

"Then, and this is the real crazy part, but I…had what I would call a vision one day, I guess. It was a few weeks after the crash, right here on this terrace." Thomas paused for a moment, looking over at the spot that he had just mentioned; a distant look shimmered in his eyes.

Daniel sat there in a sort of daze. He listened intently.

"I remember it being sunny and hot, around two in the afternoon. I began feeling dizzy and nauseated, and all of a sudden, I was just somewhere else. I know it sounds crazy, but I just wasn't here. I was in some sort of big room, like an old library, or office of some kind.

"I remember feeling really sick; everything seemed…distorted. But after a while, I guess I adjusted to it, and then I didn't feel so bad. I remember feeling a huge sense of curiosity, yet I felt frustrated, not knowing what was going on.

"While I was there, while I was in this place, I remember looking at rows and rows of shelves, bookshelves, full of books. There was a desk, and a couple of old chairs facing a huge picture window. Then, I was looking over toward the shelves again. They had all sorts of strange things on them: little statues, odd-shaped mechanical-looking things, bluish orbs of some kind of crystal or metal. And then I noticed several pictures on the shelves, you know, framed pictures. I remember being drawn to one of these in particular. It was sitting next to one of the bluish, orb things. It was a picture of a boy sitting on a porch.

"I leaned forward to get a better look at it, and then I realized that the boy in the picture was *you*, except that you were real young—and you were in a wheel chair. I recognized you right off. It was unmistakable. You were looking up at the sky, and tears were running down your face.

Daniel still just sat there, stunned at what he was hearing.

"Anyway, again, you'll probably think I'm crazy, but, this guy came up to me from the side. He put his hand on my shoulder, real friendly like, and said to me, 'That one's going to change *history*. Just tell him to believe he can!' The man smiled at me, and then invited me to sit down. So, we sat down and talked for a while, about different things.

"All I remember after that was, that I was standing right about there." Thomas pointed to a spot a meter away. "I was just standing there, looking down through the valley. My wife came out of the house and asked me where I'd been all afternoon. She said that she figured I went on one of my long walks again. I just nodded, kind of dumb-like. It was then that I realized that the sun was setting. The last I remembered, it was two in the afternoon and the sun was still high."

He paused and shook his head from side to side.

"I always get the sneaking suspicion that that strange man and I had a long conversation, but I can only remember bits and pieces, and only at certain times. The whole thing seemed like it only took ten or fifteen minutes or so. Crazy, huh?

"For the longest time, I thought I was over the edge. I thought I'd cracked. I couldn't explain it. Then, one day, I got it in my head to go visit Godfrey's Drop Zone—in hopes of seeing you, actually, for whatever reason I wasn't sure. I just felt like I needed to, I guess." Thomas dropped his eyes from Daniel's.

Daniel seemed frozen in space and in time. Thomas was more than slightly embarrassed in telling the story, but he continued as he looked down at the fire.

"When I heard about CD—you know, from Godfrey—I…I just couldn't believe it. The way it happened and all, about all those people. I was mortified. For some reason, it didn't surprise me that you'd left town. No one knew where you'd gone, so I just went back to Oregon."

Thomas paused and looked fixedly at Daniel. After noting Daniel's intense gaze, he continued.

"Then there's, well—and this'll probably really blow you away—I had this dream about skydiving. You were in a small plane and you were afraid to get out and jump. The closer the plane got to altitude, the more your mind went into a state of frenzy. I could feel what you were feeling, think what you were thinking, it seemed. Like I was you!

"Your mind was jumping back and forth between anger and joy, pain and pleasure, fear and courage, sanity…and insanity. You felt sick, dizzy, disoriented. Your face kept changing expressions, like a mime doing some sort of…of, emotions routine. And then the door of the plane opened. That's when I woke up.

"Daniel, I had that dream the night before last. And then today, well, you just showed up, stranger still, huh? All these years, and here you are!" He shook his head, smiled, and shrugged his shoulders. "You tell me?"

Daniel continued to sit there, staring.

His pupils were as big as black marbles.

He wasn't exactly looking at Thomas; he was looking through him. Through to the memories he had of those visits with that Professor character. Daniel's mind was swirling with thoughts. What was all this supposed to mean? What was going on?

"You know, Daniel, I know this sounds strange. I really didn't think I'd tell you all this, right at this moment, all at once. I had kind of wanted to ease into it, but, there it is! I guess it's because I don't have much time. I guess I wanted to, no, I guess I just had to…to say it, due to my situation. I don't know, maybe I…"

Suddenly, Daniel returned from his thoughts, sparked by Thomas' last statement.

"What do you mean by…by '*your* situation'?" Daniel asked, as his eyebrows furrowed.

Thomas hesitated, and then he answered, "I'm dying, Daniel. I have cancer. It's in my liver and my lungs. Don't know how much time I have left, maybe a year, maybe six months. I don't know; *they* don't really know, either. That's why I'm here. I came to finish my last book, my last work. When you showed up today, it was, well, it was like it was meant to happen, like it was meant to be. I don't know why! I got the most eerie, yet joyous feeling when I saw you. I believe that, for some reason, our paths were supposed to cross today."

Daniel was struck; he tried to speak.

"I…I'm sorry. I don't know what to say!" Daniel spoke in a stuttering, yet reverent whisper.

"It's okay, it happens to everyone. Dying, I mean. I'd rather not focus on that right now. I'd rather discuss some other things, things I haven't been able to get out of my mind for close to ten years. And apparently they concern you, I guess, or you wouldn't be here."

This was too weird to be real, Daniel thought.

"What have I got to do with anything?" Daniel asked, struggling for more words. But they escaped him. All he could do was sit there with his eyebrows scrunched tightly together.

"I don't know exactly, Daniel. Maybe, for some reason, we just needed to talk. Life is like a puzzle sometimes, most of the time, I've come to realize. We only see a few pieces fitting together, the ones we do have don't seem to make much sense, and then one day, a random piece comes out of nowhere and it's that one piece that allows us to catch a glimpse of what the whole big picture looks like.

"Maybe this is just one of those seemingly random pieces. Someday, another piece will fit, and then, poof! It'll all come together. Come into focus. I know my life has been sort of like that. When I look back on all the experiences I've had, I can see how they've served to steer me in particular directions, oftentimes without me even realizing it. But for the most part, I feel like I accomplished some good things because of it. Like the directions I've chosen were, on the whole, the right ones, for me, anyway. At least, *I* think.

"In my life, I've tried to help people see the other side of so-called normal everyday experience—through my writing, talks, etc. For the most part, I feel like that's what the Man Upstairs wanted me to do with my life. To help others see that there *is* more than just what meets the human eye! You know?

"Something tells me, Daniel, that you've got a lot to do with whatever is happening—or will have a lot to do with it, later on. The world is a screwed up place. Crazy stuff's going on all over, especially nowadays. Imagine what it'll be like in the outlying future. Maybe you're here to help out, in some way, I don't know! I just know, I had to tell you all this for some reason."

They both sat there, pondering everything that they had just discussed. Neither of them spoke for the longest time. It was almost fully dark now. Daniel looked in the distance towards the panoramic view of the valley. It was lit with a near-full moon, and the shine of a brilliantly adorned, star-filled sky.

<<< >>>

"You know, Daniel," Thomas paused, took a sip of coffee, and then resumed talking. "There is a delicate balance to things." He paused again to clear his throat, and seemed to wince from some internal discomfort. He took a deep breath, held it for a moment, and then proceeded. "Personally, I believe everything is being thrown out of balance. And I think it's the aberrant side of human nature that is the primary cause!

"So many bad things are happening in the world now, happening to the planet: deforestation, air and water pollution, ocean dead zones, species collapse, trash heaps the size of mountains, global warming, etc., etc., etc., all a result of our impact on the natural systems of the Earth.

"Oh, people will argue with you that the environmental changes we're seeing are just cyclic. As if we're at the end of some ten-thousand-year cooling period and the Earth is just naturally warming up. That may be! Sometimes, I wonder if we're just at the *beginning*…of some *high* garbage-collection era, and things are just naturally piling up?" He laughed and rolled his eyes.

Daniel greeted the sarcasm with a grin. Thomas acknowledged the look and then continued.

"Many people believe we're actually witnessing the beginnings of the destruction of the world as we know it, Daniel. And the difference is People. It's unprecedented in history. I mean, think about it. We've spanned the globe. There aren't any new places to go. Most people just don't realize how integrally tied together everything is. Oh, it'll take several more hundreds of years, probably, but it'll most likely happen, if things keep going the way they're going. It'll collapse—unless people work together to understand it, to stop it.

"It used to be that there *was* always somewhere else to go, you know, always a new frontier—an untouched forest, a fresh stream, or river, or ocean to harvest our sustenance from. But now, we're spread across the globe, and there *is* nowhere else to go. And everywhere we *do* go, we leave piles of waste—like at Yucca Mountain. We ignorant human beings are destroying our only home for God's sake, our only life support system for surviving out here in space!

"People are getting smarter about it all, some people anyway. Things are turning around, it seems, at least a little. But with the present economic structure, you know, expend the Earth's resources to make things, use them for a while, and then throw them away, just to make jobs and keep jobs for the ever-growing populations of the planet, it's just not sustainable, it just isn't, not by a long shot.

"How long will it continue? Your guess is as good as mine. But, it really doesn't matter if it is a hundred years, or five hundred years. Once the equilibrium is tipped, no amount of rapid response is going to stop the chaos that'll engulf humanity!"

Thomas was noticeably more animated, but he abruptly paused, held his hand to his side for a moment, as if to soothe another internal pain, and then continued.

"Honestly, I don't know much more about how it's going to unfold than anyone else. The best scientists in the world can't figure it out. But, it does seem like we're doing some really stupid things. Just look at Yucca Mountain. We're creating waste that will be toxic to all biological life for the next ten to fifty thousand years! And we're burying it virtually next door!

"My intention is not to denigrate humans, or our values, but there does seem to be some nastily recurring patterns to our behavior—when you look at it from history's point of view.

"We've enslaved others, taken from one group to fulfill the selfish desires of another. Fought wars and killed when our way of life was threatened, and we've done it all in the name of God, believing our actions are *His* will, a lot of the time.

"Most people, on average, are good and don't intentionally seek to do harm. But most are still caught up in the idea that they somehow deserve to have their comfort zones—earned or not—and will support whatever powers-that-be that might come along that promises them those comforts, no matter what the cost is to others.

"Look at our own country's history. We fought the Revolutionary War against England to win independence against its tyranny. We won, yet with the same breath, we enslaved black people for simple economic gain and superiority.

"The very land you're looking at right now used to be populated by hundreds of thousands of proud Native

Americans. We came into their homeland and took it for ourselves, and why? Two reasons: one, because we wanted the wealth of the land, and two, because we blindly led ourselves to believe that we were right in doing so.

"The human blindness that perpetrated such atrocities here in *this* country was no different than what the Romans did, or what Nazi Germany did. Or all the other countless conquests recorded throughout history, for that matter. It's the same thing, really. It's just a matter of varying geographical scales, and time.

"The motivation's the same: wealth and control, money and power. And this is what's fueling the fires. Corporations are warring against each other for dominance and power, and the governments are allowing it for the same reasons. And the excuse is that 'it's just business.'

"This way of thinking is replete throughout our history. It's an accepted part of our culture. There are hostile takeovers and mergers every day in the business world, and as a result, millions of people lose, not only their jobs, but their livelihoods—along with their dignity, oftentimes.

"Everyone struggles here on this planet to get what he or she can—competition now is rarely any different than back in the Stone Age. We just use more innocuous euphemisms to describe it, and justify it.

"Don't get me wrong here. I'm not touting some communistic idyllic society where everyone supposedly gets his or her fair share. I'm all for hard work, decent and fair compensation, on all levels. In fact our democratic way of life is the most balanced socio-political philosophy to come along. It's a lot better than it was, I can agree with that. But, it's not perfect. And regardless of what system is the most near-perfect system to dominate the planet, it won't matter if there's no habitable planet to live on.

"And that's precisely what's stirring up all the chaos in the world right now: fear about the future, and the confusion as to what to believe, along with the conclusions drawn from the Mars findings. That life once existed there on that planet, and then—for some reason beyond our present comprehension—it was destroyed. Many believe the same about the lost, ancient civilizations of the Earth. That they were destroyed, or destroyed *themselves* in some way! Some people think they're seeing the pieces of the big puzzle coming together. Seeing the past repeat itself and the future's scaring them.

"I know it seems like I'm going off on a tangent here, but I do have a point, and I want you to realize something. I've not been able to get it out of my mind since I saw that picture of you, since…since that experience I had—." Thomas paused, collecting his thoughts.

He continued slowly.

"The observations that I'm making here explain, to some degree, the convictions of the groups that set the bombs, that ultimately killed CD."

Thomas paused.

Daniel looked up at him with a quick jerk of his head, taking his gaze away from the fire. He didn't know what to make of what Thomas had just said.

"Daniel," he paused again, searching desperately for the right words. "Even though what they did was wrong—*reprehensible*—what they are fighting for does make sense. We are destroying our planet, Daniel, by a combination of ignorance, indifference *and* extremism.

"It's like the world is skidding toward an accident, and…and many people are…over-steering, locked up with fear and panic. Many are going to extremes in a desperate attempt to change it, yet they overreact, oftentimes making it worse because of their efforts.

"And some, some just choose to ignore it all—which is just another form of extremism, when you think about it. The fear of it makes them close their eyes to everything. They hide, and become insensate, indifferent to whatever is going on. They quit caring, reducing whatever chances there are of making anything any better by *their* actions, *their* choices, *their* contributions."

Daniel's eyes filled with tension.

His lips tightened.

Thomas noted the change.

"Hear me out, here! I'm telling you this because I believe that I…must tell you. All the things we see going on—well, it's a mix of things. And just because a few fools are in the mix, doesn't mean that they're *all* fools. You know what I mean? This goes for governments, the sciences, *religion*.

"Do you see what I'm saying, Daniel? Do you realize what I'm trying to tell you? Just because people's behavior may be aberrant and intolerably so at times, it doesn't mean that they should all be judged totally bad. Or that the totality of a person should be judged solely based on a few facets of their character! But yet we do that, don't we?

"Just because a small percentage of a whole harbors an overabundance of excessive zeal leading to extremism, to unacceptable behavior, doesn't necessarily mean that the whole is rotten—this applies to people, life, and, in my belief, to God!

"Whatever you believe about God, Daniel—whatever you or I think He is—there is *some* reason for all this! Some reason for you and me meeting again like this."

Chapter 43

Even after what Thomas had said, Daniel still blamed God. He didn't want to hear, much less acknowledge any of it.

God could still stop it all if He wanted to, Daniel considered. Even go back, if He wanted, and change things. He could change it all!

Why hadn't He?

Why doesn't He?

Daniel concluded, in accordance with Thomas' poignant comments, that God must be allowing it all—but why? *Why?*

Then, a word jumped out of his memory as if impaling his conscious mind:

Frustration.

He remembered the wall in the Professor's study, and his comments about the great importance and purpose it had. The Wall…Frustration…the Wall…Frustration…the Wall…

It made him angrier.

Then he remembered the glimpse he'd had of the other side of it—it was just a slight feeling now, after all that time. But he could still remember. He could still see a small, yet shimmering remnant of it in his mind.

Time, Daniel thought.

For some reason, he remembered what Thomas said concerning the vision he'd had. It sounded so much like his own experience. Except, he thought, he was there for hours, it seemed, but was apparently only gone for a few minutes. Thomas described his experience as if he were only there for a few minutes, yet he had been gone for hours.

Then Daniel remembered the ticking clock on the Professor's table.

All of these things, he realized, were rushing through his mind like converging rivers of time and experience. Every thought, every annoying memory that entered his stream of consciousness created a turbulent confluence that swirled through the center, and then around his mind's edges, creating eddies of things that, for one moment, made sense, but then didn't.

All he could think of was that it was all headed somewhere.

It had to be heading somewhere.

A simple picture entered his mind right then, the place where all rivers go: the ocean, the metaphorical harbor of life.

Daniel was in an daze.

Suddenly, all he could think about was dying.

It crossed his mind that he hadn't even considered how Thomas must feel. Thomas was facing death, his own death, soon. Daniel couldn't imagine it at first, but then he could, he thought.

Thomas looked over at him, and then down, not yet speaking.

A strange feeling suddenly came over Daniel right then, one that he couldn't quite understand. Inside, he felt like Thomas. Not like he felt empathy for him, nor even mere sympathy. He felt like he *was* Thomas. As if he was the man himself.

For a moment, he could feel everything that Thomas was feeling. The sensation was oddly familiar.

Daniel felt shock, yet no shock at all when he recognized that he could see what *Thomas* was seeing. He realized that he was looking down at his knees—Thomas' knees—yet, not quite focusing on them, or any particular outward thing, but on inner things. His eyes were blurry from tears. His emotions swirled.

Thomas' thoughts were his thoughts: thoughts of intense fear, of anger, of doubt, of hate; yet, at the same time, thoughts of hope, of courage, of determination, of faith, of *knowing* and *acceptance*.

The contrast of feelings captivated Daniel. Then, just as quickly as they had begun, they were gone, dissipating as furtively as they had appeared.

Suddenly, a question came to Daniel's mind. He spoke it without further thought.

"Are you afraid, Thomas? Of dying? Or…or are you just indifferent to it?" Daniel asked it with a regrettable measure of insolence, spawned from the now-deepened anger and confusion he felt.

Thomas looked back up at Daniel. He had no negative reaction to the question, nor how Daniel had asked it.

"Yes, I guess I would be fooling myself if I didn't admit that I was afraid," Thomas replied. "But then again, *no*. At first, all I could do was cry. Cry, cry and cry some more. I didn't want to think about it—denied it. So yeah, I guess I was indifferent, for a while, to be honest."

He smiled, even though his eyes were starting to water up.

"Then, after a while, I found a peace inside. I'm not sure where it came from. Realization, acceptance, I think…God, perhaps. We all die, Daniel. Everything living dies. In fact, the one fully-shared characteristic of all living things is that they die. I suppose no one, or *no*-thing, wants to, really, maybe some do. But most want to continue to live. It's just something that seems to be inborn in all life forms—the desire to survive, to keep on living.

"One thing I do remember, when the peace came to me—thoughts of what I've learned, and the good I've done in my life, *tried* to do in my life. Oh, I do have some regrets: all the cigarettes and booze I used to partake of back in those high-stress business days. Thinking they were helping me to stay in control—it's probably what's killing me now— but, I've wised up, at least to some degree, I guess." He laughed.

"I've been fortunate to have been able to do a lot of the things I wanted to do, and *be* some of the things I set out to be. I'm really glad of that. I think most people, at least when they get older, have some sort of list, you know, the things they wanted to do in life: travel somewhere, make a lot of money, climb a mountain, have a family, write a book, things like that.

"I think I've pretty much been able to check off most of the things on my list. I can't imagine how a lot of people feel when they get to the end of their lives and realize that their lists are still full of unfulfilled dreams, or un-realized wishes that they blame everyone else for not coming true.

"Be sure of it, Daniel, I've been through my share of suffering and loss in my life. It took a while, but I chose to use it, to use it to make things better, not worse. I remember a long time ago, I started thinking about what I wanted to be, wanted to do. At first, I wanted to be a businessman, make a lot of money, and have a lot of stuff, things like that, like I said.

"And then, along the way, I started thinking that I wanted to spend my time doing something different, something creative, like doing something for others, doing something that was real, something good, instead of just trying to beat the other 'rat' running next to me. So, I gradually started writing about various things, business stuff at first, to help others understand concepts, that kind of thing.

"Then I realized that the business principles I was writing about were universal, really. You know, going about things with a conscience, treating others like you want to be treated, having integrity in your dealings, and being honest, humble, and respectful of others if you wanted them to be that way with you. I know business has a bad reputation for being ruthless and heartless, but it's not always so.

"Anyway, I kind of naturally drifted toward writing books about these things—about different perspectives. It was a long while before I realized that it was what I was supposed to be doing. Don't get me wrong, it wasn't as easy as it sounds. At first, I was a terrible writer. I couldn't carry a noun in a bucket. But, I became determined enough to do so, and that made the struggle doable.

"The first thing I had to do was to ask myself if I had the fundamentals to do it. No one can be a great NBA star unless they have the physics to go along with the heart, you know. I knew that I had the 'stuff' when I realized I had an analytical mind. I was always picking things apart, curious about everything, always wanting to learn why this was that way or why that was this way, always asking questions. The actual writing part took some doing, though. But I knew that I could learn. The hard part was *choosing* to learn.

"I've always been glad that I chose to believe in myself—even when no one else did. And believe me, at first, no one thought I could do it—I even had my doubts, a lot of them. It wasn't until I started looking at the...the whole—" Thomas stopped abruptly, smiling. A small, steady laugh came from deep in his throat. He shook his head from side to side.

"That reminds me." Thomas trailed off again, and then became silent, stroking his chin, looking up at the sky. "Hummm!" he exclaimed softly, with an airy, throaty sound, akin to a brief chuckle.

"Reminds you? Reminds you, of what?" Daniel asked, curiously.

"Oh, something I'm remembering. I haven't thought of it for many, many years." He paused again, thinking, then continued. "When I first decided to try writing, no one believed that I could do it. All my friends and family and business associates raised their eyebrows when I announced my decision. I didn't blame them. I couldn't even write a post-it note without misspelling simple words, or saying stuff that didn't make any sense—at least to anyone else. It's no wonder they thought I was just a dreamer.

"Around that time, there was this old man who came into our office late one night. I worked as a night shift supervisor back then for a manufacturing company. I didn't know who he was or what he was doing there so I just ignored him. Day shift guy, I thought. I remember I was the only one there. I was on my dinner break and I was trying to write something in a word program. I was struggling with how to express a thought about getting the hourly workers to become more interested in our new Continuous Improvement Program, as I remember. From across the room, the man looked over at me and, out of the blue, he said, 'If people could just see how important it is to just try to look at the big picture, then everything would improve immensely!' He smiled, shook his head, and then went out the far door.

"I sat there, and for that moment, it all seemed to make sense. I remember thinking, if everyone could just try to look at the big picture, whether it had to do with Continuous Improvement in an industrial setting, or politics, or human relations, or about the planet, things would surely improve immensely.

"I remember that I finished the writing. It turned out that it really did help our situation there. Although they did have to correct several of the misspellings I made in the first *three* drafts," he said, with a measure of self-sarcasm and a slight laugh.

They both grinned.

"It was strange, that coincidence, that old man. I never saw him again, and I was there at that company for years afterwards. No one seemed to be able to place him when I described him, either. Anyway, that was just one of the things that seemed to steer me in this direction. So, you see, I feel like I did some good in my life, *with* my life. Like at least I tried to make things better by what I did. So, I don't feel like my life was a total waste. I imagine some people feel that way. That'd be really hard to live with—especially, to die with."

Thomas sat silently after saying that. So did Daniel. They both sipped coffee and just looked up at the sky for the longest time before either spoke another word.

"You know, Daniel, in all my research, I've learned that most people at some time in their lives—young, middle age, or old—ask themselves if what they are doing in their lives is what they should be doing. What about you? Have you asked the question, yet?"

Daniel sighed, noticeably uncomfortable.

"Yeah," he said, pausing to examine his thoughts on the subject. "Yes, I have. I used to want to be a teacher, maybe do some writing, too. CD wanted to do that. She was ready to start her Masters. I guess I...kind of lost the desire after she...," he struggled with the words, "after she was gone. I don't know. I guess I just quit caring." He stopped talking and lowered his head, staring into his cup, squeezing it hard with both hands.

"Still hurts a lot, huh? Even after all these years. It was the same with my wife," Thomas said softly, caringly. "You're a framer now, I see." Thomas sought to quickly redirect the conversation.

"You build structures. That's a good thing. Nothing wrong with that, it's a good trade. It helps provide one of the basic needs of people—shelter. It's kind of a metaphor for life, too. You have a foundation to build on, and then over a period of time, you construct the framework in connection with the foundation. And it's that framework that supports all the various characteristics—the finishing touches—that make the whole thing unique, makes the big picture.

"But you know, something tells me that what you're doing now is still only putting together the framework—metaphorically speaking. I've hesitated in saying this, Daniel, but," he paused, perceptibly reticent, "but, I must.

"There's something you have to do, something you're meant to do! You're going to change history, Daniel, where, when, how, I don't know. But, it'll happen, once you bring yourself to believe that you can. I—I.... "

Thomas suddenly realized that it was time to stop. He had said what he knew he needed to say, and more than he probably *should* have said.

He could see the war raging behind Daniel's eyes.

"Hey, I didn't realize what time it was. I—I apologize for carrying on." Thomas looked at his pocket watch. "I need to get up early, so...I'm afraid we're going to have to call it an evening, if that's alright. I sure have enjoyed your company and our conversation—even though I guess it was me doing all of the talking. But you see, I've been waiting for this for some time, Daniel.

"You may not understand this—hell, I don't even understand it—but I felt *driven* to say all this to you, Daniel. I'm not sure why, I, well, anyway, so there it is. I hope I haven't offended you in any way, and I mean that. I truly do. It was just one of the things on my list, if you know what I mean." Thomas smiled, hoping the point was understood.

Daniel somewhat calmed after the humble comments. He assured Thomas that he hadn't offended him, and that he didn't understand any more than Thomas did, but then that was okay. There were a lot of things in life that he didn't understand.

The deep conversation ended there. It then took on a more casual tone.

Daniel helped carry the evening's leftover refreshments inside, and they both talked superficially as Thomas walked him to the parking area. They shook hands one last time, and said their goodbyes.

Daniel recalled the look in Thomas' eyes as he pulled away, a peculiar look of sadness, release, and satisfaction—.

Daniel watched Thomas through the cracked review mirror, as his image got smaller and smaller, until he was finally gone from view. His mind related the diminishing image in the mirror to Thomas' pending death. He still couldn't believe that the events of the day had transpired.

Again, his mind drifted between the past, the present, and the future. The frustration of it all squeezed on his brain— another surge of anger swept over him. Once again, he shut his mind down in an attempt to relieve the pressure of the constricting thoughts. All he wanted to think about was getting home, getting drunk, and escaping—again—to his self-appropriated seclusion.

Chapter 44

A split second before he heard the voice, all the stars disappeared and the sky turned black. He squinted down hard, and then opened his eyes wider in an effort to coax their return.

"Experiences of a lifetime!"

The sound of the voice was loud and piercing, even though it seemed somewhat distant. Daniel's reaction to it was as if a boom of thunder had gone off mere centimeters from his head. A coarse rumbling noise vibrated his bones, causing him to shudder and shake slightly.

His hands flew up in an instinctive defense posture as he flinched from the caustic resonance. He quickly turned his head to find the source of the voice, and his eyes immediately fell on the figure before him. He blinked rapidly as he brought the image into focus—it was the Professor.

"Hello, Daniel," he said.

Daniel's eyes engorged with incredulity. He couldn't see anything, anywhere, nothing above him, nothing to the side of him, nor even any type of support beneath his feet. He saw nothing except himself, and this person. It was as if he and the Professor, by their sheer presence, illuminated the existence of the other.

"Your choice is your own, Daniel, but you need not choose this self-inflicted desolation. You must know that the experiences of your mother, your father, Caitlin, your condition—the future—everything around you, everything, it's all part of the illustration; you must understand this. This lack of recognition, of acceptance, for your experiences—for your life—won't do anything but drive you further away from the purpose of your being. And you do have a purpose for being, Daniel, I assure you. Your contribution is infinitely important in the larger scheme of things, the larger future!"

The voice faded to complete and utter silence. A silence that was suddenly as quiet as the nothingness around them was dark and deep. Then, just as it had first resounded, the voice boomed once again.

"There is an inhibitor inside you, Daniel, as with all of us. Its presence is intended, but only for a time. You must experience it. It is imperative. You do sense this, don't you?

"What you are going to see, what you are going to do, who you are going to become, the fullness of your potential depends on these experiences. You must choose to embrace this reality. You must trust it. And you must know this: you are on the edge of *time*, Daniel."

Another dark silence appointed the moment.

"However, there still remains some time…time…time…time…" Daniel listened as the echoing sound swirled around in his head.

The voice faded proportionally as the image faded, and the stars slowly began to reappear. To Daniel's shocking realization, he found himself inside his truck, which had crashed into a rocky embankment some twenty meters off the side of the road. Blood was running down his forehead.

He had totally missed the curve to the left, and had crashed. He felt his head with his right hand. A gigantic knot was swelling up from where it had hit the steering wheel. The truck had died. He painfully reached over and turned off the still-burning headlights, switched the ignition to the 'off' position, and then slowly got out to survey the damage, holding onto the door tightly to steady himself.

It's not too bad, the damage, he thought. He realized that he must not have been going too fast. It was still drivable, he concluded. But that was the extent of his calm rationale.

Daniel leaned up against the fender and looked up at the stars. Then an overwhelming sense of fear and loathing began to overcome him. He suddenly felt so afraid that he started shaking. He slid down the side of the truck in one descending motion and just sat there with his back against the bulk of the tire.

He wrapped his arms around his knees, squeezed them tightly to his chest and clamped his eyes shut. All of a sudden, he felt closed in, claustrophobic, deeply anxious, and wholly afraid. Fear engulfed him like he had never felt before. It was the fear of life, the fear of *life* itself.

Daniel felt a pressure in his head, like his skull was being crushed. He began to realize that he was not only afraid of dying, but he was deeply afraid of living—afraid of being. He began examining himself like he'd never had before. The wound in his soul was opened wide now, and for the first time in his life, he was able to peer inside at its rawness.

He was finally able to admit that he was scared. Scared that another loss in his life would rip his heart out again, scared to face life's seemingly incessant need to abuse him, scared to trust life to any degree, period.

He realized that this fear had been his constant companion, always lurking unnamed in the shadows of his mind. He felt so lost now, so alone, so distant from everything and everyone. He started to weep, crying moans of long-imprisoned feelings of despair.

He felt dizzy and sick to his stomach.

Then, slowly, the tears again turned to anger, anger and hate and contempt toward existence itself. Anger at the sheer suffering life puts everyone through, anger at the constant war that drones on in the mind and eventually transfers out into this world of blindness and pain, only causing more blindness and pain.

Why are we forced to live? he thought. Why were we unwillingly thrown into life's distorted violence? Why fight to understand it? Why even care? Why can't we just stay behind the wall of ignorance, if ignorance is such bliss?

Daniel just sat there and cried, until he heard a rumbling sound and saw lights approaching. The car came closer, slowed, and then sped away, not wanting to stop.

"Figures," Daniel said in response to their cold indifference. "Just the way the F'n world is. No one gives a shit!"

The rash comment made him think of himself.

He turned his head, looked down, and tried to swallow the lump of disgust that seemed to be lodged in his throat. His nostrils flared as he attempted to blow his entire breath out through them.

After a few more minutes, Daniel pulled himself to his feet. He sighed painfully, and wiped the blood from his forehead, the tears from his eyes. He dragged himself to the truck's door, and climbed back inside. Though still feeling sick and nauseous, he started it up and slowly drove the rest of the way home.

He fell on the couch immediately upon walking in, exhausted from the effects of utter contemplation. He slept, if you could call it that. His dreams, visions and nightmares tossed him all night—.

Chapter 45

The months and years went by. They seemed like days to Daniel—sometimes like minutes. They all bled together, rushing past him like cars on a high-speed train. He closed his mind to just about everything from then on. He seemed to harden as each day passed.

He did manage to get together with Thomas Dorkin a few more times in the months following their encounter. Daniel liked to talk to Thomas, but he would always block out Thomas' attempts to encourage him to open up and find a peace that would allow his bitterness towards life to heal.

Daniel showed the man a lot of respect, but after a while, he didn't go there anymore. He just couldn't watch as Thomas withered away from his cancer. He did call him one last time before Thomas' family came and got him, and said goodbye.

Thomas went back to Oregon for his final few months.

He died on a Sunday evening, Daniel had heard. He'd chosen to employ the Death with Dignity laws of the state of Oregon—he ended his own life with the assistance of his doctor and the blessings of his family.

Thomas did manage to finish his final book shortly before he left Nevada. *Finishing Touches* was its title. It was about a person's last conversations and activities when one is facing imminent death. It was a short book, to the point. It was almost two years before it was published. Daniel read it when it came out. One part talked about his many conversations with Daniel—although it didn't mention him directly by name.

But Daniel knew that it was referring to him. He even felt that Thomas must have included it in the book, just knowing that Daniel would read it one day. It brought tears to Daniel's eyes every time he thought of it.

The inference Daniel took from the book was that the best we can hope for is to leave some part of ourselves behind through the sharing of our experiences, our loves, our creativity, and that in doing so, we become part of the "…framework of the Big Picture" itself.

Daniel had to really work at putting that thought out of his mind. It was harder than most.

<<< >>>

Daniel was a builder back when Thomas was still alive. But the construction work around the nuclear waste facility had started to dwindle and the only real work after a while was at the facility itself, underground mostly. Fortunately, through knowing Thomas, and Thomas' knowing one of the executives that ran the place—the guy that Daniel built the house for all those years back—he was able to get on the maintenance and construction staff at the facility.

He had to go through all sorts of government-required background checks, physical and mental evaluations, etc.— he barely passed the mental ones. Daniel succeeded, though, in getting a job there. The pay was great compared to the average for the same kind of work—basic labor—in other parts of the country.

Actually, Daniel hated it.

Working underground, the darkness always contrasted with the bright, glaring lights, the dust, the extreme heat, the closed-in spaces, and the long laborious hours, but he counted himself fortunate for getting the job.

Plus, it would most likely be a long-term thing. There was so much nuclear waste around the country that needed to be disposed of. It would take several lifetimes to do the job. The first week that Daniel worked there, he remarked to himself, "If I wanted, I could work here for the rest of my life."

He had said it out of a sense of pride and satisfaction: pride, in that he had landed the job, when there were hundreds, perhaps thousands who hadn't; and satisfaction that he had a *decent*-paying job, when there were so few available anywhere around the country. But then he realized the implications, the stark truth of the statement: this was where he *was* going to spend the rest of his life!

He blew it off—thinking too far into the future, or into the past, was something to avoid in his mind. It just brought the pain back. It was like a natural reaction, like when you instinctively draw away from a flame; it just happened without thinking.

He was extremely proficient at it now.

<<< >>>

Daniel did go back home to see his uncle and his friends, but only a couple of times. He only visited twice in that fifteen-year stretch, and then he only stayed for an afternoon each time. And when Finley died, he didn't even respond to his uncle's insistent prodding that he come back to Indiana for the funeral.

When he *had* shown up, some months later, they couldn't believe that the man was their Jeremy. He looked so old and haggard, hunched over from the years of grueling physical labor and lack of concern with correct posture or a healthy diet.

The last time they all saw him, Daniel had broken the forty-five year mark, and he was obviously not in the best of health—mainly from all the drinking over the years. He suffered from intestinal problems, acid-reflux, headaches, and lower back pain from all the physical work.

His uncle, at that time, was still in pretty good health. He hiked every chance he got, ate right, and his only apparent physical ailment was bad eyesight. He always joked about it, saying, "I can't see the forest, *or* the trees, now!"

The Continuum, although barely surviving over a decade of lean years, due to the tough economy, finally started flourishing again. Everyone, it seemed, wanted to start planting food gardens and growing things. He hired a manager to run the place and was able to take it a lot easier now that he was approaching retirement age.

He still had his sense of humor, and wit.

It hurt Paul tremendously when Daniel blew off several of his attempts to make him laugh like he did when he had been a young man. Still, something in his uncle found enough love and understanding to forgive him for it. He knew Daniel had been through a lot. He just wished that things had been different. He wouldn't have guessed it would have worked out this way in a million years. Daniel seemed to have the world by the tail back when he was younger. He held so much promise, had so much drive.

Paul figured Daniel would have become a teacher, maybe even a professor, or something like that. But he hadn't. Daniel just wanted to keep it simple. Just do what he had to do to get along, and not think about the rest until his life was over. A lot of people seem to do that lately, Paul thought, as he watched Daniel drive away after only a short two-hour visit. He wondered if that would be the last time he ever got to see him.

The notion led him to tears.

Bass had become a successful businessman, just like his father had been, Daniel learned. He'd started an environmental products company that sold things all over the world: no stores, no warehouses, everything was drop-shipped from the original manufacturers via an online ordering system—very environmentally friendly.

In his free time, Bass played basketball on Parks and Rec's Men's teams, although he nursed a somewhat disabling nerve problem in his right leg. And he coached two youth basketball teams. He still loved basketball. Bass had married; they had a couple of kids, a daughter they named Caitlin, and a son they named Jordan. They were a happy family.

Scott was still in the motorcycle business. With all the economic problems in the country and around the world, motorcycles were a hot item since gas prices in the states had reached over ten dollars a gallon. He was also doing some stunt coordination for a local advertising and media company, small stuff for commercials and the like. And once a year at the county fair, he'd jump over a car or two on his custom-built motorcycle, to entertain the crowds and help drum up business.

He and his dad had built that particular motorcycle together from scratch out of spare parts, just for that purpose. It wasn't in the movies like Scott had wanted, but it was still living his dream, he would brag. Like Bass, Scott had gotten married—no kids, though. Their choice, due to the condition of the world, they'd say. They, too, were happy.

As happy as they could be, in a world that seemed bent on madness.

Chapter 46

Time went on, and Daniel spent most of his days at home when he wasn't working. He didn't have many friends. He didn't really want any. He had only been on a couple of dates in the previous five or six years, both with the same lady. He had met her at a company training session, and she appeared to like him, because it was *she* who asked him out in the first place.

She had lost her husband many years back, and was at a point in her life when she was ready for another relationship. She'd said that to him during one of their conversations. But she was too much like CD, he had ultimately concluded— caring, thoughtful, and ambitious. Even though he was lonely most of the time, he stayed away from people in general, and he never went out with that woman again after those two dates.

His free time over the years was filled with watching TV, reading newspapers, and drinking beer—lots of beer, when he could get it. He watched news programs incessantly. For some reason, he couldn't stop watching them; he was drawn to them like a drug.

The world had become an even more confusing, debased, and dreadful place. Every day seemed to be filled with inestimable stories of pain and suffering: hurricanes and major storms were hitting all over the world, causing flooding, starvation and famines with a frequency unparalleled in history.

When the big-Big earthquake hit—not in California, like everyone thought, but in the heartland of America—nearly half a million people died, with ten times that displaced from their homes up and down the Mississippi valley.

Concurrent with those events, the country had also been involved in several major wars, and countless other minor "Military Assistance Deployments"—as the media would euphemistically put it. The largest conflicts were those in the Middle Eastern countries. Governments and religious leaders seemed to cyclically rise and fall in that part of the world like the sun and moon.

New leadership, often people or groups that no one had ever heard of, would come into power in what seemed like just a few weeks or months. People would put their faith in these new *Select*, hoping they could make a difference. Then, something would happen and they would be assassinated, or die mysteriously, or be overthrown in some sort of a coup d'état or revolution.

And then, it would start all over again.

Most people at that time were in some sort of self-surviving, stoical daze. Not wanting to believe what was happening, yet somehow still convinced that it was only going to worsen. The four small nuclear detonations that occurred that year and the year before in South Korea, Iran, Israel, and on the East Coast of America, was, as the world collectively seemed to believe, the prelude to a massive war that would plunge the planet into uncontrollable chaos.

It seemed inevitable, a full-blown, self-fulfilling prophecy coming true. People still tried to live their daily lives; they worked their jobs, bought and sold, had families, and tried to ignore what was going on around them. But there was still this deep inner-sense that it was all going to explode at any time. Cases of individual and collective suicide in the United States alone increased by a factor of ten, and the rest of the developed world's averages were even higher.

It was strange. Daniel had numerous opinions about all of it, but when it came to conversations with his friends and coworkers about the subjects, he would always decline commenting about any of them. In fact, he avoided all conversations that tended to go anywhere toward the deep end.

The few people who knew Daniel considered him to be a nice person—someone who would help out if asked—but for the most part, they considered him closed up in himself, short-tempered, and oddly eccentric in his behavior. Especially when it came to the TV that his friends knew he had at home.

They couldn't understand why anybody would want one of the largest big-screen TV's made, taking up all that area in their tiny 10' x 12' living room. They would joke about it amongst themselves, saying that Daniel must think he was 'Captain Kirk of the Starship Trailer-prize, sitting in his big chair in front of his big-view screen, watching the world—the universe—as it went by, holding true to the "Prime Directive"—stay away, only observe, don't get involved, don't change anything.'

That was Daniel's life.

Chapter 47

One particularly hot weekend, Daniel was trying to stay cool in his little run-down mobile home, the air conditioner barely lowering the temperature to around the eighty-degree mark. In the late afternoon, tired from working extended hours that prior week, he sat down with yet another can of cool liquid thought-stopper and began watching a news documentary.

The program was about the major events of the preceding twenty-five years. Daniel had anticipated the program for days, and when it had started, Daniel was stuck to his big-screen television like glue. He turned it up loud with his arm-chair remote and sat on the edge of his seat. He watched the whole program, staring at it intensely, barely blinking. The past, the present, and the future were swirling again in his mind—.

. . . .

"Choices and consequences…causes, and effects," the announcer said in a Rod Serling-esk dramatic tone. "Our planet's history is replete with stories of innumerable choices, and their resultant consequences. Where we were…where we *are*…and where we'll most likely be going, are steered by these laws of cause and effect.

"We, and I speak of all humanity, have contributed to these choices—these causes. And, as a result, we have inherited our dubious and currently precarious consequences—as depicted in our presentation tonight. The past is the past. It cannot be changed. Time, for us, is linear; its constant rhythm drums a steady beat.

And it drums on, whether we choose to pay attention to it or not.

"The only past that can be changed, is tomorrow's past. For our future lies down the road we choose to create, today. How we choose to create it, from this point on, is what will make all the difference. Thank you for joining us...."

....

The program was over. The announcer's voice faded and was replaced with the eerie ticking sound of hundreds of old pendulum clocks.

Daniel just sat there in a daze, listening.

His mind was swirling again. He realized that he was starting to feel nauseous. He remembered the feeling. It had been a long, long time, but he recognized the growing sensation.

The blank screen before him started to enlarge.

The ticking grew louder.

He felt his head spinning.

His body jerked.

No...no...I don't want this! he thought.

Then, bells and chimes exploded in a cacophonous eruption of sound.

Chapter 48

Everything in his peripheral field started turning velvety black. At first, it was like he was being sucked backwards down a long tunnel, the light from the entrance shrinking ever increasingly before him until it was little more than a flicker of a flame. And then, with a near-silent, airy whoosh, the flame blew out.

There was nothing but darkness and silence and stillness, for a brief moment.

Then, in stark contrast, the next instant enshrouded him with the sense of faint motion, delicate sound, and subtle light.

Daniel felt himself tremble.

He blinked, checked his senses, and took a slow, deep breath.

He saw that he was sitting in a large, brown-leather, high-backed chair. Immediately, he sensed the eerie presence of someone else near him. His head slowly turned to his right. There next to him, sitting in a similar chair, was what appeared to be a young man.

The man was hunched over, his face in his hands, head close to his knees. He was rocking back and forth, rhythmically. Just as Daniel looked at him, the young man began noticing Daniel's presence and slowly started to look up.

They both jerked back in utter disbelief.

Daniel was now looking at someone who looked just like himself—but when he was much younger. The two stared, wide-eyed, and then the eyes of the young man swiftly looked past Daniel's head to something behind him. The look on the young man's face suddenly morphed from one of disbelief, to one of terror.

Daniel immediately sensed another presence and turned his head in response. His eyes fell on an old, gray-haired man sitting in another brown-leather, high-backed chair to his left. The man, much to his own shock, also looked like him, just older—much older.

Daniel quickly looked side to side, focusing on one, and then the other, and then back again. All were uttering gasps of Astonishment.

Immediately, the young man stood up, nearly falling over his feet in his hasty attempt to distance himself from what was before his eyes. Nervously, with a jerking motion, he stepped backwards away from Daniel and the old man, almost tripping over himself again.

He attempted to speak, his voice tremulous with fear.

"Who…who are you? What am I doing here?" the young man said, the look of dread contorting his face.

"I'm Mr. Sayer. Who in God's name are you?" the old man replied, trepidation also evident in his voice.

Daniel again panned his vision between the two. He was awestruck, unmoving, and speechless.

"What? What did you say?" the young man replied, with a curious tone.

"I said my name is Mr. Sayer. Why, why do you look like me? And you!" The old man pointed to Daniel. "What's going on here? Who are you people?" he said in a raspy, tired, yet sturdy voice. His gaze turned from the young man then back to Daniel, then back to the young man again.

"I'm Jeremy…Jeremy Sayer. What…what's going on? What am I doing here?" He repeated it again.

Daniel just kept looking back and forth between the two. He felt small, his head dizzily spinning.

"Well, if this don't beat all!" the older man exclaimed. "You've got my name, and my looks?" He pointed back and forth again. "You…you…you guys look and sound like, like me? This is impossible. What in space-nation is going on here?" he asked wryly.

"What do you mean, *I* look…sound, like you. What are you talking about?" The young man was really scared now. He looked pale and traumatized, like he was going into some kind of shock. His eyes were full of fear, his voice full of anxiety, his breathing labored and shallow. He looked at Daniel. "Who are you? What's going on? Tell me what's going on!"

"I'm Daniel…Daniel Sayer." Daniel finally spoke, slowly, listening to his own voice as the words came out. "I don't know what's going on, either. I don't know what's going on any more than you do! But," He paused and started looking around, now overcome by the familiarity of the surroundings.

"The Professor's study," the old man said. "It's the Professor's study. We're in the Professor's study."

"What, we're where? What," Jeremy said, also beginning to look at the surroundings.

Simultaneously, the old man and Daniel, as if they both thought the same thing at the same time, looked over at the shelves across from the chairs. There was the picture of that young boy looking up at the stars and crying—it was Jeremy, it was them, from a long, long time ago. They both looked at each other, then at the young man. Their eyebrows rose high on their foreheads, and then they looked back again toward the picture. Their gaze ended with both looking up at the young man again, at the young Jeremy Sayer.

Jeremy saw the picture, stepped closer to it and noticed that the boy in it looked like him. This confused him, and scared him even more. He was on the edge. He jumped back in shock, grabbed both sides of his head with each hand, distorting his eyes as he pushed his cheeks up to his temples.

He began to mumble.

"I…I'm! Aaah! Aaaaah! Aaaaaaah." His cries grew louder as his brain pulsated inside his head. He was dizzy, and suddenly realized he was feeling sick.

"Calm down, young man," Mr. Sayer said to Jeremy. "It's all right. You're looking a little shook-up there. It's going to be all right. Everything's going to be all right. I'm not sure exactly what's going on here either, but…but don't worry, we'll figure it out." Mr. Sayer looked back toward Daniel with a questioning, disconcerted look on his own face.

"That's right, uh, I...I, *we*, don't know what's going on either, but, there's a reason, there's a reason, and I'm sure we'll figure it out." Daniel looked back at Mr. Sayer. He raised his eyebrows inquisitively, and then both lowered them at the same time and shook their heads side-to-side, both astonished at what they were seeing.

"This is crazy," Jeremy spoke. "I must be going insane. That's it, I'm insane. My mind is blown. I've cracked. I...."

"Now hold on there." Mr. Sayer started talking again. "We're all, all of us here...here for a reason, like *he* said, I suppose. I don't know why. But, we're going to figure it out." He paused again to think. "What...what was the last thing you remember? What was the last thing you were doing before you came here, before you showed up here? Let's start there, just calm down a little, okay!"

The old man searched for more words, any words, to calm the young man down, seeing that he was becoming hysterical.

Jeremy started pacing in front of them, and then spoke, still holding his temples.

"I was...on a plane. I am—*was*—going skydiving with my friends. I was just sitting there, and I couldn't breathe. My heart was pounding. I felt a pressure on my head. I felt like I was getting sick to my stomach, and then I just showed up here, in that chair."

Skydiving? Daniel thought. He then whispered it to himself, while his eyebrows scrunched down hard. Daniel looked up at Mr. Sayer, again with a questioning look on his face, and then asked, "What about you? Where, or, what were you doing before you came here?" Daniel asked the old man.

Me?" he answered, and then thought for a moment, looking off in the distance as if he was caught off guard by the question.

"Well, I was, on my way home, getting ready to go into my house, actually." He paused and looked to the floor, seemingly reticent about continuing. "I...had just been to the doctor. I had some tests done, just some tests." He paused again, looked down at the floor again, then back up.

"I was standing in my driveway, leaning against my truck. I was just standing there, you know, just thinking, getting ready to go in the house and see my wife and kids, and then I was here, in the Professor's study, it seems. It's been a long, *long* time." He said the last words slowly with a raspy voice as he glanced around. A deeply introspective look washed across his face.

He continued.

"I remember being here, before, a long time ago. At least, I think I was. Unless it was a dream, or…or something, but, it couldn't have been. I don't know! I never quite figured it out. And now, I'm here again." He took a sighing breath. He was speaking to himself, as much as to the others. He grew quieter, solemn, and then spoke again.

"So, what about you?" Mr. Sayer asked Daniel. "Where were you before you showed up here?"

Jeremy spoke before Daniel could answer the question.

"The Professor's study, you've been here, *here* before? What do you mean? What is this place? Who's this…this Professor? What are you talking about?" the young Jeremy asked curiously, still holding his head.

Daniel was stunned. He was thinking about what the young man had said about skydiving, and the older man's having gone to the doctor. Then the part about a wife quickly turned his attention.

"You're married? You've got kids?" Daniel asked, gulping with a dry throat, now looking at Mr. Sayer intently.

The old man returned Daniel's look. It took a moment to shift his thoughts regarding the question. He was remembering the Professor and those experiences.

"Yes…*yes*, for, well, almost twenty years now. Why? And yes, we've got two kids. Why?" he asked.

"Kids!" Jeremy interjected. "Aren't you too old to have kids?"

Mr. Sayer gave the young man a grimaced look.

"Actually, we adopted!" he replied.

"Twenty years!" Daniel exclaimed. He struggled to grasp what was happening, then the question exploded in his mind. He blurted it out without hesitation. "To who? CD, are you married to CD?" Daniel asked, the unexpected intensity of the eruption surprising even him.

"CD...*CD*? Caitlin Dobbs? Are you talking about...about *Caitlin Dobbs*? No, *no*, of course not," he answered, beguiled by the question. "CD died, well, she...she died some fifty years ago. I guess it'd be. How do you know about CD?" He paused with the question. "Oh, that's right, you're me. I mean, I'm you! I... I... I don't quite know what I'm talking about here," Mr. Sayer said, confused, now staring into space with a blank look on his face.

"CD...Caitlin Dobbs? She's that good-looking girl at the Drop Zone. She's real nice. She *died*? When? What are you guys talking about? And who's this Professor-guy again?" Jeremy said, now more confused himself.

Everyone's eyes were squinting down hard, tension contorting their foreheads, each trying to grasp what was happening.

"CD, I haven't thought of CD for a long time. I really missed her when she died." Mr. Sayer said, looking down at the floor, remembering. Then he looked up toward Daniel, cocked his head, and then asked again, "Like I said, what were you doing, before you ended up here?"

Daniel's head was really spinning now. Everyone's head was spinning.

"Adopted, you adopted?" Daniel asked, still amazed. "You *adopted children?*"

The old man looked back and forth between the two, somewhat incensed that his question was not being answered, but he addressed the query.

"Yes, we did, my wife, Anna, and I." The old man realized that Daniel was intent on learning more, so he continued, "It was my Anna's idea, at first. I can't imagine not having them, now—or her! We chose to adopt. Too many kids in the world already." He gave Jeremy another look, and then continued, "We adopted two kids that were orphaned from the war in Israel—one nine, a girl, and her brother, he was twelve when we took them in. Lazaell and Efrain are their names. They're the greatest kids. They're twenty-one and, let's see, twenty-four now, both in college. Efrain's joining the WRS this summer—Lazaell's not really sure, but she's probably going to do the same."

Daniel just sat there and stared. Everyone sat there, silent for the moment.

<<< >>>

"Like he said, what were you doing?" Jeremy asked, now becoming more curious.

Daniel tried to pull himself out of the daze that his mind was in, but he was having a really hard time doing it.

"Me? Uh, I…." He took a deep breath, blew it out, and then continued, "I…I was watching a documentary. It was over, and then I was here. That's it, that's all."

"A documentary. A documentary about what?" the young Jeremy asked, for no other reason but to keep talking.

Daniel wondered what importance the question had. He felt like he didn't want to answer, but then he answered it anyway, mechanically, hearing his own voice as if he were somehow separate from himself.

"Uh, it was about the world, what the planet was like before the Mars announcement. And, what it's like now: politics, economics, wars, the storms and disasters. It was about consequences…consequences as a result of…people's…choices." Daniel's voice was choppy and it quickly trailed off. He looked down at the floor, remembering. There was silence again for the moment.

"*Mars* announcement? What are you talking about?" Jeremy asked inquiringly. Daniel just sat there, his mind still spinning.

"Oh yeah," Mr. Sayer said, "when they got the first evidence. I know what you're talking about. I remember that. That was like, like close to fifty years ago—before they sent the colonists."

Daniel's mind grabbed hold of the thought. He spoke abruptly.

"Colonists? They send colonists to Mars, they really do? They did, I mean?" Daniel asked, fuddling his words, suddenly struck by the notion. "In…in your time, people go to Mars?" This time it was more of a statement, than a question.

Jeremy just sat there in awe, listening.

"Yeah," the old man replied, "they eventually sent colonists. Eventually, after the wars died down a little, and people started using their brains again."

He cleared his throat before continuing

"Things got pretty nasty there for about twenty years, after that first announcement, but things usually have a tendency to get torn apart until there's not much left to tear apart anymore, and then it gets better. It'll happen again, though, I suppose, always does!

"When everyone gets tired of peace, it turns to chaos, then when they get tired of the chaos, things settle down, get rebuilt, and then it starts all over again. I've often wondered what holds us back from seeing that truth. It's like something in the minds of people get pulled down by something that just blinds us, until we see the light again."

He paused for a moment, looked down into his thoughts. He took a deep breath, and then went back to the original point.

"Yeah, they sent people to Mars, seven people actually. It kind of brought the world back together again, at least kept us all occupied, for a while," Mr. Sayer said.

Daniel sensed a strange distance in the old man's eyes.

"So you guys are from the future? You're me, in the future?" Jeremy asked, awestruck, his voice trembling slightly.

Daniel and the old man looked at each other, eyebrows once again raised high. Both shrugged their shoulders at the same time, the same way—both pulling the left shoulder up, dropping the left chin slightly down, while raising the left corner of the mouth, all in a naturally choreographed physical flow of simultaneous motion.

Both realized the mannerism was mimicked perfectly by the other. Their eyebrows dropped at the subtle notation.

"I guess," Mr. Sayer said, still staring at Daniel. "It seems that way. And you're all from the past, *my* past, somehow?"

Their minds were really swirling now.

The future, the present, the past, if this were so, then Daniel was right in the middle. He was there, in his present, with his future and his past—but how, why? It was like a Dickens fairy tale.

Something didn't make sense, though, he suddenly thought. The old man seemed different from him, different from whom he would turn out to be, he thought. Different from whom he would *want* to be—a wife? Adopted kids?

This made Daniel acutely curious.

Jeremy appeared decidedly calmer, taken over by his own deep curiosity. He walked over to his chair, grabbed it, and pulled it around in front of the others, and then seated himself. All three just sat there in a triangle, staring at each other, trying to figure it all out.

Jeremy was the first to speak again.

"So what are we supposed to do? Just sit here and stare at each other? Doesn't anybody know what's going on?" He shook his head as if he already knew that no one else knew the answer. "So then, if you guys are me in the future, tell me how I turn out? What do I do? Where do I live? Are you guys cool—I mean, am I cool? What do *you* do?" he asked, looking over at Daniel.

Everyone was becoming somewhat calmer now.

"Not much, actually. I'm in construction. I build tunnels and things, now, at Yucca Mountain—the nuclear waste facility in Nevada," Daniel said.

"Tunnels, like…like underground-type tunnels?"

The old man's eyebrows scrunched down.

"No, he builds *above*-ground-type tunnels. Of course they're underground tunnels," Mr. Sayer said, slightly irritated at the young man's somewhat insolent tone.

The young man blew off the comment and continued, "Okay, so, really, that's cool. It's like spelunking, caving, you know, for a living. I bet you—*I*—like it a lot, huh?" He looked at Mr. Sayer, and then to Daniel.

"Well, uh, no, I don't, actually." Daniel paused, thinking about it, and then started again. "You just have to do what you have to do, sometimes, most of the time. It's okay, I guess, sort of. Anyway, there aren't a lot of jobs out there, nowadays, in my day, where I'm from."

Daniel found it hard to speak.

Jeremy turned his questions to Mr. Sayer.

"So what do you do?"

"Me? I teach, science, sometimes literature, in the summer, and I write—I'm about to finish my fourth novel."

Daniel, again, was overwhelmingly surprised, and intrigued. He had always wanted to write, but gave up the notion years ago.

"You teach, and you write, too? You're writing your *fourth* novel?" They were meant as rhetorical questions. They popped out of his mouth, just as they were formed in his mind.

"Yes, after I finished my degree—which the government paid for while I worked at Yucca Mountain all those years ago—I started writing in the evenings and on weekends, after I became a teacher, after I met Anna."

He paused, as if suddenly thinking about something else.

"I need to finish it." He looked to the ground and paused again, then quickly looked up and continued, "I mean, it won't *take* long to finish." He trailed off and again looked down.

"That's cool. What're they about?" What's *it* about? Jeremy asked, even more curious now.

"About? What? Oh, the book I'm working on." He swallowed hard. "It's about…it's about, life, purpose, *faith*."

"Purpose, faith, what do you mean?" Jeremy asked.

"Well," he paused, collecting his thoughts, looking between the two. "We live in a universe that's full of opposites, ambiguity, uncertainty, apparent randomness, yet underlying it all, there appears to be some sort of order, or plan, or *purpose* for it being this way.

"My Anna helped me to finally see that, even though," he paused, looking down toward his chest, taking a deep breath, "even though the truth of that hurts, and causes a lot of anger. People just want things the way they want them, and when the universe doesn't cooperate, well, we get all bent out of shape—."

He stopped his words again, contemplating what he was saying, then continued with a strange mixture of anxiety and self-certainty.

"The truth of that is far from what a lot of us want to hear—the part about it being on purpose. People don't want to face that part of the truth. The truth is that people are afraid of the truth, angry at the idea of a greater purpose that includes all this crap we seem to have to go through.

"Ultimately, the theme of it is going to be this: everything we go through, everything we suffer is meant to teach us something, prepare us for something, something *after* all this. People just can't see that, until they get to be my age, or until they get to the bottom of their rope. Well, that's kind of what it's going to be about: a guy who finally faces the truth—faces life—and starts climbing back up. Like I said, it's not finished yet."

Mr. Sayer was looking down again, a solemn look on his face.

Daniel was listening intently, absorbedly. He remembered these words, knew the sentiment. This sounded so much like the author, Thomas Dorkin. Daniel felt so strange. Everything the old man was saying seemed to provoke his mind, his heart, and his emotions—*what was going on?* he wondered.

<<< >>>

"Do *you* have a family, kids?" Jeremy asked pointedly. The questions were directed at Daniel. "Why are you in the 'underground' construction business if you don't like it? Can't you do something else? Don't you want to do something else? Teaching and writing sounds a whole lot cooler than having to do that."

It was Daniel who was being probed now.

He wanted to avoid the conversation, like he was used to doing. He didn't want this at all, but for some reason, he felt like he was supposed to speak, supposed to contribute in some way to this bizarre experience.

"I don't know," he said, answering only the latter queries. "I just don't know. I wanted to do a lot of things, way back when. You know, finish school, maybe teach, and write, too." He looked at the old man. "...make a difference! I guess. Then CD died." Daniel again looked at Mr. Sayer, but then quickly to the floor.

"I guess I just lost the desire, for some reason. I suppose I just didn't, just don't, care, much, anymore, I suppose." Daniel's speech grew slow, quiet and reflective. Tears began to fill his eyes. He continued, "Life's cruel. It's not fair. For the most part, it sucks! I don't know, maybe I am afraid of it—the truth—like you said." He looked up at the old man once more. "Every time I turned around, something, or someone, was being taken from me. Something I loved, something that I trusted would always be there. Nothing stays the same. Something's always being taken away!"

All three just sat there, staring down into the center of the invisible triangle that the position of their chairs outlined, as if there were some mysterious hard-to-focus-on object there between them, but there wasn't. The object wasn't there in the middle of them. It was in the center of them, in the center of their beings, and suddenly, they all felt the anguish that Daniel was now expressing. Somehow, they each knew it intimately—they were sensing it together.

"I guess I've grown to hate." Daniel continued, softly, "I suppose, at least, I guess it's hate. I don't *want* to hate, at least I don't think so. But I guess I must hate life, or...or God, or whatever the great power is that's allowing all this—and I guess I do fear it, too, I suppose.

"Maybe that's why I hate it, I guess. Maybe I'm afraid of God, angry at God. I don't know. I mean, why can't He stop it all? You know, all the suffering, the pain that people go through. Why doesn't He stop it? Why's He allowing it?"

He held his fists clenched, knuckles digging into his thighs, as he spoke.

"Why did He subject us to it in the first place? Why doesn't He have the compassion that everyone says He's supposed to have? There's so much tragedy in the world. I'm not just talking about my life, but everyone's. Everyone, from the beginning of history, has had to endure this crap, this...this—"

"Frus-tra-tion..." The voice reverberated.

Chapter 49

All three heard it.

It came from the direction of the Wall, the Wall on the other side of the room. Their heads turned simultaneously and looked in its direction. It was the Wall that Daniel had seen, and touched, all those years ago. It was as dark and mysterious as it had been back then. They hadn't noticed it before. Strange, Daniel and the old man thought to themselves.

It had no discernable surface, just a black fuzzy-looking depth that seemed to vibrate softly. The three just sat there, mesmerized, looking toward it, wondering if they had heard what they thought they had heard.

Then, a frame-like outline began to slowly appear on its surface. It was in the shape of a large rectangle standing on its end, somewhat like the outline of a door—two meters wide, by at least four meters tall. The inside of the rectangle began to glow softly and became colorful.

They started seeing colors that none of them recognized, nor could be described in their minds. Then something began to emerge from it. Something that also radiated the strange spectrum of colors they saw. It was an enormous figure, a figure of a man, a giant man. All three were immeasurably stunned by what they saw.

The figure glowed with what seemed to be an internal light. It passed through the Wall as if melting from it, and forming out of it, at first translucent, and then appearing solid. Then, their bewildered gazes turned to overwhelming shock—the figure looked just like them.

It had the same features, except it was tall, towering three or so meters high, and clothed in a softly shimmering, colorful light, that same indescribable light that the rectangle first began emanating. Their eyes rose and focused on the figure's face; it looked just like theirs. It *was* theirs. Their mouths dropped open in unbelief.

It had the look of age, of youth, of wisdom, of sadness, of sublime joy, all at the same time. It was smiling graciously at them.

"Hello. I remember those feelings, well!" The figure spoke with a deep, yet serenely tranquil voice. "I assure you that everything is as it should be. Don't be too alarmed. And please, you need not fear this, or me." The figure laughed tenderly. "I've come to help align things, to make things clearer. So, just listen to what I have to say. I'm sure I'll— *you'll*—understand more completely." The figure laughed gently again, then continued. "You, *we*, are here for a larger purpose. I am here to help you become aware of this.

"I have been on a journey for some time now—and I only use the word 'time' for your reference, so you may grasp at least a likeness of what I'm about to tell you. Along this journey, I have learned much, and it's because of you, because of us.

"This learning has come to pass because we have chosen it. Each of you can think of yourselves right now as extrapolations of likelihoods, developing degrees of varying possibilities, entities derived of the multiple options that you yourselves have chosen, the resultant dichotomous consequences of those choices, the effects that have come about by your—*our*—own *cause*, if you wish."

The figure walked slowly toward them, and then stopped a few yards away. The three were speechless, gazing up at the towering being. It raised its arms and appeared to take a long deep breath while taking in the surroundings with a child-like joyous expression on its face. It walked over to the shelves on the other side of the room and picked up the little picture that the three had noticed upon their arrival. It looked at it, nodded its head slightly, and then turned toward Jeremy. It smiled at the young man, blinking slowly and softly.

"The past, it's good to revisit the past. It helps remind me of where I am—and where I am going."

Once again, it looked at the picture, and then carefully placed it back on the shelf.

"Yes!" It spoke again, continuing its deep breaths. Then it turned once more to look at the three. "Please, join me!"

All three blinked in what seemed to be slow motion, then they turned to look at each other as if to gain acknowledgement that what they were seeing was really there—they confirmed it through their expressions. As soon as they did so, they found themselves in another place, a familiar place.

They realized that they were standing around a campfire, in a wooded area. They all recognized it immediately. It was where Jeremy's Uncle Paul used to take him camping shortly after his mother died and his dad started going off on his long trips.

They remembered the u-shaped covering of pine trees behind them, the open view from the top of the hill looking down to the river below, and the climbing cliffs off in the distance across the field of wildflowers. The scene was now lit by the full moon floating serenely above them. All three started reminiscing about those times. They could feel the breeze, smell the field of flowers.

It was real.

The first camping trip there, they remembered, was when Paul Usher had that long talk about life being 'unpredictable and oftentimes cruel.' He was trying to help a boy, who had just lost his mother, understand that life can sure knock us for a loop. They all remembered the way he had said it.

It was in his usual, unusual way: "Sometimes, Jeremy, life will sneak up on you and hit you so hard upside the head that you won't remember who you are for days, sometimes, even years."

They all remembered the same event, at the same time, even the same way: where they sat, the sounds, the stars, and even the smell of the pine trees that surrounded the area. They were deep into their sensory experience when they realized that the being that had apparently brought them there was standing off to the side, leaning up against a large tree, just watching them.

They noticed the fire's light reflecting off of their faces as they looked around at each other, but there was no reflection from the being, not even from his eyes. It was as if he absorbed it, or it passed through him, yet he still gave off some sort of other light—they thought this was odd.

"You remember this." It was not a question. It was a statement. As if it knew they remembered. The being took several deep breaths, seemingly savoring the atmosphere, and the experience. "I remember, too," he said. "This is where I, *you*, made your initial choice to fear life." He paused as he breathed in again, and then continued.

"What your uncle said, although he meant no harm, shook you to the core, remember? You lay there that night, alone in your tent, and you became frightened, deeply fearful. You began shaking. You hid yourself inside your sleeping bag, balled-up like a newborn baby just brought into this cold, strange world. Remember?

"The darkness became darker, the sounds you heard became scarier, and deep down inside, you convinced yourself that life, at any moment, was going to reach out and hurt you again. You chose this conclusion, whether you realize it or not. Your fear—your fear of living—took hold that night. But you know this already, don't you?"

No one spoke a word. All remembered. All three seemed locked into the experience. They started shaking inside, just as they remembered they had back then, when just a boy of twelve. None could find the strength to speak at that moment. After a short time, Mr. Sayer, stammering, asked a single question. "Why have you brought us here?"

The being laughed softly again, apparently amused at their condition. "You are here because I am here, because I chose to be here. Trust me, this experience will be providential. You see, the very nature of choosing presupposes that one has at least a limited amount of experience to base their choices on. Often, the mind exaggerates this small amount of information and creates fallacies that seem based on fact, but in truth, are not. This is what happened that night. The mind—the spirit—is powerful. You have no idea, yet!

"When you one day realize that you can choose to control your own mind, and your spirit, *your very choices*, then you begin a journey of unimaginable glory. The fear you chose that night, here, in this place, has steered you for most of your life, and for the most part, you've chosen to ignore it.

"You have lived, but with a deeply-rooted *fear* of living. When this fear is overcome, you will find a freedom that no frustration can besiege. However, this is not something that happens at one given moment and becomes an eternal fortress, forever protecting your soul. It is something that is exercised for the eternity of living. This is why you—*I*—am here, why we are here together." He paused and smiled.

"Come, we have another place to go."

Chapter 50

In an instant, the being had taken them somewhere else. They found themselves standing on the edge of a gently meandering stream. They could hear the water gurgling behind them. It was dusk and the light in the sky was almost gone. They looked beyond the stream and saw a small white house with grey shutters situated in the center of a grassy clearing.

There was a large maple tree in the backyard with an old tire swing hanging from one of its large, thick, nearly horizontal limbs. On a porch ten yards from the tree sat a young boy, looking up at the softly glistening stars. He was crying, weeping. They all recognized where they were—and when.

"I see that you remember this solemn place," the being said quietly, "as do I. This is where I...*you*, chose to *hate* life. Do you remember?"

They all looked intently at the scene. Young Jeremy was the first to respond. He spoke slowly, almost in a whisper.

"That's, that's *me*, on the porch! I remember that night. I remember sitting there!"

"Yes, I do too. It was the day Dad left," Daniel said, also speaking slowly, intently. "He said that he was going away for a while, probably a long while, and that I ought to grow up and start acting like a man, instead of a...instead of a whiny child—" His face contorted with the sentiment.

Mr. Sayer continued the emotion, "Yes, and he said that Uncle Paul was coming over the next morning to get me, because I was going to be living with him for a while. Dad was drunk. He was always drunk back then."

"What, I don't understand! Why are we here?" Daniel asked angrily with a deep and throaty utterance. He swallowed hard.

Both he and Jeremy looked up at the being. But before an answer was given, Mr. Sayer, not turning from the scene, spoke again, his voice weak and distant, as if he were speaking only to himself, momentarily lost in his memories. "It was the time when I first realized that…that I, was on my own," he said, in his own raspy, shaken voice, tears now welling in his eyes. "No Mom, no Dad, just me, just…me."

"Yes," the being said somberly in a melancholy tone. "That single evening, a seed was planted, a bitter seed. It was at that moment that true responsibility was thrust upon you—upon me. It was a burden seemingly too heavy to bear. The reins that once guided and steered my life, were at that very moment, placed in my hands.

"No longer was I going to be taken care of. No longer was I going to have my life coddled and nurtured. I realized, at that moment, sitting on that porch, that I had no choice but to face the fact that I was alone in this life. I was abandoned, at least it seemed."

The being stood silent for a moment, tears in its eyes, remembering as the others were. It gazed down at the stream behind them, looked back up, and then began speaking again.

"This was a turning point, a time that all go through, in one form or another. Yet one that, in our case, came early in life, and harshly. It was at that time that hate took its root. It stuck you in the heart as if with barbs of steel, and then was ripped out, leaving you raw and bleeding. You felt hate for your father, hate even for your mother who left you, hate for the loneliness, hate for people, hate for God, and eventually, hate for *life* itself.

"The sorrow from that time left a deep scar in your spirit. Even though someone who cared about you took you in and cared for you as best he could, the aching wound was still there, festering. The frustration of not being able to understand it, much less bear it, kindled a fury that still resides in the depths of your being."

They were all in tears.

Not just from their observation of the boy on the porch, but from the re-living of the emotions. From the bitter anguish they remembered. They felt it, again, as strongly and as surely as they had felt it back then.

Their anger swelled.

"Why have you brought us here?" Mr. Sayer asked coarsely, as Daniel had a moment before. "What purpose does this serve? Why are you doing this? Why the games?"

"Oh, I assure you, this is no game. Please understand, I feel as you do! I am experiencing the same anguish, for I have the same scars. This re-visiting is purposeful, and necessary. This part of your being has been, as I have said, buried. It is imperative that you face it now with the advantage of greater knowledge and wisdom so that everything can be realigned, reconciled. All of this connects to the realization that we observed before—the deep-rooted fear of living that resides in your spirit."

The being paused.

It looked at them intensely, its eyes speaking volumes of empathy and understanding. Their anger suddenly gave way to the compassion in its eyes.

"Remember this scene. Keep it in your heart. You'll wish to bury it again, but don't. Keep it in its proper place—." The being smiled with its eyes, and then spoke softly. "Come."

<<< >>>

They were all still gazing in the being's large eyes when the sensation of change swept over them. They turned, and as they drew their sight to their present surroundings, they found themselves standing on top of a very tall bridge, a train bridge, at least eight stories high, connecting two hill tops.

The bridge spanned a wide, water-filled valley below. Off in the distance was a large lake, and part of its southern rim flowed under the bridge and emptied into a creek. The part they were standing on was over the dried-up lake bottom where the waterline had receded.

Logs and pieces of driftwood, trash and debris could be seen sticking out of the dried-up, sun-cracked lake bottom. It was hot and there was a humid breeze blowing over them from the lake's direction. The sun was setting over the hill to the left. They only looked at the scene for a brief moment before they all realized where they were. And somehow, they already knew why.

"I see that you remember this, too. It is another place, and time, that I, we, must revisit." The being took a step forward, right up to the very edge, and gazed down at the shadowy bottom below them. Then, quite slowly, it looked over into Jeremy's eyes, and spoke again. "You have the most vivid memories of this place, and the most recent, don't you, young Jeremy?"

Jeremy looked into the giant's eyes and read their content—again they were full of compassion. He stretched his body to look over the edge as the being had done, not taking any steps. He leaned back to his prior position, legs spread apart for optimal balance. He was visibly shaking. The others looked at him. All their eyes and their thoughts were on the young man. They all knew how he was feeling, why he was feeling the way he did. It had been a long time since the others had been at this place, even in their minds— but they all remembered.

"Why are we *here*?" Jeremy asked, barely whispering, struggling to speak, and feeling himself ready to choke.

"As I said, it is a place and time that must be revisited. This is where you—*we*—considered ending the anguish. Isn't it? You remember, don't you? The burden of the years prior to your coming here were seemingly too heavy to bear, weren't they? No one knew what you were thinking that evening as you stood there, alone—there, where you are standing now.

"No one suspected anything from the conduct that you displayed on the surface. But deep inside, you were so beaten down from the internal battle in your spirit that you were going to choose this way of premature retreat. You all remember, don't you?"

The being looked down at the others. Their eyes were transfixed, not just on what the being was saying, but on their own gripping memories of that time.

"It was at that moment that you came to fear death, wasn't it?" He paused, watching his own memories swirl behind their eyes. "It is the greatest of frustrations, being afraid to live, and at the same time, being afraid to die!"

The being turned and was now looking deeply into Mr. Sayer's eyes. The old man returned the gaze. He quickly realized that it was not only compassion that the being's eyes were radiating. It was knowledge, and strength, and courage. They all felt it ripple through their spirit, washing away the fear that just moments before had engulfed them. He smiled at them, and then resumed speaking

"Death has been left a mystery on purpose. When it is your time, you will come to realize this. Death's nature and meaning have been pondered since the beginning of creation, yet the true reality of it remains elusive. You must know now that this has been wrought by intention.

"All can acknowledge death's most basic of tenets: it is the '*end*' of something. However, the question has lastingly been: is it also the '*beginning*' of something? I assure you, here and now, it is!

"On that night, on this bridge, fear fulfilled its purpose and led you to a choice, keeping you from a hasty and premature graduation. From this, you set in motion a new timeline, as every choice does. So you see, there is a reason for fear. A purpose for its existence, as there is a reason and purpose for faith, courage and fearlessness. There is a reason for pain, frustration, and yes, even death. Each is necessary at its appropriate time." The being tilted its head, its eyes again penetrating Mr. Sayer's.

"Most do not yet realize that the frustration induced through life is necessary. That it is a crucial element of our lives. It is frustration that invites us, incites us, to seek knowledge and explanation. It encourages us to wonder, to ponder, to question. And it forces us to face the unknown in our quests for understanding—even when the unknown frightens us.

"Some fear is not fear at all. This type of fear should be seen as a cautious respect for the universal laws that govern physical creation. This is good. Just as there is a time to live and a time to die, there is a time to fear and a time to face fear. This is why you're here, why you exist here on Earth: to experience the frustrations and fears that are offered to you, presented to you for your education, for your growth, for your own promotion.

"The sum of our beings—our entirety—is made up of the innumerable experiences that we are subjected to, by our own choices, and by those of providence. The experiences we have had, the knowledge we have gained, the pain we have suffered, and the frustrations that we have endured, all contribute to our past, present, and future state of being.

"All of this was, is, and continues to be, anticipated as creation waits in eager expectation for the unfolding of the Grand Purpose. But even with all that I've just said, this is only a 'likeness' of the true reality that I speak of.

"Let me illustrate."

Chapter 51

As soon as the word was spoken, the three found themselves in a location where they had never been, much less ever thought they would be. Somewhere they had only briefly imagined in their wildest dreams.

It was as if they were in a bubble—a barely perceptible sphere of some sort holding them in position together. They were just suspended there, in the incredible vastness of outer space.

Around them, in every direction they looked, above, to the side, behind and below, were various-sized shining orbs of light and color suspended in an immense velvety blackness. Everything was so clear, so vibrant, so unencumbered by any haze of atmosphere or barrier of any kind.

It was breathtaking, strikingly beautiful.

They understood that what they were seeing were stars and galaxies, cluster upon cluster of light-emitting objects, things of which they had only seen in pictures. Rivers of light and energy seemingly flowed all around them, everything in motion. The colors were so rich and deep and changing. It was as if it were all alive, as alive as they were. They soon began to feel an all-encompassing joy in just being able to witness the cosmic splendor before them. Again, it all seemed alive. As if its motion, direction, and purpose were intended.

They stared in awe.

"Quite amazing, is it not?" the being asked, breaking their silent, enraptured states of wonderment.

They noticed that the being was just floating there next to them. Its own light was illuminating the space encircling them, seemingly creating the translucent sphere that held them.

Then they realized that something was different. They hadn't heard any sound. It was as if they just knew, deep in their minds, the thoughts that the being was thinking. Somehow, they even felt what the being was feeling. They marveled at the natural ease and simplicity of it.

"Life is amazing, isn't it?" the being posited. "We're all a part of this, you know." He looked around as he gestured with his extended hand. "We have the privilege of being a part of this. The same beauty, the same matter, the same energy, the same light, we're all a part of it, and it is a part of us." He smiled broadly at the implication.

"Do you remember wondering about this? Wondering, all those nights as you looked up at the stars and thought about what could be out here? Remember your thoughts, your questions: How many inhabitable planets might there be? How many different forms of life exist? Are there beings like you, or like me, out here?

"Well, even though I cannot reveal its totality to you now, I assure you, we are not alone. In fact, our universe abounds with life, such that you have yet to imagine. This physical, material, animated life is only a portion of...*sentience*.

"In between every bundle of substance, there exists life. Just as all life forms on Earth are separate yet connected, all the life forms of the cosmos, though seemingly separate, are connected as well. Just as all apparently disparate life forms on Earth, together, create and support a symbiotic ecosystem, so it is with the cosmos."

His smile was broad and joyous.

"All of this," the being motioned again with its hands toward the rivers of light around them. "All of this has existed now for a time that is beyond even my comprehension. It is ever changing, ever growing—as are you, as am I. It is brimming with unimaginable diversity.

"You have yet to realize this broad reality; you have yet to realize your part—your place—in it. You only see, only know, a small portion of it right now. You are only at the beginning of your school experience. However, I am allowed to at least show you a few glimpses of what, after the great Inhibitor—*Time*—is removed, awaits you."

The three simultaneously wondered, silently pondered the questions: *allowed*...allowed by what, by whom... *Inhibitor* ...*Time*?

Quite suddenly, the expansive view that they were observing was replaced with an entirely new scene. It was as if the whole panorama before them just flicked off for a split second, and then flicked on again. Now they were in an area of the universe that they couldn't even begin to imagine—it was completely different from anything they had ever seen in any picture or illustration. Or, maybe it was the same part of the universe, but somehow they were just seeing it in another way, perhaps, for what it actually was. Perhaps, for what it actually is.

The colors were uniquely different. The intensity of light was brighter, yet softer; even the texture seemed different— this felt strange to them, yet it was a wonderful feeling. And the beauty of it all was indescribable, for they saw it, not only with their eyes, but with their spirits, with their souls.

They were awestruck with delight at the experience.

Then, they started seeing—feeling—other beings around them, sensing other life, sensing the presence of consciousness caressing them. Their consciousness's, their intellects, were sharing and being shared with. They felt expected, accepted, strangely adored, yes, and deeply loved —loved beyond any measure of their past comprehension.

It was the most wonderful feeling.

Then, it happened once more. They found themselves in a place that flushed them with light and warmth and joy— they felt like everything around them was inside of them— they were so elated by the feeling that tears began running down their faces.

At that point, they saw an indescribably radiant being— its love and adoration for them could be felt to their innermost centers. And because of it, they now truly realized where their centers were.

The joy of the revelation was beyond any sufficient description. However, the being before them felt brotherly, motherly, and altogether fatherly. They sensed that it was softly whispering something to them. Yes, it was telling them something, telling them, patience. The sense, the meaning, and the essence of: PATIENCE. This endeared them. A catharsis of sublime emotion rushed out of them, and back into them, all at the same time. It dizzied them for a moment, like it was too much of a good thing.

Then, just as quickly as it all happened, they seemed to take off from their current position, rocketing to an extreme velocity. They were zinging past galaxies and objects that were so large and luminous that they felt like they were going faster than light itself. In the distance, a spiral galaxy appeared and they felt that they were somehow slowing down. Within seconds, they had stopped and they sensed the being's thoughts again. They knew what it was saying.

"We're back now—wonderful, isn't it?" The being again motioned with his extended hand.

As soon as his words spread into their minds, they beheld a brilliant blue planet, floating just beyond and above them. They looked up at the majesty of it. Its atmosphere glowed in fluidic translucence, glistening sharply in the vast darkness that surrounded it. Its blue oceans swirled slowly and soothingly. White and blue-grey puffs of pillowed clouds floated gently above its surreal exterior, casting dimensional shadows across its textured terrain.

The greens and browns of the landmasses looked like features of a child's three-dimensional globe, only on a colossal scale. Its slow motion movement gave them a sense of aliveness—not only from its rotation, but from its gentle surface pulsations. Its motions seemed to inform them, convince them, that the whole planet, the whole world above them, was alive.

The being gazed up at the spectacular sight, and the three saw tears welling in its eyes. Its eyes, they noticed, strangely resembled the glistening majestic sphere before them. It smiled a child-like smile again, and then resumed its internal dialogue.

"Which is greater, a tree, or the seed in which it comes from? Which is more valuable?" It paused for a moment, allowing them to think.

"Regardless of your choice, you must know, both hold the same relevance; each is the cause of the other. Both have the same origin. Both are made of the same life-giving substance, the same life-affirming essence. The tree's purpose is locked up in the seed, the seed's, in the tree, both waiting to emerge, both striving for succession.

"The only difference is that the seed is young, the tree is old, yet both are intrinsically hungry for life. Both have purpose in life. The seed, the seedling, and the tree itself, continuously grow because of this hunger, ever stretching, ever searching for its sustenance. At every stage, all life-forms absorb and exude their surroundings, as you see before you. This life and death, give and take, cycle is intended."

The being gestured again with its arms toward the vast spatial panorama that was beyond them. Then, as if the entire universe just dropped while they stayed still and motionless, they found themselves now looking down at the Earth.

The moon came into their vision just to the right. Off in the distance, it glowed beautifully, a shimmering and soft silver-white. Beyond, and slightly behind the four, the sun could be seen shining its life-giving light down upon the surreal image, casting shadows on the far sides of the gigantic spheres before them.

"At all stages, life consummates its purpose through this assimilation, this taking-in of the life around it—to make it live. In turn, its existence—its purpose—is to give back to life as well. Everything that has life acquires life, and in turn, contributes to life. Life gives back to life. This happens on the smallest of scales, and on the grandest.

"All the life you see down there." The being once again motioned toward the majestic view before them. "The immense diversity of this small planet is only a minute portion of the grandness of the rest of the universe—as you've seen. It is a seed, growing. It comes from, and is growing toward, the great source of life that begat it all. And it exists as part of the Grand Purpose. Most do not yet know this. But the Creation will find overwhelming joy in its revelation.

"This unknown, will only be unknown for a time. The Grand Purpose is slowly being revealed. It is being revealed through life, and from life, that was, and is, and will always be. Many call this life-giving entity GOD, to some, the Creator. Some use He, or She, or Father, or Mother. To the vast universal multitudes, the Creator has many names, and is even described with unpronounceable utterances. To many others yet, He remains nameless, and for the astute, all of these are the same.

"Regardless of the level of true knowledge that one possesses about the Beginning-of-Beginnings, the Creator's origin, or the purpose for all this," he waved his hand toward the heavens, "one thing is true: all things are part of Creation...*all* things! The future, the past...the good, the bad...the knowing, the not knowing...the conflict, and the frustration...the orchestration of it all, is the Creator's. Remember this: all things have their place, and purpose, in time...*all* things.

"Now, I must go. I want to thank you deeply for the help that you have given me. I would not be who I am, if it were not for you." He smiled. Glassy tears welled in his eyes. "Thank you!"

Those were his last thoughts.

The being's image began to dissipate before their eyes. If they were asked to describe it, they wouldn't be able to, exactly. But it was as if portions of the light that made up the being's image just shot out, each going toward and connecting to every other source of light that they saw around them. As if the being had just extended out into everything else.

Chapter 52

They were left there alone, just looking at each other, and at the great cosmic spectacle before their eyes. The being was no longer there, casting its light upon them. But they felt its light was still shining on them, and, strangely, shining out from them. The light from their images combined with the light from the sun, the moon, and the billions upon billions of stars and galaxies that illuminated the darkness around them, and they truly sensed that they were a part of it all.

Then, off in the distance, a small rectangular object began to appear. It was moving closer to them, gaining in size as it traveled through space. No one spoke. Each just watched as the object approached. The light emanating from it created a progressively sharper image as it drew nearer. Then, they became motionless with curiosity when they recognized what they were seeing.

The object was now directly in front of them. It stood about three meters high, four meters wide. They were looking through it, into it, as if it were a large window—it was then that they realized that they were looking into the Professor's study. They saw the brown leather chairs, the desk, the shelves, even that mysterious Wall on the other side of the room.

The Professor was sitting in the chair closest to the desk. On the other side of the small table, which held that strange clock, a young woman was seated. She looked curiously familiar. Strangely, they felt as if they all knew her, but for some reason, they just couldn't remember from where.

She had long, black, straight hair, and an attractive ruddy complexion. She appeared to be in her mid-thirties, perhaps. She had the proud, stately features of a Native American woman. When that thought entered their minds, it was immediately confirmed when they noticed her clothes.

She wore a simple dress made of supple leather, laced together with coarse, yet artistically rendered stitching. Ornamenting her petite neck was a thin leather necklace with a small, ivory-colored amulet hanging from it. A small feather-trimmed hair piece adorned the right side of her head. She was barefoot.

They watched, unnoticed for a moment, and then the Professor briefly glanced over toward them, and then at them. He smiled and then looked down at that strange clock that was on the table. He turned and smiled at the woman. He spoke, and then the two stood up and walked over to the Wall. The Professor and the woman were talking, but the three could hear no sound. The Professor's hand was on her shoulder, just at the base of her neck, and he was patting it gently, lovingly, and they were both teary-eyed and smiling.

The Professor and the woman stepped up to the wall, in front of the large, rectangular outline that the three had all seen emerge from it earlier, when the giant being had first appeared. It was glowing with those indescribable colors that they remembered.

The Professor and the woman turned to face each other. They both reached out their hands and shook the other's with a firm, lingering, double-handed handshake, and then they hugged. The Professor placed his hand on her back, again at the base of the neck, and he spoke to her once more as they both turned toward the Wall. The woman took a deep breath, and with that, stepped in to it, and through it.

Then she was gone.

The Professor stood there for a short moment with his back to the three. He appeared to wipe a tear from his eye with a handkerchief that he'd pulled from a side pocket, quickly returning it from where it came. He summarily spun around, and with a large smile on his face, walked back over to the chairs and looked straight at the three. He then motioned with his hand for them to come, saying something.

The three looked at each other, and then back at the Professor—he motioned again. They all took a deep breath and stepped through the now-apparent opening and into the Professor's study. Immediately, they could hear again. The Professor was uttering a soft joyous laugh.

"Welcome…welcome, come in, come in. What a joy, we had just finished. She is on her way now, what a joy, what a joy! Please…*please*, take a seat. Mr. Sayer, good to see you again," he said, "and Daniel, nice to see you again as well, and young Jeremy, very nice, very nice to see you, welcome." It's so good to see all of you. How was your journey? Educational, I trust, so much to learn, so much to know."

He shook each of their hands in turn, holding Jeremy's for an extended moment, and then again motioned for them to sit. They glanced back and forth at each other, back at the Professor, and then they seated themselves.

The Professor acted as if he knew what had been going on with them. This was strange, they thought. They just sat there, not knowing what to say.

"So, what do you think of the curriculum, so far?" the Professor said, sitting on the edge of his chair. "It's quite stimulating and thought-provoking, wouldn't you say? You know, the primary subjects that were covered to date have been a part of the curriculum for thousands of years now: Frustration, the Seven 'C's', Fear of the Unknown, Faith and the Grand Purpose, and all that. Foundational, don't you think?

"I particularly like the Seven 'C's' part. They all go together so well, you know. Of course, I would like those. I lecture on them quite frequently, as you probably remember. And they're all quite good at rounding-off the sharp edges. Don't you think? You know, in preparation!"

He laughed and then paused abruptly, noting their wide eyes.

"Anyway, I'm babbling on, aren't I? This is all just so exciting! The ultimate outcome from all of this is what's going to make it all worthwhile. Make *all* the difference, you see. But, we do have several points to cover before we're through with this session. And one of them is the subject of your most recent guide and tutor.

"In actuality, all of you brought him a wealth of nourishment and growth. Re-visitation was what he needed, for his next quest, you must know. He's quite the astute observer, don't you think?"

They all just sat there, stunned. They had heard so much, seen so much, and contemplated so much. They didn't know what to say or even think. They just sat there.

Mr. Sayer then spoke. "I…I'm not sure I understand. Why did all this happen? Why *is* all this happening?"

"That is a very good question, very good question. Let me explain. This happened for you, Mr. Sayer, yet, for all of you, as well. For the one who just left you, and even for me. We're all growing from it, learning from it, being made better because of it. All of us will be able to use these experiences as foundations for future knowledge."

The Professor paused. He looked directly at Mr. Sayer. With a delicate, yet piercing tone, he spoke slowly and deliberately:

"You are going to die, Mr. Sayer."

Chapter 53

The statement was blunt, and shocking. Daniel and Jeremy just stared at the Professor, their ears disbelieving.

"Die? What do you mean?" Jeremy was the first to utter the question.

Mr. Sayer looked to the floor. He realized the Professor knew his condition.

"Yes. He's dying, of leukemia," he told the others. "He doesn't have much time, maybe a few months, at the most." The Professor smiled softly.

A long silence permeated the room. Mr. Sayer looked up, and then spoke in a solemn whisper.

"That's right, he's right." He looked at the Professor to confirm what he had said, and then he turned to the others. "He's right," he said again. He took a long breath.

"That's what I found out at the doctor's, from the tests, before I was brought here. I was just standing in the driveway, leaning against the car, trying to figure out how I was going to tell Anna, the kids. I've never been so afraid in my life." Tears started welling in his eyes.

"I couldn't breathe, I couldn't think, I couldn't move. But that was then. I know it sounds strange, but after all we've seen and experienced together, I don't feel the despair that I felt then. I realize this now!" He shook his head side to side.

"Come what may, I know it's meant to be." He whispered it softly. "Somehow I just know it's going to be all right. In fact, I'm really okay with it, now. It's just my turn."

He smiled a sour smile, paused briefly, took another deep breath, and then blew it out hard before continuing.

"The doctor said it was the identical form of leukemia that Mom died from. Funny, isn't it?" he said.

"Wha…what?" Jeremy asked, now visibly starting to shake, blinking erratically.

Mr. Sayer continued.

"The doctor speculated that it quite possibly could have been caused from the same polluted stream that ran through the nursery where Mom worked, all those chemicals from that old plant. I'd probably been carrying around traces of them in my system all my life, he'd said. Of course, that's just his speculation.

"We used to play in that stream all the time, remember. A lot of people got sick around that area back then, as I remember. It's funny, now I wish I would have taken better care of myself all those years, better care of my immune system. The doctor's said that contributes to it a lot, too. You know?"

It was then that Daniel finally spoke.

"The stream that ran through our backyard, we…we were just…there." He paused with the realization, and then quickly continued with another. "If Dad hadn't left, if Mom hadn't died, I…*we*, would have most likely played in that creek for many more years. Or if a host of any other things would have happened, it could have gone a different way, or a worse way." He sat there, staring. Everyone realized the inferences.

The Professor interrupted their thoughts as he spoke.

"Very good, you're all now glimpsing how this matrix of timelines creates all the diverse opportunities we use to learn. Good does come from frustration, as you will soon find, Mr. Sayer." He smiled a sincere smile.

"And now, Daniel, this experience was for you, as much as it was for everyone," he said, as he turned to look Daniel square in his eyes.

"You grew to hate life so much that you turned your back on your future: on your talents, on your gifts, on your health, on the ones you loved, on those who loved you, on *life* itself. In truth, you are still afraid of living, of caring, of dying. Your bitterness—your hate—has held you back from doing what you could have been doing, should have been doing.

"Every step, every turn, every direction you've chosen has served to create or destroy a possible future—an alternate timeline. Only by looking objectively at your past, and humbly studying how it has made you who you are, now, can you hope to build the framework for a different future. You're all here to learn the importance of this!"

The Professor looked at all three, stopping his panning gaze on each one. He smiled broadly, and then focused his attention on Jeremy.

"And you, young man, this experience was for you as well. You have much to learn, from yourself, from these two, from life. Your fears are as real as anyone's. They only seem more intense, more frightening, because of your lack of experience. In time, you will learn to stand up to this fear and frustration, to control it, even to embrace it. And by doing so, fulfill your intended course."

He smiled again, and then quickly continued.

"Mr. Sayer, Daniel, Jeremy, you must learn, courage is not the absence of fear. Courage is the boldness to confront that which *is* feared. Courage is making deliberate choices to seek knowledge in order to condense frustrations, anxieties, and fears, and change them into awareness, understanding, and comprehension. Courage is the application of simple faith through knowledge and experience in the struggle to make the unknown, known. In doing so, you will overcome the world. All of you will! *If* you will it! These concepts are so important, so relevant. It is why they are built into the school's core curriculum.

"The being that served as your guide, your escort, and your recent tutor, is a graduate of this school. You can think of him as an example—of the fulfillment—of the potential that you all have. His presence here was for your promotion, and yours, for his. What all of you are, is truly the framework of what he is, and of what he aspires to ascend to!

"You see, he is now working on another degree, a loftier degree, actually, and a quite significant one for us, I must add. His purpose here was multi-fold: it allowed him to gain supplementary perspective of the value and importance of this school, its diverse curriculum, of which aids him in his own life and contribution; and, it has served to reinforce his courage, his trust, and his faith *in* the Grand Purpose by doing so. The reexamination of the past—which is true for all of us—is fundamental for *his*, as well as *our* collective futures.

"Undoubtedly, you remember his speaking of his own need for re-assessment? Even at his level, he is susceptible to the sometimes over-powering effects of frustration and fear. His returning here addressed this. He may appear to be a powerful, universe-savvy being, but you must realize, even this is relative. Every stage of life is accompanied by varying degrees of uncertainty and frustration—no matter how knowledgeable and influential you are.

"However so, he is considered a Guardian of the Future, a defender of the temporarily defenseless. He is also a teacher, an instructor of children, and a leader of warriors. He is in the process of assisting multitudes, which are preparing for a great conflict—.

"This conflict begins in the individual, and then expands beyond the universe. It is being allowed for reasons that are, well, at present, generally incomprehensible to children."

He paused for a moment, but then quickly resumed.

"This is not just a conflict of might and superior weaponry; its roots lie within a battle for truth, knowledge, wisdom, legitimacy, and the future. It is, quite indisputably, a fight for the very future that we all look forward to. And, as with all battles, its purpose is to free those who are in bondage."

He paused and again gazed deeply into their eyes.

"This limited explanation might not convince you of its vital need, or of its rationale. However, trust me, the Grand Purpose—in accordance with the wisdom of the *Predicate*—facilitates its necessity. And it will happen in its proper time.

"But you must recognize, the fulfillment of the being's purpose, whether you yet accept its reality, is still directly dependent upon you! This, too, you will come to understand more completely, as your course progresses.

"And, speaking of time." The Professor paused, turned, and looked down at the clock sitting on the table. It was still ticking forward a half-second, then back again, its twitching motion like a metronome mimicking the heartbeat of life itself. "We do need to cover one last thing, however, another exceedingly important concept for the students here at the school.

"Forgiveness!" He spoke it slowly, with a defined measure of reverence. Another pause followed, offered with a broad, yet solemn smile.

"Let me show you." The Professor motioned toward the large window. The scene there was still the star-dotted panorama of darkness from which they had emerged only moments before. But soon, they were seeing the Earth rotating into view, and its image was getting larger and larger as if the room they were in was a ship that had swooped down and was now flying over the surface of the planet. They were so close that they could see cities, towns, buildings, bridges and roads, all of these passing below them in surrealistic succession.

"Look, do you see the vast numbers of people?" the Professor asked, motioning to the window, "the young, the old, the amazing variety of cultures and beliefs that have made humanity what it is? For ages, they have been living and dying, dying and living, learning all they can in between. All are the same in reality, with few differences. All want to grow, to prosper, to thrive, to understand the nature and purpose of everything.

"What you are seeing is the history of this school. You are seeing the campus of the School of the Blind, where frustration and time, spawned from ignorance itself, become the teachers. You may think that all you have gone through, all that you are going through, and the future before you is unique to your experience. But, it is not. All of these things existed long before you came here, and will exist even for a period after you leave.

"Billions upon billions have suffered what you think you now suffer. They've tasted, smelled, felt, heard, and seen what you are now experiencing. This constant struggle with frustration and time is an integral part of the school—of life down there. It has been, and will continue to be, wrought by intention.

"Yes, many have suffered far less than you. But remember, many have suffered far worse. Whichever degree is your required allocation, the purpose of it remains the same. Your fears of this will not change this basic reality; however, your choice of accepting it—of applying it while you're here, as one does a tool—is what will make all the difference. Can you—*will* you—choose to accept it, to concede to its existence, to its purpose? Or, will you choose to rebel against it, locked up forever in the shackles of hatred and resentment, because of it?

"Can you choose to forgive—to forgive the very Creator—for allowing this, for subjecting us to it? Can you forgive the burden of ignorance you must temporarily bear, while being part of it? Can you forgive the pain and the suffering that results from it? Can you forgive the frustration that you are encouraged, by your very nature, to endure and learn from? Can you forgive the apparent time that it takes to endure it? Can you forgive all this, knowing that it *is*...all this...that steers you to your higher self?

"I assure you, you are not asked to endure this alone. There is a comforter, a near-still, small voice which speaks of courage, of faith, of love, of forgiveness—and concurrency of purpose. When you hear this voice, when you sense its presence, will you continue to allow fear, hate, and resentment to abide in you?

"Before you answer, I implore you to re-examine and re-consider all that you have seen—past, present and future—before deciding. Once you begin to understand the reasons for these things, you will, in effect, break the bonds of this oppressive anger and fear that now dominate your life, and by doing so, you will experience a peace that exceeds all comprehension. I assure you of this."

The three just sat there, overcome by the Professor's words. They had no words to speak. They were rapt by the significance of it all. They just sat there and pondered the essence of themselves, of life, of the past, present, and future.

Chapter 54

"Now, it is time," the Professor said.

Upon saying this, the three instinctively looked down at the unmoving hands of the clock below their faces. Somehow, they knew that it was time to choose, to make the choice. They started feeling dizzy, nauseous, and sick to their stomachs. They felt small, weak and insignificant. They couldn't breathe. The whole universe suddenly began spinning, seemingly uncontrollably, and then they started hearing a loud, vibrating noise all around them.

They felt it through their bones.

But then, they heard something else: the still, small voice. It was consoling them, encouraging them, as if it were coming from deep inside them—from their centers. It was helping them to make their choice. Their choice to trust, that no matter what happened, they could make it through.

Without any sense of individual motion, the three found themselves standing in front of the Wall. The transition happened in an instant. Then their breathing became shallower, almost non-existent as they felt—*sensed*—that something life-altering was about to happen.

Again, they heard the still, small voice telling them that everything was going to be all right. That they were going to be fine, that all they had to do was remember what they had seen, heard, and had been taught. The Professor stood behind them. He patted each on the back, his eyes glazing over with tears of joy.

They took a deep breath, and then forced themselves to look at the Wall, and when they did, a small translucent opening began to appear in front of their faces, as if they were creating it by the very attention they were paying to it.

They then saw an unimaginable heavenly beauty before them: white cloud-like structures over a background of deep translucent cobalt. The majesty of the expansive image captivated them. They were in sheer awe at the sight.

Although still there, their fear seemed to diminish, to shrink, and they felt a sense of power over it, again by their own choice. They felt proud and suddenly realized the glory that was being revealed through their new-found understanding.

They slowly blinked their eyes, and then looked back at the Professor. He was smiling, and tears were running down his cheeks. Then he spoke once more to them, shouted in excitement, and with an uplifted hand, motioned them onward toward their destiny.

Mr. Sayer was the first to step through. He did so with confidence and courage. And he had gone through with his eyes wide open, his chin up, and with the look of utter gratefulness on his face.

Jeremy was next. He looked at Daniel and the Professor and smiled, then gritted his teeth, stuck his chin out, took a deep breath, smiled even larger, and then he stepped through.

But Daniel struggled with the fear in his mind. It was squeezing the breath out of him with every spinning thought. He shook violently inside. He felt sick to his stomach. He felt cold, clammy, and as weak as a newborn baby.

The Professor stepped closer to the struggling man and gently spoke.

"Daniel, the course of your life is still yours to set—it's never too late. Every thought, every choice, every change of direction, every step, at every point, will serve to create the being you are to become. Remember this!" He smiled, turned to look at the majestic scene before the two of them, and with a forward nod of his head and a slow blink of his eyes, he silently encouraged him to take the step.

Daniel looked into his eyes. He saw truth in their gaze, comfort in their sincerity and courage in their steadfastness. Although still wholly afraid, somehow, somewhere, he found the courage, chose the courage, he supposed, and he forced himself through the immense and awesome Wall.

As Daniel stepped through, he felt like he was being squeezed down into a box of some sort. His knees were up under his chin, and he felt something constricting his sides. Suddenly, he felt a general numbness all over, yet there was a throbbing, tingling pain in his knee joints and in his hips.

He heard a roaring sound pounding on his eardrums. It was near deafening. The vibration from the sound could be felt in his bones. His whole body was pulsating from the low-frequency resonance. Daniel was really scared now. He felt dizzy, sensed a great pressure squeezing down on his head. The sourness in his stomach persisted, and he found that it was hard to breathe. He gasped for air.

Then he remembered the words that the Professor spoke about courage, and the still, small voice.

"IT'LL BE ALL RIGHT…JUST REMEMBER WHAT YOU LEARNED!" the voice shouted over the rumbling in Daniel's ears.

Was that the still, small voice…it's so loud…what did it say? Daniel screamed silently in his mind, frightened, trembling. Then the voice returned, even louder.

"YOU CAN DO THIS!" the voice screamed as it spoke again, only it was different-sounding this time.

"USE THE FORCE, JEREMY!"

Then it shouted once more, yet again sounding different.

"READY? HERE WE GO…DOOR!"

Force? Daniel asked in his mind.

Suddenly, he was hit by a blast of cold. It immediately chilled him to his core. He began quivering and realized that he was soaked with sweat. It's why he chilled so quickly. His hands and face felt clammy, sticky. Daniel raised his hand to wipe the moisture from his cheek. To his astonishment, his hand bumped into something unexpected on his face.

He felt it. Something was covering his eyes. It was boxy and had the texture and feel of plastic. Something was also on his head, something, it seemed, was enshrouding his entire head. It also had the texture of smooth plastic, and there were holes on the sides where his ears should be.

What is this? he thought. *Is this some kind of experiment, some kind of…research or something? This is what it's like on the other side of the Wall?*

Daniel tried to open his eyes, suddenly realizing that they had been clinched tightly shut. His eyelids felt like they were glued down from the clamminess that oozed out of his pores. He struggled in his mind to find out what this unknown experience was, but he couldn't think straight—he was stricken with fear. He remembered again what the Professor had said: "Courage is not the absence of fear." It helped him to focus, a little.

Then, with a deep breath and the greatest of effort, he chose to bring his mind and his senses back on-line.

Daniel took a deep breath and then forced his eyes open, challenging himself to look at the images before him. He was shocked and astounded by what he saw. He blinked again, several times, to bring more clarity to the scene. He couldn't believe what he was seeing.

There before him were four people. And one of them was right in front of his face. The man had a strange, tight-fitting, rippled-looking hat on his head. Dark goggles of some sort covered his eyes. The hat was pulled down around his ears, partly covering the sides of his upper-jaw, held tightly to his head with a chin strap.

Some sort of suit clothed his entire body. It shone with different colors: yellows and reds, the color of flames, like it was on fire. A clock-like object protruded from the middle of his chest, centered between two thick black straps. There were other straps, too, around his waist and his thighs. They looked like straps from a…from a "*Parachute?*" he thought. "It's a parachute." he said to himself in a whisper.

He looked past the man, now gazing intensely at the other people. They, too, had suits on, and parachutes, and clocks. They appeared to have hats on, too, but then he realized that they were helmets, blue-colored helmets, and they had clear goggles strapped over their eyes. They were both smiling. One of them raised a hand and gave him a thumbs-up gesture, then shouted, "THE MOMENT OF TRUTH!"

The other person did the same thing, and then shouted as well, "TO INFINITY, AND *BEYOND*! YEAAAAH!"

They were both smiling ear-to-ear.

And then, he recognized the smiles.

"Scott…Bass?" he whispered. "…SCOTT… BASS!" he then yelled.

There before him were his two old buddies. They were in a plane. They were all in *the* plane.

What? he thought to himself.

He noticed the pilot next to him, and then looked back up at the man in front of him. It was their Jumpmaster, Thomas Bond.

They were all in the plane.

He looked to the side.

The plane's door was open and he was just sitting there, next to the opening. He felt the wind tearing through the cabin with a cold, whirling ferocity. Every strap, every flap, every lock of hair that wasn't tucked under something was flapping around uncontrollably in the powerful blast of air.

He looked through the opening, and down.

He saw small, yet familiar shapes: buildings, roads, a bridge, and huge fields. The buildings and cars looked like they were mere toys. Everything looked tiny, minute, and insignificant. And he suddenly felt as if he were a giant looking down at a miniature version of the world, and everything down there was going in slow motion. Like time had nearly stopped.

Then, Daniel Jeremy Sayer felt a slap on his right knee, and heard the man in front of him shout, "PUT YOUR FEET OUT AND STOP!"

He looked back at Scott and Bass.

They were still smiling. Both gave him another thumbs-up, and Scott rolled his eyes from his left to his right, and then stopped his gaze on the open door, his eyebrows going up and down rapidly.

Jeremy suddenly realized where he was, and who he was.

Had he been there all along?

Right there on the plane.

All those experiences, all that time.

Had it all been in his mind?

Had it been?

He felt as if he were two people for a moment.

He remembered that feeling.

Could it be? he thought again.

Had it just been his imagination?

It couldn't have been.

But, what if it was?

Somehow, it was all making sense, but then it wasn't; it just wasn't.

Why did he have all these memories?

It was then that he looked at his hands.

They were young, smooth—weak.

The scars?

He remembered the scars: from the knife, from the hammer, the splinter of wood.

They weren't there. they weren't there.

The transference of the sense of reality, from one perspective to the other, was difficult. His body jerked to the erratic rhythm of his thoughts as his young torso easily turned and his feet dropped out of the opening and onto the small metal step.

Something inside him didn't want to return, but he knew the transition was almost complete now—like waking up from a dream-state into the real world, and experiencing that strange feeling that one gets as one exists on the twilight-edge of both.

He was almost in reality now, in utter shock at the tick-of-time that divides the two worlds. Then, he heard the man in front of him shout again, as loud as he could, "JUST REMEMBER WHAT YOU WERE TAUGHT! YOU'LL DO GREAT...GO ON OUT AND HANG!" The man motioned with his hand to the great expanse outside the door.

Jeremy realized what was going on now.

He felt a stabbing pain in his gut. It twisted and jabbed at him. He gritted his teeth and resisted the pain. The fear started to wall him up like he was being crushed by a great weight. His feet were on the edge of the precipice, and the bottom was a long way down. And he was as scared as he had ever been in his life.

He then heard a voice. It whispered clearly above the high-decibel horror that was swarming around him. It was soft, and calming:

"Life…has its reasons!"

Jeremy took a deep breath, looked back at his friends, then reached out and embraced the strut of the plane, just as he was now embracing the fear.

He remembered what to do.

He grasped the strut with both hands then slid them out until he was standing up on the step and was leaning out into the chilling air. The prop blast hit him hard, but he became determined to fight it.

He turned his face to the wind and gritted his teeth even harder. Its cold force cut into his cheeks. With a grunt of exertion, Jeremy held on tight, and then stepped off. He was now dangling in the air, swaying forward and backward like the ticking pendulum of a clock. He squeezed hard on the cold, painted steel of the wing's support.

Jeremy was determined now.

He did half a chin-up and held it, frozen, his muscles taut. He looked back through the door at the Jumpmaster. The man looked down then gave a hearty thumbs-up, pointed at Jeremy with two extended fingers, and then yelled, "JUUUUUMMMMPPPPP!"

Jeremy heard it as if it were spoken in slow-motion.

He faced the stinging wind again. He took another deep breath. Then, with the confidence of a warrior, he let go with a deliberate, coordinated effort. He was now falling through the cloud-filled sky.

He had made the choice; he was now embracing the fullness of that choice.

The violence of the opening parachute was somehow diminished from what his mind told him it was going to be, and it only lasted a few seconds. He was now hanging there in the air.

A great calmness came over him.

The experience was surreal at first, and then slowly, as he flew through the sky, it all became very real to him. And it felt familiar. He felt that this was exactly where he should be right at that moment. It was a feeling that could only be described as correctness, rightness, an experience that was supposed to be.

The trip down for Jeremy was joyously exhilarating.

He steered his path by the command of the voice on the radio: "Right, left, now straight. Hold."

It was a familiar voice, a firm, yet gentle, guiding voice. He was allowed to steer where he wanted, but only with a modicum of self-direction. He was instructed by the voice to stay within the parameters of where it would allow. He was told why: Don't go too far this way, or that way, or you may not make it back—and might not enjoy the consequences.

The wisdom that came from the voice guided his path, and his turning. Jeremy felt comfort and confidence in the knowledge that the voice possessed. He trusted in it, yet, he knew that he could learn this knowledge, and one day steer himself on to his own destinations. He believed it now.

It all seemed to make sense to him.

This is what the school is all about.

This is what this life is all about.

Chapter 55

Jeremy came down confident and sure-footed, keeping his balance and staying on his feet upon landing. A small crowd surrounded him as soon as his parachute touched the ground. He stood there for a moment, like a proud statue, an unmoving force amongst the chaos of motion around him, succumbing to the full power and influence of gravity, yet finding satisfaction in being back home on the Earth.

His eyes were filled with the tears of triumph, and his heart was filled with joy. He was tired, exhausted, feeling that he had just battled the entire universe for his place in it, and that it had yielded to his victory, even honored him for his faith and courage.

Uncle Paul was in the back of the storm of people that swiftly encircled his nephew. When finally noticing him, Jeremy saw a face beaming with joy and pride. His uncle clenched his lips together and nodded in admiration of his nephew's achievement. Jeremy returned the nod, his joy unbounded in just knowing that his uncle was there.

They held an extended gaze and Jeremy told him with his eyes that he loved him with all his heart. Paul understood immediately, read the beaming sentiment in his nephew's expression. Nodding back again, he bit his lower lip in an effort to control his own emotions. They both smiled as the tears welled in his eyes. As Paul approached, Daniel Jeremy Sayer couldn't help but reach out and embrace his uncle; he hugged him as if he hadn't seen him in twenty years.

Soon, the others landed. Once back together, they all hugged and laughed and cried their own tears of elation. All felt that they were men now, blaming the tears, of course, on the wind and on the sun.

"If we can do this, then we can do anything!" Bass said adamantly.

They all nodded, acknowledging their own sense of triumph, especially Jeremy as he stared back up toward the sky and into his memories.

Once the jumpers and their helpers were loaded up, the driver carefully steered the open pick-up truck back to the hanger. A small crowd of dedicated supporters and helpers trailed alongside and behind. Once stopped in its designated parking spot just inside the hanger, and once everyone had stood up to exit out the back of the recovery truck, the whole place erupted into whoops and hollers, hoorahs, hand claps and whistles!

Virtually everyone, people they didn't even know, yelled congratulatory comments and phrases at them, many patting them on their backs as they each stepped down from the truck's tailgate. The boys were somewhat taken aback by the attention.

Everyone, they'd just then come to learn, recognizes the first-time students. It had been a tradition there at the Drop Zone since its first few days of business. Everyone remembers their first time, and congratulating others was not just an offer of honor, support, and respect, it was a genuine acknowledgement and conveyance of brotherhood.

As Jeremy zombie-walked through the crowded hanger, making his way to the rigging table, a familiar voice spoke to him.

"You freaked out, didn't ya? Told ya! It's good to freak out, sometimes, you know! Ha! Ha! I knew you would! It's great, isn't it? Congratulations, dude!" The long-haired, tattooed man giggled as he had done before. He smacked Jeremy on the shoulder, and then he walked away toward the training rooms with another student. Jeremy watched him as the man shot him a thumbs-up, and disappeared through the door. Then, another familiar voice grabbed his attention.

"So, how'd you like it, Mr. Sayer…*Daniel?*" The person behind the voice was looking at her list, having read the name as she spoke it. "Over here, if you would," she said, looking up and smiling cutely, and then added. "Was it worth it?"

Jeremy turned his head to greet the person. It was Caitlin Dobbs—it was CD.

Jeremy momentarily froze. He just stared at her with his mouth hanging partially open. She smiled more broadly and motioned him closer to the table. Trembling, he slowly stepped towards her. As he drew near, she proceeded to undo his parachute rig. He clumsily tried to help her, but he was still shaking, and he couldn't stop staring at her as she moved around him, summarily loosing straps, while simultaneously checking the gear.

He needed a glass of water right then, badly.

"Yes," he managed to mumble. "It…it was worth it!" He paused, looked into her eyes, gulped down his fear, and then spoke softly. "I'd do it all over again, if I could!" His eyes began to well with tears, but he held them back.

She locked her gaze on to his for a brief moment, considering his choice of words. Her delicate brow lowered slightly with curiosity. She smiled strangely, yet nicely at the comment. She halted her subtly inquiring gaze, and then proceeded to take Jeremy's helmet and his goggles from his hands.

She spoke again.

"Could you, could you see alright?" she asked, holding the goggles up, though still thinking curiously about his odd statement. She sat the goggles and helmet down on the table next to her and began to take off his rig, motioning for him to step out of its leg harnesses.

Jeremy thought about what she asked. He thought of what the words meant, thought about a deeper meaning. He acknowledged the question with a nod of his head. He struggled for something to say. He just stood there in silence, looking at her. He wanted to speak but wasn't able to.

He thought about that glass of water again.

"Okay, cool. I'm glad you had a good time. Congratulations," she said genuinely, holding out her hand, offering a handshake. Jeremy quickly raised his to reciprocate the gesture.

He about passed out from the warmth and softness of her hand. His eyes began to moisten further.

"Come back and see me—*us*, I mean—again, sometime. Okay?" she said, letting go. She looked into his eyes once more, smiled, and then winked at him. She turned and walked away and started helping the other students who were filing into her area. She glanced back once more, although briefly, a curious look of bewilderment apparent on her face.

Jeremy desperately wanted to speak to her again. He awkwardly searched for the right words, but was interrupted by the sounds of Bass's and Scott's whooping and hollering. He shifted his gaze toward them and saw that they were walking over to him, having been de-geared as he had just been.

Then, Brake, the Drop Zone owner, walked over and stood in front of the three. He shook all of their hands and gave each a Certificate of Accomplishment, rolled up and tied with a crimson ribbon—it looked like an ancient scroll.

He told them how each had done an outstanding job, and then, with an upward nod and a focused stare, motioned their attention toward one wall of the hanger, and to a large poster that was tacked to it. He then recited the words in a dramatic tone:

"...and once you have tasted flight, you will walk the Earth with your eyes turned skyward... for there you have been, and there you long to return. ~ Leonardo da Vinci"

Brake gave them another large smile, congratulated them each once more, and then told them that he hoped to see them again sometime. He then walked off toward the other students. They all just stood there and stared at the poster for a moment, each remembering the freedom they had felt. They partly felt like they were supermen, having just flown through the sky; now, they stood there, tall, chests filled with the breath-of-triumph, feeling unique among the crowd, yet, strangely connected to everything somehow because of the experience.

The sensation was interrupted when Paul suggested they go have a bite to eat over at the picnic area. He had brought sandwiches and sides, knowing that they would be hungry after their jumps. They all liked the idea.

Together, they walked out of the hanger.

Jeremy paused to look back. He couldn't help himself. He wanted to see her again. He finally spotted her over by a parked airplane next to an adjacent hanger. She was helping a lady with some camera equipment. Then, with the feeling that she could sense his looking at her, she looked up, seeing him in the distance. She smiled, waved, and then continued helping with the equipment.

They all sat down together around the picnic table and ate their late lunch as they watched plane-loads of other students and skydivers take off. They sat and stared with awe as they watched the little black streaks fall through the air and then blossom into colorful, flower-like rectangles, eventually swooping in and skimming the ground as they landed their canopies with the grace and natural finesse of birds.

They talked about the plane ride up to altitude, and how nervous they all were, and how Bass and Scott had thought that Jeremy was going to vomit on the way up. His face, they said, looked happy one minute, and then all of a sudden, it looked sad and contorted like he had felt sick, remarking that he would only look out the window briefly, then he would close his eyes tightly like he was about to pass out.

They teased him, saying that they didn't think he was actually going to do it. But then they, too, admitted that they had felt the same way, and that they weren't sure if they could do it either, until that last second.

After eating, Bass and Scott left the table to take a leisurely walk amongst the hangers, to check out all the different airplanes and assorted flying machines. Jeremy said that he just wanted to sit there for a while, so he stayed at the picnic table with his uncle. He actually wanted to keep an eye out for one more glimpse of CD as she occasionally roamed in and out of sight.

It was then that Paul found the opportunity to give Jeremy the letter—the letter from Jeremy's father.

"This, reminds me. I've got something for you," Paul said nervously, then unzipped his backpack and pulled out the envelope. Jeremy looked at it curiously. His eyebrows furrowed, wondering what it was.

"Your dad sent you a note. It was in the mail this morning. I didn't want to give it to you until after the jump. You know, you needed to keep your mind focused on what you were doing and all, so I waited. I hope you don't mind, anyway, here." He scrunched his eyebrows and handed the letter to Jeremy, searching for more words to say. He couldn't find any. He knew the letter would stir up a lot of emotion. Nothing he could say would change that.

Jeremy slowly took it, looking at it with a blank stare on his face. He noted its usual thinness. His dad's letters were always thin, as they were rare, usually just a store-bought card with nothing more than a signature on them. His dad never had much to say.

He opened it.

Wrapped in a single hand-written page of notebook paper, he found a cashier's check made out to Daniel J. Sayer for the amount of forty-thousand dollars. Jeremy showed the check to his uncle. Their eyebrows were now set high.

He silently began reading.

. . . .

Jeremy,

I know it's been a long time. Awhile back, I was delivering some lumber to a job site out here in Nevada, and I saw someone who kind of looked like you, except a lot older. He looked really tired and withered. From that day on, I couldn't get you out of my mind, Jeremy. And I couldn't quit thinking about things.

I can't begin to tell you how sorry I am, for all these past years. I can't think of one decent excuse for how I've been. All I can say is that, I'm sorry! Sorry for losing your mom, sorry for putting you so far out of my life, and sorry for being so selfish!

I've been getting some help from a doctor this past year; he's more than a doctor—he's kind of a teacher—a psychologist, actually. He's helped me to see that my own past—things that you've never ever been told about—has bent me and twisted me into who I am. Who I was— I really want to say! He's helped me to see that even though life unfolds in ways that we can't begin to imagine, we still have the "choice" to make it better! I know, now, that I didn't choose wisely.

I just wanted you to know, Son, on your 18th birthday that I have been going through some changes lately — it's sad that some people have to find out that they're going to die, before they realize what their life should've been.

I have heart disease, Jeremy. And, apparently, I don't have too much time left, even with an operation. But there's always hope, huh?

Anyway, I sold my truck and have settled down in a small town in Nevada—I like the warmth and the clear night skies here. I'll be facing an operation sometime soon, but the doctors say I only have a small chance of beating this. We'll see.

I'm sending this money to help you make it into a good school. I know it's not enough—to make up for anything—but it should help in getting you started. Please go! Please use it to learn that you don't have to stay in the same "box" that you were born in…or, that you were left in. I just hope that you'll become a better man than what I turned out to be! I know you will.

Someday, when—if— you feel it's right, maybe we can see each other. I think I would really like that now!

Happy Birthday, Son!

....

Jeremy's eyes engorged with tears. He handed the letter to his uncle so he could read it, too. As he did, emotion washed across his face. Both struggled to keep the feelings they were experiencing at bay—they were in a public place.

<<< >>>

Jeremy didn't see Caitlin Dobbs anymore that afternoon. She was busy in the hanger, somewhere, helping with gear, and videos, and the people, he supposed. He wanted to go to her, to speak to her. But something in him knew that he couldn't. As he sat there, watching the crowds of people live their lives, he was entranced with the memories that raced through his head. They were so real. They had been so real.

It was odd, he thought, how he had imagined it all, how he could have thought all those thoughts in such a short amount of time—*lived* an entire lifetime, it seemed. Yet, strangely, he realized that because of it all, because of the jump, because of his dad's letter, he was a different person than he was the day before—.

He was a man now.

Yet, he was more than that, something inside told him.

He had a new sense of understanding about things, about life. And he felt a peculiar sense of acceptance—acceptance of all he had been through in his life up to that point, and perhaps, acceptance for whatever the future might bring. Jeremy was tired, more tired than he could ever remember being. And even though the day was over, somehow he knew that his whole life was just now beginning.

They settled into the vehicle with a long drawn-out sigh coming from each of them. Paul inserted the key into the ignition, and then looked over at Jeremy who was sitting in the passenger seat next to him. He smiled, and Jeremy smiled back. Then, noticing something, Paul quickly looked past Jeremy's head.

"Shhhhhh," he whispered softly. Moving in slow motion, he pointed to the window.

"Cool," Bass said, in a whisper, seeing it too.

"Awesome," Scott added quietly.

Slowly, Jeremy turned his head.

Outside the window, there was a tiny hummingbird, just hovering there in mid-air. As his eyes fell upon it, it rose slightly in elevation, and then flew up to within a few inches of the window. It hovered for a moment, its wings vibrating a rhythmic hum. Then, it flew backwards, stopped, looked once more at the window, and then turned and swooped out across the flat terrain.

"It probably saw its reflection in the window, like a mirror. It must've thought it was another bird," Paul said as he put the car in gear and began driving away.

Naturally following the diminutive creature's path of flight, Jeremy watched as it got smaller and smaller, eventually disappearing into the haze of the warm summer air. Then, he caught a glimpse of something farther off in the distance.

As he narrowed his eyes to focus, he saw the image of a man: a suit-clad, gray-haired, older man with glasses. He was just standing there by himself in a grassy area at the far end of the airport's single runway. The man appeared to be looking directly toward Jeremy. A smile could just barely be seen expanding across his face. Jeremy squinted harder, but the image, as with the bird's, became lost in the haziness of time and space.

The trip home was a mostly quiet one. They all quickly realized just how exhausted each of them was from the lack of sleep the night before, and the post-effects of adrenaline that had coursed through their veins that afternoon. Few words were said until Paul broke the silence.

"Oh yeah, we'd better drop off those books you wanted, Jeremy. I'll run by the library real fast, put 'em in the night box."

Jeremy was struck with the comment. He had totally forgotten the books. *The books,* he thought. He just sat there, in a daze.

A short time later, Paul flipped on his turn signal, indicating his intention to turn down the road which would route them to the library.

Jeremy realized what he was doing.

"No, Uncle Paul...forget the library. I'll take the books back...tomorrow," he said, pausing, looking out the window. Tears of fatigue glistened in his eyes. "I need to pick up some other books anyway—on careers, stuff like that, a good one on becoming a writer, and...and maybe...one on hummingbirds."

Paul flipped off the signal.

They all sat silently and stared straight ahead, down the shadow-covered road as their small corner of the Earth rotated out of the sun's light.

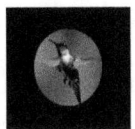

354

"A musician must make music, an artist must paint, a poet must write, if he is to be ultimately at peace with himself. What a man can be...he must be."

~Abraham Maslow

G. F. SMITH

SUBJECTED (the entire three-book series) explores a topic that has been considered extraordinarily controversial throughout humanity's history: Creation and Evolution; Science and Religion; God and Aliens, Life and Purpose, etc. First and foremost, I did not write these books to propagate, promulgate, proselytize, or in any other way, preach the supremacy of any one perspective. I'm truly just a humble, genuine man with more questions than answers.

I do suppose though, to quote the books that, *"Life has its reasons..."* I think, and it is deeply related throughout the entire series, that there *is* more going on than what we know. We all came from somewhere, and the flow of Time is apparently taking us somewhere. Where is that? I don't know, exactly. But, I do believe the following:

We (all those science guys, actually) have discovered that everything is made of energy and exists in a universe of the extremely BIG: quadrillion, trillion, gazillion Stars, Galaxies, Clusters, Nebulae, Black Holes, etc., which exist in an envelope of space that is not only apparently growing, but accelerating in its expansion. We have also discovered a universe of the small, which, in and of itself, appears to contain just as many sub-components as the big universe has large ones. And we, mysteriously, have found ourselves smack in the middle, looking up, and looking down, consciously considering it all as we scratch our little heads asking Why.

The *amazing* part, is that we learned all of this *through* our little three-and-a-half-pound brains. Wow! How'd we do that? Which has led me to think that, there's more to *us* than just these little three-and-a-half-pound brains.

--------- < O > ---------

G. F. Smith is married, has four talented and successful grown children, several awesome grandchildren, and lives in the picturesque, forested hills of Brown County, Indiana, near the renowned Pioneer Artist Colony known as Little Nashville.

New Release!

NEW CONSUMER TECH: SMARTPHONE STREAMS DIRECTLY INTO HUMAN BRAIN

Smart*brain*
An eerily predictive, 2-part Novel…

Part 1: *Mind*

Sarah Whiting, young, attractive, techno-savvy homebody, accepts a potentially lucrative offer to join a product/market analysis team that is performing the final evaluation of the believed technological breakthrough of the century before its release to the public.

As the incredible opportunity unfolds, Sarah finds herself smitten with the technology, as well as with the project's lead engineer. Even with the contrast of taking care of her Alzheimer's-ridden father, it all seems like a dream-come-true for Sarah. That is, until she abruptly learns that she may now be unwittingly mired in a dangerous ruse of international deception, and that the man she's fallen for, as well as this new, highly transformative technology may originate from somewhere else, other than Earth.

Part 2: *Matter*

Sarah's world is further thrown into chaos and confusion when she wakes up with little memory of her recent past and is told that she is a victim of severe brain injury brought on by the very technology she had been working with. Sarah is lost in the revelation, loath to accept the reality being told her, and soon falls into a downward spiral fueled by a husband she doesn't remember, along with the abysmal fear that she may actually be losing her mind.

What Sarah doesn't realize is that as she fights to gain a hold on what *is* real, others are in the process of risking their lives in a desperate attempt to free her from her perceptual prison. Filled with guilt, the very man who blames himself for Sarah's cerebral incarceration begins to work with a group of highly trained professionals who might just be Sarah's only hope of ever returning to her real life.

Book One of The…

Smart*brain* Universe
-and the *Penchant Series*

Smart*brain*, a two-part novel and the first in the *Penchant Series*, introduces the Reader to a burgeoning, future universe where new, uber-immersive consumer technology creates the potential for worlds of augmented realism that exceeds ordinary, high-definition reality by inestimable measures.

This universe, achieved by a technology that streams data directly into the human brain, just as our array of normal senses do, initially seems to offer endless possibilities and new frontiers of personal, as well as social experience. However, as with most things, the dichotomous contrast of the human essence also apparently has the potential to present itself anew—for good, and bad.

Hence, the *Penchant Series*, in its present as well as future iterations, promises to highlight, and perhaps portend—within and through this new universe—many of the recurring topics and curiosities that a vast number of people in the world are not only wondering about, but also are understandably deeply concerned about.

Is technology truly leading us to a better world?

Will innovation and technology ultimately save our environment from self-induced catastrophe?

Are we, because of technology, losing an important part of our humanity?

Will this new universe of technology be just another contributor to the separation of the classes?

Would technology like this help balance, or destroy world economics?

Will we become so dependent on technology that we can no longer survive in the natural world?

To what degree, or limit, can technology and biology combine?

Can, or will, AI—artificial intelligence—actually supersede human intelligence?

Will technology truly help us reach out and colonize the heavens?

Will technology enable us to learn that we are not alone in the universe, or ultimately to find out that we are?

Technology has already defined an entire new epoch in Earth's history; will this be the final one? Moreover, if not, what could possibly come next?

Dear Readers,

Thanks for reading! I sincerely hope you enjoyed the book and will enjoy my others as well. Also, if you do find them interesting, and/or compelling, a quick online review would be most appreciated; it's really easy to do actually, and one or two sentences would be more than fine. My thanks go out to you again! Stay curious, and all the best to you and yours!

~GFS

www.ingramcontent.com/pod-product-compliance
Lightning Source LLC
Chambersburg PA
CBHW060349260626
47160CB00006B/2250